The Ballad of Grégoire Darcy

The Ballad of Grégoire Darcy

Jane Austen's
Pride and Prejudice
Continues

MARSHA ALTMAN

Ulysses Press

Published in the United States by
Ulysses Press
P.O. Box 3440
Berkeley, CA 94703
www.ulyssespress.com

ISBN: 978-1-56975-937-0
Library of Congress Catalog Number 2011922509

Acquisitions Editor: Keith Riegert
Managing Editor: Claire Chun
Editor: Kathy Kaiser
Proofreaders: Lee Micheaux, Lauren Harrison
Production: Judith Metzener
Front cover design: what!design @ whatweb.com
Cover photo: *The Lukin Family* by Charles Biggs from Felbrigg Hall in Great Britain; photographed by John Hammond © National Trust Photo Library/Art Resource, NY

Printed in Canada by Transcontinental Printing

10 9 8 7 6 5 4 3 2 1

Distributed by Publishers Group West

When I was a little kid playing with my toys in the den,
my grandmother, Helga Franklin, sat down with me and I
proceeded to explain to her the complex backstories of all
of my assorted action figures in great detail.
"Marsha, how do you come up with all these stories?"
she asked me. I've never been able to answer her.
This is for you, Grandma. It'll have to do.

"Everybody likes to go their own way—
to choose their own time and manner of devotion."

JANE AUSTEN (1775–1817), *MANSFIELD PARK*

Introduction

WELCOME, READERS! Quite a bit has happened in the world of the Darcys and the Bingleys since Jane Austen left off with them, so let's do some summaries to help everyone catch up.

After their most joyous coming together in *Pride and Prejudice*, Elizabeth Bennet married Mr. Darcy (of Mr. Darcy fame), and her older sister Jane Bennet married Mr. Bingley (of Darcy's friend fame). Seriously, if you're a little foggy on your *Pride and Prejudice*, I suggest some freshening up. At least rent the movie or something. Anyway, the Darcys and the Bingleys proceeded to have a whole mess of kids. (Fortunately, not all at the same time.) The Darcys' oldest child is Geoffrey Darcy, and the Bingleys' oldest child is Georgiana Bingley.

Caroline Bingley, Charles's unwed sister, became involved with a Scottish earl, who then turned out to be a rake, and by that I mean a nineteenth-century scoundrel and not a gardening tool. This was all exposed in time for her to also reveal she was actually in love with the impoverished Dr. Daniel Maddox. Dr. Maddox lost his social standing when his older brother Brian gambled away their family fortune. After some sword fighting and the bad guy getting clobbered with a candlestick, Dr. Maddox and Caroline Bingley were married.

Mary Bennet, Jane and Elizabeth's unmarried sister, returned from studying in France and brought the news that she was with child, the father being an Italian seminary student. Darcy and Elizabeth traveled through Europe to find him, on the way discovering that Darcy had an illegitimate half-brother named Grégoire Bellamont-Darcy holed up in a French monastery. Mary's would-be suitor was found and he offered her a settlement. Mary had a son, Joseph, and is currently unmarried and living with her parents. Darcy also discovered that George Wickham (the villain in *Pride and Prejudice* who seduced and married Lydia Bennet, the youngest Bennet sister) was also his half-brother. Their family reunion went the worst possible way, with fratricide and a complete lack of potato salad. Lydia got over her husband's death rather quickly but was left with two children, George and Isabella Wickham. Brother Grégoire, still a monk, went to live in Austria. Dr. Maddox and Caroline Bingley had a daughter, but also adopted a son—the bastard child of the Prince Regent and a prostitute—named Frederick (the son, not the prostitute).

(There will not be a test. Just so you know.)

When Napoleon invaded Russia in the tumult of war, Darcy lost track of his brother, Grégoire, and Dr. Maddox lost track of his brother, Brian, who was supposed to have married a Transylvanian princess but then disappeared. The two of them traveled to Austria to find them, but ended up in a Transylvanian dungeon as hostages, and their wives ended up rescuing them after locating Grégoire. Brian Maddox and his wife, Princess Nadezhda, reappeared after being missing for two years, having taken the long way home to England via Russia and Japan. So it turned out they had been fine all along. No one was thrilled to hear that the happy couple had been so thoughtless. They brought with them a mixed-race Japanese convict named Mugin, whom I only mention because he pops up from time to time.

Lydia Bennet remarried and had a whole mess of kids with her new husband, Mr. Bradley. Kitty Bennet, the last remaining

Bennet sister to be mentioned, got married to a Mr. Townsend, a story really not worth going into because she isn't a very interesting character so I don't like to spend a lot of time with her.

After the war, Grégoire Bellamont-Darcy moved to Spain, his previous monastery having been dissolved by Napoleon.

There is also a Bavarian saint named Sebald buried in Darcy's graveyard instead of his traditional home in Nuremburg, but there's a long story behind that, so just take it for what it is.

Marsha Altman
New York, NY
2011

Family Tree

Bold face indicates living, *italics* indicates deceased.

THE DARCYS

Henry Darcy
(with unnamed wife)
Gregory Darcy (never married)
Geoffrey Darcy
(children with *Lady Anne Fitzwilliam*)
Fitzwilliam Darcy
(children with **Elizabeth Bennet**)
Geoffrey Darcy
Anne Darcy
Sarah Darcy
Cassandra Darcy
Georgiana Darcy-Kincaid
(children with **Lord William Kincaid**)
Viscount Robert Kincaid
(children with *Mrs. Wickham*)
George Wickham
(children with **Lydia Bennet)**
George Wickham the Younger
Isabella Wickham
(children with Miss Bellamont)
Grégoire Bellamont-Darcy

Assorted:
Lady Catherine de Bourgh – **Mr. Darcy**'s aunt on his mother's side
(children with *Sir Lewis de Bourgh*)
Anne de Bourgh-Fitzwilliam
(children with **Richard Fitzwilliam**, now Lord Matlock)
Edward Fitzwilliam, Viscount of Matlock

THE BINGLEYS

Charles Bingley (I)
(children with *Mrs. Bingley*)
Louisa Bingley-Hurst
(married **Mr. Hurst**, no children)
Caroline Bingley-Maddox
(children with **Dr. Daniel Maddox** – see The Maddoxes)

Charles Bingley (II)
(children with **Jane Bennet**)
Georgiana (Georgie) Bingley
Charles (Charlie) Bingley (III)
Elizabeth (Eliza) Bingley
Edmund Bingley

THE BENNETS

Edmund Bennet
(children with **Mrs. Bennet**)
Jane Bennet-Bingley
(children with **Mr. Bingley** – see *The Bingleys*)
Elizabeth Bennet-Darcy
(children with **Mr. Darcy** – see *The Darcys*)
Mary Bennet
(children with **Giovanni Mastai**)
Joseph Bennet
Kitty Bennet-Townsend
Lydia Bennet-Bradley (formerly Wickham)
(children with *Mr. Wickham* – see *The Darcys*)
(children with **Mr. Bradley**)
Julie Bradley
Brandon Bradley

Assorted:
Mr. Collins – nephew of **Mr. Edmund Bennet**
(children with **Charlotte Lucas-Collins**)
Amelia Collins
Maria Collins
Eleanor Collins

THE MADDOXES

Stewart Maddox
(children with *Mrs. Maddox*)
Brian Maddox
(married to **Princess Nadezhda of Sibui**, no children)
Dr. Daniel Maddox
(children with **Caroline Bingley**)
Frederick Maddox (adopted, son of the **Prince of Wales** and *Lilly Garrison*)
Emily Maddox (same age as Frederick)
Daniel Maddox the Younger

CHAPTER 1

The Miracle Worker

~ ~ ~

"BROTHER GREGORY," said Prior Pullo, "the abbot requests your presence."

Grégoire hadn't even seen Prior Pullo's approach. He had been consumed by his gardening, and his wide straw sun hat blocked most of his vision of the world above the soil. "I am at the abbot's disposal," he said, pushing himself to his feet and setting his tools aside. The patch was coming along nicely, despite the heat; the fauna seemed to have more of a resistance to the Spanish summer than he did.

Grégoire Bellamont-Darcy had worn the cowl eight years now as a Benedictine, with the past four spent in the ancient monastery on the hilltop in Vila de Bares on the Iberian coast. He had thought he might feel lost in his new surroundings. But he had been born in France and had already lived in England and Bavaria, so he knew how to make himself at home. At home was the Rule and the daily rhythms of monastic life, which had been in place for centuries. Some came to run from the world, but he had come to give his life to God. That his accent was different, that he was used to colder climates, or that he was the bastard mix of an English gentleman and his French maid could not stand between Grégoire and the contemplative life in this place

He went happily to the abbot, a kindly old monk who had been appointed by Rome and who would keep his seat until his death or reassignment. Beneath him was Prior Pullo, who did not have the same smile for Grégoire that the others had, despite what he owed him. Grégoire had been offered the position as brother prior the year before, and turned it down. He was not a political animal, and he had the sense to see that path for what it was and avoid it.

It was a long walk up the steep hill to the abbey gates, where he deposited his laughably wide hat and followed the brother prior, taking on a more serious air. Behind the door he sought was a man of great stature and spiritual insight, and he wanted to look at least as though he had not had his robes trailing in the soil. It was not to be. The abbot would take no note of such material concerns, no? How foolish of him to think otherwise.

Grégoire was still chastising himself as he entered. The abbot's office was not particularly grand, but the twelfth-century fresco of saints never failed to astound him in their medieval beauty.

"Father."

"Brother Grégoire," he replied, nodding for the brother to take a seat. The abbot had a busy schedule and this was not the confessional, so he was politely to the point. "There is a rumor on the wind."

"I am not much for rumors, Father. You must enlighten me."

The abbot smiled in a sad sort of way. "It is concerning your conduct with the Valencia house visit."

"I am at a loss, Father." His mind was truly blank. "Is Pablo all right? Has something happened?"

"No, the child is doing quite well, or so I am told."

"Blessed be the Lord," Grégoire said, and crossed himself. This left him to guess, and he did not like to guess. "If this is about the christening, the father was so very insistent that his son would relapse and be damned—" but the abbot raised his hand. This was not the problem.

"You were authorized to perform that christening, and it was overdue." From the day of his birth, Pablo was so ill and covered with sores that the priest was afraid to go near him, much less christen him. It was only during Grégoire's third visit and increasing insistence that the child had recovered enough for the ceremony had the priest been convinced, and Grégoire had been honored to hold the baby for the ceremony so that it could be performed that very night, so late it was almost morning, and save the child from the fires of hell. "The question on some people's minds is how the child was restored to health so quickly."

Still not understanding the situation, Grégoire said, "On the first visit I bathed the child with soap, which had not been done before. He was still very yellow, so I put him in the sun for several hours, as I heard that the sun's rays have restorative effects on a child. On the second visit, he was less so, but he still had the blotches, and I happened to inquire as to where his blanket had been made. His mother said it had been made for her previous child, a girl who had died within days of her birth. I thought it best that they discard the blanket, and they agreed. I bathed him again. The next day, he was restored."

"So I have heard."

"Is…there something wrong with that, Father?"

"Please close the door, Brother Grégoire."

Increasingly uneasy, Grégoire did so, and returned to his seat.

The abbot sat up. "There are people who are calling the child's recovery a miracle. I am seeking the source of these rumors."

This is the first I've heard of them," he said. "Yes, it was a wondrous act of God to return the infant to health. But I believe it was merely a matter of a blanket giving a newborn a rash. I would not call it a miracle, Father."

"Neither would I, though the Good Lord's help is needed in every act, even the most simple." The abbot rubbed his chin. "However, this is not the first case of a quick recovery under your care."

Grégoire swallowed. "Father, I cannot apologize for something that I was sent to do. Nor do I understand why I must."

"You are wiser in the ways of God than in the ways of the world. Although this is generally beneficial, I do not think it aids you here," the abbot said. "Grégoire, the people are willing to believe in miracles—but the word is a precarious one when constantly mentioned concerning one person."

"Father, I did not mean—"

"I know very well what you meant and what you didn't. However, the people may not see it with the same eyes. I wish to protect you from what you will bring upon yourself—or at least make you aware of it. The choice is before you then—whether to continue your visits with the potential of gaining a reputation, for good or ill."

He did not hesitate. "Father, if I am the most qualified to work with the ill and infirm, then it would be most beneficial for everyone involved for me to do so."

"And you are willing to face the consequences?"

"There cannot be bad consequences for doing good work."

The abbot smiled. "It is not for us to know what the consequences of our actions will be."

Grégoire colored, humbly lowering his head. "Forgive me. I do not presume to imagine myself in such a position—"

"Of course not. I will give you time to contemplate your decision. Do not presume lions to be lambs before you throw yourself to them."

~ ~ ~

Walking always settled Grégoire's mind, and unsettled it was. As simply spoken as the abbot had been, the subtlety had not been missed. To be a good monk was one thing. To be a miracle worker was another. "Lord in Heaven," he said, "let me not lead the people toward idolatry."

After Vespers, the air began to cool, but it was not dark yet, and would not be so for a few hours. He set out immediately after supper. He liked the abbey grounds very much. Some fields were sown and some were untouched wilderness. There was a point, not far away, where one could see the coast, and smell the salt in the air.

Little houses populated the area near the cliffs. The residents had lived there for generations, perhaps believing the air to be beneficial, and they worked the abbey lands beyond what the monks themselves could do for a good wage, often in kind. He had been in almost every home and knew almost every family. It was impossible not to.

"Brother Gregory!" someone called out. He turned to see the approach of Señor Diaz, a carpenter responsible for most of the new wooden construction in the abbey. He spoke nothing but Spanish, like most of the people in the area. "Why are you out so late?"

"There is light yet," he said, bowing. "Señor Diaz, how are you?"

"I am well, thank God."

"And your wife? Your daughters?" Diaz had three daughters.

"They are all well." Diaz slapped him on the shoulder, and Grégoire was good at hiding his wince. "Brother, will you carry a message to the abbot? I will tell you first that it is not good news."

"The abbot is an understanding man," Grégoire said. "What is the matter?"

"I am supposed to build the new pews for the chapel, to replace the ones that were eaten by mites last winter. But I do not know how I can do it. The price of the wood the abbey requires is so high—"

"I am sure the abbey will reimburse you for the expense, Señor."

"It is not just that. I will have to travel all the way to Oviedo for the wood, and I do not have the time or the money. You know the storm we had at the beginning of the spring? The very beginning? Right before the days of rain?"

"Yes."

Señor Diaz seemed to be pleading with him. "They destroyed so many houses—I am so busy rebuilding them."

"Business is good for you, then. I am sure the pews can wait. It is only a few that were damaged. Helping the people is more important."

"Yes, but the people have no money to pay me, and I cannot work for free. I am the only carpenter here—I am exhausted. I do not know what I am going to do."

"You say the families are in financial distress?" Grégoire said

"Yes—not for food but for stable roofs. Just yesterday, Señora Alvarado's kitchen roof caved in. She was fortunate to be in the other room, or she might have been killed."

"Why did you not inform the abbot? It is not fair for good people to be without shelter while we live in a castle."

Diaz looked relieved. "I am glad you see it that way, but the abbey already feeds us—we cannot ask for more. I am sorry, but we have our pride."

Grégoire nodded. "I see." He put a hand gently on Diaz's shoulder. "Trust in God, Señor. I assure you that you need not worry about the pews or acquiring the wood."

"Thank you, Brother Grégoire."

He bowed. "I have done little to earn your thanks. But now I must return for Compline. Go with God, Señor Diaz."

"Go with God, Brother Gregory."

He smiled and was on his way. Already a plan was forming in his mind, distracting him from his earlier conversation with the abbot. The families on the coast were in financial distress, but if the abbey gave them the money to rebuild, their pride would be injured. (And Grégoire knew enough about pride from his brother.)

But then there was his ten thousand pounds, most of which lay at his disposal for the year. The English pound was strong, and only a tiny fraction would cover all of their expenses in rebuilding their homes. The abbey did not know about it; Darcy had advised Grégoire to tell the abbey when he was in Bavaria and again before he had left for Spain. Grégoire had seen the wisdom in that. Besides, Benedictines, unlike his previous order, were not averse to dealing with wealth. The only matter was to contact his banker in Madrid and figure out a way to distribute the money anonymously, but by the time he returned to the abbey, he already had some idea of how to go about that.

Feeling considerably more settled, he sang with his brothers at Compline and was dismissed. It was eight, and in seven hours he would be woken for morning prayers and another day. He was hot and tired from the day's work and the walk, and in the privacy of his cell, he removed his cowl and robe, and then painfully removed the vest beneath it. He cleaned away the blood—caked in some areas and wet in others—and then rubbed a lotion over his chest, where the damage from the cilicium—the hairshirt—was most severe. His back was too scarred from previous injuries to be much affected. After the soothing balm set in, he found an easy sleep. He was at peace with the world around him.

CHAPTER 2

Bride and Prejudice

~ ~ ~

"YOU SEE?" MAHMUD SAID as his servant fired the rifle, which emitted only a large sound and smoke but no bullet. "I cannot make it work. This it does, every time. I am afraid to do it myself. Nizam has burned his hands several times."

Mahmud Ali Khan's English was very good, and by now Charles Bingley and Brian Maddox were used to the local accent. Bingley's trade with the East India Company in Calcutta was purchasing dye, but he was in talks to open a cotton plant. The company promised astronomical returns on such an investment, but Mahmud said he was hesitant to introduce a new crop to his extensive lands. Somehow Mahmud had obtained a Baker rifle from the local Sepoy Battalion—Indians employed as soldiers by the British—and was utterly fascinated by it.

"It's the cartridge," Charles Bingley said immediately. "Let me show you—when it cools down."

Tea was brought for them, and the three men—the mogul lord, the fair-haired trader and the Englishman dressed in Japanese clothing—sat beneath a red umbrella. They looked out over their host's gardens, all neatly arranged into rows of plants neither Bingley nor Brian could recognize, but which seemed more colorful than anything they had in England. Beyond them, not far north but out of their direct sight, lay the Ganges. They were trying to purchase tickets for a boat to Agra. Bingley was desperate to see the Taj

Mahal, having heard its virtues extolled many times before he left England. Brian found himself in a more tentative position when exploring the Indian mainland. All of their stops so far—Bombay, Madras and Calcutta—had been coastal and sufficiently English. A thorough Orientalist himself, Brian had weighed his own interests against the fact that he had promised to deliver Bingley safely home. And Brian was not keen on committing seppuku because his cousin had drowned in the sacred river, or had gotten his head bitten off by a tiger, or had been knifed by an insulted shopkeeper because he had mispronounced something in Hindustani and insulted the shopkeeper's daughter. The first threat had been on the boat itself, when Bingley's fair skin had gotten sunburned quite badly in one afternoon. He had spent the rest of the trip wearing one of Brian's bowl-shaped gasa hats, at the expense of Bingley's dignity before the crew.

Bingley had done his best to prepare. Once he had secured his wife's approval for the trip—which he had obtained at a cost he refused to mention—he went to Bath, where the legendary ex-Sepoy Dean Mahomet had a bathhouse. There, Bingley had spent many hours with the bathhouse owner attempting to pronounce languages he had only read in books and never heard spoken. He had also hired a drawing instructor. His penmanship was still hopeless, but to everyone's surprise, he had turned out to be quite talented with a charcoal pencil when using his left hand, mainly because there was no ink involved. He was most dutiful about sketching all that he saw in India as he assumed that life would never bring him to these parts again.

Brian, who had already ridden their company's boat once to the Orient with his wife a year earlier, focused on planning the route. They would be gone easily eight months, and the only communications possible would be from the Cape or Bombay back to England. He had never left his wife for that long in their entire marriage, but she had reassured him that keeping Bingley from getting himself killed was of paramount importance, and she would be fine. She was a samurai's wife, so he had no doubt of it.

So far, no incidents had occurred on the trip that succeeded in taking either of their lives. That was why Brian had accepted the invitation from Mahmud Ali Khan to visit his palace beyond the boundaries of British Calcutta.

Now they sat on pillows as the gun cooled before Bingley. That gentleman, who was familiar with guns from his love of the sport of shooting, picked it up and demonstrated how to load the powder and the cartridge, just as the servant had done. "The key is to make sure the cartridge is all the way in. Sometimes you have to do this..."

He set the gun down, took the ramrod in both hands, and shoved it hard into the barrel.

"...to get in there."

He removed the ramrod, brought the rifle to his right shoulder, and fired high into the sky.

"Perfect!" Mahmud clapped with delight. He stood up and clasped his hands together. "I am grateful to you, Mr. Bingali."

"It's no trouble," Bingley said, handing the rifle back to him.

"No, let me invite you to my daughter's wedding tonight. Surely you will come?"

Bingley cast a glance at Brian, sitting with one of his swords resting on his right shoulder. Brian nodded.

With his patented winning smile, Bingley said, "We'd love to come."

The male crowd that gathered for the wedding of Mahmud's second daughter (out of eight) were largely Muslim moguls, the earliest arrivals arriving in time for evening prayer. The rest were a diverse group of people—Afghans, Hindu Brahmins, a few British officers from the nearest base, and higher-ranked local Bengal troops. The spoken language was mostly Persian, with a surprising amount of

English, and, of course, Hindustani, Punjabi, Urdu, and some scattered Arabic—or at least what Bingley was fairly sure was Arabic.

Neither Brian nor Bingley had ever seen such a display of Oriental pageantry, and they had seen quite a bit of it in the past month. The houses and pavilions were adorned with green branches and bright orange flowers in an elaborate fashion. They passed rows of musicians, and lowered seats, and had been instructed not to speak to the people on the lowered seats beneath them. "Lower class" was a term taken quite literally in India.

The bridegroom was carried in on a palanquin, followed by a train of servants with lit torches, leading him from the house on one end that was his to the place where the bride sat, whom he had never met. Brian had to be careful not to lose Bingley in the crowd of overexcited people thronging to the raised *semiana* for the ceremony, though it was not terribly hard to keep track of a person with red hair in this particular crowd.

The music ceased as the mullah, the priest, entered. He read the wedding ceremony, rings were exchanged, and the couple joined by tying the ends of their shawls together. A glass of sugar water was passed to the bride and groom, and then around to the immediate audience of personal friends and family.

"Whatever you do, don't draw this," Brian said as the dancers entered. They wore embroidered silks and muslins. In some ways, their dress was flowing and modest, not like a tight bodice, but the way they moved did all of the work for them.

"Oh, I promise," Bingley whispered back. Each man brought his palms together at his chest and bowed to the passing Mulna as he sprinkled perfumed water on them.

As the bride and groom were ushered away, the festivities truly began, complete with fireworks that put to shame any of the regent's proud displays in Town. There was a man who seemed to swallow fire, but did not understand Bingley when he asked how he did it, the language barrier being too much or the entertainer not accustomed to being questioned.

The British were officers who had come because they never passed up a free meal. One of them, Kingston, was old and already retired from the military; he now worked as a translator. He claimed to have served under Wellington when he himself had been a colonel and Wellington a general. At that time, the gentleman who was now a duke had led the outnumbered British forces to storm the fortress of Gawilghur during the Anglo–Maratha War.

"He could inspire us to do anything," said Kingston. "Even get ourselves killed. By God, he could do it with a single speech. I wonder whatever became of that man?"

Brian and Bingley shared a laugh as another guest showed them the correct way to smoke a hookah, not like "you bloody foreigners"—hold the pipe just right and do not exhale until the precise moment. They watched the man in a turban bigger than his head puff smoke in rings and were entranced. The mild buzz of tobacco was the only intoxicant there, because their host was religious and did not serve spirits. Instead, there were trays and trays of sweet cakes, bananas, fruits, and bread with honey.

"I would still give anything for a good plate of ribs," Brian said in Japanese. Bingley understood the language adequately, thanks to three months of education on the boat, and they used it when they wanted to talk privately.

"I thought you were an Oriental," Bingley said. Brian had not brought a single piece of English clothing in his trunks.

"An Oriental who would go for a cow right now," he replied. "But don't translate that to this guy," he said as a man in Hindu dress sat down. He had a bright red turban and a red dot on his head. He spoke only Hindi.

"'The eye that spies,'" Bingley translated for Brian. "I think."

"You mean 'all-seeing.'"

"Maybe I do," Bingley said, and then returned to his conversation with Shalok. "What? Yes, I have daughters—well, one of them is, the other is blonde, No, I will not sell the red-haired one! What, 5,000 rupees? No sale. Understand? No sale! Not selling!"

What Brian understood made him fall over sideways with laughter.

~~~

"When did I become the responsible one?" Brian said when they finally made it back to their guest house. It was now well into the morning, and the muezzins were already making their calls for prayer. *Prayer is better than sleep! God is great!*

"Compared with that, my wedding was positively dull for the guests," a sleepy-eyed but still hyperactive Bingley said. He had eaten a great deal of sugar that night, so he was still *quite* awake. He washed his face in the washbasin, scraping off the red body paint on his forehead. "It was fine for me—I honestly don't remember a thing."

"I remember not understanding anything," Brian said, removing his swords and carefully setting them on the cushions. "It was all in Russian, I think. Papist ceremony. And I thought, *What I would give to have Danny see* me *here—wearing a crown and marrying a princess.*"

Bingley lay down on his own bed. He was wearing an orange silk kurta that he used for both sleep and activity, something he found very convenient. "Darcy was at my wedding, but I don't think he was particularly paying attention to me." He sighed in exhaustion. "Maybe we should do something with flowers and fire-eaters for my daughters instead of a vicar going on and on about marriage and sin."

"I'm sure Mrs. Bingley will take well to that." Brian disappeared behind his screen and removed his *hakama,* letting his robe fall down. "And where are you going to get all those tiny flowers?"

"I suppose we'll have to start growing them when we get back. In ten years, they might be ready."

"Ten years?"

"Something tells me Georgie isn't going to be begging me to go out, much less be eager to marry. Eliza, I don't know, but she's only ten, thank goodness." He paused. "May I ask you a personal question?"
~~~

"You may."

"How old is Her Highness?"

"Four and twenty."

Bingley put a hand on his head. It was too early in the morning to be doing these calculations. "So when you were married her, she was—"

"Young, yes. Certainly not anything objectionable, but I am nearly two decades her senior." He sighed. "I've never been good at planning. In fact, I think my entire life has been one happenstance after another."

"Turned out fairly well anyway."

"Still. It would not have been the safest bet. But then again, I was never any good at betting, which was what got me in trouble in the first place."

Bingley laughed. "You should become a Muslim, then. They forbid gambling, so you wouldn't be tempted."

"*And* spirits. No, I would not survive long without a good shot of whiskey, or maybe gin, or beer. I won't be sitting at the dinner table, drinking milk. Like a child."

"I like milk."

"My point exactly."

CHAPTER 3

To the Ends of the Earth

ALTHOUGH ELIZABETH DARCY privately held the opinion that *her* children had been the most beautiful babies in the world, she said otherwise as this particular newborn flailed his tiny limbs around. "He is the most adorable boy I've ever seen." And Viscount Robert Kincaid was indeed a little treasure, still rather pink and often refusing to open his eyes. His hair—what little of it there was—was brown, like his father's.

Lady Georgiana Kincaid (née Darcy) beamed with motherly pride, as could only be expected, and well deserved after the nerve-racking and life-threatening experience that was labor. Despite everyone's fears, all went well, and Baby Kincaid came into the world after just six hours of labor. Within only four days, Georgiana was well enough to stand at the christening, with her brother and sister as godparents.

The Darcys had arrived in the last weeks of Georgiana's confinement, children and all. The mansion was not how Elizabeth remembered it—it had been renovated to be more livable, but you could make a castle only so modern. Lord Kincaid was in fine form. He was good at hiding his nerves, expressing them mainly in fencing with Darcy and Geoffrey. The latter had recently been allowed to take up the sport and seemed to relish it with his father's old enthusiasm. Between Darcy having to fight on his weak side and Geoffrey's age and inexperience, Kincaid easily bested them both, but was good enough to make it not seem as such. Darcy was not so much determined to see his son a fighter as he was to see the future master of Pemberley engage in all forms of masculine activity, and not be overwhelmed by the influence of three younger sisters. Fitzwilliam Darcy loved all of his children as much as a father possibly could, but there were moments when they were all in a room together that he felt he could sympathize with Mr. Bennet. And his daughters weren't even near puberty yet. He didn't wish to imagine it.

Darcy had worried obsessively about Georgiana's state during her entire pregnancy. He had been relieved that she did not conceive during the first few years of marriage, and the earl did not seem to mind in the least. When she did conceive, she was five and twenty, and it was obvious that she was ready, physically and emotionally. Still, during her labor, he had to steel himself with a full glass of whiskey. Their mother had died giving birth to her. He had little memory of the labor—it was a woman's thing—and had been thoroughly confused by this small thing that was supposed to be his sister, though where in the world she had come from, the young Master Fitzwilliam could not tell and no one had enlightened him. But when his mother had taken ill the next day, he noticed. He would have stayed with her, but they mostly kept him out of her room. He saw her only twice before her death two days later. He had lost his mother and was left with this tiny thing that made noises but did not seem as though it would ever be a person. It was not a fair trade. Only his father could assure him that some good had come of it, and as Georgiana grew to be his darling sister, he came to believe him.

Georgiana did survive the labor, and by all appearances remained in good health as Darcy held his new nephew in his arms. William Kincaid stayed with Georgiana as soon as he was allowed back in the room, even while she slept and he sat awake. It was a happy time for all of them. Only one person was missing.

"Mr. Darcy," Lord Kincaid said to him on the third day, "I've asked for a painter to come and make a small portrait of Georgiana and Robert for her brother. Do you think he would take it?"

"I think he would love it," he said. "I will send it with my next correspondence, as soon as you say it is prepared. Did you tell Georgiana?"

"Not yet."

"I'm sure she will be glad to hear it."

Grégoire was missed, but by all accounts he was happy in Spain and very busy there, working with the community. When he could arrange it, he would escape the hot Spanish summer to England, but that didn't happen every year. Surely, this year, with the birth of a nephew, he would get permission.

The Darcys stayed for the christening and for the next few weeks. Georgiana would not be traveling for some time and was reluctant to have them leave. Elizabeth found herself unaccustomed to being without her sister, especially with Mr. Bingley abroad, but Jane was in London with her children, and the Hursts stayed with her, and of course the Maddoxes were in Town until the Prince left for Brighton. The Bingleys (sans Mr. Bingley) would be traveling to Longbourn for the summer as soon as Georgiana Bingley returned. Jane had been cajoled into allowing her daughter to accompany Princess Maddox to Ireland for a brief tour of the coast. The princess had never been to Ireland without her husband nor had Georgie been there without her father so they stuck together while Mr. Bingley and Mr. Maddox made a business trip to Japan (with a stop in India). Their last correspondence had been from a post office in Johannesburg, to say their ship had rounded Africa's coast safely. Beyond that, correspondence would be unlikely, as it would move no faster than they would.

The adults adjusted to the scattering of the family with the knowledge that it was brief, but the children, so accustomed to one another, complained bitterly. Geoffrey was not eager to go to Scotland. He had already lost Georgie and now he would not have Charles, only three younger sisters. Lord Kincaid, whom he had always liked, filled that void to some extent, although Geoffrey remained frustrated that the man he had to spar with was so much taller than he was.

"One day, my boy, you'll grow as tall as your father and you'll be ducking under doorways and bumping your head," his uncle said. "So don't go complainin' now. You'll hit it soon enough."

Geoffrey scowled, but his uncle was right. Geoffrey was twelve. His voice had already dropped an octave (even if it didn't *stay* there all the time) and he had cramps in his legs from rapid growth. He could pick up any one of his sisters, even Anne. But he still couldn't look up at his father and think, *That is what I'm going to be someday*. Or, at least, he couldn't believe it when it did strike him.

And then, of course, there was the *question*. He knew it was awkward, but he didn't know why. He could just sense it as he held his cousin Robert. "So babies come from stomachs?"

His father's immediate response was stony silence, which was what his father did when he was uncomfortable. His mother's response was to laugh and lean into his father. "Essentially," his father finally said, staring out the window instead of at him. And that was it. That was all he was going to get. Geoffrey looked back down at Robert. If Uncle Bingley were here, he would explain it to him. Uncle Bingley couldn't keep a secret. When he returned, Geoffrey would ask him.

"What did he say?" Anne asked him immediately when he left the room.

"Nothing."

"He's Papa. What did you expect?"

And so that mystery remained unsolved. At least, that is, until Uncle Bingley came home.

~ ~ ~

"It's a boy," Jane announced to her audience of the Hursts and the Maddoxes. The post had arrived after luncheon, but she had held it for dinner. "Robert Kincaid."

"*Viscount* Robert Kincaid," Louisa said.

"Perhaps we should give him a few years before he is required to use his title," Dr. Maddox said.

"And at least five before he must attend a ball," said Mr. Hurst, raising his glass of whiskey in a gesture for the newborn.

"Does he take after his mother or his father in appearance?" Caroline asked.

"Lizzy says that he has Lord Kincaid's hair and Georgiana's eyes."

"Is he a lively child?"

"I don't seem to recall any newborns being interested in anything other than eating and sleeping," Dr. Maddox said to his wife.

"I believe she is asking if he is a screamer," Louisa said.

"She doesn't say," was all Jane offered. Even if he were, Lizzy would not write it to be read publicly.

"What you don't want," Caroline said, "is twin screamers."

"Oh *goodness,*" Dr. Maddox said. "*Yes*. God, yes."

"Unhappy memories, Dr. Maddox?" Mr. Hurst said with a smile.

"I remember leaving for work in the evening with both of them screaming, and then returning in the morning to the same state of affairs."

"But you weren't there at night!" Caroline said indignantly. "You had somewhere else to be!"

"Oh, hush, Caroline," Louisa said. "Whenever you complained about Charles, Mama would remind you that you were the loudest of all of us as an infant."

Caroline Maddox stared down her sister as her husband covered his mouth with his napkin to prevent her seeing his expression. "I don't recall any such nonsense."

"You were four—how would you? But *I* remember it."

Mr. Hurst burst out laughing, which was a godsend. Most of the rest of the room did the same as Caroline silently fumed but would not, even after much prodding, admit to it.

~ ~ ~

"It's so hot out," Georgiana Bingley said, looking up at the sky. "Why is the water so cold?"

Princess Nadezhda Maddox shook her head. "The ocean is always cold. Don't be a baby." She had already waded in ahead of her niece, holding up her kimono to her knees so her bare feet could soak in the salt water. "What would your father say?"

"That it's not proper for a girl to play in the ocean without a suitable bathing costume?"

"Well, good that he's in the Orient, then, and not here to say that," Nadezhda said. Her English was very good, and she retained a charming Romanian accent. "Now come in. You get used to it."

"My dress will be all messy!"

"Georgiana Bingley!" her aunt said with mock indignation. "When have you *ever* cared about a dress being dirty?"

Georgie could offer no opposition, so she stepped out of her sandals and splashed into the water, which went up to her knees much quicker than it had for Nadezhda. "It's rocky."

"Not if you know where to step. Look down and see how beautiful the water is," Nadezhda said, and Georgie did so. "The first time I ever saw the ocean was in Russia, on the coast. The port was half frozen and the water was so dark it wasn't blue. It was almost black. Not like this." She kicked at the water, splashing Georgie, who cried out and then laughed. "The second time I saw the ocean from land was when I came to the docks at the filthy Thames. Look how beautiful this is." All around them was green—the rocky coast and the rich shades of the Irish fields. It seemed to color the water an odd and perfect shade of blue.

"Will yeh be needin' anyt'in' else, Yer Highness?" called O'Brien, their coachman, as he doffed his dirty cap. "'Sides from da towels and da tea."

"No, thank you."

He donned his cap and walked off, leaving them alone on the shore. Technically, he was their bodyguard, but Nadezhda's sword was intimidation enough, especially when she walked as though she knew how to use it, instead of being an aristocrat carrying a sign of her office. She was a samurai's wife, and she took that as seriously as her husband did. No one questioned her odd dress when they heard her accent—how were they to know the difference between a Hungarian princess dressed as a Hungarian and a Hungarian princess dressed as a Japanese?

Nadezhda and Georgie eventually tired of standing in the water and played on the shore. Nadezhda set up a branch in the sand as a target and had Georgiana hurl coins at it. Few of them hit their target. "Some did," Nadezhda said encouragingly, before taking down the makeshift tree with one good flip of the wrist to its lower trunk. Georgie picked up all the coins, large circles with pointed edges and a hole in the center, and Nadezhda put them back on the string in her pocket. Wet from the splashing of the waves against the rocks and the sea breeze, Nadezhda toweled off Georgiana's hair. Her own was protected by her headdress.

"Can I braid your hair?"

"Tonight," Nadezhda said. "Not now. Someone might come along and see us."

"But they can see *my* hair."

"You are not married and you are not from Transylvania," her aunt responded. Georgiana had shot up in the past six months. She was still quite short, but Nadezhda did not have to kneel to be at her level. "My hair is for my husband, not other men."

"Did you let him see it before you married him?"

"I did not. He was most curious about it," she said with a smile as they collected their things and made their way back to the path that would take them up to their coach. "If you hide something, it makes people curious. If you show it all the time, they get bored. Men, especially. I cover it and it becomes special, something only for him." *Among other things,* she added silently. "And you. But if your brother asked, I would not let him."

"What about Uncle Maddox?" Georgie said, referring to her proper uncle, the doctor.

"Only if I had a scalp wound."

"What about Papa?"

"No."

"What about the King of England?"

Nadezhda smiled and looked down at Georgie. "It would never come up, but no. Not even for the King of England. For my husband only."

The sun was setting when they returned to their inn. From the room, they could see the water and hear the waves. Despite the beauty of it all, Georgie was noticeably melancholy as she watched the skyline turn red and then a deepening blue.

Nadezhda put a hand on her shoulder. "We'll be home soon."

Georgie nodded.

"You miss your father?"

She nodded again.

"I miss my husband," Nadezhda said, taking Georgiana into her arms. "But they'll be home soon."

"Do you think they're all right?"

"I'm sure that Brian will take good care of your father."

~ ~ ~

"It says *what?*" Brian said. He hadn't heard the first time over the din of the crowds, who were cheering as the wushu master on the platform defeated yet another opponent by pushing him off the stage.

Mugin, who could speak Chinese but not read it, had to have it read to him by the man offering the sheet of rice paper. "It is a death contract. In case the challenger dies in the fight, it is legal."

"We've not seen a single person die in one of these fights," Bingley said, his eyes still on the champion.

"We've witnessed only limbs broken and heads bashed. Nothing *serious,*" Brian said to Bingley.

"I still want to do it."

"Of all the stupid things I've let you do on this trip—"

"I told you, I did not know the word meant 'prostitute'! I

thought I was saying that she was a dancer! How good do you expect my Punjabi to be the first time I hear it spoken?"

"For God's sake, man, you put your head in a tiger's mouth before I could stop you!"

"The handler said it was safe," Bingley shouted. "And I emerged with my head intact."

"Because I saved you!"

"Arguable. Other times, you *definitely* saved me. But that one is up for debate." Bingley turned to Mugin. "Is it safe? The contest?"

"You can't win, Binguri-chan."

"Of course not. I just want to try it."

Brian growled. "Will you please find things to try that don't involve wild animals, compromising situations, or experts in martial combat?"

"Oh, *Brian Maddox* has never done anything daring or outright insane."

"Not while I was guarding a relative, no." He paused. "Well, yes, but not *this time*."

"I will take care of it," Mugin said, and began to argue with the official in Chinese. Eventually, money changed hands and he handed the contract to Bingley. "Sign."

Before Brian could lodge a protest, Bingley signed his name. The wushu master, a young man with a surprisingly pleasant disposition, given his violent trade, smiled and helped him up into the ring.

"He's just going to knock him around a little," Mugin said, grabbing Brian's kimono to stop him from following his charge, "not hurt him."

"I hope the bribe was big enough," Brian said.

Bingley stepped up on the matted dais. The announcer began to speak to the crowd of men with identical queues, and raised Bingley's arm. "*Hongmao Guizi!*" he bellowed.

There were boos from the crowd, and a little laughter. Mugin just laughed.

"What'd he call him?"

"Red-furred demon," Mugin answered.

Bingley, clueless as ever, was not put off at all as the announcer raised the hand of the current champion, and the crowd cheered. The champion bowed with a hand gesture that Bingley copied incorrectly, with his fist on the wrong side.

"Five dago he lasts more than three seconds," Mugin said.

"You know I don't gamble anymore, Mugin-san, don't try to tempt me," Brian said, watching as Bingley assumed a fighting position. "Though it is tempting."

Brian would have won the bet. Bingley succeeded in throwing a single punch, which, of course, was sidestepped by the champion, who grabbed Bingley's wrist and pulled him forward as he kicked his challenger's feet out from under him. Bingley landed on his back as the crowd gave their noisy approval.

"Ow," Bingley said. He looked up, and the champion was offering a hand. "What? We're still going? Fine, I'm a sporting man."

"So do you give up?" the challenger said in broken Japanese. He assumed a different but still complex stance as Bingley slowly got to his feet and tried again. And again. After landing on his back three times (the third in a full flip, with the champion somehow sliding under him entirely as he did it), he tapped the ground.

"Ow. Winner," he said in Japanese, pointing to the champion. Smiling, the master helped Bingley to his feet again, and Bingley raised the master and still-champion's hand up. That was as long as he could manage to stay standing before he collapsed again, and Brian and Mugin leaped up to help him off the stage.

"That was...I think I need—to be ill," Bingley said.

Brian stifled his own smile as the cheering continued. As he helped Bingley to sit down on the stands again, he watched Mugin and the champion exchange some words before Mugin jumped off the dais and rejoined them. The official presented him with a certificate of his defeat, which Bingley probably would have appreciated more if he hadn't been vomiting into a porcelain vase.

The day's fights were over, and the crowd began to disperse as people returned to their businesses. The champion stepped off the dais and approached the three of them, saying something to Mugin.

"He says he was most interested to fight a foreigner," Mugin said. "He would like to invite us to dinner."

"Of course," Brian said, and bowed to the champion.

"His name is Ji Yuan," Mugin said, and translated their answer in more formal terms to the champion, who took his leave. "You are all right, Binguri-chan?"

"I'm going to be a bit—ow," he said, trying to stand, "—sore in the morning, but I think so, yes." He squinted. "Do they have, say, doctors in China?"

An hour later, they were back at the inn, where a terrified Bingley was lying with needles in his back, a prospect he found far more intimidating than fighting a wushu master.

"Don't complain; you got yourself into this," Brian said, stepping into the other room. Bingley was bruised, but not harmed, as promised. In the next room, Mugin was drinking whatever the local vintage was. "What did Ki Yun say to you?"

"Ji Yuan," Mugin corrected. "He challenged me."

"And you said no? *To a fight?*" Brian leaned against the doorway. "What is wrong?"

"Nothing," Mugin said. "I did you a favor, you know. You should give me the money."

"What money?"

"The prize money. For winning."

Mugin was being amply compensated for serving as their translator during their visit to Hong Kong and their minor expedition into mainland China, so that was hardly the issue. "You would have won that fight, wouldn't you?"

"He is wushu master here. If I beat him, I take his title, his honor. His students abandon him. He has no reputation until he beats me," Mugin said, taking another swig and launching into his meat dish. "It would have been big trouble for all of us. More trouble than fighting is worth."

"I never thought I would hear you say that," Brian said. "Thank you, Mugin. But how can you be sure that you would have won?"

Mugin took a mouthful, swallowed, and followed it with the liquor. "Ah, spicy. His technique was good, and he knows more about the use of chi than his competitors, but he doesn't know how to use that to make himself faster." He offered Brian the bottle, but Brian turned it down with a gesture. "I studied wushu for three years in a school in the north. I'm faster; I would beat him."

"Do you think he knows it?"

"Yes."

"Then we do owe you a favor," Brian said. "But before you say it—I am *not* buying you a prostitute."

Mugin scowled at him and turned away in a huff.

CHAPTER 4

The Scholars

~ ~ ~

DANIEL MADDOX, LICENSED PHYSICIAN and surgeon, was not known to take part in the many pleasures offered to him at Carlton House. Even in the riotous atmosphere of the Prince Regent's grand parties, now almost nightly, he did not socialize with the upper crust, keeping his professional veneer intact. This evening, having just come from his own meal in his own home, he did not sup with the guests—even though he was told repeatedly he was welcome to do so. Around midnight he did partake of a light dinner, which he took alone in the kitchen. While the upper crust of English society drank and feasted and did things that would surely make the *Courier*, he sat quietly with a medical journal from the Continent. He sat awaiting his usual cue. The Regent or a guest would pass out, and he would be called in to resuscitate the reveler. On one occasion, the sixth Duke of Devonshire, who would have been the richest man in England but for his gambling habit, tripped against the outer corner of the Chinese-style pagoda, and Dr. Maddox put three stitches in his knee. The soused but nonetheless grateful duke gave him his diamond-encrusted snuffbox on the spot. Not a fan of snuff and not wanting it around his sons, he had the diamonds removed and made into a necklace for his wife, the silver box paying for the expense. Caroline walked on air for a week, which was the only joy he had from the entire exchange.

Tonight, there was nothing. Despite having eaten and drunk too much, and been liberal with his snuff, the Regent was still on both feet well into the early morning. Dr. Maddox had finished the *French Medical Monthly* and the *Prussian Medical Review*, and had fallen back on the new edition of *Sir Gawain and the Green Knight*. He was sipping tea and enjoying his reading when a servant approached. "His Royal Highness, Prince William, to see you, sir."

"The Duke of Clarence?" he said, but before he could receive an answer, the third son of King George and the Prince Regent's brother, entered. Dr. Maddox quickly rose and bowed. "Your Highness."

"I understand that you are my brother's chief physician."

"I am, Your Highness."

When he looked up, he saw the duke eyeing him skeptically. "Where was your training?"

"Cambridge, sir. And then the Academy in Paris."

"You can *see* my brother, can you not?"

He held back a smirk. "Yes, Your Highness. I assure you that I can."

"So you are either grossly incompetent or he refuses to take your advice. Knowing George, it is the latter."

"I cannot discuss my patient's behavior. I can say that every man is master of his own fate."

"Have you ever met my father, Doctor?"

"I have, sir, but only briefly."

"His doctors control his fate entirely, though I suppose it does little good."

"I am not his doctor, sir, and therefore cannot make an assessment."

"You are discreet indeed," said the duke. "I can see why he employs you—that and whatever medical skills you may have." He stepped closer to him. "Please do me the favor of keeping my brother alive. I care not for the prospect of the throne. It seems the most tedious job in the kingdom."

Never one to interfere with family (especially royal family) squabbles, Dr. Maddox merely nodded and said, "I will do my best, Your Highness."

Without a word of good-bye, the duke turned and took his leave.

~ ~ ~

It was well past dawn when Dr. Maddox walked home. He did not live far, the streets were easily navigated in the morning light, and the carriages leaving Carlton House were filled with people returning to their homes in a drunken stupor, so it was more convenient to walk. There was a beggar on the corner—a boy with one leg—and he dropped a shilling in the boy's upturned cap before ascending the stairs to his townhouse. The servants were, of course, expecting his arrival.

"Is my wife by chance awake yet?" he asked as the doorman removed his overcoat. It was still early for a normal person.

"No, Dr. Maddox."

He sighed and headed to his own room, where he threw some water on his face to clean off the London smog before climbing into his clean sheets, and into a dreamless sleep.

When he woke at about two, he was informed that his wife was entertaining friends. He had a tray brought to his study, where the post was already in, but nothing seemed important. Seeing as his wife was still engaged, he unlocked his laboratory door and checked on his poppy plants. They were lodged next to the window and beneath glass to protect them from Town air. Despite his daily watering, he could not seem to get them to stay alive for long. The delicate things withered away. He plucked a leaf from one of them, put the plant back in the case, and put the leaf under his microscope. He was still inspecting it when he heard the door open. The children and most of the servants were not allowed in the laboratory, and he always kept watch on the door when it was unlocked. "Good morning." It was his first smile of the day.

Caroline Maddox kissed him on the cheek. "Good afternoon."

"I know," he said playfully, taking his seat again next to the microscope. "I think I'm going to have another crop failure this year."

"Are these the seeds that Brian gave you?"

"Yes, and they were straight from the Orient. Nonetheless, they don't seem much good." So far, he was still buying raw opium the traditional way—in a shadier section of East London. "I spoke with a botanist, but he didn't know much about poppy. Or wasn't willing to admit to it." He looked up. "How are the children? I've not seen them today."

"Emily has writing instruction, and Frederick is pretending to study with the Greek tutor."

"Not everyone likes Greek."

"Or any other challenging subject."

"Well, I wasn't going to say it unprovoked," he said. "He's a boy. If we were at Kirkland, he would be out in the woods, enjoying the weather."

"And making trouble."

"It is the primary occupation of boys."

"Your sex will protect its own to the very end," she huffed.

"I would say the same of yours, but I prefer to be polite," he replied, which softened her countenance just a little. "I haven't heard a peep from Danny all day. Did you take away his recorder?"

"I had the excuse that you were sleeping."

He smiled, but it was a sad sort of smile as he fumbled with one of the more harmless instruments on the table. "The Prince is set to go to Brighton at the end of the month."

She didn't miss it. "So? You just said that Frederick was suffering from cabin fever. Brighton will clear that up. And Danny loves playing in the ocean."

He just nodded. This would be their fourth summer trailing the Prince Regent to Brighton, all expenses paid for the entire Maddox family, for most of the summer. It had its pleasures. Nonetheless, he said, "I am thinking about resigning my post." Before Caroline could whip her head around with an indignant question, he continued calmly, "We have the money to do it. Even if the Prince refused to pay my retirement salary, which he is under obligation to do, we have enough put away to provide Emily with a decent inheritance. And if you wanted a manor in the country, we would only need to sell the stock in our brothers' company. I'd probably have the best patient list in the whole Royal Society of Medicine. And you know that I was offered a position at Cambridge."

Her indignation melted. "If he even *let* you resign—"

"I think he would, if I agreed to find a suitable replacement and still occasionally checked up on him."

Now Caroline had reason to pause. "You've considered this."

"I prefer to consider everything I do."

"Is your job so terrible?"

His expression probably said enough. "I enjoy my profession. What I do not enjoy is spending hours in a sitting room waiting for my patient to pass out because he did precisely the opposite of what I told him to do for his health. The last person I actually helped was the Duke of Devonshire, and only because the edges of the pagoda were sharpened to look exotic." He frowned. "I sleep most of the day. Frederick needs more instruction, but I'm not awake to give it. Danny hates Town life and is off at Kirkland or Brian's estate whenever he can secure my approval. And as ungentlemanly as it may be..." he said, "I'd rather spend my nights sleeping in your chamber."

"You do make a very convincing argument," she said, kissing his hand—the one with all the fingers. What would otherwise have been a lovely moment was broken by the sound of something shattering. "*Frederick!*" his mother shouted.

There was scurrying in the hallway, and Frederick Maddox appeared at the door. "I know what you're thinking, and Danny—"

"Your brother is asleep," Caroline said.

"Noble effort," Dr. Maddox added.

Frederick's next plan was to run as fast as he could up the stairs. This scheme worked until Nurse found him hiding in the attic. For his punishment, he spent an hour sitting on a pillow.

~ ~ ~

After briefly stopping at Pemberley, the Darcy family headed south to London, where they would spend a month before the real heat set in. There were relatives to visit and business that had been put off for practically the entire time of Lady Georgiana's confinement. Mary and Joseph Bennet, who rarely left Hertfordshire, were visiting the Gardiners while Jane and her three younger children stayed at Longbourn with Mr. and Mrs. Bennet. They would all gather at Longbourn for Edmund's birthday. Mr. Bennet, never much of a traveler, stayed on his grounds for everything but church now, owing to his great age. Elizabeth's one regret about moving to Derbyshire was the fact that her father was denied the presence of his two favorite daughters. He wrote often, and they in turn, but that would not fill the gap. Mr. Bennet wrote that he was staying alive merely to confound Mr. Collins (who now had *four* daughters).

The Darcy children were eager to be in town and ecstatic the whole way, which was why they had their own carriage. At last, Geoffrey begged admittance to his father's carriage, and with a smile, Darcy agreed. "Why is it that our children never seem to remember how hot, smelly, and dirty town is? They'll be complaining within a week."

"I want to see George," his son announced. George Wickham, who was turning thirteen the following week, now lived with his sister and mother in an apartment on Gracechurch Street with Lydia's new husband and their infant son. "Do I have tutoring today?"

"Of course you do," Darcy said without taking his eyes off his ledger.

"George doesn't have tutors. Why?"

"Because George teaches himself," Elizabeth said, exchanging a glance with her husband. It was the most polite reason to give. Now out of Longbourn, the Wickham children's formal education was limited. "Did he ask for anything for his birthday?"

Darcy had a semi-regular correspondence with this particular nephew. "He wants a set of Homer in Greek."

"*So* boring," Geoffrey said, leaning back against the cushion.

"People have different tastes," Elizabeth said, stroking her son's hair. He had his father's coloring and his mother's curls. "Uncle Bingley likes to read about foreign countries. Your father likes to read his ledgers."

Darcy gave her a look. She smiled.

George Wickham (the Younger or the Third, depending on one's perspective) sat on his bed next to the window that overlooked the row of apartments lining Gracechurch Street. He was lying on his bed, with his feet kicked up on the dresser. Having recently outgrown the cot, he was forced to sleep with his feet sticking out until the new one arrived. Mr. Bradley had said it was on order, and would surely be there by his birthday. His mother had told him he should ask his uncle for a bed, but fortunately, her new husband thought otherwise.

He was still trying to make his way through the *Divine Comedy*—which was confusing enough even with his Latin dictionary handy—when Isabella Wickham burst through the door and slammed it behind her, without knocking, of course. George only turned his head sideways. "What did you do, Izzy?"

"Oh, for heaven's sake, am I to be chastised by *everyone* in this house? Even *you?*"

"What did you do?" he repeated, his voice not at all stern, but nonetheless serious.

She sat down on the remaining space of the bed, next to his legs. "It's not my fault that the baby cries every time I pick him up!" she huffed.

"Did you hold him upside down again?"

"No, George."

"Did you forget to support his head?"

"No! Of course not. He just cried. There's no reason. He always cries."

"He's a newborn. What do you expect of him?"

"Are you taking Brandon's side?"

He put his book down on his chest. "I cannot take a side with or against an infant. 'Tis impossible."

"Mama is so tired," Isabel said, "and she's so cranky when she's tired. Why did she have another baby so soon after Julie?"

"I don't know. I don't think she had much to do with the decision."

"What does that mean?"

"It means I will explain it when you are old enough. Or Mother will. God, I hope it does not fall on my shoulders to do so."

"*George!*" She tugged at his vest. "Tell me!"

He shook his head. "It is not for people our age. I merely read it in a book."

"Then I'm going to read every book in your room until—"

"A *French* book."

Isabella stuck her tongue out at him. "No fair."

"I'm sure there is a time—probably before the wedding—when all good mothers sit down with their daughters and tell them all about how to have a baby."

"And sons? Would Mr. Bradley tell you if you didn't already know because you read it in one of those picture books of ladies?"

"You don't know about those!" he said. "I paid you a sovereign never to mention them again!" "I know," she said and giggled. "I just wanted to see you blush."

George picked up his book again, mainly to hide his face.

"Fine, be like that. Will you lend me a shilling?"

He lowered the book again. "Why would I lend you a shilling?"

"Because there's a new ribbon colored with Indian dye, and I want to get it and look pretty for your birthday. I know you have the money because you got money for Christmas and you haven't spent a farthing of it. And I'm your little sister and you love me."

He sighed, mainly in defeat. "Why do you need so many ribbons?"

"Why do you need so many books?"

They were surrounded by books. He had overloaded his bookcases and, in desperation, started piling them up in neat stacks on the floor. He could expound on the virtues of learning over the importance of looking pretty, but he knew it would get him nowhere. Instead, he reached over to his dresser, opened the top drawer, unlocked the small box inside it, and handed her a shilling.

She kissed him on the cheek. "Thank you."

"The way you could really thank me would be to spend at least a few farthings of this on a gift."

"What, a book?" she said. "I'll do my best." She did always get him something he actually liked, and she would use her own spending money to do it. "I'm going out, if anyone asks."

"Do you need me?"

"No, Lucy Gardiner is going to join me. I won't be *unescorted*." Coin in hand, she got up and headed for the door.

"Be careful anyway."

She rolled her eyes. "You worry too much." She left, slamming the door again. One of these days, it was going to come right off its hinges, and Mr. Bradley would have to repair it.

There are worse things, he thought, and returned to Dante.

CHAPTER 5

The Infamous George Wickham

~ ~ ~

"NO. ABSOLUTELY NOT."

Dr. Maddox sighed. The refusal was not unexpected. His formal letter of resignation was still in the Regent's hands, fluttering in the wind. Somehow, he had succeeded in getting his patient to walk in the park, but the Prince of Wales was so afflicted with gout and extra weight that he had made it only to a bench not far from the house. "Your Highness, you know that I will eventually need to retire on account of my—"

"You would be a better doctor blind than half the Royal Society of Medicine," the Regent said.

"You are underestimating the intelligence of my colleagues, sir."

The Prince put down the letter, squinting in the sunlight. "What's this all about, then?"

"I want to do more charity work. I want to maybe write a paper or two." He frowned. "I want to spend more time with my family."

This gave the Regent pause. "I suppose your current schedule doesn't much suit theirs."

"No, sir, it does not."

"That does not change the fact that I need your medical advice—not that I take much of it," the Prince said and chuckled. Dr. Maddox said nothing to that. "But when something serious does happen—and you keep diligently warning me that it will—I will need you." He handed the letter back to the doctor. "Nonetheless, the subject of one of my father's constant lessons, when he was still capable of lecturing us, was the importance of family. And not listening to him—well, you see how that turned out for the House of Hanover."

Again, Dr. Maddox had no comment. He looked down at his shoes.

"I will be here another month. Less, if I can help it; more, if Parliament can help it. You have that time to find a suitable replacement. But you will remain my chief physician and will be expected to respond—at a moment's notice, when possible, and as quickly as you can, when not possible—if something dire occurs. You will remain at the same salary, and will be expected to keep in regular touch with the attendant physician—correspondence at least once a week—so that you are apprised of my current condition. You are still forbidden to work in the cholera wards, or any public hospital in London. I won't have you dying on me just yet. Otherwise, you may do as you please."

He bowed. "Thank you, Your Royal Highness." Though he had expected at least some kind of new arrangement, he was still overwhelmed. This was the best he could have hoped for. "Thank you very much, sir."

"I heard you were offered a position at Cambridge. Will you take it?"

"I—I don't know. It depends if my wife and children wish to live there."

"Do you make any decisions for yourself, Dr. Maddox?"

He colored. "I made this one."

The Regent laughed. He was generally a jovial person—when not horribly depressed. "If you do decide to take a position at Cambridge or Oxford, let me know immediately."

"Yes, sir."

"Go forth, my good man, and do the world some good. I loosen your chains, though I have not broken them," said the Prince, who had a flair for the dramatic. "And if I find you in estrangement from your beloved family, which you hold above your sovereign, I will hang your words from the highest tree, I shall!"

"I will not disappoint you, sire," Dr. Maddox said with a smile.

The first sound that greeted Dr. Maddox was not the sweet voice of his wife or the laughter of his children. It was the harsh, loud, metallic sound of a recorder note. After his coat and wig were removed, he immediately headed up to the nursery, where he found his three-year-old son sitting angelically on a blanket on the floor. "When I said I wished him to learn about music," Maddox said to Nurse, "I did not wish him to be quite so enthusiastic." He pulled the recorder out of his son's mouth, and prevented a tantrum by immediately picking him up. "Daniel, I love you very much, and although it is not lessened while you are playing that instrument, I suggest you take up a new one."

"*Father*," his son said, squirming in his arms, "I like it."

"Because you enjoy music or because it is loud?"

His son looked up at him, but either did not understand the question or did not know the correct answer.

"I thought so," Dr. Maddox said, kissing him on his head of curly red hair before setting him down. "You can have it back tomorrow, preferably when your mother and I are out."

"Finally, the voice of reason," Caroline said in the doorway. She told Nurse to put their son down for an afternoon nap, and they moved into her chamber. "How was your discussion with the Prince Regent?"

"I am still to be his well-paid chief physician," he said, "but no longer his nursemaid. I have to hire a new one before he goes to Brighton, but otherwise..." His voice trailed off as his wife embraced him. "Not many wives would be so eager to have their husbands at home all day."

"I was assuming you would be spending it at White's," she said, kissing him on the cheek. "Drinking and gambling and leaving us all well enough alone."

"I am sorry to disappoint you," he said. "He was reluctant to relinquish me."

"I assume you were persuasive."

"I said something about wanting to spend time with my children."

"You know how to manipulate a Prince as well as anyone on the Privy Council."

"Just *that* prince," he clarified, and kissed her. He was not the dashing man of one and thirty that he had been when they were married—not that he had ever considered himself *dashing*—and he had come home from his trip to Austria with more than a few gray hairs. But Caroline still loved to run her hands through his bushy hair, and he still loved her creamy white skin.

"I invited the Darcys for dinner," she said when she had a moment to breathe.

"Very well," he said and nodded. "Of course, I'll have to rush off after dinner."

"Then let's make the most of our time now," Caroline responded.

Their door remained closed until it was time to dress for dinner.

The Darcys arrived on time as usual, bringing with them their two eldest. Geoffrey and Frederick got on well despite their age differences, while Emily and Anne were best friends the way only ten-year-old girls could be, which involved a lot of giggling and squealing. In other words, the children entertained each other as the adults sat down for dinner. They toasted the Darcys' newest nephew and Dr. Maddox's semi-retirement.

"No, he is still not permitted to talk about his patient," Caroline said.

"I doubt that I know any more about His Royal Highness's physical state than half of the town," Dr. Maddox replied.

"Are you to go to Brighton?"

"We are searching for somewhere else to summer," Caroline said.

"Few people can boast of being bored with Brighton," Elizabeth said.

"Some places in Wales are very fine in the summer," Darcy added.

"You say that because you went shooting there once with Charles," Caroline said. To Elizabeth she said, "He was going to buy a house there before we both talked him out of it—too distant from society."

"There's always Bath," Elizabeth suggested, "and it has all those positive health qualities."

"Not Bath," Dr. Maddox grumbled.

Because he rarely grumbled, she added, "Do you have a professional assessment of the healing waters of Bath, Dr. Maddox?"

Before Caroline could attempt to stop him, Dr. Maddox answered: "If you were in your own home and you bathed while ill in water with another person who had a different illness, would you consider that healthy? Or even sane?"

"You always have to go ruining medical fashion with your logic," Caroline said. She and Elizabeth had a laugh at that, and the husbands exchanged amused glances.

"I rest my case," said the doctor.

With no great fanfare, George Wickham turned thirteen. He did receive a larger bed from Mr. Bradley, for which he was grateful. His mother, consumed by attending to her smaller children, did not host a family gathering. It was George and Isabella who received visitors who came to drop off gifts. The Gardiners came by with their children, now of age except for the youngest, Lucy, who was Isabella's closest companion. George was given new clothes—which he desperately needed, having grown nearly six inches in six months—and a pocket watch. His grandparents and Aunt and Uncle Townsend sent their presents by post—books from Grandfather and Grandmother and handkerchiefs from the Townsends, sewn by Aunt Kitty herself. (Mr. Townsend included a small envelope with two sovereigns for George to use "as you see fit.") Aunt Bingley had left her present at the house, to be given to him that day.

"How many books are you going to get?" his sister said. "You can't *eat* them."

"You could make furniture from them at this point," Mr. Bradley said, and slapped his stepson on the back.

In the afternoon, the Darcys visited. George had already spent time with Geoffrey since the arrival of the Darcys at their townhouse. Geoffrey was adept at using George as an excuse to get out of his lessons. George didn't mind; he could count the number of friends he had on one hand, and not use all his fingers.

To his surprise, Aunt Darcy sat with her sister and Mr. Bradley while Uncle Darcy offered to take him out to a club for lunch. He had never been to one before, and Geoffrey rather noticeably expressed his annoyance at not being invited. "Your time will come to eat bad food and watch rich men make fools of themselves," his mother had said when he complained.

George knew Uncle Darcy cared about him more than his father ever had and more than Mr. Bradley ever would, and part of him was now old enough to realize why. He had been six when his father died, and unlike his sister, he remembered him and he remembered the funeral. Uncle Darcy had spent it in an armchair because he was too weak to stand and had nearly died of his own injuries in the fatal duel with George's father. George's mother had never made any secret of how her first husband had died, and how much Uncle Darcy owed them for "killing my husband." Thankfully, that had died down when she married Mr. Bradley, because it always brought Isabella to tears of disbelief. How could their father have been a bad man? How could Uncle Darcy have killed him in a duel? George was old enough to remember some details. And Uncle Darcy had never denied it, but never looked pleased when Lydia brought it up. Actually, Uncle Darcy had always looked horrified, and unconsciously tried to hide his right hand, which bore the scar from the fight. Young Master George was not very talkative, but he was a good observer.

Despite all the history between them, he saw no reason not to like Uncle Darcy. He liked all of the Darcys, he had decided long ago, despite all of the evidence not in their favor. He closed his ears to his mother's complaints, though it made him uneasy to do so. But he swallowed these anxieties with the small amount of whiskey offered to him as he sat down at White's with his favorite uncle.

Though he still had to return to the Bradley house on Gracechurch Street to reclaim his wife and children, Darcy was relieved that the visit had, so far, gone well. Lydia Bradley had been too distracted by her infant to complain to him. He knew she always applied to her sisters for money (and got it, though in measured amounts), but since Wickham's death, she had been relentless about hounding Darcy for money. He felt that his debts had been settled; he had paid for the funeral, and had been more than generous in sitting up trusts for both the Wickham children. His financial penance would go only so far. He would not give her access to either child's account, explaining again and again the nature of a *trust fund* and how the money could not be gotten at for ten years. But it would fall on deaf ears. So he would sigh and go back to his old habit of ignoring her.

When Lydia had lived at Longbourn, Mr. Bennet had provided for her, but to an extent she deemed unsuitable (he had apparently learned the lessons of time). It had been a relief for everyone when she married Mr. Bradley. He was a former colonel who had been injured in the battle of Toulouse in 1814, and discharged with an eye patch, thereby escaping the carnage at Waterloo the following year. Aside from his injury reward and retirement pay, he had inherited thirty thousand pounds from his aunt upon her death and quickly sought a bride, and the fact that he did not have to provide an inheritance for Isabella Wickham made the marriage possible. He was a pleasant fellow—not overly bright, but sensible enough to limit his wife's pin money to something manageable. His redeeming qualities were his love for Lydia and desire to support her, and his general concern for the well-being of the Wickham children he had inherited with the marriage. Although not flawless, he was good enough to be liked by the family as a whole. Lydia had done her wifely duty of providing him with two children, one male, in the space of three years, so she must have been inclined to him as well. It was a relief to the family.

That left George and Isabella in a somewhat awkward position. Their financial futures were secure—more secure, in fact, than the rest of their family's—but even though he was a better father, Mr. Bradley was not *their* father. They would forever be "the Wickham children."

Young George's appearance had stunned Darcy; the boy had shot up like a weed in spring and looked very much like his father. He needed only his side whiskers to complete the picture, but was too young to grow them. He had his mother's eyes. Unlike the rest of the guests, the Darcys had enough tact not to discuss George's resemblance to his late father. In personality, the young man was pleasant, but quiet and often anxious, and his current stage of rapid physical changes did not aid his social development. George had lost his cousin Joseph when George moved out of Longbourn, and Geoffrey and Charles were in Derbyshire most of the year. Young George was not to go to Eton or Harrow. He would go straight on to university, and then probably the church or higher academia.

Darcy gave him a rare smile to reassure him, but there was only so much that he could tell a young man of three and ten. So he employed neutral conversation over lunch. "How is your sister? Does she enjoy living in town?"

"Very much," George said, dissecting his intimidating steak. "She prefers it to the countryside, though I think she misses our grandparents and Aunt Townsend. And she's positively sick of being escorted everywhere."

"It is better for her to be sick of it than not have it," he said. "And how do you find town?"

"I don't go out much," George said. "Dr. Maddox took me to a lecture at the Royal College of Physicians."

"Really? What was it about?"

"They were debating the new vaccines. There was a speaker, but at the end they were all shouting over him. Dr. Maddox said it's usually like that. Everyone has their own opinion."

"And Dr. Maddox's opinion?"

"The doctor thought they needed more testing before they could be deemed safe, but he barely said a thing the whole time. He said when he voiced his opinions they were unpopular, and he didn't appreciate being yelled at for what he thought was a good idea by old fogies. So he said that he would wait until he was a fogy to put forth his ideas."

Darcy smiled. "Dr. Maddox is a brilliant man. What did *you* think of it?"

"It was interesting, but I don't know how they do it. I can't stand the thought of performing surgery. It makes me feel ill."

His uncle chuckled. "If you think you are the only person with such thoughts, you should ask the esteemed Dr. Maddox what he thought of his first surgical lecture at Cambridge. Ask him how long he made it into the lecture."

For the first time, George smiled. "I will. Thank you."

George was too young to fence or gamble, so there was little else for him at White's, and they left after dinner, walking back up the lane beside the Thames. It was an early summer day, and it was during the season, so girls under white umbrellas were going up and down the lanes with their friends. More than once, Darcy saw George turn his head.

He colored when he saw Darcy's smile. "I don't like girls—people—staring at me."

"I think you were more looking at *them*, young Mr. Wickham," Darcy said. "And do not flatter yourself. You are still quite young. Chances are, they are looking at me, a rich gentleman, as a better match, and wondering if I am single. Who knows? I could be a widower."

George frowned. "I still don't like it."

Darcy stopped. He could see George fidgeting with his hands. "If you think people are staring at you, you are right. Everyone looks at everyone else in town; it is the only regular activity some of these people get. People look and talk and gossip. It happens to everyone and there's nothing to be done. But unless you are doing something ostentatious, it is mostly harmless." He no longer had to bow down to look George in the eyes. "Do you think those people out there mean you harm?"

"No!" George said. "I mean, yes, all right. Maybe sometimes. How do *you* know what I think?"

"Because I'm your uncle, George," he said, "and I have the same thoughts sometimes. But they're not rational. No one means you harm. Or, at least, they rarely mean you harm. And usually that harm is a social slight—something that you can brush off. If it is more, you have your family—me, for instance—to defend you. Understand?"

George nodded.

"Let's be going," Darcy said, not wanting to linger on a topic that made even him uncomfortable. "I can leave your aunt Elizabeth with your mother for only so long before someone is likely to suffer spontaneous combustion."

They resumed their pace, walking in silence for a while before George said, "Can I ask you something, Uncle Darcy?"

"Ask me anything, George."

"How much money is in my trust?"

Darcy glanced at his companion. "Why do you ask?"

"I'm interested." He added, "And my mother asked."

"You have a right to know, I suppose," Darcy said, "but not because Mrs. Bradley wants to know. The money has nothing to do with her."

"But—she is my mother. I should support her if she is in distress."

Darcy had a hard time keeping his voice even. "Your mother is not in any sort of financial distress. Mr. Bradley supports her, as is his legal and moral obligation as her husband." Darcy did not add that Lydia's sisters secretly sent her money out of their own pockets, so secretly they thought their husbands none the wiser. "I put that money away for you, so that *you* might have standing and a level of comfort when you are of age, and I did the same for your sister, so that she will find a decent marriage. When you turn sixteen, you may do with it as you please, but I advise you to regard her pleas more skeptically than you are inclined." He softened his tone. "I know that it's very hard to think that your parents aren't perfect. I believed so until I was nearly five and thirty. It was as shocking then as it would have been when I was a child. But it was true nonetheless, and some good came of it." He looked at George, who seemed to be half-nodding, understanding on some basic level that this concept might be true. "In answer to your question, I put money away and it did very well, and you will have about sixty thousand pounds, and your sister about forty as an inheritance. Only you or I will be able to touch either of those accounts."

He saw fear and a wary respect—not greed—in George's eyes at the sum. This was comforting to Darcy, because it meant George understood the value of money and that there were responsibilities that came with it. On the other hand, it was a burden to lay on an essentially fatherless boy. "You have no obligation to tell your mother. It is not your responsibility yet. There is no need to be concerned now."

George looked up at him, his expression one of wanting to believe him, but not quite being able to do so.

CHAPTER 6

The Newlyweds

~ ~ ~

THE NEXT WEEK IN TOWN passed quietly for the Darcys. Fitzwilliam Darcy was buried in financial affairs, and spent a little time at his fencing club. He was frustrated that he had to work with his left hand, as his right hand was not responsive enough for the subtleties of swordplay, and he no longer had the energy of youth to make up for it. But he was determined to learn, and his coach thought he was admirable in his attempts. Geoffrey was not old enough for a club, but he would be soon. He loved the sport as much as his father and he looked forward to facing him as a serious opponent.

Upon returning one day from a meeting with a banker, Fitzwilliam found Elizabeth waiting for him with more eagerness than usual, a letter in her hands. She was not, however, in tears, so that was a good sign. "What is it?"

"Jane," she said, but he had recognized her sister's handwriting from afar. They moved into the study, and the servant shut the door behind them before Elizabeth started speaking. "She suggests that I visit Longbourn sooner than we had anticipated going, while you finish your business here. Everyone else is fine, but Mama is out of sorts."

"She is ill?"

"No—not precisely. She just—well, Jane is at a loss to describe it, but her habits have changed. She says odd things."

"What does your father say?"

"He actually thinks her temperament has improved, or so he said to Jane—but he also called for a doctor."

"Did he call for Dr. Maddox?"

"Darcy, Dr. Maddox is not our personal doctor, at our beck and call for every minor scrape. You know that he is swamped with his own work."

"So Mr. Bennet thinks it is serious enough for a doctor, but not serious enough for Dr. Maddox. That is a good sign, I think." He put his hand around his wife's shoulder, and she leaned into his embrace. "I'm sure that if it were serious, there would be an urgent letter to everyone. Why don't you go on ahead with the children? I can be finished in a few days and then I will join you." He kissed her on her forehead. "Your mother is not as young as she used to be, but she is not obviously ill or suffering. Go see her, and you will feel better."

She nodded, but stayed in his arms for a long time.

Dr. Maddox appreciated the irony that he sat behind the very same desk at the Royal Society of Medicine where, fifteen years earlier, the man who had just approved his license had told him to stick himself in a dark hole and not come out. Brian had ruined their family fortune, and their reputation had sunk with it; the ink wasn't dry on the license certificate before young Daniel Maddox was not fit to show his face in decent society and was carrying around more debt than he could pay. But they couldn't revoke his license, and he had survived, and here he was, interviewing applicants for the royal service.

It had been two long weeks. He was a man of high professional standards, and he knew the Prince Regent expected nothing less of him. He was not willing to take people based on their reputations; he quizzed them on technique and found them lacking. Some of King George III's former doctors applied, and were furious at being turned down by this young upstart. Anyone who mentioned bleeding as a method of treating fever was immediately dropped; the Prince hated being bled and Dr. Maddox did not believe in it, except in rare cases. Also, he wasn't going to have the Prince Regent sitting in filthy water at Bath, so those experts were turned away. By the end of the first week, he wondered whether he was being too exacting. The new man, after all, would essentially be in charge of resuscitating the Prince after his nightly overindulgences. But then he reminded himself that eventually the prince was bound to come to more serious harm from his intemperate habits. Also, the new doctor would likely replace Dr. Maddox down the line, when he became incapable of working because of his failing eyesight.

He began looking through the applications of surgeons with licenses, having been one himself and having a healthy respect for a doctor willing to get his hands bloody. Most were too young, or blatantly lied about their age before showing up for the interview.

He had the card of a young doctor who had been a surgeon at Waterloo. Many people had made that claim, but he backed it up in writing. He was young but experienced in fieldwork. His degree was from St. Andrews, a very respectable medical school, and his license was on record.

Dr. Maddox took a fresh cup of tea before sitting down opposite the visibly nervous Dr. Bertrand. The man was young, maybe five and twenty, but not ridiculously so. He seemed even more edgy than he should be. "So Dr. Bertrand," Maddox said after the formalities, "you treated the wounded at Waterloo. Were you on the battlefield or in the tents?"

"Both, sir."

"I assume you didn't keep track of the number of men you treated. What did you do to fight infection among the wounded?"

It wasn't a normal interview question. Dr. Bertrand was quiet for a moment before answering, "Honey."

"Honey?"

"Yes, sir." He went on to explain, "It's a temporary method, but it keeps dirt from the wound."

"Old medieval trick, isn't it?" Dr. Maddox said, trying to contemplate how it would work. It did make sense, however ridiculous. "What were the results?"

"I did not have time to do a general study, but I think the rate of infection was lower. Though…a few delirious men licked their wounds."

"Gives a whole new meaning to the phase, doesn't it?"

Dr. Bertrand finally smiled. "Yes, sir, it does."

Dr. Maddox leaned back. "So you did your surgical studies at St. Andrews." He looked at Bertrand and at his application again. "How is Professor Maurice? Is he still around?"

"He is, sir. I heard him lecture on sutures."

"Yes, I remember him." He added, "He's not a professor at St. Andrews. He's a professor at the Academy in Paris, where I studied."

Bertrand sank. He had been caught.

"Your parents were French nobility, I assume?"

"Yes, sir. I am sorry, sir. I'll go. Please don't tell—"

Dr. Maddox raised his hand. "Now, now, I'm not going to hold your family's history against you. You are applying because of your medical skills and little else. Now please sit down and answer my question."

Dr. Bertrand swallowed, and did so. "My parents had an estate near Toulouse. During the Revolution, they expatriated to England. When I was eighteen, they repatriated because Napoleon had suffered his first defeat, and they felt he was on the way out. So I completed my education in France, but I didn't feel at home there. I had been born and raised an Englishman. After the war, I came back."

"We have no prejudices against French doctors here. You are well aware of that. French culture is the most fashionable culture there is. This has been true for centuries. So the conclusion I must draw from the falsehoods on your résumé is that you were a surgeon at Waterloo for the other side."

Clearly terrified, Bertrand nodded.

"Well, you'd do best not to mention that if the Duke of Wellington is ever in the room." He closed the folder with the application and took a sip of his tea. "I assume from your soldiering days that you are capable of lifting a grown man and carrying him?"

"Y-Yes, sir."

"Good. I warn you, the Prince is very fat. Not as bovine as the *Courier* would have you believe, but not far from it. When he falls, he usually breaks whatever is beneath him, and it takes two men to get him up, so you'll need someone else to help you. That is assuming you want the position of babysitting the Prince Regent every night while he drinks himself into oblivion." Before Bertrand could answer, he continued, "There will, of course, be a field test next week. I'll send my card with instructions." He rose, and offered his hand. "And no, I won't say anything. Honey. Why didn't I think of that? Exemplary thinking."

The young doctor shook his hand. "Thank you, sir." He seemed to notice that half a finger was missing, but he said nothing. "Thank you very much."

"The pleasure is mine," Dr. Maddox said, and was not lying.

One could never go home again. Every time Elizabeth Darcy came to Longbourn, it had undergone some new renovation. Mary's inheritance, in Mr. Bennet's possession, was no small sum, and on the interest alone they could do as they pleased to make the estate comfortable. Although it was true that it now had fewer occupants than ever, it also hosted more guests who needed the space, so another wing had been added. The real question was how Mr. Collins expected to keep it all up when he inherited the estate. He could not sell it, and Joseph Bennet was not legitimate and had no claim to it. Mr. Bennet dismissed these concerns with his staunch refusal to keel over.

Mr. Bennet was very old, but in good health, and his pattern of living had not altered much in the many years since his daughters (most of them) had married and moved away. He read, he ate, and on occasion he went to church. Joseph Bennet was eight, and between his grandfather and his mother, he had two accomplished tutors.

Mrs. Bennet had been sad to see Lydia go when her favorite daughter remarried, and she spent much time talking with Mrs. Philips and the Lucases, and whoever else was available. With the war over, there were fewer redcoats these days, just men in shabby versions of their old uniforms, drinking and making trouble. Otherwise, life in Hertfordshire continued as normal, only thirty miles from London but far away in its way of life.

"Aunt Darcy!" cried a horde of children, who were the first to greet her carriage. Joseph Bennet, the Bingley twins, and Edmund Bingley came charging out the front doors of Longbourn before the servants could stop them.

"I am glad to be the object of so much attention," she laughed as they surrounded her before going to greet their cousins. Then she could finally turn her attention to Jane, who was following her children. "I came as soon as I could. Mr. Darcy will be here in a few days."

"It is not urgent," her sister said. "Though it is good to see you." She threw her arms around Elizabeth and the two hugged.

As the children were rounded up, the two sisters walked inside, where Mrs. Bennet was in the sitting room, working on some new embroidery. "Oh, my dear Lizzy! How are you?"

"Very well, Mama," Elizabeth said. "Mr. Darcy will arrive in a few days."

"Mr. Darcy! That insufferable man!" Mrs. Bennet said, and then smiled pleasantly. "Jane, where are the children?"

"Outside, Mama."

"And the grandchildren?"

At a loss, Jane said, "Also outside. They will be in soon."

"They shouldn't stay out—the sun will ruin their complexions. You know how Georgiana freckles!" she said. Georgiana was in Ireland, but that didn't matter to her. "I must find Edmund. Edmund!" she shouted, and walked slowly down the hallway, in the direction of Mr. Bennet's study.

"Edmund?" Elizabeth said, picking up the dropped embroidery circle. The stitches seem to be randomly placed, a spider's web of confusion.

"I know! She's been doing that since I arrived." Jane frowned and then dismissed the servants. "The doctor said she may have had a stroke."

"A stroke! When?"

"We don't know. Sometime after Mary left. It hasn't inhibited her speech or movement, so it was minor, and Papa said he did not notice it for a few days."

"Can anything be done?"

"No, but it won't get worse, unless she has another one. Oh, Lizzy, these things are so unpredictable!" Jane leaned on her shoulder.

"Now, what's this? Unexpected guests?" said Mr. Bennet, announcing his presence in the doorway with a heavy tap of his cane.

"Papa!" Elizabeth said and hugged her father. He was perhaps a little older (and shorter, it seemed) and more wrinkled, but very much alive. "I came as soon as I heard."

"Thank you, my dear," he said, taking a seat in the armchair. "I admit I did not notice anything amiss until your mother started calling me by my Christian name. The last time she did that must have been around the time that Kitty was born!" He chuckled. "Well, there's nothing to be done about it. The doctor said it could have been much worse. She has no significant loss of memory, although she gets *confused* about names and dates. And you will find her nerves in good working order, perhaps the best they've been in years! So, my daughters, the news is not all bad."

"Has anyone told her?"

"She might suspect. But we haven't told her. It would just embarrass her," Jane answered. "Or so the doctor said. We may apply for a second opinion, but there really is nothing to be done for a stroke."

"A very minor one, he said," Mr. Bennet added, "Though if I have to hear about Netherfield being let one more time, I may have one myself!"

"*Papa!*" they said together.

He sighed. "It seems the only one who is allowed to joke around here since this happened is Mrs. Bennet herself! I know it gave us all a good scare—and still does. But, my dears, watch carefully. Mrs. Bennet!" he called.

"There you are!" she said, re-entering with the children tugging at her dress. "Where have you been?"

"I've been looking for you, my dear. I assumed you would be in your own sitting room."

"I am sorry to disappoint you. Please forgive me, my darling husband." She leaned over and kissed him on his head more tenderly than they had ever seen Mrs. Bennet act around Mr. Bennet.

"You are forgiven, my dear wife," he said. "I believe you will be besieged by grandchildren if something is not found for them to eat before long."

"Of course." She kissed him again, which he returned, and left. The children who were old enough to bow or curtsy did in passing to their mothers and grandfather.

"You see?" Mr. Bennet said with a sly grin. "It's not *all bad*. If she'd lost her wits entirely, she might be wondering why her betrothed was an old man!"

CHAPTER 7

The Protégé

WHEN DR. ANDREW BERTRAND received the card, the instructions were confounding: *11 p.m., outside the Royal Society of Medicine house. Wear your worst clothing and bring best equipment.*

Not one to question orders, he did precisely that, putting together his oldest, most threadbare outfit aside from his field uniform (which would hardly have been appropriate). Fortunately, his parents were not around. They had left long ago for their usual tour of evening entertainment. Aging ex-nobility, they lived the life expected of them in town—that is, well beyond their means. The most fashionable pastime of the rich was the avocation of incurring debt. This meant that he was unlikely to inherit anything other than his name, so the young ex-viscount had decided to make his own way. This post would legitimatize his profession in his parents' eyes—although the way that he was dressed at the moment would not have impressed them.

He had been surprised to discover when he applied for the sought-after position that the man making the decisions was no older than forty-five or perhaps fifty. Bertrand had expected an old man in a wig who had served the king. When he asked around, he found Dr. Maddox had a good reputation although he had never published any papers or spent much time at the clubs the other doctors frequented. Also, he never gossiped about his patients. So they knew little about him and didn't care much for him.

Either way, Maddox seemed a reasonable man to be employed under and the position was no doubt a comfortable one, so Dr. Bertrand had no objections and made it to the society house right on time. The doors were shut, and the doctor was sitting on a bench, hatless and dressed in black. "Ready, Dr. Bertrand?"

"Yes, sir."

"Are you armed?"

"Yes, sir. A small pistol." It would have been foolish to go about London without one.

Dr. Maddox stood up. "I have always believed in the benevolence of humanity. From that axiom, I have earned most of my scars. Nonetheless, I can't bring myself to actually use a weapon, so I am glad you brought one," he said, and called for their carriage.

They rode in silence for some time before stopping at the edge of East London, where one wouldn't want to be seen in such a nice carriage. "Wait here," Dr. Maddox told his driver. "Now, Dr. Bertrand, I assume you've had all of your vaccinations."

"I have, sir."

Dr. Maddox had left his walking stick inside the carriage, and he carried only his satchel. He reached into his coat and removed a piece of paper. "I know the street at least. Perhaps not the exact address, but we shall find it. And take off your hat—you look like a man of wealth."

Blushing, Bertrand did so, and left it with the driver as they proceeded up the foul-smelling streets of some of the worst sections of London, well outside of the Town proper. "Now, whatever I say, you just follow my lead," Dr. Maddox said as they came to a wooden door that was nearly off its hinges. "Here we are." There was no doorknob, so he knocked with his fist. "Hello? Mrs. Potter?"

There was some noise before a fat woman in an apron opened the door, holding up a candlestick. "Who is it?"

"You requested a surgeon for a Mr. Potter," he said. "I am Dr. Maddox and this is Mr. Bertrand."

She looked at them both skeptically. "I can' afford two doctors."

"The fee is the same, I assure you. Mr. Bertrand is my apprentice."

"A shilling."

"Yes."

She hesitated and then stepped back to let them in. The apartment had maybe three rooms—a kitchen, some kind of sitting room, and a bedroom. The sitting room was outfitted with cots and there were children sleeping on them. When some of them stirred, they were hushed by a stream of curses from their mother as she led the doctors into the bedroom.

Sitting up was a man in a bloodied white shirt, with an old soldier's jacket from the Continental War over his shoulders. His beard was brown, his hair filthy. One of his arms was cut off about halfway up the forearm. "I can' afford two."

"There's no extra charge, Mr. Potter," Dr. Maddox said, bowing to him. "I am Dr. Maddox and this is Mr. Bertrand. Do you mind if we look at your wound?"

"Just make it stop with the gunk, wouldja?"

Dr. Maddox pulled a chair close to the bed. "Light, please, Mr. Bertrand." Bertrand held up the light as close as possible as Dr. Maddox removed his glasses and looked very closely at the wound. It was an old amputation, probably done hastily on the battlefield. The sewing job was only adequate, and it showed. Parts of the arm were dead or dying slowly. Dr. Maddox covered his mouth with a cloth and probed the wound with a metal tong, and though there was no clear opening, pus seeped out as Mr. Potter cried out. Without flinching, Dr. Maddox let the pus drip into a small tin, and held it up to the light for them both to inspect. "A moment, please, Mr. Potter." He stood up and they walked to the corner of the room. "Your assessment?"

"He wasn't sewn correctly in the first place, and whatever happened since, the limb's dying. It needs to be done properly."

Dr. Maddox nodded. "How much would you amputate?"

"I would try to do it cleanly around the elbow. I've done that before—I think it looks better at a natural stopping place."

"You've done it before? In the precise place?"

"I almost always went for just under the elbow and sewed it there."

Again, Dr. Maddox nodded. "Get your saw ready. If you don't have one, I do." He put his glasses back on and turned to Mr. Potter as he opened his bag on the dresser. "Mr. Potter, my apprentice and I must operate on your arm again."

"Oh, God in heaven," Potter said. "I just—I don' think I can do that again."

"It will be different this time, I assure you. I'm going to give you something to make it far less painful, and we're going to cut it cleanly. If you keep the wound uncontaminated and have the stitches removed properly, it should heal just fine." He removed several tiny bottles of powder and measured out part of their contents before pouring them into a small bottle of water. He put a lid on the bottle and shook the contents. "Do you have any other amputations?"

"No, Doctor."

"Good, good. Have you been bleeding a lot recently?"

"No, just this awful mush."

"Have you been drinking excessively in the past few hours?"

"Just a little gin maybe…I don't know, an hour ago."

Dr. Maddox poured his mixture onto a large spoon. "Open your mouth. And yes, I know, it tastes very bad. For that, I apologize." He gave him two spoonfuls, neither of which Mr. Potter cared for, but he put up little protest. "All right, here's some sugar to change the taste." He fed him a spoon of sugar. "Now you may feel a little drowsy—there is no reason to fight it. Tell me, under whom did you serve?"

As Bertrand readied his equipment, he watched Dr. Maddox make conversation with Mr. Potter, who had been a private at Waterloo and been shot in the hand, which was gangrenous within a week. He had been treated in the tents in France before returning to the mainland. Over the next few minutes, his answers became increasingly slurred to the point where he was incoherent. "It's time," Dr. Maddox said.

Dr. Bertrand was ready. This was different from the battlefield—despite Mr. Potter's screams, as drugs could have only so much worth. It was rather quiet. There was no one around him shouting orders in French, or people running back and forth. Dr. Maddox sat quietly, watching his work while holding Mr. Potter's hand, keeping one finger on his wrist for a pulse. "You're doing well, Mr. Potter," he would occasionally say, even if Potter gave no answer. His voice was remarkably gentle.

Bertrand was used to doing quick work, and even at his leisure it didn't take long to make a clean cut. Stitching it was actually a longer and more complex process, but he managed that in a few minutes.

"Pour this over it," Dr. Maddox said, handing him another vial. "It's not honey, but it will do."

Bertrand smiled. Mr. Potter, meanwhile, had actually fallen asleep, and was snoring. Dr. Maddox wiped his face as Bertrand packed up his items. Mrs. Potter entered as they were tying the final bandages. "I will be back or send my assistant in a week to remove the stitches and check on the patient. Don't give him anything tonight, and be liberal with the alcohol tomorrow, but no more than two glasses an hour."

"He's sleepin'!"

"He is drugged. Let him sleep as long as possible—he won't feel very well when he wakes up, but he will live."

She paid him the shilling, and they made their exit. They walked back down the street in a casual stroll. "I'm sorry for the demotion," Dr. Maddox said, "but she wouldn't have believed *two* doctors were charging only a shilling."

"Why were we charging only a shilling?"

"Because that's the going rate for surgeons, and I have no desire to interfere with their market, having been one for many years myself."

"What did you give him to make him so peaceful?"

"A mixture of raw opium and some other ingredients to make it drinkable. With the quality of opium I tend to use, and the amount

I gave him, we barely broke even tonight." He handed the coin to Bertrand. "You did most of the work."

"I'll give you this back for that recipe, Dr. Maddox."

The doctor smiled. "I don't give it out often. It is highly addictive. You must use it sparingly. But of course, only the best for the Crown."

Ahead, they found the carriage waiting, and began the ride back to the decent part of the city. "I should be available to do the return visit next week. If not, I'll send you a note. This is why I requested a partial retirement, anyway. I wanted to do more charitable work, not pick up drunken lords." He shook Bertrand's hand. "Good work, Dr. Bertrand. If you can stand it, you can have the job I just so lovingly described."

"Gladly," Dr. Bertrand replied.

~ ~ ~

"Mama!"

Jane stepped out of Longbourn's doors to greet her eldest daughter, running toward her. She barely had time to get her arms out before Georgie embraced her mother. She was twelve and growing quickly. Her expression of affection was rare and therefore all the more felt, regardless of how long she had been gone. Georgiana Bingley was not always an easy child to manage, sometimes strangely compliant and other times disobedient to the very end. No one knew quite how she would take to going out—either she would be begging for it or be dragged kicking and screaming into the social sphere. "I missed you, too, dear."

As Georgie greeted her Aunt Darcy, Jane turned to Nadezhda Maddox, emerging from the carriage. "Your Highness."

"Mrs. Bingley," Nadezhda said. She was dressed in standard Romanian clothing, which was far less revealing than their gowns. "Thank you for letting me take your daughter. It would have been lonely without her."

"I hope that she wasn't any trouble."

"None. She is a treasure." She curtsied to Elizabeth. "Mrs. Darcy."

"Your Highness."

"Would you like to stay for a few days?" Jane offered. "All the children will be here tomorrow for Edmund's birthday anyway."

What Nadezhda did with her time when Brian was not with her, they did not know. She was not part of the London social circles. She spent time with her Maddox nephews and niece, but the month-long trip to Ireland was the longest she had spent with any of them. "I would be honored."

The Maddoxes arrived in time for Edmund's birthday, which had somehow turned into a regular social gathering in Hertfordshire. Dr. Maddox was immediately consulted for his expertise, despite Mr. Bennet's words against it, and he spoke with Mrs. Bennet for some time before reaching the same conclusion that the original doctor had.

"She probably had a minor stroke," he said. "She will not get worse. She will probably stay just as she is now."

"Is there anything we can do to prevent another one?"

"I'm afraid not, Mrs. Darcy. Cerebral apoplexy is impossible to predict. Though, considering that it is likely her brain was involved, you'd best try not to upset her nerves."

Despite their concern, nothing could prevent the former Bennet sisters from bursting into laughter at that statement. Mr. Bennet stood up, putting aside his glass, and said, "Well, I'd better be off to bed, then. Everything I say and do upsets her nerves. But wait! Every time I disappear, it also upsets her because she comes looking for me! So I guess I must sit quietly in her presence and say or do nothing. A precarious position, is it not, Dr. Maddox?"

"Indeed," Dr. Maddox said.

Edmund Bingley celebrated his birthday without his father but surrounded by his siblings, cousins, aunt, and uncles. Georgiana Bingley had done the same in March. Bingley said that a return before late summer was highly unlikely, but he would try. Jane did her best to hide her melancholia, and the others did their best not to appear to observe it and be supportive all the same.

As the adults sat down for luncheon, Mr. Bennet announced, "I do hope my far-traveling son will return soon, selfish as it may be for me to say it, because I have decided to hold a celebration next month for all of my daughters and their families, and my brothers and sisters. In other words, an army will march on Hertfordshire. We'd best alert the authorities beforehand, so they don't become alarmed."

"What is the occasion, Papa?" Elizabeth asked.

"I am going to attempt to do something I have never done before, and doubt very much I will ever do again. I am going to turn seventy. And do we not love to celebrate round numbers?"

This came as some surprise, as Mr. Bennet was not in the habit of mentioning his age or celebrating his birthday, and none present (aside from Mrs. Bennet, it was presumed) even knew it. Mr. Darcy gladly initiated a toast to the idea.

"Edmund!" Mrs. Bennet said. "That means our anniversary—"

"It will be almost half a century. Fifty years of me hiding in the study and you talking about 'our girls.'" He paused. "My goodness, now I do feel old."

Their laughter was broken only by the doorbell. Mr. Bennet nodded for a servant to answer it, and that man returned with a package. "For Mrs. Bingley," he announced.

The paper wrapping was worn and dusty, and there were stamps all over it—but no return address. She tore it open immediately to reveal a cover letter. "It's from Mr. Bingley!" she said. After scanning it, she read it aloud:

Dearest Jane,

By the time you read this, I will, hopefully, be speeding home. At the time that I am writing this, however, I am sitting on a hill overlooking the Ganges, which is a river in India much larger and longer than the Thames. Across from me is a Hindoo temple, where they worship a god with the head of an elephant. The sun is setting and it is the most beautiful thing I have ever seen, marred only by the fact that my family is not here with me.

Enclosed are letters for everyone and gifts for the children. Do apologize for me for missing their birthdays and assure them that their birthdays will come around next year at the same time. Mr. Maddox also is reminding me that we have to move now, because it gets terribly buggy here at night, and we are going to retreat behind a screen. He sends his love to everyone.

Yours,
Charles Bingley

P.S. A man tried to buy our daughters for sixteen goats but I refused. I hope you find this to your approval.

It was hard to recall when, of late, there had been such a display of joy at the Bennet table. Jane was in tears when she removed the cover letter to reveal an entire sketchbook of drawings, the last being no doubt the scene he had described, complete with tiny figures in the corner that were crudely drawn caricatures of Mr. Bingley and Mr. Maddox, with CB and BM written under them. It was passed around with great care. It would be inked and colored in by a professional when he returned home. The buildings on the pages were something out of a fairy tale, with unimaginable shapes and spirals. There were also letters for everyone, including Nadezhda from her husband, and the luncheon was recessed so that the children could be called in.

"Just in time for your birthday," Jane said as she handed Edmund his gift box and kissed him on the cheek. "As your father promised."

Edmund Bingley, now seven, opened his box to reveal a small set of wooden toy soldiers. Unlike his cousins' sets, these soldiers were Indian ones, painted in bright colors and carrying bayonets. He immediately abandoned the adults to start setting them up on the drawing room table. The twins, who had their father home for their birthday, received puzzle boxes made of a strange wood, and spent hours figuring them out.

Georgiana Bingley opened her box to reveal a locket set on a chain. The locket was a tiny glass box contained in a metal case, which was molded like the temples of India. She quickly discovered the upper spire could be pushed down like a button, but it did nothing but click. She was about to set aside the box when she found a note, which she read.

"What does it say?" her mother inquired.

"It says it's magic," Georgie said. "He said the man in the shop made it a charm, and it will work only for me, and only when saying one name."

"Whose name?" Elizabeth said.

"Papa says I have to figure it out for myself," Georgie said as her mother helped her get the locket around her neck and the clasp fastened in the back. It was just the right size for her. "Georgiana Bingley," she said, and pushed down. Nothing. "Charles Bingley." Nothing. "Fine. Charlie Bingley the Younger." Still nothing. "Jane Bingley." Nothing. "Jane Bennet." People interrupted with suggestions, which varied from "Grandfather Bennet" to "King George III," and she cycled through all of them, and the names of her siblings, and the names of her aunts and uncles. "Her Highness Princess Nadezhda." The box remained unchanged. "Nadi-sama." Still nothing. She leaned against her mother on the couch, clicking away with increasing annoyance.

Geoffrey Darcy, whose birthday had also been missed, received a wooden dog that looked just like his, painted to resemble it exactly. He turned his attention back to his cousin. "Does it have to be a person's name? Or is it supposed to be the name of a place?"

She looked at him and then back at the locket. "Geoffrey Darcy." It lit up in a brief array of circling lights of all colors—red, and then orange, and then pink, and then purple and blue—until shutting off after about ten seconds. "Yay! Thank you!" She hugged her cousin, who had no idea what he had done precisely, before running off to show the rest of her family.

Geoffrey turned to his Aunt Bingley, who only said, "I have no idea, either. Your uncle has a rather strange sense of humor."

CHAPTER 8

Primate Concern

JULY WAS PLEASANTLY QUIET for Dr. Maddox. The Prince Regent was in Brighton, and for once, he was not. There were no emergencies to call him there, and Dr. Bertrand's letters indicated that their patient was still in his fine, fat form.

The summer was not particularly hot, but bad enough that most of society had departed with the season to their summer homes and coastal resorts. Daniel and Caroline had the names of a couple of places but had no time to look at any of them, and were due to be in the area for Mr. Bennet's birthday in a few weeks. Nadezhda stayed with them, and on especially hot days they went up to her house just outside London, where at least the air was breathable.

"Why is it that Aunt Maddox can shoot a gun and you can't?" Frederick asked his father, who was sitting in a lawn chair, watching Nadezhda pick off fowl with stunning accuracy.

"I never learned. I don't care much for the sport." He didn't want to add that he also couldn't see that far. "I mend things, not kill them. Most of the time, anyway."

"Then who's going to teach me?"

"Your Uncle Bingley, I suppose. Brian's a terrible shot." He looked over Frederick's shoulder and called out, "Daniel! Stay where I can see you!"

Danny Maddox waved his stick around and came back up the hill. "There are toads by the water. Can I keep one?"

"That wouldn't be very nice to the toad. I don't think it would care for London."

"It's really hot in London. Is that why your plants always die?"

He sighed. "I think so, my boy."

In the evenings, it was cooler, and Town was strangely quiet. Frederick didn't want to be read to anymore, or that was what he said, but sometimes he would sneak into Emily's room and listen to his father reading to her.

Upon his unofficial retirement, the servants fully expected the master would spend most of his day at a club. But even though Dr. Maddox belonged to a few, he went out only to lectures and to see patients, mainly charity cases. During the day, he spent much of his time in the laboratory, where the heat and foul air had not succeeded in killing every plant he was growing. The laboratory was of endless interest to his children, mainly because they weren't allowed inside except to look. When he heard a low knock on the door one afternoon, he called out, "What is it?"

"Can I come in?"

"Not right now." He was mashing up a raw stem of poppy, and his mouth was covered with a scarf so that he would not accidentally blow on it. "Later."

"Mama says it's important!"

"One moment and I'll be out."

"She said it's *really* important."

He spilled the contents into a jar and put the jar and the rest of the root in the bottom drawer, which he locked. He opened the door. "What—?"

Brian Maddox was holding Emily in his arms. "Your child for your opium."

"That's a tough one. Opium is very expensive these days."

"Papa!"

"I told you your father was capable of joking," Brian said. He set her down so that he could embrace his brother. "Hello, Danny."

"Welcome back," he said. "I hope you brought Bingley with you."

"He's downstairs."

"I hope he's in one piece."

"One overly excited piece, yes."

Dr. Maddox stepped into the hallway, locking the door behind him. "You look good. What kind of trouble have you been in?"

"Mostly, I was busy keeping my business partner *out* of trouble. Ask him about the tiger sometime."

"You know that your wife is here?"

"I got an enthusiastic greeting. If you hadn't been cooped up in that study, you'd have heard it."

Downstairs, the Maddox sitting room was in an uproar as servants carried in trunks and Caroline embraced her brother, who apparently had not gone native and was dressed like a dignified Englishman.

"Mr. Mugin," Dr. Maddox said and bowed to his guest. "What a surprise. I never thought you'd be back on this side of the world again."

"I need to be in place—" he said something in Japanese to Nadezhda.

"He says he needs to be somewhere where he's not wanted for any crimes," she said. "And China was apparently *not* an option. Mugin, what did you do?"

"It's not so much that he committed a crime as that he's being hunted by a group of martial arts students because he defeated their master," Brian said. "And then spit in his face. Which he had said he wouldn't do."

Mugin shrugged. "I lie. And give you *plenty* of warning to run."

"You knew Bingley couldn't run! I had to carry him halfway across—"

"Gentleman! Please!" Bingley said. "I've had to put up with this for two months." He turned to Dr. Maddox and offered his hand. "Doctor."

"Mr. Bingley." Maddox took it. "You look—" Bingley was sunburned and he had overgrown hair and the beginnings of a beard, but his eyes were bright. "You look as though you've been on a boat for a long time, but otherwise well."

"You also, minus the boat part. I understand my family is still in Hertfordshire and the Hursts are in their country house."

"Yes. Mr. Bennet is throwing a party in a week or so."

"Terrific. Well, if I could trouble you, I need your medical advice. And no, we didn't pick up any Indian diseases. It's about an animal."

"What? Did you buy one of those talking birds?"

"No," he said, "not a bird."

By the time Darcy was done with his final meeting with his steward and his accountant, the post had already come to the townhouse, which he viewed as a good sign. He despised staying alone in London when his family was away, but business had arisen the night before and it had carried over into the next day. He wanted to read his letters and be gone.

The brown envelope from Madrid drew his attention. He rarely corresponded with the banker in charge of receiving Grégoire's yearly income, except when actually making sure it had gone through, which it had in January. As his father had before him, Darcy managed the fund set up for Grégoire's welfare. He had altered it only by basing it in London instead of France, and lowering the amount to something more manageable for Grégoire, who only gave it to charity anyway. The rest stayed in the account to accrue further interest.

Concerned, he motioned for the servant and had him call back his departing steward. "I need your advice. It seems my brother withdrew one hundred pounds from afar and that money did not make it to the correct location."

His steward was familiar with the situation. "Who was responsible for the transfer, and where was it going?"

"It seems a man was hired to take it to a local noblewoman, who was to distribute it to needy residents. This man has been in the bank's employ for many years and has always been trusted to see the job through."

"And the noblewoman?"

"I don't know." He handed the letter to his steward. "Will you have someone look into this immediately?"

"Yes, sir."

"And give me a minute to pen a letter to my brother, if you'll be sending mail to Spain."

"Of course, sir."

He never was quite ready to assume that Grégoire's mail would be read unopened, even if Grégoire insisted the seal was still intact when he received it. He wrote a quick letter about some family account business being unsettled, and would he please write back, or contact the banker? He had written Grégoire only a few weeks earlier, and had little else to say, so he sent it off and told his manservant to prepare to leave for Hertfordshire. The steward was opening the front door when he faced a bowl-shaped hat.

"Darushi-san."

"Mr. Mugin," he said. "What a surprise. Is this to say that Mr. Bingley and Mr. Maddox have arrived?"

"Binguri-san, he go to country soon."

"And you're to be their servant again?" he said, not sure that it would rile Mugin, but hoping that it would.

"Lazy *gaijin*, too slow," Mugin said, bowed, and ran off back down the road, his wooden shoes clacking all the way.

Darcy had never trusted Mugin, but had no reason not to believe him now, and followed him to the Maddox townhouse, where there were many trunks in the hallway and a great commotion. The first person he encountered was not Bingley or Maddox, but a disconcerted Mrs. Maddox, her bonnet off and her normally perfectly tied hair askew. "Mrs. Maddox." He bowed.

She stopped only to curtsy. "Mr. Darcy. Excuse me." And then she rushed into the sitting room and shut the door behind her.

"What! He's not that bad, Caroline—"

Darcy could vaguely hear Bingley's voice from up the steps, but it was not Bingley who emerged first. It was a small animal, like a cat but not quite, covered in soap suds. It squeaked, and then without warning, climbed right up his clothing and sat down on his head.

Bingley did catch up, looking a little wet. "Hello, Darcy."

"Bingley."

"Sorry about—"

"Bingley, what precisely is on my head?"

"It's a monkey."

Calmly, he said, "A monkey."

"Yes. He won't harm you."

Coolly, Darcy said, "Though it has been an honor to be your companion these many years, our friendship will come to an abrupt end if you do not get this animal *off my head*."

Bingley did not need to be told twice. "Monkey! *Kinasi!*" The monkey leaped from Darcy's head to Bingley's outstretched arm, where it climbed up onto his shoulder and squawked. "I am sorry about that. It seems he doesn't much care to be bathed."

Darcy was going to say something, but Mr. Maddox came barreling down the stairs, towel in hand. "Here you—oh, hello." He bowed. "Mr. Darcy. You have suds in your hair."

"I know."

Bingley took the towel and wiped off his little monkey, which was not much bigger than his head and brown in color. "Dr. Maddox said we should bathe him. In case he had some bugs in his fur. Have you seen my sister?"

Darcy gestured to the closed double doors of the sitting room.

"You can come out now. Caroline?"

"I am not going near that thing!" she shouted from the other side of the door. "He screamed at me!"

"Well what did you expect him to do? You were screaming at him!"

"Monkey see, monkey do," Mr. Maddox said.

"She doesn't like animals—other than dogs, that is," Bingley said. "Louisa had a cat when we were children. It used to scratch its paws on her dresser."

"And on my leg!" Caroline said. The monkey shook itself out on Bingley's shoulder as Dr. Maddox appeared, followed by his children.

"A monkey is not a dog."

"Has she locked herself in there?" Dr. Maddox said.

"It's not her fault she yelled at it."

"You could have told her you were bringing a primate in the house, Mr. Bingley."

"I told *you*."

"What's a primate?" Emily Maddox asked.

"It's a monkey," her father explained.

A truce was eventually reached; Monkey (the animal's name) went back in his cage and into the wagon bound for Longbourn, and Caroline Maddox agreed to come out of her fortress.

Darcy still had to make his way to Hertfordshire and Bingley was eager to see his wife and children, so they bid their adieus, stopping for a moment outside before they would depart in their separate carriages.

"It is good to have you home," Darcy admitted. "You didn't do anything insanely idiotic while in the Orient besides buy a monkey in the notion that your wife would accept such a thing in the house?"

"I have spent months practicing my pleading look," Bingley said. "And as for anything else you hear I may have done, please don't believe everything you hear from Brian or Mugin."

"I never do."

~~~

It was Mr. Bennet who greeted Mr. Darcy as he stepped out of his carriage. His father-in-law was sitting on a chair in the sun. "Mr. Darcy."
~~~

"Mr. Bennet. I apologize for being late."

"I doubt Lizzy will be any less eager to see you."

"Yes, well, I doubt I will be the main attraction today," Darcy said as Mr. Bingley got out of the carriage.

"Mr. Bennet."

"Mr. Bingley!" Mr. Bennet stood up a bit straighter. "So my wayward son has arrived."

"How are you, Mr. Bennet?"

The old man shook Mr. Bingley's hand as firmly as he could. "Busy frustrating Mr. Collins every day. Your wife is…frankly, I don't know where she is. But at least one of the children will shriek loudly enough to get her attention when they see you, which I'm sure will be soon enough—"

"*Papa!*" Eliza Bingley came running out the front doors, her embroidery cloth and ribbons still in hand.

Bingley picked up his younger daughter. "You've grown tall! You look more like your mother every day." He kissed her cheeks. "Speaking of—"

The quiet did not last long. Edmund was quick to follow, and then Charles, and finally Georgiana, until he was almost toppled over by all of his children. "I cannot carry you all! Edmund, there's no reason to be pulling on my coat, I don't—" He stopped when he saw his wife, emerging tentatively into the sunlight. "Mrs. Bingley."

She curtsied. "Mr. Bingley."

He pulled her into his arms. "Jane," he whispered, his eyes tearing. "My beautiful Jane."

"I missed you," she said. "Don't ever go away again."

"I will do my very best," was his reply.

Fortunately, only the Darcy family was currently in residence, with everyone else in London or at Netherfield. So Mr. Bingley had to endure only so many reunions with everyone present before he could excuse himself to get something from his carriage. He took Jane with him.

"I have a surprise," he said. "Well, several, but this one I think will adequately distract the children for a little while."

"Now, why ever would you—Oh, my God." Jane covered her mouth as Bingley uncovered the cage. "Is that thing alive?"

"Of course he is. And he's tame. Well, relatively, for a monkey." He opened the little door and put out his arm, and the monkey instantly went up to his shoulder. "And he's not dirty or diseased. We bathed him at the Maddox house. My sister would be glad to complain to you about it."

"Charles, you can't be *serious.*"

He turned to the simian on his shoulder. "Monkey, what do you think? Am I being serious?" It squeaked in response. "Monkey, shake." The monkey held out its tiny arm. "He just wants to shake your hand."

Jane looked at her husband, and then at the monkey, and then at her husband again. He did seem to be serious. She held out her fingertips and let the monkey grab them. "He has such tiny hands."

"He likes you. Monkey, do you like Jane?" Bingley said. The monkey howled. "Well, you had better like her, because if you don't get on her good side, you don't get to stay with us."

"Charles—"

He held the monkey in his arms. "Look at him. The children will adore him."

"He's a wild animal."

"He's not *that* wild. Are you, Monkey?" he said. In response, the monkey squeaked and grabbed his nose. "Ow, ow, that's enough. I told you not to do that!"

Jane broke into laughter, perhaps at the sight of a small monkey trying to capture her husband's nose. "We'll *try* it."

"A trial basis. I understand." He kissed her. "Thank you. Oh, and you might want to cover your ears."

It was good advice. The children collectively screamed in excitement upon seeing the animal perched on Bingley's shoulder, and it screamed right back at them. It took him a full minute to shush eight children.

"Is that a monkey?"

"What's its name?"

"Can I stroke it?"

"Can we keep it?"

"Does it have to live in a zoo?"

"Can I hold it?"

"Does it bite?"

"Children," he said calmly, with as much authority as Charles Bingley could muster, "this is Monkey. Yes, that is his name. Not very original, but you will remember it. He doesn't bite unless you hurt him, so as with any pet or person, you must treat him with respect. That means no tossing him or tugging him or pulling on his tail. You can hold him *one at a time.* Georgiana?" He dealt with the crowd of boos. "She's the oldest."

"Not by much!" said Geoffrey.

Georgiana smiled triumphantly as she took the monkey into her arms. One by one, they all met Monkey, though Cassandra and Sarah were frightened of him, and Edmund was too proud to admit that he was, but passed him off rather quickly. Perhaps the most excited person was the last person in line, Mr. Bennet. "Now here is something I never thought I would see," he said as the monkey climbed up onto his bald spot and sat down.

"If he gets upset, just let him run up a tree or something, and I'll come get him down," he told Elizabeth before disappearing with Jane. Darcy mysteriously did not offer to help with monkey wrangling and vanished into the library as quickly as he could.

Jane and Charles found a spot far away from the house, where they could see Oakham Mount, a place where they had regularly walked during their engagement. The view had not changed, but they were not interested in the view.

"I missed you," he said between kisses. "I'm sorry I'm a little hairy—and burned. And freckled."

"You're perfect," she said.

They sat together on a large stump, looking out at the wild and content to just sit together with Bingley's arm around his wife's shoulder. "I would regale you with stories, but to be honest, I am utterly exhausted." He chuckled. "What happened while I was gone?"

"Lady Kincaid had a son. His name is Robert."

"It went well?"

"I think so. Mr. Darcy seemed pleased at his sister's good health. Lizzy was ecstatic, of course. They stood as godparents."

"Was Grégoire there?"

"He did not come in time. He should be here in a month or two, maybe. It is not set." She looked up at him. "My mother had a stroke."

"I'm so sorry—"

"It was minor. Papa said he didn't notice it for a few days."

"Can anything be done?"

"No, aside from not saying anything when she says something strange."

He put his other arm around her. "I'm sorry I wasn't here."

"It was only a few weeks ago."

He kissed her on her forehead. "I'm still sorry."

"We always assumed she would outlive him. Do you suppose it would be better if—"

He hushed her. "We don't know the future. All we know is your parents are both alive and relatively well. For now, that is enough."

CHAPTER 9

A Long-Expected Party

~ ~ ~

MR. BENNET, NOT KNOWN to be a stingy man with his family (which had almost proved to be his ruin with his youngest daughter), spared no expense. And anyone with even the slightest connection to the family was invited. Though Hertfordshire was no Derbyshire, by its own standards this was a grand celebration. Mr. Bennet did not host a ball ("My daughters are well settled, thank you very much"). Instead, it was a daytime celebration, mainly to accommodate his seventeen grandchildren, four nieces and nephews, and four great-nieces.

Aside from planning the menu and the accommodations, Mr. Bennet had one unpleasant duty. At Mrs. Philips's insistence, he sat in a gathering with her and Mr. and Mrs. Gardiner about Mrs. Bennet, whose condition remained unchanged. She was still given to periods of confusion, but was hardly an invalid.

"I see no cause for concern," he said to his sister-in-law. "If anyone says anything of note, it will hardly be heard over the screaming army of children to descend upon us."

"I do not want my sister exposed to public denunciation."

"Then perhaps you should have lodged a complaint between now and when my first daughter came out a month ago," Mr. Bennet said, to which the Gardiners could not help smiling. "Mrs. Philips, my wife has not complained about her wits for almost six weeks now—and I have been counting. I can hardly lock her away for such a crime. Nor am I remotely willing to do so," he said. "If anything, she is to be commended."

The widow Mrs. Philips was overruled by the Gardiners, who agreed with Mr. Bennet, and then by the man in charge, and she silenced herself.

"There is, however, cause for more general concern," Mrs. Gardiner said, and her husband nodded.

"I am at the moment too happy and foolish to fathom it," he replied. "If this is to be her twilight, then I have decided to enjoy her now and wallow in misery later. Putting off important business has always been my proficiency."

In early August, the mass descended on Hertfordshire. Already the Darcys and the Bingleys were in residence, and everyone delighted in comparing notes about the differing accounts of Mr. Bingley's travels that he gave, depending on his level of intoxication at the time. He showered his children and relatives with odd gifts. Indian goods had been available in Town for years. But it was quite another thing to get an Indian trinket as a gift from a traveler who could say where he had gotten it, how long he had bargained for it, and whose heritage had been more insulted by the end of the bargaining before an actual price was affixed. "I verbally slighted many shopkeepers' mothers," he said. "And I am a dolt with the hair of a demon."

"That was already known," Darcy said, and was already looking out the window innocently when Bingley turned his head.

Another amusement was the fact that Mrs. Bennet could never seem to grasp the presence of Monkey, and was surprised every time she saw him. "My goodness, there's a wild animal in this house!" Such repeated proclamations did not put her on either side—those who despised the monkey (Darcy) and those who loved him (everyone else). Darcy had found an ally with the arrival of the Bradleys and the Wickhams in Isabella Wickham's cat. Fortunately, Monkey was a better climber and took refuge on the nearest person's head whenever the gray tabby entered the room.

It was on a shooting expedition with Mr. Townsend at Netherfield that Bingley said, "What happened to young Mr. Wickham?"

"The same thing that will happen to Geoffrey soon enough," Darcy replied.

"May I say it?"

"Yes, he does look like his father," Darcy said. "Even more every day, it seems."

Mr. Townsend, who had not known Mr. Wickham senior, replied only, "Looks are not everything. Especially when his father has been described to me as dashing. And George is a sensible boy."

"He is," Darcy said, and Bingley's anxious look softened. "Very sensible. He is set on Oxford as soon as he can manage it."

"Oxford?"

"Yes," he replied. "Probably for the reason we think." (Mr. Wickham's alma mater—like Darcy's—had been Cambridge.) "And probably because Oxford was his grandfather's university," he said, referring to Mr. Bennet.

Done for the day, they set a time for the following week, a day before the party.

"Am I inviting the Maddoxes?" Mr. Townsend asked.

"Only if you want to be eating fowl for months," Darcy said. "Her Highness is quite a hunter."

The Collins family arrived in time for services on Sunday, and for Mrs. Collins to spend time with her parents and also with her sister, now married to another retired soldier (perhaps England's most popular occupation). Trailing them were their four daughters, who were no doubt loved with the same subtle frustration that Mr. Bennet had loved all his unmarried daughters. Nobody dared to say "The Bennet Curse" in earshot of either of them.

Indeed, the dynamics had changed much since Mr. Collins' visit to Longbourn more than twelve years prior. He still stood to inherit Longbourn, but whether he would have the finances to keep it up was an unanswered question. If he died without a son, the entail would die with him, and the property would be sold, presumably to Joseph Bennet (who could not inherit because of his illegitimacy). Mr. Collins' benefactor was none other than Mr. Darcy, master of Rosings, who set his pay. Fortunately, Mrs. Darcy and Charlotte Collins remained friends despite the change in fortunes, and Mr. Collins was in no great financial trouble.

Mr. Collins' desire to please his patron and patroness with a deluge of compliments had not changed. Fortunately, a plan was quickly developed to divert this; Mr. Bingley trained Monkey to jump at Mr. Collins whenever the vicar spoke to Mr. Darcy. Mr. Bingley, however, had yet to receive thanks from Mr. Darcy for his effort.

~ ~ ~

Final arrivals included the Earl of Fitzwilliam, his wife, and their three-year-old son, Henry. The Kincaids sent their regrets, but Lady Georgiana could not be expected to travel so far with a newborn. At last, the Maddoxes arrived, all four adults and all three children, with one lost Japanese thug in tow. True to Darcy's predictions, Prince and Princess Maddox were happy to join the hunting party, and Her Highness felled what seemed to be an entire flock of pigeons. Brian brought a gigantic painted bow and succeeded in hitting many trees and other relatively wide, inanimate objects. His wife was all encouragement.

Mr. Bennet was in high spirits as the adults sat down to a massive luncheon—not lacking in game meat—while the children played outside. In theory, they were under watch by an army of nurses as the adults toasted Mr. Bennet's good health.

Outside, one adult refused to sit down for a long dinner with a bunch of barbarians, and instead slept off his own meal (which had been considerable) and drink (also considerable) against a tree while the smaller children tugged at his feet. "Mr. Mugin! Mr. Mugin!"

"Go 'way," he said, lifting his leg and taking little Cassandra Darcy on a ride as she grabbed his ankle. "Little gaijin."

"Why do you wear sandals?"

"Why do you have tattoos?"

"Can you see like normal people?"

"Can I get a tattoo?"

"Can I see your sword?"

"Do you have a wife?"

"Do Japanese people get married?"

"My dad says you're a convict. What does that mean?"

"How old are you?"

"Can you carry me on your back?"

He moaned and opened his eyes to the little children. "Ugh. Children loud. You know what children do in Japan?"

"No!" they collectively shouted.

"Children scrub floors! Like servants! You want be in Japan?"

The children screamed and ran away, or at least the youngest and most gullible did. Mugin went back to sleep.

The older children had gathered by the fence, which was as far as they were allowed to go without supervision. Anyone older than seven had an air of authority and tried to shoo away their younger cousins.

"So when Grandfather dies, Mr. Collins gets all of this?" Charlie Bingley the Younger asked, gesturing to Longbourn.

"Grandpapa's not going to die!" Anne Darcy cried, clutching her older brother. "Geoffrey, say it's not true!"

Geoffrey sighed and looked to Georgiana Bingley, who just shrugged. "Everybody dies, Anne. It would be weird if everybody didn't. There would be too many people."

"She's right," Geoffrey said to his sister.

"It's still not fair," Charles said. "Someone should *decide* who gets Longbourn. It shouldn't go to Mr. Collins just because he's Mr. Collins."

"That's the way it works," said George, who was sitting on the fence. "You shouldn't talk. You get Kirkland."

"Of course I get Kirkland. What do you mean?"

"You get Kirkland and Edmund doesn't, because you're older," George huffed.

"What about Georgie? What if she wanted Kirkland?"

"She can't have it. She's a girl." This earned him a cold stare from Georgiana. "It's just the way the law works."

"You don't know everything, you know," Geoffrey said, in an attempt to soothe Georgiana. "Just because you're older."

"Fine. Look it up. Or ask your father."

"Why can't we make a system where everyone takes what they want?" Charlie said.

"Because then we'd be barbarians," George replied, but was ignored.

"Fine!" Geoffrey said. "I'm going to take Kirkland then, because my dad can beat up your dad."

"He cannot!"

"Can too!"

"His arm doesn't even work!"

"His *hand*," Geoffrey corrected him. "And your dad doesn't even fence."

"He shoots."

"Stop it!" Anne shouted. "Our dads would never fight. And Dr. Maddox wouldn't fight because he can't see, so if we all had to fight, Mr. Bradley would win. So he gets everything!"

"He has *one eye*," Frederick Maddox said, referring to Mr. Bradley. "My dad has *two*, and they sort of work, so my dad wins."

"At what? He doesn't fight and he doesn't shoot," Geoffrey said.

"Shut up!" Frederick said, already angry. "He could trounce your dad! He's taller!"

"No, he couldn't!"

"Yes, he could!"

They were shouting now, and soon Frederick threw a punch.

Not a particularly good one (he was eight), but it didn't even connect before he fell on his back, and Geoffrey Darcy was knocked into the soft grass. Georgiana Bingley had gotten between them and instantaneously pushed them both down.

"*Stop fighting!*" she said. "Or I'll beat you all up! And then…I take everything!" She turned to the stunned George. "And don't even say it, because I'll throw you over that fence faster than you can finish your sentence!"

"She'll do it, too," Geoffrey said from the ground.

There was a scared silence, and then finally, clapping.

"Good, good," Mugin said, shambling into the crowd as the boys picked themselves up. He patted Georgie on the head. "Now, children, stop fighting. Is no reason. Your parents *all* weak. Huge weaklings. I beat them all, take everything."

The long day of feasting, chatting, gossiping, and herding the children (and some of the more inebriated adults) to bed by the women ended with a fiery crescendo of fireworks, supplied by Charles Bingley and Brian Maddox. Mugin insisted that lighting the Chinese rockets would not be dangerous until one blew up in his face, and he ended up dipping his face in the pig trough to cool it. In the end, he had only ashes irritating his eyes to contend with, as it had been a small rocket, but the rest of the rockets were handled with much care. The children were allowed to stay up for the fireworks, including the final one, which vaguely made the shape of a dragon in its red and purple journey to the sky. Then the children were all put to bed, and the servants dismissed for their own party (as they did certainly deserve one), leaving those adults still awake and aware to quietly enjoy the evening of one long and memorable day.

"Thank you all for joining me," Mr. Bennet said in a final toast. "I doubt I shall turn seventy again, but with any luck, I will hit another nice round number and still have enough wits to realize it." With that he retired, his tightly held wife by his side.

"I am off to bed, too," Elizabeth said and kissed her husband.

"I will be there soon enough," he said, holding back his yawn until she was gone. He really was getting older. He looked around; Bingley was asleep in the armchair, with Monkey curled up on his head, having made a bed out of his hair. Dr. and Mrs. Maddox had retired after their children were put down. Nadezhda was doing embroidery while Brian stoked the fire.

"Mr. Maddox," he said, approaching him.

"Mr. Darcy," he said and bowed. "You have the good fortune of being limited in your intake of spirits, or you would be already asleep or else dreading tomorrow morning like the rest of us."

"True," he said. "I heard a rumor from Bingley that you are off to the Continent soon."

"Yes, for business. Nady and I are going to France to make a deal with a vendor. And she has never seen Paris. Why do you ask?" Even at his least alert, Brian Maddox had a knack for knowing when something was on the wind.

"Is there any chance you could use your company's ship to visit Spain?"

"It could be arranged," he said in a lowered voice. "Why?"

"There was some kind of error with the bank in Madrid that supplies my brother with his income. Apparently, the money never made it there. I'm not overly concerned about the money and I'm sure it will be sorted out or chalked up to a highway robbery, but I wrote Grégoire about it weeks ago and he hasn't written back."

Brian nodded. "He lives on the coast, doesn't he? Very far north?"

"Yes."

Brian was quiet for a moment, and then said to his wife, "Nady, would you like to go to Spain?"

CHAPTER 10

Ghost in the Chapel

ABBOT FRANCESCO CHIARAMONTI was guardian of thirty-two souls in the ancient monastery overlooking the Spanish coast. This particular afternoon, his concerns focused on one of them. Turning away from the window, he looked at the ancient mosaics of the saints—Benedict, Gregory, and Peter—as the bishop sat in his chair, perusing the documents the abbot had now nearly memorized. St. Benedict looked heavenward, a book in his hand, believed to be the Rule he had written for his monks. Peter had his hands outstretched and his head bent down, with the keys to heaven in golden illumination hanging from his belt. Only Gregory looked straight ahead, his eyes facing the window, his halo seeming especially brilliant because it was in the right position for the sun to hit it just right. All of them were serene in expression—and yet, how they all had suffered. Beneath the altar in their very sanctuary was a reliquary with a tooth from Peter's head, which, by history's count, was resting in four different places. How were they, in death, so unaffected by their experiences in life?

"Where is he now?"

He was pulled from his reverie. "What, Your Excellency?"

"Where is the monk?"

"He is at the threshold of the oratory, of course."

Bishop Fernando Valerano of Oviedo removed his spectacles and rubbed his eyes. "Does he know all of the charges laid before him?"

"I was not aware of the extent of them when he was excommunicated. The details should be fully explained and he should answer for them."

"Do you think he will answer truthfully?"

"He will, Your Excellency. I have no doubt of that."

"You have great faith in this monk who has disobeyed the Rule and lied to his elders in two different monasteries now."

"This I will not deny," he said. "Nonetheless, if we ask him, he will not lie. Especially now that he has been given time to meditate on his sins."

The bishop did not look impressed, but the abbot had no way to impress him. Bishop Valerano did not know Brother Grégoire, and probably never would have known him, if not for this.

"Your Excellency," the abbot said, "I do not think this situation will become any less untangled without the aid of the soul in question. I will not rely on stories on the wind."

"Fine." The bishop rose from the abbot's chair, and though he was a much younger man than the abbot, who was a former archbishop himself, he moved as if he were exhausted. "Then let us hear what your monk has to say for himself."

As the bishop walked through the monastery, wearing his cap and miter, the monks bowed in reverence and hurried out of his way. The bishop and the abbot found Brother Grégoire where he was supposed to be, on the stone floor before the oratory, in silent prayer.

"Brother Grégoire," the abbot said as they stood over him. "The charges laid against you should be heard again before your penance is decided."

Because the abbot was old and hard of hearing, he had a bench brought for himself and the archbishop.

"As you know, we have information that a certain noblewoman was given 200 ducados for the distribution among the poor of this diocese. How we came upon this information is not relevant," the bishop said, and the abbot resisted the urge to cross himself.

That poor noblewoman, thinking she was doing only good, had happened to mention it in conversation to her priest, who had then reported it to the bishop. "We now also have the confession of the man who delivered the money, a courier who had been hired before for similar purposes by a banker in Madrid. This, we have come to understand, was done at your command. Is this true, Brother Grégoire?"

"Yes," Grégoire said, his first word in a day, since he had been sent into temporary excommunication.

"And you are in contact with this banker in Madrid? He is in your employ?"

"He is not in my employ, Your Excellency. He is in the employ of my brother, but he does carry out my requests as part of his employment."

"Are you the owner of the money in this account?"

"I am."

"And how much is it?"

Grégoire stopped to reflect. "I d-do not know, precisely. It should be—maybe f-four or five thousand English pounds."

The abbot looked at the bishop, very aware of how his eyes reacted. His mouth must have been watering as he continued, "And this is your savings in Madrid?"

"No, Your Excellency. It is my yearly income."

"For how many years?"

"This year alone, Your Excellency."

"How is that possible?"

"My father, God rest his soul, left me a great deal of money in hopes that I would become a gentleman. When I told him before his death that it was my ambition to enter the church, he insisted that I have savings of my own. When I refused, he closed my access to them. They are sent to me every year, whether I want them or not." Grégoire swallowed and continued. "The controller of this account is now my brother, his legitimate son. The account is in London, and every year he sends some of the interest to Madrid."

"Did you have similar situations in your previous monasteries?"

"Yes."

"Were the abbots aware of them?"

"In Mon-Claire, where I was only a novice, yes. When I took the cowl in Bavaria, no."

"Why not?"

"My b-brother appealed to me not to."

"Your brother is an Englishman?"

"Yes. Anglican."

"Is he religious?"

Grégoire seemed to weigh his answer. "To the extent within his sphere that he can be, he is, Your Excellency."

"Brother Grégoire," the bishop continued, "are you aware of how much money is in your account in London?"

Grégoire flinched. "Roughly, Your Excellency."

The abbot did not think this was relevant, but he would not raise this issue here. He wanted to see how it affected the bishop.

"How much is it?" the bishop asked.

"It is—fifty thousand pounds, Your Excellency."

The abbot sighed for all of them, giving Bishop Valerano time to drool. Even to Valerno, a bishop from a noble Spanish family, and Chiaramonti, an abbot from a well-off Roman family, this was an extensive fortune. When he finally recovered, the bishop said, "Father Abbot, do you have the brother's petition?"

"I do." The only reason he had it ready was because it was necessary to perjure Grégoire; otherwise it remained locked in a box beneath the altar with the rest of the brothers' petitions. He unrolled it. "Brother Grégoire, you do not need to be reminded that this is your petition to join the Brotherhood of St. Benedict, and your promise to obey the Rule to all of its extent. This includes the chapter about giving all of your worldly possessions to charity upon taking the cowl, or presenting them to the church to do such. In this case, I feel we may consider your said 'income' to be a gift from your brother to you because you have no legal control over it.

However, you seem to have forgotten what you wrote here, which is that you would present all gifts to myself for approval and any money would be dispersed by the church, and not by you."

"Yes, Father. I know, Father."

"Your wealth is not your own, and so you testified in Bavaria and again here in Spain, and both times it was not true. Did you fail to understand the Rule, Brother Grégoire?"

"No, Father. I was in error. I should not have done so."

"The Rule is not to be taken lightly, Brother," he said, more insistently.

"I know, Father."

"Did you not trust the church to manage its own wealth and give it appropriately to charity?" the bishop interrupted. "Do you believe the words of a heretic over the Vicar of Christ?"

Each sentence seemed to fall like a blow on the monk before them. "Your Excellency, my brother—he is not a heretic."

"You said yourself he is a member of the Church of England, which denies the supremacy of Rome."

"That is true, and in our eyes, he is. But he does not believe he is, and he is my brother. I will not slander him."

"But by protecting him, you—"

"Your Excellency," Abbot Francesco interrupted. "This—Señor Darcy is not on trial here. His soul is not our concern. I will not ask Brother Grégoire to speak ill of his own family."

Grégoire glanced up with red eyes only briefly before bowing his head again.

"You will write the banker in Madrid," the bishop said, "and tell him to send the five thousand pounds to the abbot, who will distribute it himself. Then we will discuss the rest of your 'inheritance.'"

"Forgive me, Your Excellency, but I promised my brother I wouldn't."

"You promised him you would not give your money to the church?"

Grégoire could not seem to bring himself to speak. Instead, he only nodded.

"You did not swear an oath," the abbot said, hoping it was not true.

"I did, Father. I am sorry, Father."

"Brother Grégoire, you cannot swear contradictory oaths!"

Grégoire fell on his face. "Please, Your Excellency, Father Abbot, do not make me choose between my father's wishes and the Holy Father's! Please, have mercy on this sinner!"

The bishop was going to say something, but Brother Grégoire was the abbot's charge. "Brother Grégoire," the abbot said, standing up to tower over his monk, "you have sworn falsely, you have deceived the church, and you have disobeyed the Rule in writing and in action, knowing full well what you were doing. However, you told me previously that you wished to repent fully. However, I must punish you, so that you may see your error, as St. Benedict prescribed. Today, you will return to your cell, and take bread after the rest of your brothers. Your excommunication stands and you will remain in silence until tomorrow, when you will submit to the discipline of the Rule. Then you will write to your brother, explaining the situation, and beg to be relieved of your oath. From there, we will go forward with the financial matters that remain." He put his hand on Grégoire's head. "Have faith in Christ, who has forgiven greater sins. You may go."

"Thank you, Father. Your Excellency." He bowed again and, holding his rosary tightly, hurried off to his cell, passing other brothers, who were forbidden to look at him.

The heaviness that had descended upon Abbot Francesco did not lift as they returned to his office, the bishop once again taking the abbot's chair and leaving the abbot to stand. "I will call for a doctor. I want him on hand tomorrow."

"What about the funds?"

"You had best forget about them, beyond the five thousand in Madrid. And even there, you are chasing a ghost," the abbot said. "His brother will freeze his assets as soon as he hears of this, if he has not already. The banker in Madrid is an Englishman."

"Who is his brother?"

"Aristocracy, I believe. He owns land in the north of England." He paced, hoping it would relieve the pain in his heart. It did not. "I have allowed Brother Grégoire to visit him twice since taking the cowl here. He is attached to his English family."

"Even though he is a Frenchman."

"Yes. It seems Grégoire is the child of the elder Señor Darcy—his father—and a French maid. She was sent home to have the child, who was named after someone else in the family, presumably. Despite his illegitimacy, Grégoire was acknowledged by both his blood father and his half-brother, the heir to the fortune. He also has a half-sister he is very fond of, now married to a Scottish earl," he said. "Grégoire has admitted to me that his brother and sister tried to persuade him from a life in the church many times, before he took his final vows and after the monastery in Bavaria was dissolved. They begged him to enter the Church of England, but he refused. He wanted the contemplative life and would settle for nothing else. He has been a pious monk and perhaps the greatest apothecary our monastery has ever seen. He has saved any number of lives with medical knowledge he picked up in England. And he is all humility."

"He is also quite wealthy."

"Yes." The abbot put his hand on his head. "There is that. We will not ask him to choose between the church and his family. Some deal will be reached with the brother and this will all pass."

But something told him it wouldn't.

"Darcy, you're kicking me."

That brought him out of his sleep. Or at least, it brought him to more awareness, for he had not been asleep for some time. He had woken in the middle of the night and had not been able to return to sleep, and tossed and turned to the point of accidentally kicking his wife. "I am sorry," he mumbled, kissing her nearest available limb. It turned out to be her shoulder.

"Are you all right?" Elizabeth said, stroking his cheek.

"Yes. I just—feel restless." He kissed her again. "I'll have a bite of something, perhaps."

"Try not to wake the children."

"Is that all you will say to me?"

"Oh," she said, "and I love you."

He smiled and dressed himself in a robe and slippers before leaving the chamber, armed with a lit candle. Sometimes he had nights where he could find no sleep or had a disturbing dream; some Austrian ghosts continued to haunt him. But he usually solved that with a cup of a special concoction of Dr. Maddox's. This was different. Finding himself not hungry, he wandered the halls of Pemberley like a ghost. The moon was full and its light shone through the windows of the great hall. In days past, he had often walked outside with his dogs; how he missed them.

Somehow, he found himself in the chapel. He was rarely there when his brother was not in residence. He considered himself a faithful Christian, but he felt he fulfilled his obligations by weekly church attendance and being a charitable man. The candles for the chapel were not lit, and the cold stone made it a soothing room in the late summer warmth. Those castles of the Middles Ages must have been drafty.

He was not alone. Anne Darcy was sitting on one of the hard wooden pews, wrapped in a blanket. "Anne?"

"Papa!" she shouted with delight, and lifted her arms. He sat down beside her and lifted her onto his lap, which she was getting a little big for.

"What are you doing awake? Where is Nurse?"

"She's sleeping."

"What are you doing here, then? Why are you not in the nursery?"

"I was talking to somebody."

"You were?" His alarm was rising. "Who?"

"I don't know him. He said he was one of Uncle Grégoire's friends."

"Anne," he said much more seriously, "what did he look like?"

"He had a beard and a funny accent." She whispered, "I think he was a ghost."

"What makes you think that?"

"He said he was *really* old," she said. "Older than Grandpapa!"

"Did he say his name?"

"No."

"Anne, darling, you know you should not speak to strangers, especially in the middle of the night." He didn't want to frighten his daughter. So he said calmly, "Just promise me that if you see a stranger in Pemberley, you will tell someone immediately. Promise?"

"Promise." She hugged him. "He was just a ghost."

"And you're not scared of ghosts?"

"He was a *nice* ghost."

He sighed. She had imagined the whole thing, or fallen asleep and dreamed it. "Very well. What did you talk about?"

"Uncle Grégoire."

"Of course. He's Grégoire's friend, is he not? What did he have to say about his good friend?"

"He said he was worried about him." She looked up at her father. "Is he in trouble?"

"I—don't think so," he said. "But I suppose if a ghost said so—well, he might know something we don't."

"Are ghosts smart?"

"I suppose that they're as smart as they were when they weren't ghosts, sweetie." He rose, picking her up with him. "Why don't we discuss it with your mother in the morning? Someone is up past her bedtime."

"*Papa!*"

But he would not listen to protest. He carried his daughter, with her head resting on his shoulder. By the time he reached the nursery, she was already asleep, and he laid her down on her bed, not disturbing her sleeping younger sisters.

Back in his warm bed, with his wife by his side, he finally closed his eyes, but sleep was slow in coming.

CHAPTER 11

The Discipline of St. Benedict

FOR THE REST OF HIS DAYS, all Abbot Francesco Chiaramonti could truly recall of the exact moment he knew something was wrong, was the color red. It stained the steps that he ascended.

"Father! We must not touch blood!" Because they were monks.

He did not listen to the prior. He knew it was true and he did not care. He did not touch blood—he stepped straight in it, kneeling before Grégoire's collapsed figure. The layman hired for the job (the church did not spill blood) had already stepped back with his flail. The bonds holding down the monk had come loose and he had lost consciousness, his head hitting the stone. The doctor had declared the young and relatively healthy Grégoire good for no less than ten strokes, but he had only made it to three.

"Don't just stand there!" the abbot shouted to the doctor. "Help me!" With his own withered hands he tore apart Grégoire's bloodied shirt. His intention was to get the wounds in view of the doctor, but that was not what happened. The cloth came apart to reveal the coarse cloth of a hairshirt.

The effect was instantaneous. The monks and even the bishop got on their knees, crossing themselves. "My goodness," Bishop Valerano said, "we've killed a saint."

He would not believe it. He could not believe it. He refused. Instead, he felt for a pulse. He did not have adequate words of praise for God when he found one. "Almost, Your Excellency, but not quite. Now we must save his life, or we are all damned."

~~~

"Father," said Brother Martin, "please." He held up a change of robes.

This shook the abbot from his stupor enough to realize that it would be prudent to change out of his blood-soaked robe. "Thank you," he said quietly.

"The brothers—we have circulated a petition that we might fast for Brother Grégoire's recovery until he is out of danger."

Normally, he would not want an entire abbey of lethargic, hungry monks, but he said, "Yes, of course."

He stood up from the bench outside Grégoire's cell for the first time since the door had been closed and the doctor had set to work. He returned to his own cell, where he changed his robe. The old one would probably have to be discarded. "Forgive me Father, for I have sinned," he said in the darkness before returning to his vigil. The bishop had said nothing, but removed his cap and was pacing nervously.

Finally the door was opened, and the abbot let himself in, closing the door behind him. Grégoire was on his mattress, asleep or unconscious, and on his side. He was wearing nothing above his waist and his back was covered in bandages.

The doctor was still cleaning his hands of blood. "Father."

"Doctor. Will he live?"

"I've done all I can, Father. I've sewn him, but his flesh was weak—from the um, shirt, I presume." He was clearly out of his element with this, even though he had treated many punished monks. "He has lost a great deal of blood; probably too much. As soon as he wakes, he should drink something."

The abbot nodded numbly. "How long do you suspect he was wearing the cilicium—the hairshirt?"
~~~

"I-I do not know, Father. There is no way to tell."

"But—it was not new."

"No. He has scars from it on his chest. He must have been wearing it for—a year, at least." He whispered, "Father, if you had known—"

"We would have suspended the sentence, of course. But we did not know. *I* did not know. Brother Grégoire, why did you prescribe your own penance? Why did you not tell me?" He looked at the still monk, and then up at the doctor. "You have my blessing for all of your work, Doctor. We will call you again for the stitches to come out, yes?"

"Yes. In two weeks. There were—many of them." He bowed, and excused himself as quickly as possible.

Not ready to face the bishop, his flock, or anyone else, Abbot Francesco knelt beside Grégoire. He knew of the boy's flagellant history, but Grégoire had said he stopped that when he became a Benedictine. Apparently, he had found a new way to torture his flesh. The abbot, watching him breathe, took the young hand in his old, withered one. "What great sin do you think have you done? What are you fortifying yourself against? You are no service to the Holy Spirit as a dead man, my son." He smoothed over the tangles in Grégoire's curly brown hair. "I swear, if you are good enough to us to survive, I will do everything in my power to protect you—from the bishop and from the church." He bowed his head. "And from yourself."

When they rose the next morning for Vigils, Prior Pullo, who had the last watch, reported that Grégoire had briefly woken to take water and some soup, but had said nothing. Nonetheless there was much rejoicing, and they all broke their fast together, though they ate in silence.

The abbot was on his way to visit Grégoire's cell after Sext when he was called to inspect gifts for the abbey. He went to the door to find baskets of goods—cheeses, milk, fresh fruit, and vegetables. "From the villagers," said the doorkeeper. "They've been leaving them all day, for Brother Grégoire."

"Who told them?" he said.

"I don't know, Father. No one's been in or out today." He shrugged. "Perhaps they suspect something because he's not been visiting the people for the past few days. They might assume that he is ill."

He nodded. "Bring the baskets inside. And if anyone comes to ask, tell them nothing. We do not want gossip."

"Of course, Father."

In the evening, Grégoire woke again. The abbot was watching this time. It was clear that the monk was in too much pain to speak, but again they forced him to drink broth, and a bit of the milk from the villagers. They called the doctor again, and he prescribed a mix of items mashed in water for him to drink.

The abbot spent much of his time in the chapel. A spiritual weight pressed down on his chest, making it almost hard to breathe.

"Father." It was Brother Marcus. "I was changing his sheets because they were soaked and—"

"And what?"

The monk held up the white sheet. The blood stains formed a broken cross, but a cross nonetheless. The abbot rose quickly and took the sheet from the monk. "Say nothing of this."

"But Father—"

"Nothing. No talk of miracles."

"There is *already* talk of miracles."

"No more talk then. I forbid it." He put his hand on the shoulder of the confused monk. "Trust me. It is better for Brother Grégoire if he is not spoken of in this manner. No good will come of it."

The monk nodded and left. The abbot went to the cellars, and burned the sheet. "Don't do this to yourself," he said to Grégoire afterward. "You will bring a whirlwind down on your head." Grégoire had no response; his eyes weren't open. "When you wake, I will tell you everything terrible of this world. You must protect your own soul from it, and not in this manner."

There were abbey matters that could not be put off any longer, and so on the third day, he returned to the paperwork and the mundane parts of being the abbot of a large monastery. It was then that the bishop, who had, no doubt, been plagued by thoughts of his own, intruded.

"I am to report to the archbishop."

"Please do not," the abbot said. "I beg of you. Let Brother Grégoire speak for himself first."

"He should at least hear."

"There is too much to hear. It is all talk."

"If Grégoire is a saint—"

"I don't want to hear that word!" the abbot shouted. "I have told people not to speak it—why don't they listen to me?"

"Do you believe it?"

He looked away. "It is not the point. If it goes beyond these walls, it will go straight to Rome, and Brother Grégoire will never hear the end of it. The church always needs another saint."

"And you think that is a bad thing?"

"You forget, Your Excellency, that I was once archbishop of Oviedo and before that, a bishop outside Rome. I will not have him sent to the wolves. He is just a young monk who is overzealous in the mortification of the flesh. Besides, it is useless to even speak of sainthood before he's been dead for decades, except for political gain." He eyed the bishop. "Do not report to the archbishop."

"I must."

"Then do not say anything of significance. The investigation is going on. That is not a lie."

"I will say as I please, Father *Abbot*."

He went to leave, but the abbot said to his departing back, "I will do everything to protect my charge, even if it means going against you."

"You overstep yourself, Father."

"Perhaps. You are a bishop and a friend of the new archbishop, who was once a bishop under me. You may do as you please, Your Excellency. And I will do everything I can to protect the soul I almost destroyed."

The bishop did not respond as he left. The abbot put his head in his hands and wept, only to be interrupted by Brother Martin entering the room without knocking. "Father—he is awake."

It took all of Abbot Francesco's strength to compose himself to kneel beside the bed of Brother Grégoire, who was being helped to finish off the last of his daily tonic.

"You may speak," the abbot said. "The excommunication is lifted. Your penance is more than done, Brother Grégoire."

"Then why do I feel otherwise, Father?"

"That blame lies with us, Brother. How long were you wearing the cilicium?"

Grégoire was not in the most alert of states, and it took him a moment to answer. "It must be—three years now, as much as I could stand it."

"And for what sin were you repenting, Brother Grégoire?"

"Violating my oath of celibacy, Father."

"You did this only once? The time you confessed to me in Munich?"

Grégoire nodded.

"You confessed and were forgiven." The abbot sighed. "Brother, you have given yourself to God, body and soul. It is not for you to decide when you are forgiven. The only thing you are guilty of is not understanding the extent of God's grace. Not something many grapple with, but dangerous nonetheless."

Grégoire closed his eyes and said nothing.

"You are to wear an undershirt until you are *fully* healed of your wounds. Everything else, we will leave to God until you recover. Now rest, Brother," the abbot said, but Grégoire was already asleep.

~~~

When Grégoire was ready to stand and walk again, there was no lack of offers to help him to the chapel. The abbot and the bishop watched as he took his first shaky steps out of his cell in a week, one hand on the wall and the other arm being held up by Brother Martin. Whether the monks following behind him did so in brotherhood or in reverence was debatable, but he seemed unaware of it. He only gazed at the gifts, all of them new from this morning, lined up along the wall in confusion.

"From the villagers, Brother Grégoire," Prior Pullo explained. "They miss you."

He nodded, not completely comprehending.

The reading for the day was from the Letters to the Corinthians. The abbot wondered if there was anyone who could not help but be distracted. Grégoire himself was nodding off at various points, and did not break bread with them. The next day, he made it to two services, and it seemed as though he was on his way to finally mending. Still, he said little unless spoken to, either because he was distracted by pain or addled by his experiences.

"Do you remember anything between the time of your injury and when I spoke to you days later?" the abbot said in privacy.

"I remember…an anvil. And fire."

"Brimstone?"

"No. Just fire." He toyed with his rosary. "Am I still to write to my brother?"

"It will be sorted out in time," the abbot assured him. "There is no need to worry of it now."

"I would like to see the ocean. May I have leave to sit outside?"

"Of course, Brother Grégoire."

The next day, the weather was fine, and the brothers helped him venture outside the abbey doors and sat him down in a chair overlooking the coast. He was on the other side of the abbey, and therefore did not hear the procession with the arrival of the archbishop of Oviedo.
~~~

~ ~ ~

The archbishop was a Spanish native and a Dominican, like Bishop Valerano. He had been bishop when the abbot was assigned to the post of archbishop, a requested transfer from his post outside Rome, and had been raised when the abbot requested another transfer, this one to a monastery. The archbishop still looked to the abbot with some reverence as he listened to the facts of the case, repeated to him, including all that had occurred since the bishop had written him a letter.

"If all you say is true," he concluded, "then he must go to Rome."

"No," the abbot said. "Please, Your Excellency. He is my charge and I do not believe it best for him."

"Surely a pilgrimage, at least," the bishop suggested.

"He has already made a pilgrimage to Rome. It was some years ago," the abbot said. "He still wears the cross purchased at St. Peter's Square."

The archbishop rubbed his chin. "What does the brother think?"

"He is unaware of it. He is not in a condition to comprehend it, I think. His wounds are still great." The abbot also knew that Grégoire would humbly bow to the authority of the archbishop.

"With respect, Father, I do not come rushing for every monk who disobeys your Rule," the archbishop said. "Let him come and speak for himself."

God protect him, the abbot prayed. *I am throwing him to their den.* But still the hierarchy had to be respected, and he requested that Grégoire be retrieved. After some time, the monk entered, his shuffle lopsided.

"Please," the archbishop said. "Be seated, Brother Grégoire."

Uncertain at first, Grégoire took the wooden seat across from the abbot's chair, in which the archbishop sat while the others stood.

"Brother Grégoire," the archbishop began, "upon reviewing your case, we believe it is in your best interest to make a pilgrimage to Rome as soon as you are able, and perhaps be transferred to a monastery in the papal lands."

Grégoire automatically looked up at his abbot, who quietly shook his head. "Your... Your Excellency. I have—already been to Rome."

"Not everyone makes the journey but once. Some people even live there. Like your father abbot, before his residency here." The archbishop continued, "You should consider what is in the best interest of your soul, Brother Grégoire. Take as long as you need to decide. Do you understand?"

"I—" He was struggling to keep his eyes open. "I—Father?"

"Yes?"

Grégoire motioned for him to come over, and he whispered in his ear. Alarmed, the abbot put his hand against Grégoire's forehead. "Excuse us, your Excellencies. Brother Grégoire is not well."

"What did he say?" the bishop insisted as the abbot raised Grégoire from his seat.

"He said he needed to be ill, *Your Excellency*," the abbot said. "That is your answer for now."

~ ~ ~

The doctor was called as the brothers tried to soothe Grégoire's raging fever with cold cloths. The abbot refused to leave his side, and said his prayers in the cell with Grégoire instead of with the choir. "I have failed you again, Brother."

Finally, the doctor arrived, and this time the abbot did not leave the room, and saw the extent of the damage himself. The stitches had gone bad, and his wounds were infected, and had to be reopened and sewn all over again. The abbot silently questioned the competency of this local surgeon. But there was no one else in the area, and Grégoire could not be moved. When the doctor cut the old stitches, the wounds reopened and blood poured out with a foul stench. Grégoire, fortunately, was unconscious.

Lord, how much blood must your humble servant bleed? the abbot prayed. He assisted the doctor with clean towels and water until he was finished.

"If the fever breaks, he will live," the doctor said. "If it doesn't, he won't." He deliberated for a few moments. "Father, you do not look well."

I am a tormented man. "I am an old man. Old men do not look well."

"You should rest, Father."

"I will rest when I can find some," he answered.

Grégoire survived the night, and for that they were all grateful, but his fever did not break. It would occasionally go down and he would have moments of coherency, but otherwise, he was incapacitated.

Abbot Francesco had not slept at all when he entered his own office to find Bishop Valerano and the archbishop poring over unfamiliar documents. "What is going on here?"

"Good morning, Father. We require your signature."

He took a seat and the scroll was passed to him. He read the Latin in disbelief. "This is a transfer. You expect me to sign this? He is not well enough to stand! He might not live!"

"There are arrangements for his body to be interred in Rome."

"His body will *not* be interred in Rome!" he shouted, and then he retreated from his own outburst. He was so tired. Softly, he said, "When he came to this monastery, he said that he wished his body to be returned to England to be buried with his family. Unless he is well enough to testify that he has changed his mind, I will honor his wishes. As for the transfer to Rome, it is hardly time to think about that."

"Do you intend to challenge this?"

He knew a threat when he heard one, however quietly it was spoken. After all, the blood of Roman senators coursed through his veins. "I will challenge it, yes. Apparently, you have both forgotten that the broken monk in this monastery is not without his own alliances, church *and* family." He looked up at the bishop. "Yes, I am from *that* Chiaramonti family."

Bishop Valerano turned to the archbishop, who nodded. "His brother is the Vicar of Christ."

"I will reassess the situation when Grégoire is well," he said. "If he becomes well. If he dies, God help us all, because I am sure we are all damned for this."

With that, he excused himself, and returned to his vigil beside Brother Grégoire. The other monks had found excuses to abandon their chores and were camped outside the cell. The abbot knelt beside Grégoire and kissed his hand. "If you are going to work any more miracles, Brother Grégoire, work one for yourself."

There was a knock on the door. "Come."

It was the doorkeeper, Brother Pedro. "Father, there is a couple at the abbey gates."

"Villagers?"

"No, Father. They speak only broken Spanish. It is a man and his wife. They are armed."

"Armed?!"

"Yes," he said. "They say they are Brother Grégoire's relatives."

CHAPTER 12

Grégoire's Cousins

~ ~ ~

"MY GOD, IT'S HOT," Brian said, readjusting his gasa hat as they stood outside the closed gates of the abbey. "And I'm just back from the Orient."

"You were on the ocean. It was different," Nadezhda said. She was wearing a gasa hat, too, and a summer kimono, instead of her heavy wool Romanian dress. "Have you ever been inside a monastery?"

"Not an active one, no." He looked up. The gates were at least four stories high. The entrance was actually a small door carved in one of them. "This building must be hundreds of years old and still used for the same purpose." He glanced at the heavy doorknob again. "Do they keep all their guests waiting? Maybe they do when those guests show up armed. And one of them a woman, no less."

"A good Christian woman."

"If you don't answer to Rome, you might as well be a heathen, and worship trees and statues, like Mugin."

"Mugin worships himself."

"Even better," he said. "*Your Highness*."

Still nothing. The doorkeeper was taking his time. "Maybe we should have offered to give up our weapons," the princess said.

"You can do that, but I am about to take my wife into a castle of men who probably haven't laid eyes on a woman in decades. I'll be keeping my swords, thank you." He heard a creaking sound on the other side. "Speak of the devils."

"Hush."

Brian smiled for the man who opened the door, and the older man who stepped out. "I am Brian Maddox. And this is Her Highness, Princess Nadezhda Maddox," he said in his best Spanish.

"Abbot Francesco Chiaramonti of the Benedictines," said the man, bowing to them. It was not very hard, because he had a bit of a hunch from age. "I am the abbot here. I understand you wish to see one of my monks."

"Yes. Brother Grégoire."

"Yes." He switched to French. "Is this better, monsieur?"

"Yes, thank you."

"How are you related to Brother Grégoire?"

"To be brief," Brian said, "my sister-in-law is the sister of his brother-in-law. So we are distant cousins, but Her Highness and I were the ones most willing to travel."

"Have you come…for a particular reason?"

Brian's smile disappeared. "Should we have?" The abbot was clearly in distress. The doorkeeper was keeping an eye on him as if the old man were going to collapse at any moment. Brian glanced at his wife in silent understanding. "We wish to see Brother Grégoire," he repeated.

"We normally do not permit arms or women within the abbey walls, but…" he trailed off, as if his own spirit was failing him. "But I see you are tired and thirsty. Please come in."

Taking off their wide gasa hats, they ducked under the door frame, and entered the abbey courtyard. The place smelled of age—of old stones and ancient prayers. The monks milling about were curious about these strangely dressed visitors.

"If you would, please," the abbot said, "your weapons. This is sacred ground."

"I was given these blades and told not to relinquish them," Brian said. "This is an abbey. I will have no cause to use them."

"I beg of you, please."

Brian turned to Nadezhda and said in Romanian, "What do you think?"

"Don't be a braggart. Give him your *katana* at least."

"Excuse me," the abbot said in Romanian, to their surprise. "Please. Many people would feel more comfortable if you at least gave up the larger ones, and you will certainly not be attacked."

"You speak my tongue?" Nadezhda said.

He bowed. "I was raised speaking Italian, Latin, and Spanish. It took only a brief summer in Bucharest to learn some scope of Romanian. But that was years ago."

Brian pulled the longer blade out of his sash and handed it over to the doorkeeper with both hands on the blade. "Will I have cause to be angry?"

"It is good you are here," the abbot whispered. "Please wait until you have the entire story to pass judgment."

Nadezhda handed over her *wakizashi*. "Show us to our cousin, Father."

The abbot nodded and led the way. Brian kept a hand on his tanto as they walked down the colonnade, past monks scurrying about and baskets of food lined up against the wall like offerings.

"Father."

The abbot bowed to the man with the jeweled ring and church clothing, apparently a bishop. "Your Excellency," he said in French, "these are relatives of Brother Grégoire."

"His Excellency" was about to say something, but he could not meet Brian's cold stare, and moved out of the way without a word. The abbot turned at last to a small wooden door. Monks were sitting outside the door, whispering prayers. The abbot unlocked the door.

"Father," said a monk in Spanish, rising from his position next to the bedside, wet towel still in hand.

"Leave us," the abbot said, and the monk slipped past them, allowing them entrance to the cell, which had only a tiny window in the corner to allow light in. The abbot immediately knelt beside the bed, crossed himself, and took up the towel, dipping it in cold water and putting it on the head of what was recognizably Grégoire.

Brother Grégoire was turned on his side, with his eyes closed and his breath heavy. Despite the light covers, his face was covered in sweat.

Brian reached over the abbot and touched Grégoire's forehead. "How long has he had this fever?"

"Two days now."

"What is he sick with?"

"He has wounds—they are infected."

"Show them to me."

With trembling hands, the abbot removed the covers to reveal a torn mess of flesh that had once been the skin of his back, sewn every which way. Much of the flesh was green or a sickly yellow, or covered with dried blood. Nadezhda covered herself with her veil and even Brian had to look away. He took his wife's arm to reassure her.

When he could think straight again, he asked, "Did he do this to himself, or did you do it to him?"

"Both, monsieur."

He could see why the abbot had insisted on disarming him. He grabbed the old man and picked him up by his cowl. "*Why would you harm him?* What could he *possibly* have done?"

"Please—we did not know—we were in error!"

Brian looked at his wife, who shrugged and voiced no objection to his behavior.

He allowed himself a mean grin. "You are lucky that his brother did not come. He would have struck you so hard that you would have broken. Grégoire's wounds are badly infected. Will he live?"

"With God's help, monsieur, and yours. Please, let me explain."

Brian figured he would have to do it eventually, so he let the abbot down. The old man did not retreat. He held his ground, bowing to him again. "I will tell you everything, from the beginning, if you promise to take him away from here."

"Of course we will take him! Grégoire Darcy will not die in a cell for any reason, and I have a feeling the infraction was minor—

by any standards but your own. Now sit down, Father, and begin this *explanation*."

They prodded Grégoire, but he was not near consciousness, and if he woke, he would probably be in great pain. He needed better medical attention; that much was clear. If he could not survive the journey to England, they would have to take him to a major city and find a good surgeon. Nadezhda took up the duty of trying to cool him down with water on his brow and arms as Brian paced angrily.

"Are you all right, Father?" called a monk through the door.

"Yes, yes," he said. "We are not to be interrupted. Even for the archbishop, understand?"

"Yes, Father."

As the old man sighed, the years seemed to weigh down on him, pushing the air out of his lungs as he fiddled with his rosary. "Sadly, it all began with an act of charity. How odd, now that I think of it...."

~ ~ ~

The tale he told was incredible in its intricacies. He held nothing back, even private conversations. He was terrified of them both, but also of himself, and his own actions—he said as much. "I pray that I am not damned, but I will settle with the Holy Spirit when Grégoire is safe or safely from this world, whichever it shall be." He crossed himself again. He had no good words for himself, or the bishop, or the archbishop, explaining how the bishop and archbishop had first sought Grégoire's money while the abbot remained more concerned with Grégoire's adherence to the Rule (which, in all fairness, had been violated). The discovery of the hairshirt changed everything—after all, the same thing had been found on the English saint Thomas Becket after his murder by the knights of King Henry. Now they were after Grégoire, a shining example of piety, to be paraded around in some horrible political arena beyond his understanding.

"If we take him," Brian said, "will they pursue us? Our ship is not very far, but we may have to stop in France if Grégoire is too ill to continue."

"They might. Or they might seek claim on his body, if he should die—which is a very real possibility. And they may get it, if they reach him before you reach English soil, or they could sue the Anglican church. If he dies now, surely, they will go for beatification within the next few decades, and they will want his remains for that. An English Catholic saint—it would be a triumph for Rome. You must understand, I was a bishop outside Rome—I know how they think." He stopped to think. "There is one way I can make sure they cannot pursue, but it is terrible."

Brian said immediately, "What do you want done?"

"No, there is nothing you can do. Brother Grégoire's soul has been my charge since his entrance to this order. I have the power to excommunicate him. The bishops will not touch him then."

"*Excommunicate?* Doesn't that involve a papal bull? And damning his soul to eternal hellfire and all that?"

"No, this is excommunication from his order. He is removed from the order of St. Benedict, and all other monastic orders. He can seek re-entrance at a later date, but only with my permission. His soul is not imperiled—he is not damned. I am casting him out to save his life."

Brian did not know what to think. It was Nadezhda who spoke up. "It will break his heart. He loves the church."

"The church does not love him back," the abbot said. "If he stays, it will kill him—body or soul, I know not which. Yes, it will be hard on him. For a while, it will be impossible for him to understand. He may join the Anglican church if he wishes, but I doubt he will. He may attend Mass and he may have his confession heard. He can have a life—and, more important, he can live." He was near tears. "I will write a letter to him—apologizing and explaining all of this. I hope it will be some consolation."

Brian sighed. It seemed the only way. Grégoire's life or his spirit. If he stayed, one would be broken. "What about you?"

"I will face my demons on my own. I made a vow to protect Grégoire from everyone, and I will endure whatever I must to do so. At most, they will remove me from my position, but they cannot excommunicate me. Not with my brother on the throne of St. Peter." He was not surprised by their looks. "Yes, my brother is pope. But he is not the only person in Rome, and I have not contacted him about this. This is my doing and I will attempt to mend it as best I can. And maybe someday, even if God will not forgive me, Grégoire will."

"I would say that we should wait for Grégoire to agree to it," Brian said, "but I do not believe we have that time, do we?"

The abbot shook his head.

"Write the order of excommunication, and the letter, but don't sign until we're ready to leave. If Grégoire wakes in that time, we will tell him."

The abbot nodded.

"Hang on, Grégoire," Brian said, taking his hand. "Your brother will kill me if you don't."

~ ~ ~

As the light receded from the Spanish coast, Abbot Francesco was so consumed with his writing that at first he did not hear the knock on his door. "Come."

Not unexpectedly, it was the archbishop and the bishop. "There are rumors, Father."

"There are always rumors," he said calmly, looking at them over his spectacles. "This is a monastery. We have little else to do."

"Brother Grégoire's relatives intend to take him with them. Did you explain that they could not do that without your permission?"

"I imagine they could do that without anyone's permission—physically, at least. And because they do not answer to me or Rome, they will do as they please." He added, "If and when they go, they will have my permission." He held up the finished parchment. "All it needs is my signature."

The archbishop read it quickly. "You cannot be serious. You would condemn him for what?"

"It does not matter. I am abbot and it is my judgment that one of the monks here is not suitable to this monastery. I must let him go, lest one wolf consume the sheep. I am not required to state my reasons, though you are welcome to speculate as to what they are."

"If you do this," the archbishop said, "we will challenge it."

"And be involved in a long and fruitless political battle with an old monk. Who knows? In the end, you might succeed in having me removed from my post and reduced to the status of a humble brother. And by then, Grégoire will be long gone, to a country where his money and his family can protect him. So you may try. I give you permission, my son. Or you could let this end gracefully." He did not waver. "Now, if you do not mind, I am busy with an important missive and would like privacy."

Neither of them dared to challenge *that*. They turned and left him in peace.

~ ~ ~

Brian and Nadezhda's watch continued through the night. Through the door they could hear the monks singing Compline, the final service of the night. He paced anxiously. "How is he?"

"The same."

"Do you think he would survive the trip to England?"

"Do we have any other choice? If we stopped in France, how long would it take us to find a decent surgeon?"

He smiled. "Logical as always." He turned at the knock on the door, one hand on his small blade. "Come."

It was a young monk. He did not know either of their names. "Sir—Madam—we understand you are leaving soon and taking Brother Grégoire."

"It depends on his health."

"We would like to say good-bye to him."

"He's not conscious. You understand that?"

The monk nodded. "Please, sir."

Thus began the procession, nearly silent, as each monk came in, young and old, to kneel before Grégoire's bed and kiss his hand and whisper in his ear. Brian and Nadezhda watched from a corner in amazement. Some of the monks were crying, but it was all done in a dignified and orderly fashion. Grégoire had brief moments of consciousness but not coherency. He was mumbling nonsense and they listened to every word. For the last few visitors, his eyes seemed to be half open, and when the abbot entered, they opened entirely.

The abbot turned first to Brian and handed him a sealed envelope. "Will you give this to him when he is returning to health? It may bring him comfort."

"Of course."

The abbot nodded sadly and turned to Grégoire. Sitting on the stool beside him and holding forth the parchment in Latin, he said, "Brother Grégoire, can you hear me?"

To all of their surprise, he nodded, ever so slightly.

"You will not understand this," the abbot said. "You have been so good to the church, but the church has not been good to you. When I sign this document, you will no longer be part of it."

Grégoire had no response. It was doubtful that he understood.

"My son," the abbot said, "remember that you serve God, not the church, and you can do so by leading a pious life. I have no doubt you will. You are not damned. I absolve you of all your sins, real and perceived. Someday, you may see fit to forgive me for mine." He kissed Grégoire's hand in reverence. He stood and set the parchment down on the stool, and took up his quill pen. "God forgive me." He crossed himself and signed. The abbot turned to Brian and Nadezhda. It seemed as though he had aged years in those few moments. "There is a stretcher waiting. My monks will assist you. Please take him."

"He will forgive you," Nadezhda said. "He is not capable of anything less."

"I hope so." He made the sign of the cross over them. "Go with God."

CHAPTER 13

Broken Floor, Broken Man

DARCY HAD A PISTOL WITH HIM as he descended, following the trail of smoke coming from the chimney of the house at the bottom of the hill. He hadn't always gone about Derbyshire armed, but in the days since the war, he had decided it was a good precaution. He had heard stories of ex-soldiers without jobs roaming the woods in bands. He was not a man to panic, but he would protect his family, and on this particular mission, his son was with him.

Geoffrey Darcy followed a few steps behind him. He was at an age where he was unsure of his own limbs, which seemed to be growing beyond what he was comfortable with, and his voice would occasionally drop and then squeak, much to the delight of his three younger sisters, who tortured him over it.

Darcy remembered that age as well as any man did—he remembered the competition with his companion. Wickham had always been the taller one, even though he was more than six months younger, but that had changed in Darcy's thirteenth year. Suddenly, he had started winning their brawls, and Wickham worked to best him in other areas. Now he could look back and wonder if their father had watched their unconsciously brotherly rivalry with amusement or concern. It had probably been both.

He said little, other than to assure his son that the awkward age would pass. He did not mention growing up with Wickham, not willing to accidentally tamper with the friendship of Geoffrey and George, who had the fortune of knowing full well they were cousins. George was taller and older, but he took no delight in it, and there was no real rivalry there. Geoffrey was easier with other people, and had his mother's good nature.

But then again, people change. Darcy could remember thinking that Wickham was his best friend. He remembered fishing with him. He remembered learning to ride from the same instructor. How much of the blame was his that it had all gone sour? He had to remind himself that he would never really know.

"Father."

His attention turned back to his son, who was pointing at a dip that Darcy had been about to stumble into. "Thank you." *Perhaps I am getting older.* He was not a vain man—he did not dye his hair as the gray came in—but he liked to think he still had his senses about him. "My mind was elsewhere."

"Are we almost there?"

"You can see the house, can't you?"

"That's where they live? The—"

"The Jenkinses, Geoffrey. Yes, that is their house."

He had spent the previous morning speaking with Mr. Jenkins, who had petitioned against the raise in his rent. It was a fair raise—land was worth more and all of the rents went up according to inflation—but several people had complained. Darcy's steward had explained all of the cases of complaint, which Darcy had listened to with care. Only one had seemed legitimate, and the next day he had invited Mr. Jenkins, an elderly tenant farmer, for tea at Pemberley. The man had pleaded with him—his wife was sick and their heating costs were always going up. They could not afford the new rent. Darcy had said he would think on it and return with an answer.

"Why are we going to their house?"

"Because I already made Mr. Jenkins travel all the way up to Pemberley. Now I will meet him on his ground."

Eventually, they made it down to the road, and the little house that overlooked a wheat field. Mr. Jenkins was sitting on the porch, and rose in surprise. "Mr. Darcy."

"Mr. Jenkins." He offered his hand, and Jenkins took it, but also removed his hat. "This is my son, Geoffrey Darcy."

Jenkins bowed. "Hello, Mr. Geoffrey."

"Hello, Mr. Jenkins," Geoffrey said.

"You've come about the rent."

"We will get to that. First, I understand your wife is ill. May we visit?"

"Of course, Mr. Darcy. We don't have much to offer you—"

"It's not necessary," Darcy said as they entered the house, which only had a few rooms. Jenkins hurried to get them something to drink; they were offered two glasses of watery beer, which they accepted gratefully. Darcy did not impose on Mrs. Jenkins, an old woman in a rocking chair in her bedroom, exchanging greetings with her as she coughed and sniffled and apologized profusely for not being able to better receive them.

"It's no trouble, I assure you," Mr. Darcy said.

"And this is the young master?" Mrs. Jenkins said with a smile at Geoffrey. Not only was the heir to Pemberley always a subject of speculation among the locals, but the Jenkinses had a son. That young man had died at Waterloo. "Hello, Mr. Geoffrey."

"Mrs. Jenkins," he said, bowing.

That duty finished, Darcy looked around the building as he talked with the husband. "So is it just a cough or is it a cold?"

"It's a cold that comes and goes. She can never seem to be fully rid of it."

"There's an apothecary by the name of Ashworth in Lambton. He sells mainly tonics, but he has a particular brew for the cough that contains lemon. Ask him for it and tell him I sent you. It costs barely more than a bottle of gin and it does wonders. I use it myself sometimes."

"Thank you, Mr. Darcy. About the rent—"

Darcy held up his hand. "I have a question for you, if you would."

"Of course, sir."

Darcy walked to the end of the hallway, which led to the kitchen with its little stove. Several bottles of different cold remedies sat in the middle of the kitchen table. The logs of wood that were the walls were held together with plaster, and the floor was beaten wood, probably hollow, above a stone foundation. "How long has it been since work was done on this house?"

"I—I don't know, sir. We bought it after we were married, and I used to have a man come by to fix the plaster when there were holes. But he left to find work in London."

Darcy glanced at his son, and then crouched down and pushed down on the floorboard. The other end went up a little. "Your house must be freezing in the winter."

"There's always a draft, even in the summer. In the winter, it's terrible, but who doesn't freeze in the winter? This isn't the south."

Darcy nodded, pacing for a moment before halting over a floorboard that rattled when he stepped on it. "Well, I can explain your increased coal use, and probably your wife's continual cold. The cold air comes up through the floorboards from underneath the house. You need to have your floors done."

Jenkins laughed quietly. "I can't afford something like that."

"I happen to have a very good carpenter who owes me a favor. If I sent him over to redo your floors and tighten the plaster, would you agree to the new rent?"

"I don't—yes." He nodded, as if assuring himself. "But if it's still cold—"

"Then we'll discuss it again, but I don't think it will be. He's a very good carpenter. He redid all the shooting boxes at Pemberley and you could sleep in them." He offered his hand, this time for business purposes.

Jenkins shook on it. "I agree. May I have an extra week to gather the new rent?"

"You may. My solicitor will be around." He nodded for his son. "And remember—Mr. Ashworth. If he charges you more than five farthings, tell him I sent you."

"Thank you, Mr. Darcy."

They said their good-byes and walked out into the sunlight. They took the long path on the way back, on the road that sloped up gently instead of the steep incline of the grassy hill.

"Do you really have a carpenter who owes you a favor?"

"I don't," he said to his son. "And it'll be at least twenty pounds to fix that house. Far more than Jenkins could dream of affording."

Geoffrey knew what he was being asked, and counted on his fingers. "You'll lose money! The increase won't cover it for years."

"You're discounting the fact that the rent will rise again eventually, most likely, but yes, I have just lost money. Why do you think I did it?"

His son grappled with the idea. "Was it charity?"

"It was, in a sense, but it was not the same as giving money to a beggar. Besides, if I had just offered up money because he was poor and his wife was suffering, why didn't I just give him free lodging? Or hand him coin to pay for his own repairs?" He answered for Geoffrey. "Because it would have insulted him. He's a working man, my boy. He doesn't want to be treated like a beggar. Besides, I had another reason."

Geoffrey was given ample time to think as they strolled up the path at their leisure. Finally, he said, "I give up."

"There were two reasons to do it, beyond charity for his sick wife. First, the rents are going up everywhere, equally, and it is bad to show favoritism. If I made an exception for someone because I felt bad for him, word would get around and I would have everyone at our door, telling me their sad stories, true or not. People talk—they compare notes, especially about the rich and what they do. So the rent had to go up, but I brought down his cost of living—he was buying his wife those expensive miracle cures. You noticed there were a few of them in the kitchen? And, of course, there is the matter of the cost of coal to heat the house."

"But you *still* lost money."

"But I *bought* something important—respect. Landlords are despised because people have to pay them money to live in their homes. A landlord who is liked is a hard thing to find. When Mr. Jenkins works out the real price of the renovations, he'll know I did right by him, and if someone raises objections to the way I treat my tenants in some tavern in Lambton, he might say something against it." He put a hand on his son's back. "It is very important to be liked by the people who owe you money. I would not do this for every tenant, but not every tenant has such an easy problem to solve. So the larger picture is more important in this case. The master of Pemberley must be regarded as a respectable man and even-handed landlord and employer, sometimes even at his own expense."

"Did Grandfather Darcy tell you that?"

"He did. He was a good master. One of the few things I remember about his funeral was how many of his tenants came out to pay their respects." He looked at his son's expression. "Do not worry yourself—I've no intention of giving up the ghost anytime soon." He gave him a playful shake. "That's enough for today."

"May I go to Kirkland?"

"Yes. But be home before supper!"

"I will!" He bowed quickly to his father before running off ahead of him.

When Darcy had stepped into the role of father to his younger sister, Georgiana Darcy, he had felt despair and grief. When he became a father of his children with his wife by his side, he had felt only delight. Being a good father soothed his mind, which was tired from many nights of uneasy rest that he could not properly explain.

~ ~ ~

"Dr. Maddox!"

So happily was he asleep that he would have preferred to ignore the call, but it was annoyingly persistent.

"I thought you were retired," Caroline mumbled next to him as he sat up and reached for his glasses.

"I thought I was, too," he said, and shambled to the door, throwing on a robe as he did and opening the door just a slit. "Yes?"

"Your brother is here with a patient. He said to get you up immediately, sir."

"My brother?" He was instantly awake. "Who is the patient? Princess Nadezhda?"

"Grégoire Darcy."

He did not question what Grégoire Darcy was doing in his house, much less England. He secured his robe with a belt and followed the servant with the lantern down the steps, where he found his brother and sister-in-law bearing a stretcher. "Put him in a room over there, on the extra cot," he said instantly. "Is he hurt? Or sick?"

"Both."

He turned to his manservant, who was also in his bedclothes. "Get all my equipment together and my surgical clothes. I'll change in my room in a few minutes." He grabbed a candlestick and followed Brian and Nadezhda into a spare room he used for minor surgery. A narrow, plain bed sat in the middle of the room. "More light," he ordered to the servant closest. "And get a maid up to start boiling water. And we'll need ice, too."

"He's pretty badly hurt," Brian said. "He can lie only on his side."

"Align the stretcher with the bed, and we'll transfer him." He set down the candlestick and stood on the other side of the bed. "Here, Grégoire. Let's see you." Grégoire did not respond other than to shake, curled up tightly as he was. Fortunately, he was not heavy, and Dr. Maddox was strong enough to safely lift him from the stretcher to the bed. He felt his patient's forehead. "How long has he had a fever?"

"It's been up and down, but more than a week now. We found him like this in Spain. He's barely holding on."

Nadezhda stroked Grégoire's hair. He was a mess, and had about two week's worth of a shaggy beard. "You're home, Grégoire."

"Before I cut off his clothes—where are his wounds?"

"On his back," Brian said. "They beat him for some infraction; nearly killed him. Then the doctor sewed him up badly and it became infected, so the doctor cut him open again to try to treat it, and that didn't help." He looked up and Dr. Maddox saw fear in his eyes. "It's bad."

"He's alive," Dr. Maddox said. "After all this time."

"He was wearing a hairshirt."

"A hair-hairshirt?" the doctor stuttered. "Like Thomas Becket?"

"Apparently."

Dr. Maddox did not have time to pass judgment. The manservant returned with his tools, and the doctor cut away the robe and the bloodied undershirt beneath it, revealing lines of bad stitching, green with infection. The smell was putrid. "I need help to do this." He turned to his manservant, who handed him his surgical case. "Take one of my cards to Dr. Andrew Bertrand's house. The address is on my desk. If he's not there, track him down; he's probably at Carlton House. And unless the Prince Regent is *actively* dying, get the doctor. I also need a surgeon from the clinic with the Royal Society, so tell Dr. Bertrand that. He'll know how to procure one at this hour. Time is of the absolute essence."

His manservant, who was accustomed to serving the doctor, simply nodded. "Yes, sir."

Dr. Maddox turned to his guests, bowing. "Sorry for not properly receiving you, but thank you for coming."

"Thank God you're here and not in Brighton or Derbyshire," Brian Maddox said. "Is there anything we can do?"

He thought it over. "A priest, a Catholic one. I have no idea where you would find one, but there's certainly any number of them in London."

"He was kicked out of the church. You should know that. It's a mess that I'll be happy to explain when we have time, but don't call him Brother Grégoire, because he isn't."

"But he's not—he can talk to a priest?"

"So I've been told."

He nodded and embraced his brother. "It's good to see you, by the way."

"You too, Danny."

Maddox bowed to Nadezhda. "Your Highness. Could you watch him while I prepare myself?"

"Of course."

He had no time for further discussion. He hurried into his bedroom, which he had not used in weeks, and quickly dressed himself in his worst clothes and a black apron. He stepped out of the door to be greeted by his wife in her nightgown, leaning on the door frame of her chamber. "What is it?"

"Grégoire is badly wounded and needs surgery."

She was clearly not awake enough to fully comprehend, but she nodded anyway. "Does Darcy know?"

"I have no idea. Brian and Nadezhda have just arrived and Darcy is in Derbyshire, so I imagine not."

"You're nervous."

He was usually good at hiding it. "No, I'm not."

"Do you think he will die?"

He sighed. "I don't know. It will be close."

She embraced him, kissing him softly. "You're the best surgeon in England. He'll be fine."

"How do you always know what to say to me?"

She gave him a little smile. "I've been your wife for a while now."

When Dr. Maddox returned to the ground floor, he could hear the servants in the kitchen, getting water heated for him to wash his instruments and his patient. His manservant was gone and probably would be for at least an hour. He washed his hands in a bowl in the kitchen and entered the room, where Nadezhda sat next to the bed, holding Grégoire's hand.

"Is he conscious?"

"He comes in and out."

He took a seat on the other side of the bed, removing the cover and looking at the wounds again, trying to construct the procedure in his mind. The wounds were not deep, but they were so extensive that they were dangerous. He had probably lost blood when they reopened the wounds, however long ago that was. The surgical thread they used in Spain was inferior; no wonder it had caused infection. He took a sponge and slowly began to wash some of the areas of skin that were uninjured but were caked in dried blood. Grégoire cried out all the same. "I'm sorry, Grégoire, but I have to do this." He noticed the rosary clutched in the monk's—former monk's—hand was itself filthy with grime and blood. "I will give it right back," he said as he pulled it from Grégoire's hand.

"Don't—"

"I promise, you'll have it right back." He dunked the rosary in the water bowl, scraping off the dirt with his hands until it shone again. "There." He took the opportunity to open Grégoire's hand and wipe it clean before returning the rosary, cross in palm. "Just like new."

Grégoire nodded into his pillow in affirmation. He was not strong enough to speak further.

"When was the last time he drank something?"

"A few hours now; we were giving him broth on the ship."

"Then you're a better nursemaid than most of the doctors I know," he said, and left the room to call for some soup to be heated and brought to them.

Only with Nadezhda's pleading did Grégoire swallow a few spoonfuls. "You need your strength."

What is left of it, Dr. Maddox thought.

CHAPTER 14

"To Forgive, Divine"

DR. BERTRAND ARRIVED JUST BEFORE the first rooster crowed. He was quickly introduced to Mrs. Maddox and the doctor's brother and sister-in-law. Then he joined Dr. Maddox alone with the unconscious patient.

"The surgeon will be here by six," he said. "Mr. Stevens."

"I know him," Dr. Maddox said as he removed the covers over Grégoire, giving Bertrand time to make his own visual assessment.

"Who is this?"

"A monk and my cousin through marriage. Or he was a monk until last week." He frowned. "The problem, as I see it, is if we cut away all the infected flesh, there won't be much to sew back together."

"Skin from his leg?"

"Too risky. Too many veins."

Dr. Bertrand nodded. "His arms."

"I'm not happy about doing it. Have you ever done a skin graft?"

"I've seen it done," Bertrand said. "But I don't have personal experience with it. On the battlefield, many soldiers need medical attention at the same time. So soldiers as wounded as this patient usually die before I can treat them. Do we know how deep the wounds are?"

"No, but they're fairly superficial, I think we can assume. We must do this quickly. He's already lost blood twice over this. I don't know how much he has left to lose."

"Who did this? This is a mess."

"An incompetent physician in Spain," Dr. Maddox said with disgust. "Twice, too. When the surgeon gets here, we'll begin. You take skin from the arm, I'll handle the back. Mr. Stevens will monitor his pulse and his breathing." He started opening his medical case and selecting equipment. "Did you sleep or are you just coming straight from duty?"

"I went home early. I haven't slept yet, but I will be fine for another few hours," he said. "Have you operated on relatives before?"

"Unfortunately, yes," Dr. Maddox replied.

~ ~ ~

By the time Brian returned with a Catholic priest for Grégoire, the household was awake, aside from the children. Caroline Maddox was writing a letter to the Darcys, telling them to come immediately, knowing full well that Grégoire could be dead in a few hours. Father LeBlanc, who had been appraised of the complex situation on the way, was ushered into the room. "May I have time alone with him, Doctor?"

"Sadly, no," said Dr. Maddox. "Andrew, you stay. You're not his relative. Wake him up with the salts. Father, this is Dr. Bertrand, who will monitor the patient." He bowed to the priest and exited as Dr. Bertrand went back to shaving Grégoire's arm.

In the living room, Dr. Maddox collapsed on the couch and called for tea. His brother sat beside him, with Nadezhda leaning on her husband's shoulder, asleep. "It was a long ride home," Brian explained, not looking particularly rosy himself. "What do you think?"

"It's close," he replied. "I'm surprised he made it this long."

"He's a Darcy. They're fighters."

~ ~ ~

Dr. Bertrand did succeed in rousing Grégoire with salts, and the ex-monk seemed to be at least semicoherent. "Mr. Darcy, this is Father LeBlanc."

"Hello, my son," the priest said. He was an older man, without ornament aside from his black dress and his collar. He put a hand over Grégoire's, which was feverishly tightened around his rosary. "You don't have to say anything, but if you have something you would like to confess—"

"Forgive me, Father, for I have sinned," Grégoire said. He crossed himself as he lay on his side. "I—I don't know how long it has been…since my last confession." He blinked, his eyes bloodshot. "I don't know anything."

"Think. Do you know the date of your last confession?" the priest said softly.

"I—It was after the end of the month, but there was also the confession to Father Abbot; I don't know if that counts." His voice was weak, his eyes weaker. "Forgive me, Father, for I have sinned—I don't know anything anymore. I am lost."

"I was told about the incident in Spain. You were not at fault. The abbot said so to your cousin."

"I—It doesn't…," he said and trailed off. "I don't know what I did. I don't know what I'll do. I don't know *anything.* How can I confess?" He was upset. "*How can I confess?* I don't understand if I did anything wrong or what I did that was wrong—I don't know my own sins—"

"You *do* know that God's mercy is boundless," the priest said. "And that if you have sinned, you are forgiven. And if you feel you are lost, you have a family that will help you find yourself again. They went to great lengths to bring you here."

"I…am I…where am I?"

"England. You're in London, my son."

Grégoire did not understand him. "Where is my brother?"

"I've been told he's in Derbyshire. He'll no doubt rush to your side, but that will take time. You'll have to call upon your inner reserves of strength."

"And what if I can't?" he said. "What if I don't want to?"

Father LeBlanc said slowly, "For this is thankworthy, if for conscience toward God, a man endure sorrows, suffering wrongfully."

"First Peter, Chapter 2, verse 19."

"Yes, my son. You are learned. You know that you do not suffer for no reason. God has a greater plan for you."

Grégoire opened his eyes again. "I'm familiar with the theology. I don't want it to be true. I wanted to lead the life I was leading. Now that I can't, why can't I go in peace?"

"That is not for you to decide. That is the Lord's domain." Seeing Grégoire's despair, he said, "You have this moment to decide to live or die. You have to choose to go on before you can choose a new path—a new way of life—for yourself."

Grégoire did not respond with word or gesture. He did, however, remain awake, staring into space for some time.

Then Father LeBlanc removed a piece of paper from his pocket. "I was asked to read this to you. It was written by your cousin, Mr. Maddox." He cleared his throat. "'Dear Grégoire: Please do not die. If you do, you will never meet your new nephew.' Oh, dear. I should have read that first." But he looked up, and Grégoire was smiling. "You have a new nephew?"

"I had just received the letter—before this all began. His name is Robert Kincaid. My sister's first child."

"I see. You seem to have quite a loving family, there."

"Yes," Grégoire said, and he unclenched his fist to take the priest's hand. "I am not at full wit—would you please, Father, say the Hail Mary, so I don't fail to remember it."

"Of course, my son." He made the sign of the cross over Grégoire. "*Ave, María, grátia plena, Dóminus tecum. Benedícta tu in muliéribus, et benedíctus fructus ventris tui, Iesus....*"

Grégoire joined him. By the end of it, his voice had faded, and shortly after the "Amen" he had lost consciousness.

Father LeBlanc blessed him again, and stepped out. "The patient, Grégoire, is ready."

~ ~ ~

Darcy had ridden for nearly two days, stopping only when his horse was about to collapse and to sleep a few restless hours at an inn. It was the same old road to Town, and most of the innkeepers along the way knew the traveler. The barkeep's wife said something to him about appearing distressed. He ignored the remark. When he got to his room, he collapsed on the bed, waking only a few hours later.

By midafternoon on the second day, he had passed all of the major centers before London itself. It was amazing to think that just the morning before, he had been breakfasting with his wife and about to go shooting with Bingley when the express courier arrived. Pemberley had been thrown into an uproar. Darcy had insisted that Elizabeth take a carriage; Elizabeth had insisted that he not ride so fast as to have an injury along the way, as his brother would be unlikely to appreciate *that*. The letter from Mrs. Maddox said she had written Georgiana as well, but they had sent on a letter anyway, just in case the first was lost. They had told the Bingleys, who lived but three miles from them, and that couple had pledged their support and said they would join them as soon as possible. Mugin, who had been staying with them, had asked directions and taken off on foot.

"God protect you on your journey," Elizabeth had said as she kissed her husband good-bye. Grégoire, she knew, was probably already dead and had been so for at least a day. The condition Mrs. Maddox had described in her letter was not particularly encouraging (the former Miss Caroline Bingley was not very good at false encouragement, so she made no attempt).

Why hadn't he gone to Spain? Darcy went through all his reasons. The situation had not seemed dire. He had sent someone in his stead, who was probably still wandering around Madrid. He had written Grégoire and expected a response. He also didn't much care to leave England, but that was beside the point—he would have done it without hesitation if he had known Grégoire was in trouble. Again. But he had had the foresight to send Mr. Maddox, thank God. That was his only consolation on the desperate journey.

He arrived in town barely able to stand, and with his horse in a similar condition. Not bothering with anything else, he went immediately to the Maddox townhouse. The doorman was standing just outside. "Mr.—"

He ignored him. Dr. Maddox had the poor fortune to be stepping out of his study, in plain view and ready to be assaulted by a dirt-covered, anxious Darcy. But before Darcy could say anything, Maddox said calmly, "He's alive."

"Where—"

He pointed to a side room. "His fever broke this morning. He has defeated one infection; as long as he does not develop another, he should be all right." When Darcy tried to move toward the door, Maddox grabbed him by the arm hard enough to hold him back. "Take a moment for yourself. He's not well. It would be better if he saw you in a calmer state."

"What do you mean, he's not well?"

"He had a fever for more than two weeks, and though he's not senseless, his memories of what happened before and since it are not intact. Also, he's been tossed from the church."

Darcy did allow the doorman to remove his soiled overcoat and hat, and provide him with a wet cloth to wash off his face. Dr. Maddox waited patiently with him, guiding him into the sitting room and calling for tea. It was dusk now, and with the light went Darcy's energy, but it was still hard for him to break from the state of heightened alarm he had been in for so long. "What happened?"

"I don't fully understand. The church hierarchs were cruel to him about holding back his money from the church, and the abbot thought he would be better protected if he left the church entirely. Or so I have been told. The story Brian told is a convoluted one."

"But Grégoire is safe."

"He's lost everything," he said. "You know that the church was his life."

Darcy, who gladly accepted the tea to slake his thirst—he would have accepted anything wet—nodded. So many emotions ran through his head that he could not pick one. "Does he know? Does he remember?"

"Unfortunately, yes, he does remember *that*. When you talk to him, don't speak ill of the church. I know there is a temptation, but it would do him no good to hear it."

"I understand." He didn't, but he understood the message. "I assume there was—work done on him?"

"Yes. I will discuss the surgery after you've seen him. He can't be moved, and the stitches can't come out for at least another few days, but aside from his skin, he is not permanently injured."

"I don't know what you did," Darcy said, "but thank you."

"Thank my brother for getting him here in time," Dr. Maddox said.

Minutes later, Darcy entered his brother's room, more calmly than he was inclined. Grégoire was on his side, wearing a white shirt over layers of bandages wrapped around his torso. He had a small beard, and fuzz on his head from where his tonsure had been. He seemed only half aware of his surroundings as Darcy pulled up a seat beside him and took his hand. "Brother—"

"Grégoire," Darcy said. "I'm here."

Grégoire just nodded. He was not capable of much other movement. He was pale and sickly looking, but that was to be expected.

"I'm here," Darcy repeated, to reassure himself that it was true. He stroked Grégoire's hair. It was so much like Geoffrey's. "Elizabeth and the children are on the way, but I rode ahead. They should be here perhaps tomorrow night. And Georgiana—I don't know if she can come, but I'm sure she will if she can."

"How is she?"

"Radiant. She thoroughly enjoys being a mother. And Robert is...well, the second most beautiful boy in the entire world. The top prize belongs to *my* son, but do not dare tell her I said that."

Grégoire smiled weakly. "I promise. How is Geoffrey?"

"You won't recognize him. He is a head taller than when you saw him last. Anne is forever demanding rides on his back. And then Sarah does the same thing, and then Cassandra does it as well. With three sisters who adore him, he hardly gets a moment alone." Grégoire seemed to be enjoying listening, so he continued. "Bingley's children are well. Georgiana—well, I suppose she'll be out in society in a few years. I can hardly imagine it. She went to Ireland with Her Highness while Mr. Maddox and Bingley were gone."

"Bingley's returned from India?"

"Yes, he came back with Brian. Didn't—"

"My mind," Grégoire said, "is a blur. I did not connect the two events. How is he?"

"His usual overexcited self. He is coming to see you—they all are," he said. "And I'll bring George and Isabel around. George is—well, you will be impressed. He looks just like his father, but is growing into a responsible and respectable man. And a scholar. Who knows, he may end up in the church—" He cut himself off, as if some alarm had rung in his mind.

"You can say it," Grégoire said weakly, "but I have no advice for him there."

He swallowed. "I was advised not to discuss the topic with you. I know you are hurt and…" He bit his lip. "I don't know what to make of it."

"I don't either," Grégoire said. His voice was slowly declining into a hoarse whisper, but he gave no indication of wanting the conversation to end. "I am lost."

"You were wronged."

"It doesn't matter," he said. "I have not the strength to be angry. And I look ahead and see nothing."

"You are a man with a great fortune, a loving family, and no obligations. Many people would trade anything to be in your position."

"I pledged myself to God, Darcy," Grégoire rasped. "How am I to fulfill that now?"

Darcy knew not to contradict Grégoire about his obligations. Grégoire Darcy would never be an English gentleman. He would never settle for a position in the Anglican church. Darcy felt despair. "I have no wisdom for you," he said, his voice wavering. "What kind of answer is that? I can comfort my wife when she is in crisis, or counsel my son in his anxieties about his responsibilities, or reassure my sister when she needs it. But I can think of nothing for you." He pinched his eyes, mainly from exhaustion but also because he did not want to show his tears. "I have failed as a brother. I could not lead Wickham to the right path, and I don't even know what yours is. How can I guide you? How can I help you?"

Grégoire did not answer for some time. Darcy, ashamed to look at him, wondered if he had fallen asleep. Then Grégoire spoke. "You can help me by getting the doctor. I need my pain medicine to sit up, and I am eager to do so."

Darcy nodded. "Yes, of course." He found Dr. Maddox in his study. "My brother asked me—"

Dr. Maddox looked at his watch. "Yes, it's time for his medicine." He took Darcy back to the sickroom, where he shook a green bottle and fed Grégoire a spoonful of his opium tonic. "He'll probably go back to sleep now."

"I'll stay with him."

The doctor nodded and excused himself. Darcy turned back to his brother, who was attempting to sit up but failing. "What happened to your arms?"

"The bandages on my forearms?" Grégoire said. "I think—Dr. Maddox may have said he needed more skin for my back. Or I may have misheard him. Either way, the bandages are new." Slowly, and evidently painfully, he came to a sitting position, using the pillows and Darcy's arms to hold him up. "It's half past seven, isn't it?"

Darcy looked at his pocket watch. "It is. Precisely. How did you know?"

"Compline. It's time for Compline," he said. "Will you hold me up so I can say psalms?"

Darcy offered no argument. Grégoire leaned on him, whispering to himself in Latin and holding his rosary. This lasted a good ten minutes until he dropped off right in Darcy's arms. Darcy laid his brother back down on the bed, and kissed him on the head.

It was all he could think to do.

CHAPTER 15

The Abbot's Epistle

~ ~ ~

IT WAS AN UNSPOKEN AGREEMENT that Darcy would stay with his brother at the Maddox house. After he had dinner and a bath, he sat down with Brian and Nadezhda Maddox, who told the story as best they understood it, based on what the abbot had told them.

"So they beat him almost to death for honoring his father's wishes," Darcy said, holding back his emotions, "and then they decided he was a saint instead and made plans to honor him in Rome without his consent?"

"Yes," Brian said. "There were also plans to inter him in Rome if he died, but Grégoire had told the abbot when he joined the monastery that he wanted to be buried at Pemberley instead of with the other monks in the abbey graveyard. The abbot wanted to honor his wishes."

"And the abbot stood up to his archbishop?"

"The politics of Rome are complex. Apparently his brother is the pope," Brian said. "Casting him out of his order was the only way to save him—physically—without damning his soul. He can be a layman, but never more than that without permission from his former abbot."

Darcy digested this silently.

"This may be poor consolation," Brian said, "but that abbot did everything he could for your brother. After the fact, yes, but he still did it. He was very upset about the situation."

It was little consolation, but Darcy nodded. He excused himself to check one last time on Grégoire, who was asleep, and then headed upstairs. He met Caroline Maddox on the way. "Mrs. Maddox."

"Mr. Darcy."

"Thank you for writing," he said. "I wrote to my sister, but I do not know if she can come down."

"If you haven't been told—Daniel's new assistant for the Prince Regent was called in, along with a student surgeon. Daniel was terrified that he wouldn't save Grégoire."

"I am grateful to your husband."

They nodded to each other, and Darcy took his leave, retiring immediately. Caroline continued down the hallway, where she heard her husband talking to Brian and Nadezhda.

"I noticed you didn't mention the hairshirt." The damage from it was obvious to a doctor like Maddox.

"I'm not going to be the one to tell him that," Brian said. "I think it's better if he doesn't know. If you want to tell him, that's another matter."

"I've always believed in patient confidentiality."

Feeling a little guilty for listening in on a conversation (something she rarely felt guilty about), she joined them quickly. "What is this about?"

Dr. Maddox looked up at her from the armchair. "He was wearing a hairshirt for years before this. That was why his wounds were so severe."

"What's a hairshirt?"

"It's a device made to mortify the flesh—you wear it as an undershirt and it slowly tears at your skin," Brian said. "Thomas Becket wore one."

"The English saint? The archbishop?"

"The very one," her husband said. "After he was murdered by the king's knights, the men sent to strip him found he was wearing a hairshirt, presumably as penance for almost giving in to King Henry's demands for more power over the church. For his suffering, he was made a saint." He added, "Which was probably the precise thing on the church hierarchs' minds after Grégoire's initial punishment."

"The abbot was right in sending him away," Nadezhda said. "Politically for Grégoire, it was the right thing to do."

"But that doesn't make it easier," Dr. Maddox said.

~ ~ ~

As he could not expect his wife and children to arrive very soon in their carriages, Darcy rose in the morning after a fitful sleep and ventured to the Bradley household. George and Isabel Wickham immediately offered to visit their uncle, having not been previously informed (the former Mrs. Wickham showed no particular interest, but that was expected).

"Uncle Grégoire!" Isabel Wickham shouted as she ran into his room. He did his best to welcome her, but could only manage to shake her hand. They had managed to flip him onto his other side, because his arm was getting sore. "Why didn't you tell us you were sick?"

"Some things sneak up on me," he said, his voice barely above a gasp.

George was next. He bowed. "Uncle Grégoire."

"George." He smiled. "You look just like your father."

"I know," he answered.

"It—it isn't a bad thing," Grégoire said, not apologizing. He was speaking naturally, if in a very weak voice. "Your father gave his life to save Darcy and me. He was a great man for that alone. Whatever...anyone else says...is nonsense." He reached out and touched George's face. "I have heard from Darcy about you. You would make your father proud."

"Thank you, Uncle," George said, not sure what to make of his comment. People either said bad things about George Wickham the older or nothing at all. "When you recover—will you help me with some Greek? Because I'm not going to Eton or Harrow—"

"I would be honored," Grégoire said with a smile.

George observed his uncle was drifting off. "I'll be back tomorrow, or the next day. Rest, Uncle Grégoire."

"Bless you, George."

George nodded and stepped out of the room, making way for Dr. Maddox to enter. Outside, his sister was waiting.

"He's going to be all right, isn't he?" Isabel said.

"I think so," he answered.

"He doesn't look good."

"I know. He's been sick for a long time, but he's better now."

"I have so many uncles and he's the nicest." She was instantly aware of shuffling in the background. "Oh, Uncle Darcy, I did not mean—"

He smiled. "No matter. Grégoire is gifted with the most generous disposition of us all. I won't deny it." He gave her a reassuring pat. "He will be fine."

"Can I bring my cat? Do you think he'd like that?"

"Perhaps. Ask Mrs. Maddox first."

She curtsied and ran off to do so, leaving Darcy with George. "How is your mother?"

"Fine. Brandon has started sleeping through the night."

"Good for all of you, I imagine."

George nodded. "Is everyone else coming?"

"Yes, I just rode on ahead in a panic. Aunt Darcy should be here tonight or tomorrow morning with your cousins."

He said in a lower voice, "Is he going to be all right?"

"Physically, I'm told, yes. But he needs support that no one knows how to give him. Beyond that, everyone has to find their own way." That wasn't true, entirely; from his first breath, Fitzwilliam Darcy had been destined to be master of Pemberley and had time for no other occupation. Younger sons, sons without estates but with money—they had freedom, but little occupation for them.

George might be happy in the Church of England; Grégoire would not. Or maybe Grégoire would surprise them all. He was certainly quite capable of doing so.

Their reverie was interrupted by Emily Maddox. "Mr. Darcy! George!"

"Hello, Miss Maddox," Darcy said. "What do you have there?"

She had in her hands a sheet of paper. "It's a gift—for Grégoire." Before either of them could protest, she ran straight to the door and opened it on her father, who was just exiting. "Papa, can I see him?"

"He's just had his medicine, so you can try, but he might not stay awake."

"She seems rather eager to try," Darcy said.

Dr. Maddox could deny his daughter nothing, and they re-entered the room, where Grégoire looked at Emily with glassy eyes. "Hello."

"I made you a picture. Mama says I have to learn drawing, and I was tired of making pictures of flowers and buildings."

"Oh." His eyelids closed.

Dr. Maddox plucked the picture out of her hands, which was fairly well drawn for an eight-year-old. "It seems to be you, Grégoire, and—a man I don't recognize. He has a halo."

"Papa! He's Jesus. Don't you know what Jesus looks like?"

Grégoire, who had not gone to sleep quite yet, smiled. "Let me see." He opened his eyes as Dr. Maddox held the picture up. "I seem to be—yes, I am holding hands with Jesus." It was a drawing of him in a monk's brown robe and Jesus in a blue robe, with a beard and a halo. "Why are we each holding boxes?"

"I asked Father LeBlanc what a monk was, and he said a monk was a man who devoted his life to God the Father. So I thought you must be friends with his son."

"Yes," Dr. Maddox said in amusement, "but why are they holding boxes?"

Emily grinned. "Because they're going shopping! Don't you know *anything*, Papa?"

Grégoire laughed into the pillow. "Why…why am I going shopping with Our Lord and Savior?"

"Well, it's what Mama does with *her* friends."

Dr. Maddox had a hard time containing his laughter. "Would you like me to put it up, Grégoire?"

"Please…*after* you show Mrs. Maddox."

The rest of the day brought something they had not expected—rain. It descended on London from the north, so they could only assume the carriages from Derbyshire would be further delayed by weather. A well-muddied rider arrived to say just that—that Mrs. Darcy and the children were stuck at an inn until it relented; more waiting, and another restless night for Darcy. He had slept without Elizabeth before, but not in Town when he was so disturbed and needed her. More important, Grégoire needed her. He needed to see the children—he loved the children. *Maybe Grégoire could run an orphanage*, he thought. *Or run a school. He would enjoy a life of charity and he adores children*. But Darcy could not bring himself to start discussing possibilities. Grégoire slept most of the time, waking mostly when his medicine wore off,, clearly in terrible pain. He would grapple with things later. Darcy bothered him no further. Darcy spent the afternoon watching him sleep, wondering what else he could have done. *Maybe now I can convince him to get married and have some children of his own. I would have to be subtle.*

Brian and Nadezhda had not returned to their home outside Town yet. Brian had business to attend to, and they wanted to hover over their former charge as much as anyone else. It was Brian who produced a letter during one of the hours when Grégoire was both awake and aware. It was still sealed. "This is from the abbot. He said it would bring you some comfort. Do you wish me to open it?"

Grégoire nodded.

Brian broke the seal, revealing several pages of Latin. "This may have to wait. We have your spectacles—we were allowed to take your spectacles and portraits of your family."

"Can someone read it to me?" Grégoire asked. "If it is not too much trouble."

"I haven't used my Latin since Cambridge," Darcy said.

"I didn't go to Cambridge," Brian added. "I'll get Daniel."

They summoned Dr. Maddox, who was, of course, obliging. "My pronunciation will probably be terrible, but I think I can read it aloud."

Grégoire begged for him to do so. Darcy and Brian excused themselves, shutting the door behind them. Whatever was between the abbot and the monk whose life he had destroyed was certainly private, even if it was in a foreign tongue.

Dr. Maddox cleared his throat. "My apologies for any horrible mispronunciations."

"That is fine," Grégoire said. "I am a most willing listener."

The doctor nodded and began, not entirely understanding the lines he was saying, but getting the general sense of it as he went along. If Grégoire did not understand anything, he gave no indication.

Dear Grégoire Bellamont-Darcy,

I can imagine what you are going through, though I am old and I may be entirely incorrect in my assumptions, and you may find yourself already well and happily settled in England. If this is true, then you will find no comfort in these words, but they may not be upsetting either. My intent for this missive is twofold: to explain fully my actions, so that you know how and why you came to be where you are now, and to confess to you my sins, for I cannot be forgiven otherwise. You have no obligation to feel any tenderness toward me, for I deserve none, but I cannot find any solace until I have at least begun my confession. If you do not wish to hear it, toss it in the fire. But I wish to write it.

I must begin in Cesena, where I was born and raised with my younger brother, Barnaba Niccolò Maria Luigi Chiaramonti, now the vicar of Christ, Pope Pius VII. To the subject at hand, my brother went into the church, as was our family's tradition for younger sons, or even older sons if they aspired to power. He became a Benedictine and wrote home about his life in the monastery of Santa Maria del Monte of Cesena. I was never much one for politics, which are the bread and butter of an Italian family of wealth and power, and the quiet life was an attraction to me for the same reason it is to many people—an escape from the requirements of a normal life. My father did not oppose me becoming a novice even at a very young age, as he already had one secular son and two daughters, and the church could be a secular occupation as well as a religious one, should I ever incline in that direction. It was decided, however, that I would not join the same monastery as my brother, lest it be thought that I was merely following in his footsteps. I went instead to San Gregorio (coincidentally, this was the name my brother took for himself upon taking his vows—your name, Gregorio) and I took the cowl at fifteen. I confess that though I enjoyed the community to which I had vowed my life, I longed for other experiences—I confess to you now, not all were good, especially when I was a man of eighteen. My abbot sent me abroad, thinking I would either abandon my order quietly and respectfully outside the Roman sphere, or I would work out my feelings there and return satiated. I traveled first to the Holy Land, and was blessed to see the site of our Lord's crucifixion. There was no doubt in my mind that I would never leave the church, though I might think about straying from it or feel frustrations, as does any human being.

I was sent north to the Turkish empire's capital, and failed in my mission to convert the Turks to Christianity. They remain Muslims to this day.

That summer, I continued my journey to Bucharest, where I was charged with delivering messages to the brothers and bishops there, who were in conflict with the Orthodox church. I lodged in an apartment, and every morning, a young Slavic woman brought me fresh milk. Needless to say, I was as tempted as any man my age, and proved that summer that I was no saint. At the time I regretted it, but put no stop to it; that was brought on by the order for my return to my monastery, which precipitated a great depression. This seemed to surprise my lover, who said she had known many a priest (though, she said, none so handsome as myself) who unmade himself as easily as any married man who promised never to stray from his wife, broke his vow, and then, of course, returned home for supper, so to speak. At this, I dropped to my knees and began to pray for God's forgiveness, and she said something to me that has stayed with me. "You think you are so pious—the apostles all sinned and you cannot?"

Our parting was tender, and I learned a good deal more humility from her than I ever learned from the Discipline. When I returned, much to my surprise, the abbot asked me to perform penance for my sins (which I most dutifully did) but was not impressed by my tale of sinful woe. "I do not know anyone in the church who has not done the same thing at one point, except those who have never left the doors of the monastery since their entrance—and they are often guilty of much greater crimes of the flesh." He was as forgiving as was permitted within the Rule, for which I am forever grateful.

I had now been ten years in the Brotherhood of St. Benedict and my brother fifteen, and our father was growing impatient. My esteemed brother seemed interested in nothing but his daily labors of copying manuscripts, and my father desired that at least one of us aspire to a cardinalship. I was feeling particularly eager to please someone, and so against my instincts I accepted a small bishopric near the papal lands, which required me to often be in Rome, and there I lingered for the most miserable years of my life. His Holiness Pope Pius VI was a good man, but very political, and concerned with Jesuit policies and agricultural reforms, and throwing off the yoke of France. None of this interested me, and all of the other things the city offered me were not to my taste, besides the usual pilgrimage sites and prayer. Rome, as you no doubt saw while you were there, was a city like any other city; it proposed to be something different, but there was sin there. It was nothing like the horrible tales from the days before the Reformation, of which there remained daily reminders, but it was still not what I sought. I do hear that His Holiness appeared rather unfavorably in some fiction by the Marquis de Sade, which is unfortunate. I would never read such literature, but I would assume, based on the barest of things I have heard, that he was not given credit as a vicar of Christ.

It was upon my father's death that I, when finished grieving, was free to request a transfer. I accepted a bishopric near Oviedo, and as you know, eventually became archbishop of the region. At the same time, my brother emerged from monastic hiding. As he rose through the ranks of Rome, apparently without being tainted by anything there, I wrote to him of my own despair even at the politics of Spain, and he encouraged me to do as I pleased with my life. Eventually, I gathered the courage to request the position of abbot at what is now my abbey. I had dined there on many occasions and spent time with the monks, and knew the former abbot, and was there at his death. It was an easy transition, and I was happy again, and marveled at how I had ever fully served God while in a state of misery, for is this world not created to be loved as a work of the Lord?

My life from then was as you know it, until your arrival, though that did not at first bring a great change. Over the years, many monasteries had been dissolved for one reason or another, and I had seen many monks come looking for lodgings, Benedictine and others. You I saw as another child of the world, of mixed parentage, heritage, and culture. How little I understood, to think there was not something greater in you, though you were in the first year a delight in the earnestness with which you took to your chores.

You will perhaps recall the conversation we had some months ago concerning your work with the people. As to the rumors being spread about you working miracles on the sick populace, I had my doubts for the same reason that you denied them being miracles—people are easier to take to superstition than scientific fact. How strange for a man of faith to say that, but it is nonetheless true. And we both know that some, perhaps all, of the miracles you worked were mere coincidence, or your wonderful herb garden, which I fear will wither away in your absence. I was not surprised when you turned down the job of prior, but I was saddened that I would see less of you, as you were so often out with the people, doing your work there and not within the monastery walls.

I do not know how the talk of miracles reached beyond the abbey gates, but it could have been any brother passing on information he had heard. There were those who spoke against you, saying that you were proclaiming yourself a miracle worker. These claims were easily dismissed. The townspeople denied you made such claims, instead assigning it all to God and medicine, so no fault could be found. I thought then, Lord, if you would see fit to continue Brother Grégoire on this path, he would do much good for the poor of the coast.

It was in innocence that the matter of your yearly inheritance and its use as charity was uncovered. A certain person along the chain of people in the banker's employ (whose name I will leave out) happened to mention it in a conversation with his priest, and that priest told the bishop, and the bishop wrote to me

I confess that I understand your motives completely. Your brother's advice is sound; handle your own money and give it as you see fit, rather than put it in the pockets of the church, where it might disappear. (Your brother and I see with the same eyes here.) However that is not the Rule, and I must and do take the Rule seriously, so I knew you could not escape punishment, but I hoped that it would simply be a matter of confession, punishment, repentance, and absolution, and some change in the agreement with your brother in England. I told the bishop that he would never see your entire fortune, which he did seek, for I knew enough of the world to know that your brother would simply freeze the funds, and be right to do so. I thought that would temper the bishop's thirst. I shall never know if it would have; the events that followed took us on another path entirely.

The revelation of the cilicium—the hairshirt—was devastating to me. It was very noble and pious of you, and done only with the best intentions, and to some extent brought out the best in us, but the worst of us as well. I have no doubt that had you died from your injuries, you would have been taken to Rome and canonized as quickly as possible. And had you lived and stayed here, you would have been hounded by church hierarchs to go to Rome. I could not see a life so young ruined by a simple misunderstanding of what a miracle is. Excommunicating you from the order was the only way I had to protect you from Rome, be you alive or dead, without indicating that your soul was damned.

You are not damned. There is no stain on your soul, and you should go forth and live a pious life without fear because of what I wrote on a document. I did not mean half the words on them; it was a protective measure. I bless you in thoughts and prayers every day and will continue to do so, and I doubt anyone touched by your presence here at the abbey would do otherwise.

I will tell you one final thing, which I cannot properly account for. On the day the infection was discovered, a week after the punishment, the doctor reopened his own stitches and you bled terribly, so much that we had to collect it in a basin beneath your bed. Feeling ill myself, and knowing you were close to death, I wandered to the herbarium, looking for a little ginger for my beer. There was a monk there I did not recognize. Oddly, I did not become alarmed at seeing an unfamiliar person in the abbey, though I did question him. He said he was a friend of yours, a fellow Englishman. He had a beard and spoke Latin in a strange accent, if that is any significance to you. I asked him if he would pray with us, as the bell had just rung for Vespers, and he said he would pray for you, but that he was sure that by God's grace you would live. We walked to the chapel together, but somehow I lost him along the way, and never saw him again. I am not overly inclined to question this event, for I was so overjoyed with the news that I felt I had good reason to believe, and lo, even now I do not entirely question whether you survived the journey.

Go and do as you will. If you ever see fit to forgive me for my sins in my treatment of you, I would be most honored. Go with God, Brother Grégoire. You will always be my brother in Christ.

Abbot Francesco Chiaramonti

When the doctor was finished, he saw, to his surprise, that Grégoire's eyes were still open and aware. "That is it," Dr. Maddox said.

Grégoire nodded. "My mind…cannot fully comprehend."

"You've been ill for a long time, Grégoire. You need to rest and recover."

"I have a request, but it is an imposition on your time, Dr. Maddox."

Maddox smiled. "I'm partially retired, Grégoire. Go ahead."

"Will you come tomorrow, and read it again?"

Dr. Maddox smiled. "Of course."

CHAPTER 16

Demons in the Night

~ ~ ~

THE STORM CONTINUED into the night. Darcy watched Grégoire fall asleep after his evening dose of opium. He did not head to his room, even though he was tired. He saw no reason to get into his bed without Elizabeth, when he needed her so badly. Instead, he nodded off in the chair in Grégoire's room, sleeping uncomfortably for some time before he heard glass smashing. Instantly, he was awake, his eyes turning to the hazy source.

The glass on the table beside the bed had been knocked over and shattered on the floor. Grégoire, in a shirt and bedclothes, had attempted to stand up, and failed, hitting the ground and taking his sheets with him.

"Grégoire!" Darcy grabbed him by both arms and hoisted him back up. "You're not supposed to be—"

Grégoire spat in his face and tried to break free. His eyes were bloodshot and wild, and with his beard and unkempt hair, he looked unwell. "Let me go!" He said something else in what was probably Latin. "Please, let me go!" he repeated.

"Grégoire, I would gladly let you—"

"You can't do this to me!" his brother shouted, pounding his fists into Darcy's chest. "*Amitte me!*"

"You're not well," Darcy said with a quiet forcefulness. "You have to sit back down."

"*Noli me tangere, fili meretricis!* He left me! Everyone has left me!"

"I am here," Darcy said. "I will stay here. The others—"

"*You did this to me!* You bastard, I was happy!" Grégoire cried. "I was so happy…" There was madness in his watery eyes. "So happy."

Darcy was getting a little desperate, and hoped someone had heard them. He could hardly leave his brother in this condition in order to find a servant to wake Maddox. "You were killing yourself!"

"How do you know what it is, pain? It brings us closer to God—" He went almost limp for a moment, and Darcy succeeded in lifting him back up on the bed so he was at least sitting. "Even when…there's so much of it—"

"You need to lie back down!"

"*Subsisto is!* Stop telling me what I need! I didn't need Father's money. I didn't need it from you. I told you to stop it, and now you're going to kill me, just as you killed George—"

Darcy swallowed his first reaction, and instead said, "Grégoire, listen to me. You're sick—"

"I'm not sick! Just because I want to be a pious person, that makes me sick?" He grabbed Darcy's face. "I can see into your eyes. You're just hiding—you're afraid. *Ego sum non! I am not afraid!*" He pulled back, and swung what was meant to be a punch, but it was slow and weak and Darcy easily caught it.

He saw the red staining the shirt. "You're popping your stitches. Do you want to kill yourself?"

"Yes! Would that make you happy?" Grégoire said, struggling under Darcy's increasingly firm grip. "Napoleon's soldiers couldn't kill me, the church couldn't kill me; do you want to try?"

Darcy did the only thing he could think of, which was to kick over the table with all of the metal instruments, which clattered in a noise loud enough to be noticed by anyone nearby. "No one wants you dead." He pushed him down again, and Grégoire cried out. Maybe he really *was* killing him.

"Mr. Darcy," said a voice from behind him. "What is—oh, goodness."

"Wake up the doctor. *Now,*" he said without looking back at the servant. "And send someone to help me in the meantime." He turned back to Grégoire, who was still managing to struggle. "I will save you from yourself."

"The abbot said that. Right before he cast me out. Grégoire, the rich bastard, can't be seen in the house of God!" He was weakening, having exerted himself more in the past few minutes than in many days. "I saw him. I saw the abbot, I saw the abbot in Munich, there was a terrible fire—he said something about a forge—I am not to be hammered!" He cried, "God forgive me, what good does God's forgiveness do? Am I to live or die?"

"Live!" he said as two servants burst into the room, where a bleeding madman was screaming at Mr. Darcy. Sizing up the situation, they quickly helped Mr. Darcy subdue the patient.

"Demons! Oh, God, please—I am to be forgotten and now damned?"

"You are not damned," Darcy said. "You are just delirious—"

"*Vos es totus everto ex abyssus!*" he screamed. "*Diabolus genitus!* Where is my cross? Where is the merciful God?"

To that, Darcy did not know the answer. Fortunately, Dr. Maddox rushed into the room and he didn't have to. The doctor was still tying his bathrobe. "Oh, dear. Give me a moment." He looked at the instruments spilled everywhere. "Give me two."

"He's bleeding, Maddox!"

"I know! I know!" Dr. Maddox knelt on the ground and collected his things. "Candle!" One of the servants brought him a candle, which he held under a spoon, but Darcy was too distracted to observe the procedure. He smelled something burning. Then Dr. Maddox produced a cloth and put it over Grégoire's screaming mouth.

"Breathe," he said, which was not an order that even his patient could disobey. In fact, Grégoire was gasping, and breathed very deeply. He collapsed quickly onto the bed, which was stained with his own blood. Maddox removed the cloth and put a hand on Grégoire's forehead. "He has no fever, at least. Turn him over."

With care, Darcy and the servants flipped Grégoire over. The shirt he wore buttoned in the back, and it was easy to open. Dr. Maddox had his tools ready now and looked at the wounds as more light was brought to them. "He managed to pop only a few. Turn away, Mr. Darcy," he said, threading his needle.

"I won't leave him."

"I don't want two patients," Dr. Maddox said with his usual calm. "Just turn around."

Darcy did as he asked, not relinquishing his hold on Grégoire's hand as he waited for Dr. Maddox to work. It was very brief, and then Dr. Maddox called for hot water and various other things from his lab, handing the keys to his manservant. "He will be all right."

"He wasn't all right a few minutes ago."

"He had a lot of opium and probably a bad dream." He looked up at Darcy, trying to read his face. "Whatever he said to you, he didn't mean it."

"He wanted to strike me. He tried."

"Why not? I'd be angry if I were him and you were the closest person available." He added, "He holds himself to an impossible standard. We, in turn, unintentionally do the same. He's only human, Darcy. Let him be angry for a little while. What else should he be?"

The manservant arrived with the ingredients and the others with the hot water and dishes, and Dr. Maddox carefully mixed a tea that smelled familiar. Grégoire, who was slowly returning to consciousness, was approached by a soft-spoken Dr. Maddox. "Please drink this. It will help you sleep."

For whatever reason—probably pure exhaustion—Grégoire did not resist, and swallowed it in full. He took another cup, and then settled back on the pillow, not to stir again. Dr. Maddox ordered Darcy from the room. "Let someone else watch him."

"I couldn't—"

"Leave him for a few hours," Dr. Maddox insisted. "If you want, I'll keep watch."

"You've done enough."

"I have a patient who thinks otherwise. Now go. Clean yourself up a bit."

Darcy could hardly take it as an insult; his sleeves were bloodied from holding down Grégoire. "May I—this is selfish of me, but may I have some of that tea?"

Dr. Maddox replied, "Of course."

After a bath and a cup of that soothing concoction, Darcy finally slid into bed. He had taken care to wash off the grime underneath his fingertips from the fight, but they still did not look clean. Slowly, he dropped off into a dreamless sleep.

~ ~ ~

In the morning, the rain abated. As London began to dry, Darcy braced himself to greet his brother. Not that he was afraid for himself—in fact, he had no idea whether Grégoire would even recall the incident—but it remained unsettling nonetheless. And that Dr. Maddox had been witness to it—well, the doctor had surely seen stranger things than a delirious patient.

Darcy had breakfast with Mrs. Maddox, as Dr. Maddox had just gone to sleep. The servant instructed him that Grégoire was in confession, and after a few minutes, a priest emerged. "Father, I am Grégoire's brother, Mr. Darcy."

"Father LeBlanc."

"How is my brother this morning?" It came out satisfactorily emotionless.

"Through God's mercy, he is less burdened," said the priest, and excused himself. It only then occurred to Darcy that if Grégoire had said everything in confession, then the priest knew everything of the events previous to this.

Swallowing, Darcy entered Grégoire's chamber. The linen had been changed, as well as his clothing, and he lay on his side, awake and alert. "Good morning."

"I apologize for my actions," Grégoire said, never one to mince words. "I did not know what I said."

"In a way, it needed to be said," Darcy replied. "If I had known how to handle things differently, I would have. My road was paved with good intentions…and we know where that leads."

Grégoire was silent.

"With any luck, Elizabeth and the children will arrive today," said Darcy. "They must still be in horrible suspense about your condition and will be relieved to find you very much alive." He paced as he spoke. "I was thinking—perhaps you would want to be shaved before you see the children. Otherwise, my younger ones might not recognize you."

"That is true," Grégoire said with a smile. "But I could not burden the Maddox servants—"

"Nonsense," Darcy said. "You have no idea how good it will feel to lose a beard that you did not intend to grow. I will do it myself."

Slowly, and without aid, Darcy shaved his brother's beard. He also shaved the sides, though there was some issue about whether those would be done. No, Grégoire was not willing to look like a sensible person just yet and had his sideburns shaved smooth. He had lost weight in his ordeal, and was not the picture of health, but years were taken off his appearance with the hair removed. Darcy was no barber and the hair on his head was left untouched, including the fuzzy remains of what had been his tonsure. "I am no longer allowed to have the crown of the church."

"Uneasy lies the head that wears a crown," his brother consoled him. "If Shakespeare can be believed."

Grégoire laughed. It was a wonderful thing to hear.

Darcy sent for his townhouse and the Bingley house to be opened, but his family came straight to the Maddoxes. Tears fell as Darcy embraced his long-lost wife. To both of them, it seemed as if five days of separation had been months. "He's alive. He will recover." He added more softly into her ear, so the children could not hear, "He is having a hard time. He has been tossed from the church, and no one knows quite what to say to him." He added, "Not even me."

"The Bingleys are here," she said, kissing him in reassurance. The pain must have been etched on his face. "They did not want to swamp the place."

"He will be happy to see them, I'm sure," he said.

"So he is awake?"

"Yes, but he tires easily and cannot be moved." He would not release his embrace quite yet. "I missed you." *I needed you.*

"I am here now," she said. She laced her fingers with his as she stepped back. "And what do you ladies have to say to your papa?"

"Hello, Papa!" they said, and all curtsied—Cassandra making her best attempt at it, this time managing not to fall over.

Behind them, Geoffrey emerged and bowed. "Father."

"Can we see Uncle Grégoire?"

"Is he still sick?"

"Can he play with us?"

His children's incessant questioning was not an annoyance. If anything, it was a relief. "You may see him—one at a time. He is weak from his illness, so do not overtax him. Now, in order—"

"Aww!" Anne and Sarah said. "You always do that and Geoffrey always wins!"

"I did not say in *which* order of age," he said. "Cassandra, would you like to see your uncle?"

Cassandra Darcy, who had not seen him in two years and was unlikely to remember anything about him, was nonetheless eager to see the man they were all talking about. "Yes!" She lifted her arms, and Darcy picked her up and kissed her. "I missed you."

"I missed you, too, my darling," he said. "Geoffrey, watch your sisters. Oh, and I believe Frederick is in his room."

Geoffrey nodded, leaving Darcy to escort his wife and youngest child into the sickroom. Grégoire had sat up for some time in order to be shaved, but whatever exhaustion was apparent on his face at first dissolved with his smile. "Elizabeth. And is this Cassandra? I... can hardly recognize her, she's grown so much."

"Uncle Grégoire!" she cried out, somewhat mangling his French name, which sounded more like "Graywar" than "Gregwa." Apparently, she did remember him, and delighted in playing with his rosary as Elizabeth inquired about his health.

"I am in the care of good Dr. Maddox," he said, "and, I understand, a Dr. Bertrand and a Mr. Stevens. I don't remember it, but the Prince of Wales was lacking almost his entire staff that night, or so I am told."

"And yet the monarchy survives," Elizabeth said.

"Much to the frustration of Parliament," Darcy added.

The children were paraded in, each in turn, and Grégoire was no less happy to see each one of them. "I remember when you were born," he said to all three daughters, having had the good fortune of being present at their births. "What is this bracelet?"

Anne held it up. Her wrist was barely large enough to wear it, and he squinted to read the inscription: "To my darling Anne."

"It was my mother's," Darcy said proudly, "from our father."

"It looks beautiful on you," Grégoire said to his niece.

Geoffrey was last. "Hello, Uncle Grégoire."

"Do you want me to say how much you've grown?"

"No, sir."

His uncle grinned. "Then I will not. But you are a sight. And I hope I will never be a 'sir' to you, nephew," he said, his voice dragging. By now, Dr. Maddox was awake, and he announced that it was time for them to let his patient rest. Only with Grégoire's reassurance was Darcy willing to leave the Maddox house for the first time since his arrival and ride to his own, where his staff were waiting to greet him and wish his brother well. He was not feeling particularly sociable, and nodded politely to each well-wisher. Elizabeth and he had luncheon while Nurse took care of the children. Later on, Elizabeth, sensing his anxiety, sat with him alone in their chamber.

"He blames me," he said at last. "He said it when he was out of his senses from exhaustion and drugs, but it is true."

"Darcy," Elizabeth said, taking his hand, "he does not blame you. He is not capable of such a thing."

"I have done all the things he accused me of. I removed him twice from abbeys where he was happy, and ruined his monastic career by insisting on sending him a fortune every year and then insisting he hide it from his abbot. I have ruined his life."

"You have *saved* his life," she said. "We both remember the boy we found in that awful monastery in France. Whatever has befallen him since, I am still grateful we found him and persuaded him to leave. Bavaria had nothing to do with you—it was a matter of politics. And this," she said. "You were honoring your father's wishes. You were trying to protect him."

"So easy to explain," he said. "So logical. And yet he was at death's door when he arrived in Town. He can't sit up for long. He can't stand—"

"All of which will pass—"

"He has nowhere to go. He has nothing."

Elizabeth leaned into him, letting him rest on her shoulder as they sat on the sofa. "He has us."

CHAPTER 17

The Adventures of Mugin-san

THE BINGLEYS WERE WELCOMED the next day, and Grégoire greeted them with the same affection with which he had greeted his nephew and nieces.

"How is he?" Bingley asked Darcy as the children took their turns.

"Not well," he said, and that was enough. Charles Bingley nodded as if he understood everything, and went with him into the study as their wives chatted.

To Bingley's surprise, when Dr. Maddox offered them brandy, Darcy actually accepted a glass. The doctor was his usual calm self, and if he made any note of it, he gave no indication. Darcy was a quiet mess, with dark circles around his eyes. It was not unusual for Darcy to suffer in silence when he could do nothing (or did not know how to do something) for a loved one, and Bingley searched for words to say but found none. Darcy's mood would pass as Grégoire grew stronger.

"Bingley," Brian Maddox said as he entered, "hello. Have you seen Mugin?"

"He said he wanted to walk to London. I hope nothing has happened to him, but I assume if something had, we would have heard some news of it, considering how he's so distinctive."

Brian actually looked less concerned than Bingley. "He's probably fine, then. You didn't give him any money for the road, did you?"

"Of course I did. For emergencies."

"Well, you have your answer. He is off spending it." He smiled. "He will be fine, I assure you. Though I hope he was not any trouble while we were in Spain."

"No, none at all. He spent most of the time fishing, or at Lambton."

"You realize the next generation of Lambton bastards will be foreign looking," Darcy said.

"I'm not going to dignify that with an answer, old man," Bingley said, noticing his friend had drained his glass. "Anyway, he's good with the children."

"For a homicidal thug."

Bingley turned to Darcy and then to Brian, who only replied, "I won't deny it." Dr. Maddox kept his eyes on his paper as a servant entered the room.

"The Duchess of ____shire has arrived, Dr. Maddox."

"The who?" Bingley said.

"I think her title amply described her. Doctor, we ought not get in the way of your profession," Darcy said.

"She is not a patient," Dr. Maddox said, putting down his paper and pushing his glasses back up his nose. "Has she given a reason?"

"No, sir, but she is talking with your wife."

Dr. Maddox excused himself to see to his unexpected guest.

"Have you ever met the Duchess of ____shire?" Bingley asked Darcy.

"Unfortunately," was his reply.

Dr. Maddox was met with a shriek from a diminutive, stout lady stuffed poorly into her bodice, standing in the sitting room with Mrs. Maddox.

"I know you! You're that man who's always skulking around Carlton," said the apparent duchess.

He bowed. "I am His Highness's physician, Your Grace."

"I did not know that! You've not been very public about it," she said. She was decked out as if she were about to head to a ball, complete with diamonds and an oversized hat.

"I suppose not," he said quietly. "I see you've met my wife. Allow me to introduce my brothers, Mr. Maddox and Mr. Bingley."

"How exotic a family you have," she said, looking at Brian, who was dressed in his usual outfit, his longer sword held in his right hand. "And Mr. Darcy! Don't go hiding behind the stairs! I remember your first season!"

For she was indeed a bit older than Darcy, maybe in her mid-fifties. He emerged with his usual emotionless expression. "Your Grace," he said and bowed.

"You were such a shy boy. Your poor father had to practically drag you to all the dances, and you danced with no one!" If she was aware of the stifled laughter from the other men or Darcy's mortification, she cared not. "I heard you had married—"

"*Mrs.* Darcy, yes," he said, cutting her off.

It was Caroline Maddox, of all people, who rescued Darcy. "It has been an honor for us to be graced with your presence. Are you making an inquiry?"

"Oh no! I was merely directed here by my little savior! Where did he—Mr.—oh, his name is so strange, I can hardly expect to remember—"

"Mugin?" Brian offered, for just then the lost Japanese man appeared in the doorway. His clothing was soiled from the road but he was not. For some reason, he had a gold chain around his neck. He bowed and removed his shoes, which made him considerably shorter, even shorter than the duchess.

"This wonderful Oriental—oh, I am very thankful!" She grabbed Mugin and pulled him into her full front, which he did not particularly struggle against, but did look a bit uncomfortable.

The little, portly lady continued: "We were coming down the road—my carriage and my maids, of course—and we were attacked by bandits. Bandits! In these years of peace! I suppose that former soldiers have nothing better to do, now that they're not off killing Frenchmen. One of them was even in a shabby, dirty uniform. The coachman tried to fend them off, but he was no match for six men, and they demanded of me all of my little treasures—even my wedding ring! To take the ring off a widow's finger! I would have lost all of my traveling items, which I intended for the theater next week.

"But then this man, Mr., er, *Munin,* came out of *nowhere—the woods,* it must have been—and attacked them—and him with only a sword and them with good English rifles. The same rifles that defeated Napoleon! In fact, he just kicked most of them, and came out from it without a nick."

She turned to Mugin, who had no particular reaction. "Of course, I was so very grateful—and he was so very muddy from the weather we'd been having, that I offered for him to return with me and get cleaned up. Unfortunately, we could not mend his Japanese fabrics, but he was a most honored guest! And now he insists that I return him—"

"*Orewa, mascoto janai,*" (I am not a pet) Mugin said to Brian.

"So I've given him my husband's chain—he has no use for it now—so why should it not go to my little Asiatic savior?" She grabbed Mugin again and kissed him. He quickly slid out of her grasp, but with a mark on his lips as a battle scar. "I hope you will bring him to at least one ball while he is in the country."

"If he wishes," Brian said. "Your Grace."

"I must be getting on, but here is my card." She snapped her fingers and her maid handed it to Caroline. "I insist that you come to dinner sometime, now that I am in Town."

"We will try," Dr. Maddox said. "Thank you."

They said their good-byes, and the duchess was shown out.

"You are in my debt, Mr. Darcy," Caroline said. "Or I will return the call and ask her all about your first Season. Just remember that if I ever have a favor to ask of you."

"I will remember," was all he said, and disappeared to check on his brother. The other men returned to Dr. Maddox's study.

"So," Brian said, "you came to the rescue of the duchess?"

Mugin shrugged and opened his bag. "I fight. Not get many

chances in England." He unceremoniously dumped a pile of jewelry and expensive trinkets on the desk. "How do you say—for money?"

"From pawning them?" Bingley said. "Goodness."

"I hope this was from the bandits," Brian said, "and not from the duchess' jewelry box when she wasn't looking."

"You take me for thief?" Mugin said. "You wait; I *am* thief."

"I take it you enjoyed the hospitality of Her Grace?" Dr. Maddox said.

"Fat women have best food," was his reply as the others inspected his treasures.

"Some of these have inscriptions," Bingley said. "They could be returned if their owners are located."

Mugin looked at him coldly.

"How much gold do you need?" Brian said. "You'll just gamble it away anyway. And there may be rewards."

"Yes, rewards! He has a point, Mugin," Bingley said.

Mugin picked out a particularly pretty bracelet, with jade beads. "For Nadi-sama."

"She will appreciate it," Brian said.

The rest of the spoils were divided up into things that could perhaps be traced back to their owners and things that could not, which Mugin put back in his bag. He didn't make it halfway out the door when Georgiana Bingley came running down the hall. "Mugin-san! Where were you?"

"Being kissed by hog," he replied.

It was a while before Mr. and Mrs. Bingley had a chance to speak privately. The Maddox house was sizable for town, but it was no country estate. "How is he?" she asked.

"Darcy or Grégoire?" he said with a sigh.

Jane took his hand encouragingly. "Darcy tortures himself over his brother, who will mend in time. Dr. Maddox says so. Grégoire has been through the worst of it."

"Physically," he replied. "But what is he to do with the rest of his life now?"

"I don't know. What do they do in India?"

"Oh, he wouldn't—" He stopped. "Jane, I love you."

"Thank you, Mr. Bingley," she replied. She would have said more, but she was interrupted by a kiss. Then her husband ran off to find that Grégoire's room was open for visitors. The children had each had their turn, and then he had been left alone to rest. But no matter what they said or did, he rose with what they now recognized was each monastic hour. His body was tuned that way and would not so easily give it up.

Bingley had seen Grégoire before, briefly, when he brought in his children. He closed the door behind him. "Hello, Grégoire."

"Mr. Bingley," Grégoire said.

"Are you too tired for a visitor? Be honest or the doctor will have my head."

Grégoire smiled. "No. All I do is rest. Please sit."

Bingley took a seat. "I wish you well, Grégoire. Darcy is—"

"I know him well enough. He is suffering."

"He is concerned."

"Everyone is concerned. I am all appreciation, but there are pains that concern does not relieve."

Bingley nodded. "Listen, while I was in India, I heard a story that apparently is very famous in the whole Orient—everyone I met had heard it, even Mugin. The versions differed a bit, but it's—well, I wrote it down, and I don't have my notes with me, but I certainly heard it often enough—"

Grégoire nodded. "Please. I am unable to do much but listen."

"Well," Bingley said, settling himself into the chair. "First, I must warn you that it is a heathen tale. The first time I heard the story, we had just docked and procured a room at an inn in India. Each morning, a man with a shaved head would come with a begging bowl. I would give him a little something, but after a few days, I had to wonder at it, so I asked Brian, and he said he was a monastic and they believed that begging is a way to salvation. So the next day I asked the monk what the path to salvation is, or what he thought it is, and instead he told me this story. It took a long time to tell and by the end I had almost forgotten why I'd asked it, but anyway, here it is.

"There was once a prince, a very long time ago, in India. He was part of their caste system, at the very top, and his father was a great king. His father and mother loved him and wished to shelter him from the horrors in the world, so they raised him in absolute splendor, so that he didn't even see someone old or sick until he left the palace and he could not tell what was the matter with them.

"After seeing people suffer, he decided to dedicate his life to finding a way to end human suffering. So he went into the woods, where these ascetic people lived. They sat all day in meditation, eating grass or maybe dung, and starving themselves and depriving themselves of all pleasures. He did this almost to the point of death, and even though he had many disciples, he was not satisfied.

"And this is where the tale varies a bit, but apparently, he just got up and left that life. One person said a little girl offered him rice. The monk I spoke to first said he heard a woman tuning a harp and she said that it had to be tuned just right, not too sharp or too flat. Either way, he had a revelation. The people who know this story and follow him—they are called Buddhists, because he was later called Buddha, but I'm skipping ahead. Anyway, he decided to devote himself to the middle way, which is to find the middle path—not to live too luxuriously or too ascetically. So he went and washed himself and cleaned his hair for the first time in years. His ascetic disciples abandoned him, and he sat under this tree. I saw it, actually. It is very large, and it's called the Bodhi tree, and he sat under that and meditated and was tempted by the devil many times, but each time he refused until he attained what they call enlightenment. He lived another fifty years or so, and by the end had thousands of disciples, and now his religion is all across the Orient, with perhaps millions of monks. I don't know if he really lived, but

I met a man who claimed he had seen the case that contained a tooth of the Buddha, and he was very proud to have seen it. The Buddha left all kinds of teachings, some of which I wrote down, but my notes are still a mess. And, well, that is it."

He frowned, unsatisfied with his ending. He looked at Grégoire, who had not spoken through the entire telling, and had occasionally closed his eyes, but was now very much awake, if very still from exhaustion.

"Mr. Bingley," he said, "will you perhaps allow me, when I am recovered, to copy that story from your notes?"

"Yes, of course—no! Ridiculous, I'll do it myself. I have to sort them anyway. I'll have my man write it out so you can actually read it, too. Anyway, I know it's all pagan nonsense, but I don't know what else to say. It's that or the tiger story again."

"I've not heard the tiger story," Grégoire said, "but I admit I am tired now, and it is time for prayer. Thank you, Mr. Bingley. Thank you very much."

"You're welcome," he said, shaking the hand that was offered to him. "Do you need the doctor or anything?"

"No, I just want to rest. Thank you."

Bingley rose and excused himself as Grégoire closed his eyes. As he shut the door, Bingley looked up at the anxious Darcy. "He'll be all right, you know," Bingley said. "He just has to find his own way. And no, you can't help him with that. It's the basic *principle* of the thing, Darcy. Come now, you've had too much to drink."

"I've had a glass! What did they do to you in India?"

"They don't drink. Or eat cattle. We would all starve there, I'm sure."

"You may have your own obsessions, and even keep your own wild animal—but if you cast meat from your kitchen, I will never accept an invitation to dine at Kirkland again.

"I'm not likely to shun meat," he said. "But do you know that some people in Hong Kong are vegetarians?"

"What does that mean?"

"It means they eat only vegetables, I think."

"My God!" Darcy said. "That can't be very healthy, can it?"

The final family members to visit the former Brother Grégoire arrived the very next day—his sister along with her husband and child in a carriage with the colors of the earldom of Kincaid. Georgiana Kincaid would have leaped, weeping, into Darcy's arms had she not been holding her son as Darcy assured her that yes, her little brother was alive and getting stronger every day.

"We came as soon as we heard," Lord Kincaid said with concern.

"He will be very happy to see you," Elizabeth said.

Her prediction was not at all wrong. Nothing cheered Grégoire as much as seeing his sister and holding his new nephew in his arms. As he was now healed enough to lie on his back, it was less considerable a feat, and there was a light on his face that they had not seen since his arrival. He tickled the baby's tummy, which little Robert took a serious liking to, and it seemed the Scots were not so inclined to bundle their children so tightly, so Robert's limbs were free to squirm and kick. "You like that, don't you, little Robert?" Grégoire asked. Darcy and Elizabeth watched from the doorway. "What a truly beautiful child, and so full of energy."

"He gets that energy from his father," Georgiana said. Lord Kincaid didn't deny it. His hand was on his wife's back as she sat beside her brother.

"Can you grip my finger? Yes, you can!" Grégoire laughed as he held out his finger and Robert tugged on it. "What a strong grip you have, Viscount Kincaid! What was the name of that Scot, the great king who fought the English?"

"Robert the Bruce," William Kincaid answered.

"Yes, that's the one."

"Was he not one of the few Scottish kings who were not assassinated?" Darcy said.

"Yes," William said. "He lived a long and fruitful life, and died in his bed—of leprosy. Which was quite a bit better than most of them."

"Well," Grégoire said as he made the sign of the cross over the baby, "then you should live a long and fruitful life—without the leprosy part."

CHAPTER 18

Mary's Season

~ ~ ~

AS GRÉGOIRE'S HEALTH continued to improve, the Darcys and the Bingleys retreated to their respective houses, visiting every day (Georgiana and her son were regular fixtures at the Maddox house). Dr. Maddox read the abbot's letter to Grégoire no less than four times before his patient was well enough to begin reading himself. Bingley gave him all the notes he had and a few books from his own library, and Grégoire read it all, but very slowly. Most of his time was still consumed with visitors and prayer, as his body continued to adhere to the monastic cycle that began at half past three in the morning and ended at eight at night. His pain medicine was continually reduced, though Dr. Maddox was relieved that Grégoire was no longer ashamed to ask for it when he needed it to sleep.

When he was able to sit up in a chair for a short while, they had a minor quandary about his dress. Grégoire's robes had been torched, as they were bloodied and infested with disease, and he had no right to wear them anyway. He found the English method of dress scandalously immodest because of its tightness (and was not too reserved to say it, to Darcy's consternation and Elizabeth's secret delight at the expression on her husband's face). Brian Maddox, who was no stranger to dressing in a bizarre fashion, provided him with a suitable option. Nadezhda happily knitted him a long brown tunic, and he eventually consented to at least a cloth obi belt (leather was too ostentatious), and he wore an undershirt that was soft on his scarred skin. He agreed to grow his sides but not all the way down and far too wide, so that in the end he resembled an itinerant worker. But that seemed to satisfy him. He still had his cross and his rosary, so his affiliation was obvious enough, but his tonsure was gone, lost to a thicket of brown hair slightly curlier than Darcy's.

Nearly two weeks after his arrival in England, Grégoire had some surprise guests. Mary and Joseph Bennet traveled from Longbourn, bringing regards from Mr. and Mrs. Bennet (who no longer traveled) and Mr. and Mrs. Townsend. They happened to arrive on the day when his stitches were being pulled, and had to wait some time to see him. Mary passed the time with Elizabeth and Mrs. Maddox while Joseph played with Frederick. It could not be said that Mary Bennet had livened up, but she no longer had the same tendency to go on moralistic rants, as they bored her most important audience, her son. Instead, she'd been forced to tell more interesting tales as part of his education, and so expanded her own reading tastes to find them. She did not read Gothic novels, but she read Shakespeare as often as Hannah More, and there were always the comings and goings of Hertfordshire to chat about.

Meanwhile, Dr. Bertrand had been called in to help make absolutely sure nothing went wrong, as the work was rather extensive, to the point where they gave Grégoire a dose of medicine. He bled a little, but said nothing, and was already drifting off as they dressed the wounds. "An excellent patient, as always, Grégoire," Dr. Maddox said. "He is quite a tough man," he said to Bertrand as they exited the room, letting him rest.

"Indeed," Dr. Bertrand said, and if he had anything else to add, it was interrupted by the appearance of an eight-year-old boy with black hair and slightly olive skin.

"Can I see Mr. Grégoire now?"

"No, Mr. Bennet. Sadly, you will have to wait a bit longer, as he is resting. And where are your manners?" Dr. Maddox said, and bowed to him, and the little Bennet returned the bow. "Mr. Bennet, allow me to present my colleague, Dr. Andrew Bertrand. Andrew, this is Joseph Bennet.

"*Is he nice?*" Joseph asked in Italian.

"*I like to think I am,*" Bertrand replied in that same language, to Joseph's horror.

Dr. Maddox did not hide his smile. "Do not presume there are none so learned in the language arts as you, young Master Bennet."

"*Dites-lui que je suis désolé,*" (Tell him I'm sorry) Joseph said shyly in French to Dr. Maddox.

"*Vous pouvez le dire vous meme,*" (You can say it yourself) Dr. Bertrand replied. Joseph looked as if he would have liked to run away, but Bertrand only smiled. "I have a French name, you know. And all of the civilized world must speak it, apparently."

"Do you know Latin?"

"I had to learn it for my exams at University," he replied amiably.

"It's *hard.*"

Dr. Bertrand knelt down to his level. "I did not know four languages when I was your age, Mr. Bennet. If I had tried, I would have found it *very* hard."

"Joseph!" came a cry as Mary Bennet hurried into the room, curtsying to both of them. "Dr. Maddox, I apologize—"

He waved it off. "It is fine. This is Dr. Bertrand, who is assisting me with Grégoire. And the Prince Regent."

She curtsied again as she pulled her son to her. "I am sorry if my son interrupted your conversation. It is a pleasure to meet you."

He bowed. "You as well, Mrs. Bennet."

"Miss Bennet," she corrected with a shy smile, and excused herself, dragging Joseph with her.

"Good-bye!" Joseph said and waved.

Dr. Bertrand waved back. "The father is Spanish?" he asked Dr. Maddox.

"Italian," Dr. Maddox said, and then slapped his forehead. "Oh, I forgot. I was supposed to say he was an Englishman who died in the war."

Bertrand nodded. "Of course."

"You understand."

"I never heard otherwise. All kinds of things happened in the war. All sorts of confusion."

"Yes," Dr. Maddox said. "You wanted that recipe. If you will wait a moment, I need to retrieve it."

"Of course."

Dr. Maddox left Bertrand and climbed a flight of stairs, only to find his wife hiding in a doorway at the top. "Invite him to dinner!"

"What?"

"I said, invite him to dinner! Are you deaf?"

"No. All right, I'll invite him to dinner. But I already know he can't do it tonight. Regent's schedule and all that."

She frowned. "Well, what about tomorrow?"

"I don't know his whole social schedule."

"Well, *ask him!*"

"Yes, yes," he said, not seeing a reason to put up an argument with his wife. As he reached for his laboratory keys, he said, "May I ask why?"

"Because Miss Bennet will be in town for only a week."

"So?"

She shook her head. "Your sex is so mentally dense that I wonder sometimes if there's any brain up there at all. Perhaps you are all moving on instinct." Before he could reply, she hurried down the stairs and rejoined her female guests.

Dr. Maddox shrugged to himself, unlocked the laboratory door, quickly wrote down the recipe, and relocked the door before returning to the main level. "Here you go. Oh, and are you available for dinner tomorrow night? Mrs. Maddox *insists* on inviting you."

No bachelor in his right mind would turn down a good meal. "Thank you. Usual time, I assume."

"Yes."

They said their good-byes, and Dr. Maddox turned curiously to the sitting room, where he could hear the Bennet sisters and his wife talking. He could not make out the words.

"Huh," was all he said as the plan slowly revealed itself to him. He shook his head. *Mrs. Maddox and her schemes.*

Never one to intrude on female conversation, he made his way to Grégoire's room, where he found the door already open and Joseph Bennet sitting in the chair beside Grégoire's bed.

~ ~ ~

Dr. Bertrand did return for dinner the following evening to find Darcy in the parlor. "Dr. Bertrand."

"Mr. Darcy."

"I am in your debt, Dr. Bertrand, for what you've done for my brother."

"He is a fighter, Mr. Darcy."

That did not elicit a smile from Mr. Darcy, but as Bertrand had quickly learned, Darcy almost never smiled. The best he had ever seen was a little half grin. "We have quite a party tonight. My wife and her sister are here, as well as the other Maddoxes, of course. Speaking of which—"

Brian Maddox, who was wearing black robes and only his short sword, and an Oriental gentleman, Mr. Mugin, entered. "Dr. Bertrand. Darcy," Brian said.

They exchanged greetings as the door to Grégoire's room opened and a young man emerged, maybe ten and four by his height. From inside, a conversation in very broken Latin, between a child (presumably Joseph Bennet) and Grégoire could be heard.

"Dr. Bertrand, if you have not already met him, allow me to introduce my nephew, Mr. Wickham," Darcy said proudly. Mr. Wickham bowed and mumbled a shy greeting before exiting.

"Is he your nephew by your wife?" Dr. Bertrand asked.

"Yes," Mr. Darcy said. "But there are many former Bennets. My wife has four sisters, one of whom is married to Charles Bingley, whose sister is Mrs. Maddox."

"So we are all connected," Brian said. "Distantly."

"Four sisters? What about brothers?"

"None. Just five daughters of Mr. and Mrs. Bennet, who live in Hertfordshire," said Brian.

Dr. Bertrand knew enough about English property law to see the problem there. "They are close in age?"

"One after another. If you want the full story, you'll have to ask Mr. Bingley, who unfortunately isn't here tonight. Darcy won't tell it because apparently it involves a rejected proposal."

Darcy replied only with a cold stare and then pointedly turned to gaze out the window as Dr. Maddox joined them. "Dinner is served. Or is about to be. Honestly, I have no idea how this house runs."

Andrew Bertrand liked dining with the Maddoxes. Dr. Maddox, when he was not shy or overly formal, as he was when speaking to a patient, was a cheerful man, clearly happy with his station in life. His wife was a bit haughty, and did not mind teasing her husband, but always in a friendly way. How they had ever come together, Bertrand had no idea. Mr. Maddox, despite his appearance, was an overly gregarious Englishman, far more talkative than his brother and with far more to tell. His wife, Princess Nadezhda, was quiet at first, and then quite open when not among strangers and did not hesitate to express her opinions. She seemed to endlessly exchange glances with her loving husband, and so the foursome made for good company.

Tonight, they were joined by Mr. and Mrs. Darcy. Mrs. Darcy was lively and witty, and her husband was reserved but amiable. He was suffering the strain of having had a beloved brother at death's door. The addition to the table was Miss Bennet, who resembled her sister in some ways, but was not the same at all.

It did not take him long to figure out the plan. However, he respected Daniel Maddox, and he trusted him not to throw him into the fire. Besides, if Andrew had stayed at home, his parents would have done the same. He had sat at many dinners with many friends of his parents and their young daughters.

Miss Bennet neither fawned over him nor showed disgust with her relatives about the unexpected dinner guest. Her manners were mild, but she was not silent, and not afraid to speak up on any matter religious. He judged, based on her quotations, that she bordered on Evangelical—she was certainly no Methodist—or had been Evangelical at some point in her life. However, she was not obnoxious about it. From what he gathered from snippets of conversation, she had studied in a French seminary about nine years earlier. Usually, daughters of gentlemen engaged themselves in frivolous society concerns. Or they studied religion in a vague and sentimental way. But Mary seemed to be a scholar, even of traditional Catholic texts. Andrew Bertrand, a lapsed Catholic by circumstance, was impressed.

The dinner, he thought, went well. If anyone was pushing Mary on, it was subtle, or she was reluctant to comply. She could, however, be engaged in conversation. Unfortunately, the conversation ended with dessert, as after-dinner entertainment did not interest the Darcys. Princess Nadezhda never sang or played in mixed company (she was very modest). And Mugin usually left to do whatever it was he did at night after saying several things in Japanese that Brian would refuse to translate. Dr. Bertrand had to leave anyway, to attend His Highness at Carlton, so the party was dissolved without the usual port and gossip, and he left to go to work, hoping there would be no medical disasters that evening. He already knew that his mind would be elsewhere.

~ ~ ~

For Mary Bennet, who was staying with the Darcys, her mind was not on its usual track either. She held her tongue until she saw Joseph to bed. Then she unleashed her fury on her sister, whom she found reading in the library.

"Do not ever subject me to that again!"

"What?" Elizabeth said innocently. "Was the company so objectionable? I thought you liked the Maddoxes."

"You know very well what I mean," Mary said, sitting down in a huff.

"If he was really so unappealing, then yes, you have no reason to see him again, except by happenstance. However, you did not seem so inclined during the meal."

"I was being polite!"

"There were many guests at the table, all near or distant relatives, with whom you could have made conversation—or none at all, if you really wished."

Mary fumed silently.

"Please, if you object to Dr. Bertrand, I would be most interested in what you have to say. I would wish any distraction these days."

"I—I have no *objections,* but you know that is not the point."

"If you have no objections, then there is no point."

"I'm a mother," she said, "with a *young child*."

"If that caused him any disquiet, he showed none. In fact, from Caroline's account, he seemed to like Joseph."

"And how long do you think the story about his father will hold up?"

Elizabeth smiled. "Considering the doctor's intelligence, I doubt it was believed in the first place. After all, if you had married an Englishman before the war and were carrying his child, why did you not take his name? Unless he objects, it is not fair to assume he opposes choices that were made years ago."

Mary said nothing, but her face was not the emotionless page that it normally was.

"Mary, I may sound like Mama for a moment, but Father will not live forever, and Joseph needs a father. He might even *like* one. Have you ever asked him about it?"

"He knows his father is never coming to England."

"Have you ever asked him if he would like a father who is around?"

She turned to Elizabeth and said coldly, "He is a child."

"That does not mean he is without opinions, fleeting as they might be sometimes," she said. "Ask him, Mary. If not because of Dr. Bertrand, just because you should know what his thoughts are. You can at least do that quite harmlessly."

Mary stood, effectively announcing her exit. "Perhaps you are right—about speaking to Joseph. I will sleep on it. But please—tell me next time."

"I would have, but you would have objected, and we would not be having this conversation," Elizabeth said with a smile. "Good night, Mary."

"Good night, Lizzy."

Her anger largely abated and somewhat turned to confusion, Mary went to her room and lay down, but it was a long time before she found sleep.

~ ~ ~

Elizabeth Darcy had only one thing preventing her from finding sleep—her need to talk to her husband, whether he liked it or not. He was lying awake in bed when she entered their chamber. She crawled into his ready embrace and nestled again him. "I spoke to Mary."

"I'm surprised that I could not hear the conversation from here."

She turned over, so she could face him. "She actually listened to reason about speaking to Joseph."

"And Dr. Bertrand?"

"You ask this of *me?* You know I am a terrible judge of other people's affections." She giggled and kissed him. "She did not deny being interested. And he seemed to be attracted. They found mutual conversation, which for Mary is impressive." She sighed. "She still carries the shame of her affair in France around with her. Nothing I say can change that."

"She is content with Joseph. Perhaps that is enough."

"She loves her son, as I love all my children. But that is different from the way I love *you*," she said. "Does she not deserve that?"

Darcy considered before answering. "I have learned of late that prolonged penance can do more harm than good."

"Indeed. And it would be a wonderful thing for there to be another doctor in the family."

CHAPTER 19

His Royal Highness

~ ~ ~

"DR. MADDOX!"

Dr. Maddox and Dr. Bertrand turned around to see a balding man approaching them. Dr. Maddox replied, "My Lord. An honor, sir." He bowed to Prime Minister Liverpool. "I do not believe you've met my colleague, Dr. Bertrand."

"No, I've not. Dr. Bertrand."

"Sir," Bertrand said, a little overwhelmed.

"So you have a new member of your staff, eh?"

Dr. Maddox was taller than the Earl of Liverpool and current Prime Minister. He was taller than most men, and never seemed intimidated—especially by politicians. "Yes, Lord Liverpool."

"Very nice to meet you." The Prime Minister, one of the most powerful men in England, bowed again. "I hear the Prince of Wales will be appearing before Parliament in a few weeks."

"I do not know his engagements, Lord Liverpool."

"What about His Majesty?"

Dr. Maddox said, "I am not aware of His Majesty's schedule, but I would venture a guess that he has no plans to appear before Parliament." King George had not made a public appearance in almost a decade.

"I was inquiring after his health."

"And you are aware that I am not one of his many physicians. My concern is the Prince of Wales and no one else."

The prime minister spoke in a low voice. "I would ask your professional opinion."

"You may ask, but I may not give it, sir."

"Do you think the Prince will outlive his father?"

Dr. Bertrand looked at Dr. Maddox, who wore the same calm expression he always had while going about his profession. "I am a doctor, Lord Liverpool. Not a soothsayer."

"If you had to guess—"

"I do not care much for guessing. I try to avoid it whenever possible." He bowed. "Good day, sir."

"Good day," said the flustered prime minister, who quickly hurried away. The two doctors proceeded through the gates of Carlton, where they were admitted without a second glance.

"I think you just snubbed the prime minister, Dr. Maddox."

He smiled. "I reprimand the Prince Regent on a regular basis, so I find the prime minister far less intimidating. Besides, he knows he has no business asking the royal physician about his patients. He's been doing it for years, and before him, Prime Minister Perceval inquired regularly," he said. "If you want my job, Andrew, you will have to become accustomed to such inconveniences."

"I'm not to suppose—"

Dr. Maddox stopped in the ornate hallway of Carlton House, a more serious look on his face. "If you haven't realized that you'll have this position as soon as His Highness dies or I lose my sight—whichever comes first—then you are not as clever as you make yourself out to be."

"I didn't want to say it outright."

"Then you're just polite. That's much better." He smiled. "Don't get involved in politics, Dr. Bertrand. It will ruin you and the already-spoiled good name of our profession."

"I've no intention of doing so."

"Good. Keep it that way."

They passed by the guards to enter the private chamber of the

Prince of Wales, Regent to King George III and future King of England. That was, if he survived. With his current bad habits and terrible mood swings since the death of his daughter, Charlotte, it was going to be close. He was not even out of bed yet and already drunk, moaning incoherently about his poor, gouty foot.

"Your Royal Highness," Dr. Maddox said.

"Oh, thank God," the Prince said. "You must do something for this foot!"

"Unfortunately, that would require you to sit in a chair, Your Highness. You will have to choose between staying in bed for your foot and having it treated."

"You make everything hard for me! Why do I put up with you?"

"The decision is your prerogative, Your Highness," Dr. Maddox said unrelentingly. It took the two doctors to get the ruler of Britain into a chair so that his foot could be placed in a tub to soak.

"My medicine! My medicine!"

"Your foot is in it, Your Highness."

"You know damned well what I mean, Maddox! The tonic!"

He shook his head. "I told you it was just sugar water with a dye, sir. A dye that might actually be harmful. It will do nothing for your foot."

After some time and a lot of coffee, the Regent recovered more of his senses. "I need to lose weight before my appearance at Parliament," he announced. "Please don't bother me with the obvious methods. Here." He snapped his fingers and a servant brought forward a tray with a bottle on it. "From China."

Dr. Maddox smelled the tonic, which had little odor, and inspected the label. He showed it to Dr. Bertrand, who just shook his head, not recognizing it. "It says it's bottled in Philadelphia, Your Highness. I doubt very much that it has Oriental origins. More to the point, I cannot condone it without knowing what's in it."

"It is supposed to bring about massive weight loss."

Dr. Maddox held up the bottle. "There is an address for the agent in Town. I will look him up and find out the actual ingredients, though I have little hope of it working as much as simply not consuming vast quantities of fatty foods—"

"Oh, not that again! That isn't fair—my father's a stick, you know. And I cannot match his consumption of food."

"I have not seen him in years, but I will take your word for it."

The Regent said, "You should see my father. Make…an assessment."

"I will do anything you ask, but I remind you that I am not psychic."

"Still, you should go. To…make a sort of comparison. If I am to ascend the throne, I would like to know if I'm going to be mad while I do it." He added, "He is fond of children. Take your son. That will break the ice."

Dr. Maddox momentarily lost his power of speech. Dr. Bertrand had never seen it before; it was a curious thing to watch. But he did recover, and bowed. "Yes, Your Highness."

The doctor uncharacteristically excused himself for the duration of the Regent's soak. After that, there was a little more discussion, mainly about the Prince Regent's diet, and then they left.

"Doctor—"

"I'm fine," Dr. Maddox said to Bertrand. "I am just not thrilled at the prospect of taking my son to see a sick, blind madman." Dr. Bertrand decided to leave it at that. Or he had to, because Dr. Maddox changed the subject as they left the house. "Are you inclined to continue coming to dinner while Miss Bennet is still in Town? Because I won't subject you to the social maneuverings of my wife and cousin-in-law if you are not interested."

"Is this your way of asking me if I like her?"

"I suppose. I was always terrible at this. My courtship with Mrs. Maddox was a disaster. I still wonder how, in the end, it worked out," he said, smiling again. "But that is a story for another time."

"I …would be inclined, yes, if Miss Bennet is. I do not know much about her."

"Young Mr. Bennet seems to like you."

"He seems to be an incredibly studious child."

"I wish my sons would study so hard. They'll take a ruler to Frederick when I send him to Eton, if I can even manage to get him there." He stepped down to where his coach was waiting. "Dinner tomorrow?"

"Tomorrow."

"Fine. Good day, Dr. Bertrand."

Bertrand tipped his hat. "Dr. Maddox." If he had other questions, he put them off. There was time yet.

~ ~ ~

When Dr. Maddox came home, he was first assaulted by his younger son, who raised his hands to be picked up. "Ride!"

"Between you and me, we'll be knocking your head on the ceiling soon, my son. Enjoy it while you can." He picked up Danny Maddox and was putting him over his shoulders as Caroline found him.

"I see you've come to his rescue."

"Rescue? Is he in trouble?"

"And I see he was clever enough to give no indication," she said, folding her arms. "Daniel Maddox, would you like to tell your father what you did?"

"It was Fred's idea!"

"He isn't even home, so don't try it. You know very well he's playing at your Uncle Bingley's house."

"Your punishment will be less if you do not go about assigning blame to others," Dr. Maddox said. "Now, what did you do?"

"I painted! Just like Uncle Maddox!"

"Yes," she said. "But *where* did you paint?"

He mumbled, "On the wall."

"And what did you use?"

"Ink."

Caroline looked at her husband, who was smiling. "Don't you dare laugh! It'll just make it worse."

"I want to be a samurai like Uncle Maddox and he says—"

"That samurai paint for some reason. Yes, I know." The doctor pulled his son down and set him on the ground. "You shouldn't listen to everything your uncle says. As we've said many times, he is a crazy person. You also should not paint on things not meant to be painted on. Now go to Nurse, and let her decide your punishment!"

"Father—"

"*Now*, Daniel!" he said a bit more sternly, and his son, who was not used to that voice from his father, ran back up the stairs. "How bad is it?" he said to his wife.

"Why he chose the hallway I'll never know, but at least it was the one upstairs, in case they cannot get the ink out of the wood," she said, and kissed him on the cheek. "The Kincaids are here."

"They're with Grégoire? How is he?"

"He's been sitting up for some time now."

He nodded. "I'd best check on him." He would bring up the visit to the king later. Instead, he headed into Grégoire's room, where he found Lord Kincaid sitting on the bed beside his wife. Grégoire sat in an armchair, holding Robert with the aid of a pillow to support his arms, so the infant was resting on his lap. "Hello, Lord Kincaid. Lady Kincaid. Grégoire." They still hadn't decided what to call the former monk, or even asked him. "How are you feeling today?"

"Stronger," Grégoire said with a tired smile.

"And how is little Robert today?"

William Kincaid said. "Why, my son is not little. He's robust and vigorous—"

"He's an infant, dear," Georgiana said. "He's allowed—required, actually—to be small."

Dr. Maddox hid a smile. "Lord and Lady Kincaid," he said, "would you care to join us for luncheon?" He could see that Grégoire was tiring, but it would take subtlety to get the infant out of his arms and allow him to sleep.

They agreed, and Georgiana left first to set Robert down for a nap, William following in her wake.

"Such a wonderful child," Grégoire said, as Dr. Maddox helped him stand and make it back to his bed. He still could not stand on his own, as his body continued to recover from a long illness. "So much life in him."

"Indeed."

Grégoire was settled comfortably on his bed. "You've done so much for me—and I know of no way to repay it. Aside from money, I suppose."

Waving off the remark, Dr. Maddox said, "Money is as meaningless to me as it is to you in matters of family. I am satisfied enough that we could save you."

"I heard it was very close."

"Yes," he said. "But you will be well. It is only a matter of time, now that the stitches are out."

"Who would want me now, so scarred?" he joked.

Dr. Maddox said with a chortle, "Are you wishing for intimate companionship, Mr. Grégoire?" Grégoire went red, but it was a good feeling for both of them. Dr. Maddox continued, "No one has wanted to ask if you've had thoughts about your future. When you arrived, you were quite in despair about it."

Almost two weeks had passed since his arrival at the Maddox home, and Grégoire answered, "My memories are poor of that period, but I do remember parts of it; the passage from Spain to England, not at all. Thank goodness, too, for I am inclined to be ill at sea. I remember only the abbot's voice and then talking to Father LeBlanc. There is little between that."

"You have not answered my question."

"No," Grégoire said, grasping the cross on his rosary. "I do wish to return to Pemberley, but beyond that—I have much thinking to do. Or perhaps I will travel, in the spring. Not very far, or my brother will follow me with an armed guard."

Dr. Maddox chuckled. "He would. But you realize there are questions to which there are no answers. I don't suppose I am the first one to tell you that."

"No, but there are ideas I have never heard before. Have you read *The Confession of St. Patrick*?"

"I have not."

"Darcy purchased a copy for me when I asked for anything in Latin. I doubt he knew exactly what he was purchasing or cared. It is here." He pointed to, but not did reach for, the pile of books stacked up on the table beside the bed. "St. Patrick used to pray spontaneously, as often as he felt the grace of God, while he was herding sheep in captivity. He says it was sometimes as often as a hundred times a day."

"They could not have been very long prayers, or the sheep would have all got away."

Grégoire laughed. "I do not know much about sheep. I was always more of a gardener. More a planter of men than a shepherd of men, which I realize after having said it aloud, makes little sense."

They shared another laugh. "You have the world before you, if reading is to be your occupation for a time," Dr. Maddox said. "You have that to look forward to."

"True. Now if I may have some privacy, it is time for Sext, the sixth canonical hour."

"Would you like a watch to keep track of these things?" Dr. Maddox said, looking at his pocket watch. It was indeed 12:15.

"No," Grégoire said. "I always know anyway."

Dr. Maddox nodded. "After that—get some rest. Doctor's orders." He gave him a pat on the arm and left, pondering the mystery of the former monk's internal clock.

Daniel Maddox did thoroughly enjoy his partial retirement, which allowed him to go to bed with his wife at a normal time. It was only when they were comfortably settled in bed that he said, "The Regent asked me to visit the king."

"For an assessment?"

"He wants me to see him. The Prince worries about his own mental health, after all." He added, "He asked me to take Frederick with me to Windsor."

Even in the partial darkness, where he was basically blind, he could see her alarm. It was more that he could sense it, without even touching her, as she shrieked, "*He said that?*"

"His exact words were, 'He is fond of children. Take your son. That will break the ice.' He did not bother to clarify which son, though he very well knows I have two." He reached out and she found his hand. "I've spoken to His Majesty's staff several times. He is completely out of his mind and does not look well. As a result, he has almost no visitors." He added, "I don't want Frederick to see that, even if it is his grandfather."

"Why not? You bring all kinds of gruesomeness into this house. And besides, he doesn't know the connection."

"You think the Prince is right, then? That Frederick should see him before he dies?"

"You believe that is the prince's intention?"

"Maybe. I don't know." He tightened his hold on her hand. His were so calloused that he sometimes felt almost bad touching her soft skin, as if he would mar it "I just get nervous when he mentions Frederick, however subtly he does so."

She leaned into him, resting her head on his shoulder. "I know. I do, too. But it seems to happen anyway." She said, "The Prince may be feeling sentimental." Then she added, "Is he mad?"

"The Prince?"

"Yes. Like his father."

"No. I've seen no signs of it. He is just a glutton, a drunk, an addict, and a pervert. He is not mad, however, if that is some consolation."

She responded, "That is a great consolation."

He could not disagree.

CHAPTER 20

The Noncourtship

~ ~ ~

TO EVERYONE'S GREAT RELIEF, Grégoire was at last released from Dr. Maddox's care. He was relocated to the Darcys' townhouse in London, where he was greeted by the staff with enthusiasm and seemed overwhelmed by the experience. Despite the circumstances, Darcy and Elizabeth delighted in having all of the Darcys under one roof for the first time since Georgiana's marriage. Mary Bennet continued her stay, as Joseph was often lonely at Longbourn and enjoyed the time with his cousins, even if the ones closest to his age were girls. Mr. and Mrs. Bradley finally paid a visit to Grégoire, bearing young Brandon and Julie, along with George and Isabella Mercifully, the visit was short enough to keep Mary and Lydia fr
getting into a heated conversation in the sitting room.

On the third day, Grégoire was well enough to join t
dinner, if only briefly. On the fourth, it was not Dr. Mad
called, but Dr. Bertrand. His attention was to his patien
not seem to mind when Darcy explained that the l
with Mrs. Bingley.

Dr. Bertrand sighed at the extensive scarring
and the ones he had created on his forearms
Grégoire heard it and just shook his head
fewer scars who are unable to do such
am quite blessed."

Although Dr. Bertrand did not know how this man could bring himself to say such a thing and mean it, he offered no opposition. “As soon as you are strong enough, you can return to Pemberley, if that is your desire.”

“I admit I am eager to go home,” he said. Then his eyes lit up. “Look who it is!”

Joseph Bennet stood in the door frame, half hiding behind it as Dr. Bertrand helped Grégoire roll his tunic back down. “Uncle Grégoire, you said you would do my Latin homework.”

“I said I would *help* you. But it is time for none, the fifth canonical hour. You will have to wait a bit, Joseph.”

“What is it?” Bertrand said. “What is the text, I mean?”

“He is supposed to translate some of Virgil’s poetry, I believe.”

“Very challenging. Is that true, Mr. Bennet?”

Joseph nodded.

“I can help him. Or try, at least,” Bertrand said. “And you should rest, Mr. Grégoire.”

“I know. After prayer, I will rest, if you will lift this particular burden off my shoulders, though it is not normally a burden.”

“I understand.” Bertrand turned to Joseph. “Why don’t we see if I remember anything from my exams?”

It turned out he did, and he sat on the sofa in the sitting room, helping Joseph translate a particularly difficult set of poems. He was impressed not only with the boy’s comprehension, but his penmanship. “Who is your tutor, Mr. Bennet?”

“Mother and Grandfather. Grandmother didn’t know Latin yway, and then she had a stroke.”

“I am sorry to hear that.”

“Grandfather likes it. He says she’s nicer now. She kisses him a lot.”

e blushed a little. “Mr. Bennet, I’m quite sure you shouldn’t ople your grandmother had a stroke. Or the other bit.”

ell, it’s really *evident*.”

t does not mean you should say it. But that is for your decide.” He looked up. “Speaking of—”

"Mummy!" Joseph jumped up and hugged his mother, who was still removing her bonnet as she entered with Mrs. Darcy and Mrs. Bingley. "Dr. Bertrand was helping me with my schoolwork!"

"Was he?" Mrs. Darcy said before Mary could respond. "Dr. Bertrand, I trust your patient is doing well?"

"He is."

"The patient is eager to return to Pemberley."

"I think it will be possible in the next week or two," he said. "Excuse Dr. Maddox's absence, he was on an errand—"

"That's quite all right," Mrs. Bingley said.

"Will you join us for luncheon? It seems no one else will be home in time," Mrs. Darcy offered.

Mary shot her a look, which Bertrand intercepted. The look wasn't cold, but perhaps she did not want to be in his presence. Or was she afraid? He could diagnose patients better than people. He decided to chance it. "I'd love to."

~ ~ ~

"Really, Mary. I've never seen someone so intent on chasing off a perfectly amiable gentleman," Elizabeth said when they returned to her sitting room.

Truly, Mary had done nothing to chase him off. She had not been rude at the meal. She had not ignored him. She had contributed to the conversation. She had not, however, rushed to return his affections, which, although discreet, were enough to indicate a preference. In fact, she had announced that she was leaving for Longbourn as soon as the Darcys returned to Pemberley and the Bingleys to Kirkland.

"I am not a romantic, Lizzy."

"I do not believe this is a situation calling for a romantic gesture."

Mary looked down at her knitting. "It is all ridiculous. I will return to Longbourn, where I shall remain while Papa still lives. And Dr. Bertrand is tied to town. Am I supposed to indicate that I am to remain here indefinitely when it is not true?"

"Hertfordshire is not so terribly far from town if one is a good rider," Jane said. "Especially since they have redone the roads. There is no reason to call off a courtship because of thirty miles."

"It is not a courtship!"

"Very well," Elizabeth said. "Tell us what you find so displeasing about him, and that shall be the end of the matter."

"He has no reason to court me."

"That is not a character fault. Nor is your argument logical."

Mary stared at her sister. "Must I state the obvious?"

"Mary," Jane said kindly, "he seems to like Joseph very much. Mr. Bradley was not discouraged by the presence of not one, but two, children. And he does not have to provide for Joseph, because Joseph has a trust. If he saw any reason to hesitate, he would have done so."

"He could be a fortune hunter."

"Then he is an inadequate one," Elizabeth said, "for no one has said a thing about money, and even if they had, Papa controls your inheritance and would refuse it to a rake."

The younger Bennet sister looked down; apparently, she could think of no more to say.

"Did you speak to Joseph?" Jane asked.

"I will if I need to, but not before. Speaking of him, I must make sure he is not bothering Mr. Grégoire. Excuse me." And she abruptly left her sisters, taking her needles with her.

Elizabeth and Jane exchanged glances. "Why is she so cold to the idea?" Jane asked. "Perhaps she does not wish to be married at all. Some women don't."

"I am not convinced. She would have had no reason to continue a charade of pleasantry with a man she did not like." She sighed. "Perhaps her heart still belongs to another person."

"Can you mean two people?"

"I do. And one of them is gone and never to return," Elizabeth said.

~~~
~~~

Grégoire's health improved steadily, partly because he was able to eat more and more. He could walk on his own, and one day he ventured outside the townhouse. The next day, Darcy took him to a bookshop, where, with his own money, Grégoire purchased a number of books in Latin, Greek, English, and French—whatever suited him that they were sure Pemberley did not have.

As soon as they were given leave to return to Pemberley, they made ready to depart. Dr. Bertrand called a final time to advise them to go slowly. It happened that Mary was set to depart later that afternoon, and somehow, with all of the servants and children running about, she encountered him alone in the library. Or perhaps the meeting had been carefully arranged behind their backs.

"May I call on you in Hertfordshire?" he asked bluntly.

"Why?"

He blushed. "For all of the reasons a man normally calls on a woman, Miss Bennet. And I would like to see Master Joseph." When she did not answer, he lowered his voice. "Are you really so averse to me?"

She clutched her locket. "No."

"Then may I ask you a question?"

She looked up at him nervously. "You may, Dr. Bertrand."

"Did Joseph's father give you that locket?"

Her response was a look of horror, but she did relinquish her tight clutch on the locket. "Yes."

"Are you still in love with him?"

"I don't know—I knew him only briefly." She added, "But he *is* Joseph's father."

"So he is alive, then, with no intention to return to you."

She was caught in her own lie. She hadn't actually said Joseph's father was dead, but it was the official story. "No, he is not coming back." She continued, "His family meant him for the church. He may well be a bishop by now for all I know." She looked up to find no horror or disgust on his face.

"You are not the only one to have done something that has since plagued you," he said. "I was a surgeon at Waterloo."

"That is a very noble task!"

"For the French."

There was a silence.

"My parents were nobility. They came here to hide during the Revolution. My relatives stayed and were slaughtered. I was born and raised here, but in the final years of Napoleon's reign, my parents repatriated, and so did I, to finish my education. I served in the army because I needed the clinical experience."

"Does Dr. Maddox know?"

"He is the only one—except for my family—who does."

There was another silence.

"My parents will be somewhat disappointed if I tell them I am courting an English girl from the country," he said, "but as we *are* in England, they cannot be all that surprised."

She murmured, "I have some money. Giov—Joseph's father provided him with a trust and me with living expenses. My father keeps hold of it. It is to be my inheritance. If you want it, you will have to impress him."

"I do not want it," he said, "but I will try to impress him anyway."

~ ~ ~

Dr. Bertrand left and was not there to see Mary off, but judging from her expression, no great rift had occurred between them. She even admitted, after much inquisition by her sisters, that he had asked to call on her, but made them swear not to say a word. And with that, and all the good-byes, Mary and Joseph were gone.

The next day began early; the Maddoxes called—all of them, actually—as the doctor gave Darcy various powders to be mixed with water if Grégoire lost his health on the road.

The Kincaids would return with the Darcys to Pemberley. It was on the way and Georgiana was eager to spend more time with both her brothers, and William was eager to please his wife. It took three full coaches to fit everyone and then other vehicles for the servants and nurses, but they were off. The passage took four days, instead of three (it could be done in two, with luck and speed). Dr. Maddox's instincts had been right—the bumping of the carriage tired Grégoire easily, and made him ill by the side of the road, for which he was embarrassed. Darcy shooed away the coachman and attended to his brother personally. They spent three nights at the inns along the way, encountering one innkeeper's wife who knew Grégoire from his previous wanderings but did not recognize him; he had to be reintroduced.

Darcy sent a rider ahead to inform Mrs. Reynolds of Grégoire's return. Mrs. Reynolds was to instruct the servants not to fuss over him, even though they had all heard something of his poor health and return to England. Instead, they were to focus on the former mistress of Pemberley and her husband. He was also just Mr. Grégoire now—or Mr. Bellamont if they were uncomfortable with that name (with his irregular parentage, he could not truly claim the Darcy name). His old servant, Thomas, was there to greet him and help him out of the carriage. Even without his monastic appearance, Grégoire was recognizable. They got him inside without incident, and he rested until dinner while Viscount Robert Kincaid was admired by the maids who had once attended Georgiana. The rest of the servants welcomed their master and mistress, and the heirs to Pemberley who followed them, eager to be home and not uneager to show it.

The Darcys always found a wonderful solace in returning to their own apartments, bathing in their own tubs, and having the luxury and privacy that Pemberley afforded them. It was only then that the two of them could fully acknowledge (without words, which were unnecessary) that London had been an ordeal. They retreated in peace until Thomas came knocking at their door to tell them, with impressive tact, that his charge had gone to the chapel and perhaps could use a "visit."

Darcy found Grégoire weeping on the stone before the altar that he had restored himself a decade ago, when he had first come to Pemberley. Why Grégoire would so readily subject himself to so many memories, Darcy had no idea, but thinking on it clearly, he imagined he would do the same. He knelt beside his brother, letting him lean on him as he sobbed.

"I have been abandoned."

"You were turned away from the church, Grégoire. Not God. The abbot made specific mention of that."

"Where is the Lord to be found outside the church?"

Darcy said, "Our Lord and Savior had no church. He went on journeys and spoke to the people."

"Like St. Patrick."

Darcy had no idea but he said, "Yes."

"I want to visit our family—and the saint, if I can bear to show my face to him."

Darcy just nodded, and escorted him to the graveyard. He had not been there himself in quite a while. Though he loved his parents and did his best to honor their memories, it was not one of his regular stops when traversing the grounds. They had gone long ago, and he had made his peace with that. Grégoire had known his father only in the barest terms, and his mother was buried at Mon-Claire. The only graves of people he knew were ones he had dug himself or had overseen the completion of. They passed by Wickham's grave and nodded.

"You would be proud of your children," Grégoire said to the headstone.

"Believe it or not, I agree," Darcy said, which served to lighten the mood. And it was true.

They came to St. Sebald's grave, relatively unadorned compared with some of the others and hidden away in a corner. Grégoire said something in Latin, and when Darcy requested a translation, he replied, "'Forgive this poor sinner.'" They also visited their father's grave, where Grégoire seemed to ask very much the same thing, despite his father not being a stolen Bavarian saint.

"Come. Dinner must be almost ready. There is a wonderful selection of French wines this year, and you may drink all that you like while your poor brother can have none."

"I forget—is Geoffrey old enough to join us?"

"Not yet, thank goodness, or we would have to temper our speech." He sighed. "That day will come soon enough."

"Temper what speech? You say nothing in company, nothing at all."

"I wouldn't say *nothing*—"

"Almost nothing. Monosyllables."

They slowly walked back to Pemberley proper. "If my doctor permitted me to drink—I tell you, it would be a different story. I am a lush."

"So I have heard from Mr. Bingley."

"Bingley! We should give him strong drink and find out what he *really* did in India. I keep hearing a tiger mentioned and still know nothing about it."

"Why would Mr. Bingley have a story about a tiger?"

"Precisely."

They laughed their way back to the house.

CHAPTER 21

The Letter from the Island

~ ~ ~

DARCY HAD BEEN BACK at Pemberley for less than three weeks when he called Elizabeth into his study, where the day's mail was piled up. He had been perusing a note about an offer on an estate holding when he noticed the letter from Longbourn, sorted accidentally into his pile. "From your father," he said to her. The missive, he was sure, was not urgent, or it would have come by an express courier.

Mr. Bennet rarely wrote; he had a passion for the written word, not for writing, and often lamented that there was little to say about life in Longbourn that mattered enough for the cost of the letter. Elizabeth immediately opened the letter and sat down to read it. She giggled. "It seems that Mary has had a caller."

"Ah, yes. The protégé," Darcy said, relieved that at least one Bennet romance was going as intended without his aid; he was eager to leave it that way, if at all possible. "What does your father make of this development?" he said, as she was sure to tell him anyway.

She happily read him the letter, likely omitting some words, but the letter was not long to begin with.

Dearest Lizzy,

You will perhaps take some pleasure in the fact that your maneuverings in London were not without result. Mary was here not two days before Dr. Bertrand rode to Hertfordshire to make my acquaintance and formally ask for my permission to court Mary, though he hardly required it. You can imagine who is fleeing and who is pursuing, but the way to a woman's heart is through her child, and apparently the doctor has discovered this. Joseph has a great fondness for him, and would not stop blabbering about him as soon as he returned, which was how I came to hear the name in the first place.

I do not know much of the particulars of Dr. Bertrand's service to the Crown and if he intends to sever that, for Mary has declared (and in front of him) that she has no desire to leave Longbourn. Nonetheless, he is a persistent fellow, and she has done nothing else to discourage him. So I imagine that should things continue as they are moving, I will go to my grave having safely married off all five of my daughters; no small accomplishment, considering I hardly left this study while doing so.

Mrs. Bennet wishes you well, of course, but her penmanship is not what it was, and she is forever urging me to write notes for her to her sister and brother. At her insistence, I will keep you updated about events.

My love to my grandchildren, and my sons—when they behave themselves. The sons, not the grandchildren.

Mr. Edmund Bennet

They decided it was good news (they could hardly decide otherwise). "He is a sensible young man," Darcy said, "and they are always in short supply." He rose and kissed his wife on her cheek. "I must find my brother. Do excuse me."

"You are excused," she said with a smile. She rose to leave moments after he disappeared, and stopped only to glance at the torn envelope, one of the documents that her husband had been reading when she entered. It had not escaped her notice that he was bothered by them. The name in the upper left corner of the envelope brought no recognition, being an address from the Isle of Man. *How odd*, she thought to herself. But then again, he had many holdings, inherited from both sides of the family (including Rosings and portions of Kent), so she put the thought aside to seek out her sister, who was there for lunch, to share the more interesting news.

~ ~ ~

The gun fired but missed its target, a passing bird. The shot was so wild that the fowl was in no danger of it.

"Maybe you should try stationary targets," Georgiana Bingley said.

Geoffrey Darcy put the gun down to reload it. "All you *do* is hit stationary targets."

"When they make an archery target that moves, I will be happy to shoot it," she said, and loaded and fired her bow in less time than it took him to push down the canister for the next shot. It hit the red circle in the middle. Only three shots out of ten had failed to do so. "This is so boring."

"You could hunt."

"You know Mama would never let me do such a thing. Can you imagine me tramping through the woods with a bow and arrow after a deer? I would ruin my dress and never hear the end of it."

"I can imagine that, actually."

She frowned in annoyance. "I mean, me tramping through the woods with *permission* to do so. Quite a different thing. Plus, I think my father would be suspicious if I returned with a fawn slung over my shoulders."

"Not ladylike."

"No."

Geoffrey's dog returned, having had nothing to retrieve. "Sorry, Gawain," Geoffrey said, petting him on the head. He put his rifle down and picked up one of Georgiana's arrows and tossed it. "Fetch."

"Hey!"

"Considering all the arrows you've lost over the years, you can afford to give one to poor Gawain."

"He's poor only because he never has anything to bring back but things you toss him."

Geoffrey did not respond to the jibe, accustomed to her sarcasm as he was. Instead, he just let his errant dog return and tossed it again. Sir Gawain was four, and most energetic, which Geoffrey's father liked. His father did not much care for the name, but he had been overruled by his mother, who thought it was more amusing than a traditional name for a pup.

"Do you have anything else to do but insult my marksmanship?"

"Oh yes," Georgie said. "I must learn to dance, sew, draw, paint, sing, and if I have time before supper, play the pianoforte; all casually, of course. It would be indecorous for me to attempt to become a professional at anything."

He said, "You know how to do some of those things."

"But they must be perfected."

"And after that?"

"That's the part I haven't worked out. Everyone I know who is unattached seems so terribly bored."

"I like your drawings," he said. "It's a shame your governess burned them. They were…imaginative."

"There are only so many flowers in this world to be drawn," she said. "Should we wake your uncle?"

"I don't know how he succeeds in sleeping through the racket this rifle makes," he said. "Probably because he wakes at half past three every morning—terrifies the servants every time."

"Still? Did anyone tell him he doesn't have to keep monastic hours anymore?"

He glanced at her. "Do you want to be the one to tell him?"

To this, she had no response. They gathered their materials and headed down the hill, where Grégoire was asleep against a tree, his head lolling to one side. Fortunately, they were able to rouse Grégoire before Geoffrey's father showed up, because he was supposed to be watching them, not the reverse.

"There you are," Darcy said as he arrived. He nodded to his niece. "Miss Bingley."

"Uncle Darcy," she said with a curtsy.

"Father."

Grégoire wiped his eyes. "I am sorry. Am I late for something?"

"No, not at all. There was something I wanted to discuss with you. Geoffrey, you're late for French—"

"*Auw*—"

"And Miss Bingley, I am sure you are late for *something.*"

She did not reply, but merely curtsied and ran off, back toward Kirkland.

"Shoot anything?" Darcy asked his son.

"No."

"Did you at least fire in the general direction?"

Geoffrey colored. Grégoire tried to hide his amusement. But Darcy patted his son on the shoulder. "When I was your age, I couldn't hit the broad side of a building. Most of what I know, I learned from your Uncle Bingley—and to this day, he can still best me. But that will be our secret. Mention it in front of your uncle—whichever one you like—and you will regret it."

"Of course, Father." That was his cue to exit, and he bowed briefly to them and ran back up the hill toward Pemberley, Gawain racing ahead of him. "I will not be outrun by my cousin and a dog on the same day!"

Unfortunately, he had not yet learned the value of promising himself things that would turn out to be unattainable.

~~~

Darcy sat down on the stump beside his brother. He did not ask how he was feeling—Grégoire had tired of it, even though he did not express his agitation in words. He was bordering on actually being well; it was only a matter of energy. "I trust that they behaved themselves for the time you weren't asleep?"

"They are wonderful children," his brother replied. "What brings you away from your ledgers?"

"I will endure this from my wife, but not from you," Darcy said with a laugh. "It is a proposal."
~~~

"A proposal?"

"I have a holding on the Isle of Man that I inherited with the estate—a house on a small island in the south. It has been sitting idle since Father died, and now someone has made an offer on it. Before I sell it, I want to see it again. He may have left some personal effects there, as he did in Valgones. And I must decide on a price," he said. "I would very much like for you to accompany me, if you feel up to it."

"It is a short journey by sea, is it not?"

"If we leave from Liverpool, it would not be more than a few hours at most. Plenty of time to hold your stomach."

Grégoire smiled. "Then I would be happy to accompany you."

Their journey was set for a few weeks hence. The weather was growing colder, but Grégoire wanted to spend time with Georgiana before she departed to winter at home in Scotland. He spent most of his time reading, but when he was well enough, he would accompany Elizabeth on her trips to visit the poor of Derbyshire, never without a man capable of carrying him back to the carriage if he collapsed (which he did not). It was something he had loved to do in past years in Derbyshire. He was eager to return to charitable work, even if it was just to deliver coal and cured meats. Some people recognized him and some did not, but both forced him to endure a line of questioning as to his change in appearance and occupation. He eventually found an adequate response: "Transience and impermanence are a necessary part of life." When Elizabeth asked him where he had learned this saying, he replied, "One of Mr. Bingley's Indian books."

The Kincaids were sent off with much fanfare, and a promise from them to return sometime in the spring or summer. "You will find your way; I'm sure of it," his sister said with tear-filled eyes.

Darcy and Grégoire left the very next day for their business excursion. Elizabeth, accustomed to Darcy's occasional absences for estate business, did not question it except to say, "You know, he will never be an English gentleman."

"That is not why I'm taking him," he assured her.

The servants packed a whole case of powders, tinctures, tonics, and salves for Grégoire, despite his insistence that he did not need them. He did not mind the hard back of the carriage seat. "I have hardly any flesh left there that is not scarred, so I feel nothing but the rocking," he admitted.

Grégoire read for a time, and Darcy was lost in looking out the window, watching Pemberley disappear behind him. It was not until they left Derbyshire that Grégoire closed his book and said, "So what is the real reason for our journey?"

Darcy sighed. "It is not easy for me to say this, but I think that it is time. I am not a superstitious man, but the offer arriving at the same time you returned to Pemberley was an interesting coincidence."

Grégoire nodded.

"What I'm about to say is not commonly known. In fact, the only other person who knows it for sure is Dr. Maddox, and only because, in a moment when I lost my wits in Austria, I told him to pass the time." He turned away from the window and looked at Grégoire, across from him. "Your namesake is our Uncle Gregory Darcy, Father's elder brother."

"He died young?"

"No. He died when I was already ten and five."

Grégoire mulled over the implications. "Why have I never heard of him?"

"Because there are no records of him at Pemberley, at least that I have found. He was disinherited at ten and eight, and then was said to have died in a tragic riding accident. His portraits were removed, and over the next few years, the entire Pemberley staff were changed over, one by one, so that by the time our father married my mother, no one knew of him, or else had heard rumors of a son who had died so tragically that no one spoke of him. I did not know of him until I was five, and did not fully understand the situation until it was explained to me when I was five and ten, before I saw him for the last time. Our father was reluctant to speak of him on English soil—he would just say 'we are going to the Isle of Man' and then wait until we were on the boat to say why."

"Why was he disinherited?"

"He was mad," Darcy answered, and let his words sink in for a moment. "He knew he was, as least as much as a mad person can know that. His illness was not so extensive that he was unaware of his shortcomings. According to Father's story, which Uncle Gregory then supported when I asked him myself, he asked to be disinherited. He did not want to manage Pemberley. He did not want the burden and doubted he could manage it. But if the reasons were discovered, it would mar our father's chances for a good match, despite his wealth. So instead they faked his death and destroyed the evidence of his existence, our father and grandfather. I never had a mad uncle; there is no illness in the family. You understand?"

"Perfectly," Grégoire said, though he said it with the appropriate gravity of someone who was hearing something that would take time to fully sink in. "How was he ill?"

"Hysteria, which has no specific meaning that can help us, as I have come to understand. He did not care for society; he did not trust people he did not know." He swallowed. "His distrust of strangers was much greater than my own."

Grégoire nodded.

Darcy played with his ring, the special signet ring that had not been stolen during his captivity because, on a whim, he had given it to his son to hold onto while he was gone. "I know little about whatever treatment he received, but eventually he refused it, and Father, who became his legal guardian after our grandfather's death, consented. He lived in solitude for the rest of his life on that little island, attended only by nurses he didn't trust and said were trying to poison him. And yet, when I spoke to him, we could have a completely normal conversation. He understood who I was and he told me that he was content with his life, and could not think of another way to have lived it. The fact that he…hanged himself… a week after saying so is something I will never understand." He looked away nervously. "I have never told Elizabeth, or even Georgiana. Did Father mention to you that you had an uncle?"

"No," he said. "Not to my knowledge. But I was young. I do not remember everything."

"He was good at keeping secrets," Darcy said. "It never bothered me to carry this one around. Uncle Gregory himself said that he wanted to be buried in obscurity, to not taint the family tree. He was very noble in that sense, in his loyalty to the Darcy line. This was until Austria, when it came out, and I realized—maybe I should have told someone there was sickness in my family." He was not speaking so easily now. Only Grégoire's reassuring nods kept him going. "It seems to have missed Geoffrey and Anne—the others are too young yet. But it is evident that George is affected. I have tried to counsel him—without counseling him. You understand."

"I understand."

"All of Gregory Darcy's personal effects should still be there, or so I have been informed by the solicitor, who knows him only as 'previous resident.' He is also buried there, I am quite sure. I do not know where else he would be buried, and he is not at Pemberley. I let the land sit because there was nothing better to do with it and because it would mean—going back."

Again, Grégoire nodded. "I am honored to go with you."

Darcy smiled. It was exactly what he needed to hear.

When he could put it off no longer, Dr. Maddox told his son they were to go to Windsor, to see the king. There was no way to begin to explain why—he barely understood it himself, and Frederick did not even know he was adopted. He was eight—too young for all that. Dr. Maddox withstood Frederick's barrage of questions admirably, ducking as many as he could with "His Highness requested it" and "It might not be fun, but it will be short."

Caroline hugged her son—who was dressed up in clothes purchased especially for this visit—with extra vigor before they entered the carriage. "Be good. And whatever you think, for goodness's sake, do not say it."

"Then what am I to say?"

"To our sovereign? 'Yes, Your Majesty' and 'No, Your Majesty' will suffice," the doctor said, kissing his wife. "He will be fine."

"He is not the only person I am concerned with."

Dr. Maddox smiled to hide his anxiety.

The trip to Windsor was brief. Dr. Maddox had never been there—no one went there unless compelled to, despite the massive grounds and impressive architecture. The sovereign was mad, and none of his many children called, because often they were not recognized when they did. He was seen mainly by his doctors. Dr. Maddox knew a few of them, and he had little respect for their approach. They were of an older school, and he had radical ideas about certain aspects of medicine. Dr. Maddox was against bleeding the sick—he himself had been almost bled to death as a young man when he had developed an infection following his first cataract surgery. He had had one foot in the grave when his brother, frantic with worry, finally shooed the doctors away when they came with their spikes for the daily bloodletting, and only then had he begun to recover. Or so Brian said. Dr. Maddox had little memory of the experience. Dr. Maddox was an observational doctor, believing only what he saw, and he saw patients get weaker after bleeding, with no positive effects that seemed to be connected to the bleeding itself. They had already debunked Aristotle's treatise on the humors of the body—why not do away with the entire idea of an excess of blood?

But the established doctors who had been schooled in the previous century and had treated the king for years had other ideas, and Dr. Maddox knew his place was not to contradict them. Maybe someday, when they were long gone, he would publish a paper, but he was not willing to be labeled an outlaw just yet, when his family depended on him.

Without much ceremony, Dr. Maddox and son passed the guards and greeted one of the doctors with whom he was acquainted. They made small talk as Frederick impatiently pulled on his arm. Maddox pitied his son; he had no idea why he was here and would not know for years, if he ever did. And by then, the king would most likely be long dead.

"His Majesty is in good spirits today," said the physician. "You know he is completely blind, correct?"

"I have been informed, yes."

"Not helping his stability, I'm afraid. Of course, everything he says will probably be complete nonsense. It's best just to play along or you risk upsetting him. Not that he can do much when he's that way. But it might be distressing for your son to see." He was quiet and then said, "Why is he here?"

"His Royal Highness the Prince Regent thought it would be a good idea to bring a child."

"Yes, His Majesty loves children. He loved his own when they were children. He is disappointed with how they have turned out."

Dr. Maddox nodded and looked down at his son, who was frowning at being dragged along on this mysterious errand. "Best behavior, Frederick. This is your king."

Frederick did not seem impressed, but at least he didn't say so.

The servant opened the door to the king's chamber. "Do not turn your back on His Majesty," he cautioned them.

Not that it mattered—the old man was blind—but Dr. Maddox nodded. "Of course."

The two of them were allowed entrance to a sitting room. It had the splendor of a royal palace but without any of the little touches of a man who cared for his surroundings as the Prince Regent did. In that way, it was almost as bare as the man sitting in the armchair before them. Wrapped in blankets, even though it was not cold, he shook his head, his remaining locks of white hair waving as he said, "Who is it? Who is there?"

Dr. Maddox bowed, and his son did the same. "Your Majesty, I am Dr. Daniel Maddox, and this is my son, Frederick Maddox. We are here at your son's behest."

"My son? Frederick has come?"

"No, Your Majesty. *My* son is named Frederick as well."

"Nonsense. Let me see him, and we shall tell the truth of the matter."

Dr. Maddox helped lift Frederick into the lap of King George III. "I'm Frederick Maddox, sir."

"You're very small to fight the French. Why did I ever send you to Flanders? Utter nonsense. A foolish misjudgment on my part; a man must always take the greatest care with his children." He did not bother to turn his sightless, milky eyes in the direction of Dr. Maddox, who took the seat beside him. "He is not my son, is he?"

"No," Dr. Maddox said honestly.

"A shame that I made him Duke of Cumberland, then. Wait! I know who you are!" He pointed not at Frederick but in Maddox's general direction. "You're Lord Brute! Why didn't you tell me you were coming to visit?"

"I am not Lord Brute, sir."

"How dare you say otherwise! You were a witness at my wedding! I remember it perfectly. John, I am most insulted."

Dr. Maddox said seriously, "I did not mean to insult you, Your Majesty."

"What do you have to say, George?" the king said to Frederick.

"I'm not George; I'm Frederick. I *told you* that." Frederick Maddox was not known for his patience, especially not in the lap of a mad person, even if he was king. "Don't you remember?"

"Frederick—" Dr. Maddox said to curb his son, but the king interrupted.

"Nonsense. I remember everything perfectly, except for the times that I do not. Fortunately, I do not remember them! So it is most convenient. They say I am mad, but you shan't listen to that, young George. And stop lusting after your tutors; 'tis most improper for a royal issue."

Frederick, legitimately confused, turned to his father, who gave him his most serious "mind your manners" look.

They chatted for some time, until Frederick became fidgety. The boy was escorted out of the room and told to wait outside with a servant.

"I am a physician, Your Majesty," Dr. Maddox said. "I am here because your son, George, asked me to come and see you."

"And what is your medical treatment?"

"Sadly, I have none."

"Then you admit it. That makes you more intelligent than most doctors. It is a shame you are a colonel instead of a doctor; I imagine you would have made a good one," the king said. "That was George, wasn't it? It felt like him. I know my own son."

"It was not George," Maddox said. "It was his son; your grandson."

"Really? No one told me he had been born. I am subscribed to the wrong papers. Well, I create him Lord of the Colonies in America. Tell him that, won't you?"

Dr. Maddox, despite his anxiety, could not help but smile. "I will, Your Majesty."

CHAPTER 22

A Matter of Propriety

~ ~ ~

IT HAPPENED THAT TWO LADIES were riding to Town, one an earl's wife and the other her cousin, when they spotted two people walking down the road with bowls on their heads. They were tempted to tell the curricle driver to slow down so that they might get a better look, but seeing that the couple were armed, they decided otherwise. They didn't look much like bandits—one was a woman in a silk bathrobe and the other a man walking on wooden sandals.

"How curious!"

"Oh, that's just Princess Maddox," said the driver. "She was heir to some small kingdom in Austria until she married an English gent. Comes up and down all the time. And 'er servant, I guess."

He did slow down a bit, but the travelers ignored the curricle, talking in their nonsense language so fast that the words were impossible to pick apart. "How strange, those Austrians!"

"Indeed, ma'rm."

~ ~ ~

Visiting the small village close to her home was always a pleasant walk for Nadezhda Maddox, Princess of Sibui. It was much less trouble to walk than have a carriage take her to Town for simple things, such as groceries. She knew most of the people in the village, where she felt more at home than in London's high society, despite her aristocratic blood. She usually brought a man along to carry the special items that were too small to have delivered, but now she had Mugin, at least until the next ship to sail to the Orient.

"*Sa!* Why so many? Are we having a feast?"

"Since when are you opposed to a feast?" she replied. "All you've done since you got here is stuff yourself. And, yes, we are. Binguri-san is coming to discuss business with Brian and he's staying a few days." She continued on in Japanese, ignoring the other people traveling down the dusty road, aware of their gawking. "He is bringing Georgiana."

"Is that a bad thing?"

She glanced at Mugin, laden with packages, but did not stop walking. "You know, Jorgi-chan isn't a little girl anymore." Mugin was irreverent as always. "So?" It was a good sign.

"So what I mean is, they have rules in this country about what men and women do together that are different from yours, which you ignore anyway."

"I *noticed*."

"Mugin, you're not being serious."

"What am I supposed to be serious about? Jorgi is a mere child. She is...what, ten?"

"Twelve." She sighed. "Her father is going to be more protective of her. And more suspicious of her going off into the woods with men. From now on, I go with you."

"You decided this with Brian-chan?"

"We didn't need to discuss it. Brian's English. He pretends not to be, but he is. English ladies are proper."

"Proper?"

"Respectable."

"Ah," he said. "So, you're going to chaperone me? What is the worst that could happen?"

"You're seen holding hands with her by a local, and you have to marry her."

Mugin stopped in his tracks. Nadezhda kept her expression

neutral to disguise whether she was being serious or not. Only half of her was. Georgie *was* only twelve.

"And what if I refuse?" "To what, marry her?" "Yes."

"I'll make you."

They stood in perfect silence. Not a bird chirped for that one moment. There were no passengers on the roads.

Mugin dropped the packages, drew his sword, and swung, seemingly all in the same movement. Nadezhda had already ducked out of the way. Her wakizashi was blocked only by the metal beneath his shoes as he tumbled to the ground. He kicked her sword away and rolled across the road. He jumped back onto his feet as Nadezhda charged. Their blades drew across each other with a horrible shriek and the sparks of steel striking steel, until the dust settled. Nadezhda had the edge of her blade at Mugin's neck. He had the tip of his pointed at her chest.

Without ceremony, he pulled away and replaced his blade in its sheath. "You've improved."

"I am a childless housewife. I have time to practice."

She replaced her blade and he picked the packages back up, and they resumed their journey.

"Are people really so upset about these things?" Mugin said. "If her reputation is so important, she should have a man protecting her."

"But not *alone* with her, because even he cannot be trusted."

"Heh. Jorgi-chan doesn't need a man. Certainly not a gaijin. She can take care of herself."

"Yes, but her father doesn't *know* that."

"Fine," he huffed. "Their country, their rules."

They spoke no further on the subject.

The carriage from Derbyshire arrived and three Bingleys (two human, one animal) were received with delight. Monkey went almost everywhere that Bingley did, usually because of Jane's unilateral declaration that as much as she loved her husband, she would not have his wild animal running around their bedroom and making a fuss when he was gone, which was precisely what Monkey did when Bingley went away. Georgiana was the only child old enough to manage him, and this time, she was with her father.

The young Miss Bingley was not so much traveling on her father's coattails as she was going to visit her Aunt Nadezhda. Although she was on good terms with every member of her very extended family, there were certain people with whom she felt an affinity—Brian, Nadezhda, and Geoffrey. Her father was borderline. Her mother fell in with everyone else; consequently, it was a joint decision by her parents that she would spend time with her father over her mother, as he seemed to be closer to her.

Charles Bingley was aware of Georgiana's friendship with the disreputable Mugin, but it was all managed through Nadezhda, and he held the princess's judgment in high regard. Besides, if he ever insulted Her Highness in front of Brian, Charles was quite sure he would have his head cut off within seconds. So Georgie loved to play outside with Nadezhda and Mugin. *Let her be a child a bit longer.* He believed, looking back on it, that his sisters had both assumed the position of a lady too quickly, which had had negative effects on their personalities for years.

They arrived in time to clean up for dinner, which was relatively normal English food. It was always a gamble to visit the Maddox house. You did not know whether you would be sitting on the floor, eating raw fish, or at a table, eating roast beef. He did find Oriental food interesting, but he had spent most of the trip incredibly sick from the unfamiliar spices.

"Ah, English food," Brian said. "The more tasteless it is, the better."

"He's talking nonsense," Bingley said to Her Highness, gesturing to his plate of beef. "He would have been salivating at this in India."

"There is something to be said for real meat, yes, all right. But how about our dinner with the martial arts master?"

"What, before we were running for our lives back to Hong Kong?"

"*Mugin* was running. *I* was running. *You* were being carried, because your back was nothing but bruises. And you had been foolish enough to try every dish they offered you without asking what it was." Brian turned to his wife. "I would take you there, but Mugin ruined the reputation of all foreigners *forever* in that village by beating the master senseless."

Mugin, who had not yet contributed, said in Japanese, "I refuse to lose because Bingali was injured and you run like a woman."

"I told you, I have no control over it!" He turned to his wife again. "Nady, do I really—"

But his wife had already broken into laughter. She tried to smother it in her napkin, but to no avail.

~ ~ ~

Nadezhda had succeeded in getting Brian and Charles into a sake-drinking contest, which, of course, ended with them both collapsing and having to be dragged to their rooms. The servants had all gone to sleep when she changed into old clothing and woke Georgiana. "Put this on."

They lived not more than a few miles from Town. The two adults were quite capable of running the distance, Georgie managing to keep up behind them. Fortunately, the bad section of London was closer than Town proper. Mugin had wrapped a shawl over his face; from a distance, he could almost be mistaken for an English dockworker, except for his shoes. Georgie was also dressed like a boy, which she could still pull off.

"We just watch," he said to her.

They slipped in the side door of a warehouse, or what had once been a storehouse or slaughterhouse. It was a square building, empty of furniture except for boxes, the occasional chair, and dirty straw on the floor. Gas lamps lit the middle of the room, and men (and a few women) gathered to form a ring. The onlookers were already shouting as two men entered the ring, one wearing only an undershirt and the other nothing above the waist. A man hit a bell with a spoon, but the contestants had already started pummeling each other. When it got too gruesome, Georgie covered her eyes, or Nadezhda did it for her. There was no referee; it continued until one man wound up unconscious on the floor and was dragged off, while the spectators cheered for the muscle man. As the bets got higher, there were fewer and fewer takers to fight. Georgie sat on Mugin's shoulders. "Are you gonna fight him?"

"Could get in trouble," he whispered.

"But you would win!"

That was enough incentive for Mugin, who passed her to Nadezhda. "Don't get yourself killed. Because if you do, we're running. We're not taking your corpse with us."

"Ha. I know." He stepped into the ring, still mostly covered.

This was not the kind of place where they wrote down (or even asked) the names of the challengers. Mugin got into the same pose as the champion—two balled fists up in front of his face, and the bets were being shouted against him, especially when they saw him in stilt sandals.

"Listen, Dutchman, I ain't gonna be respons'ble fer ya," said the champion.

Doing his best impression of an English accent, Mugin said, "Me neither."

"Well, little man, let's see what you can do!" said the announcer, and rang the bell.

The champion gave Mugin a moment—perhaps he felt like being a bit nice—but Mugin did nothing. So the man—apparently his name was Harry, or so the announcer called him—charged forward.

That was when Mugin dropped his hands behind his back and fell to the floor, holding himself up by his palms and letting his raised foot meet the approaching fist. Knuckles hit metal and the crunching was audible. Mugin pushed himself up, taking the fighter down with his foot, and stood over him. "Give up," he whispered.

"Or I'll break both your hands."

"That wasn't fair!"

"You are bigger than me. I do what I can."

Harry looked up at the man he was facing, but the light obscured much of his face. He pulled away, and Mugin gave him a chance to get to his feet. One arm he held up, but it was bloodied and red. The other was still fine.

"Round one for the Dutchman!" said the announcer. "Round two!"

Mugin still held his arms behind his back as the bell rang. He stood there, unmoving, before his opponent. The crowd was torn between booing and waiting to see what the wily foreigner would do. Mugin was much smaller than his opponent, and would have been a whole head shorter if not for his *geta* shoes. He was not muscular. He did not have a lot of weight.

"Fight like a man!" Mugin said nothing. He waited. He was in front of Harry, but when the muscled Harry charged, he wasn't there. He leaped on his shoulders, and then over him, landing on the ground as Harry went into the audience. There were no barriers, so it was not unheard-of for the first row to get injured. Harry barely had time to reorient himself before Mugin kicked one of his legs out from under him at the knee. Mugin grabbed the man's hair so he would not fall forward onto some smaller audience member and tugged his hair so he fell backward, flat onto the dirty floor with a thud. Mugin put a shoe on his chest again. "Hurt me, not audience." He kicked him, and Harry rolled away. Slowly, he got to his feet.

The announcer approached Mugin. "Look, Mister, if you can understand English, you have to use your hands. All right? None of this foot stuff."

Mugin kicked off his sandals. Only then did Harry get back into stance. This time, Mugin drew one of his hands up behind him and the other out flat in front of him, palm up.

"Man, I'm never goin' to Dutchland!"

"Fight like an Englishman!"

Mugin ignored his detractors and stayed in position. This time, when Harry came charging, he stepped sideways, caught the man's arm, and twisted the wrist so hard it turned Harry over and he hit the ground again. Mugin towered over him.

"All right!" Harry shouted. Mugin offered him a hand, and he painfully took it, as one hand was broken and the other wrist badly sprained. Compared with how the previous combatant had fared against Harry, beaten to a pulp in the head, Harry was still relatively intact.

Mugin bowed to a dizzy Harry, and the announcer raised Mugin's arm. "Winner!" There were both cheers and jeers, and after collecting his prize money, Mugin made a hasty exit while Nadezhda and Georgie made their own. They met up half a mile away, and began a more leisurely walk back to the house.

"You count," he said, handing the pile of bills and the coins to Nadezhda. "Well, Jorgi-chan, what did I do right?"

"You threw him down three times!"

"And how did I do that?"

"With your legs!" As they reached the edge of the small estate, Mugin stopped. "How did I really beat him? I was smaller than he was. I was weaker than he was. I was shorter than he was."

"You got out of the way."

"Right, little *ookami*," he said with a playful pat on her head. "The others, they stood up against him. One heavy object hitting another heavy object until one goes down—always the smaller one. Stupid gaijin. If your opponent wants the wall behind you so badly, give it to him." He leaned over. "You always remember that."

"What if I'm fighting someone smaller than me?" He smiled. "Then just be kind. That poor person."

~ ~ ~

Darcy felt something in the pit of his stomach as their little boat approached the island. After they had left for the Isle of Man, he had felt pangs of remorse for subjecting Grégoire to this—no, for subjecting *himself* to this. The last time he had been here was when he was five and ten, but he remembered everything, for it seemed as if nothing had changed.

The solicitor was there to greet them on the bright fall morning. "Hello, Mr. Darcy. Mr. Bellamont. We've cleaned up the place—both for the sale, and for your own inspection. It had been closed up for years, so there was a bit of work to do."

Behind them was the house, that long, strange one-level dwelling. The previous owner (before the Darcys) had just kept adding room after room, instead of building another level above. It was one long hallway all the way to the end, where his uncle had spent his days and nights.

"We brought in some food and a cook. You'll be staying how long?"

"Not more than a few days, at most," Darcy said, already wanting to leave. "Thank you."

In the immediate rooms they heard the cook singing to herself. She hurried out, curtsied to them, and asked them when they wanted dinner. Then she made herself scarce.

It was just room after room as Darcy opened the first set of doors to reveal a sitting room that had been recently dusted, but the furniture was as he vaguely remembered it. Was this the room he had sat in while his father talked with his uncle, undoubtedly about *him?* He could not remember. The next room looked the same, almost exactly—except for a pile of books in the corner that had not been dusted. "He liked to read," he said to Grégoire.

The next room was the same, except that there were more books; all in piles, none on shelves. It was not a room meant for bookshelves, just another sitting room. How much sitting could a person do?

It went on and on. In each room were more books, to the point where there were actual cases of them, and furniture shoved aside to make space. Everything looked the same—they had changed nothing, just abandoned it. There was even a chair overturned for some reason. Grégoire set it up properly before they moved on.

"This is it," he said. "They might have cleared it out, I don't know." But he opened the door, and discovered that they had not. They both stepped in, the silence impenetrable.

His uncle's room was exactly as he remembered it, except that there was no longer a mattress, just the wooden frame of the narrow bed. All the walls were bookshelves, except the one with the window, facing out to the sea. There were books piled up on the dresser, beside the bed, and under the bed—everywhere, as if he had just been finishing up a few novels the day before. But Gregory Darcy was long dead. There was a closet full of clothes, but they both coughed when the closet door was opened and the dust burst forth. The ancient garb of their father's generation hung before them, half eaten by moths.

"Brother," Grégoire said. Darcy turned around. Grégoire focused on the desk before the window, where their uncle undoubtedly had sat for hours on end. He lifted the lid and opened it. Inside, aside from the pens and bottles of now-dried ink and the knickknacks, were piles and piles of paper, all filled with writing. Some were even in hand-bound notebooks. Grégoire picked up a bound one. The title read *November 1778—October 1779*. "He wrote."

What mysteries were contained in there? Did he really want to know? Darcy avoided the question by instead opening the dresser drawers. Aside from the yellowed shirts and hair powder, there were portraits. "Look at this," he said, calling Grégoire away from the journals. He held up two portraits, connected by a metal bracket. "Our father and uncle." They looked very similar, with only their names inscribed on the back to identify them. Each one looked maybe one and ten or two and ten; they were about the same age as Geoffrey was now. Geoffrey resembled both of them, but Geoffrey also took after his mother in many ways.

Darcy looked down at the journal in Grégoire's hands. "Do you think he wanted someone to read them?"

"His death, he planned. He could have burned his writings beforehand if he chose."

"Are you so sure he wanted them to be read?"

"No," Grégoire said. "I wish to find out."

CHAPTER 23

More Notes from the Underground

DARCY BUSIED HIMSELF with the solicitor for the rest of the morning and most of the early afternoon. He was willing to sell, but he needed time to remove some personal items from the property—boxes and boxes of books. He authorized the hiring of men to package them, and wrote a quick letter to his wife, saying that they were safely arrived and would be staying for perhaps a few days to finish up some business. Only after seeing that everything was in order did he return to his brother, who was still at the desk, papers piled everywhere.

"Our uncle was quite prolific," Grégoire said. "Here." He passed Darcy some yellowed parchment.

1 August 1768

Geoffrey sent me a new book today. More accurately, it arrived, so he must have sent it some time ago. It is an original of Boccaccio's Decameron. *How coincidental, to receive a set of stories told by people who have gone into exile to escape illness. I wonder if Geoffrey read it at any point or he merely bought it because he presumed I did not already own it. The library that Father provided is already impressive, I must say. In that respect, I have not been ill treated.*

12 August 1768

My delay in writing the daily life of this madman was not of

my own design. Even now, my (blot) strength fails me.
Dr ______ came to bleed me yesterday, and I was stupid
enough to scream, which meant more bleeding, for only a madman
would scream at having a scalpel scraped across his flesh, no?
More tomorrow.

18 August 1768
I look back. "More tomorrow. "A week has passed. I could ask
Nurse ____ to transcribe my entries, I suppose, were there truly
anything worth saying other than that I hate her and I hate Dr.
____. I hate them all so much.

19 August 1768
Apologies, Journal. I spoke out of frustration, not actual hatred.
The staff believe they are doing right by me, that they are doing
only their best. What do they think—they will cure me and I
will go home? I am dead anyway in England; I cannot go home.
LET ME BE MAD!

"Were I him," Darcy said, "I would not want this made public."

"We are hardly the public," Grégoire said. "I am not proposing to paste it on the wall at Pemberley." Looking up at Darcy, he reclaimed the papers. "You need not read them, Darcy."

Darcy nodded numbly and left Grégoire alone as he returned to his sorting of the book collection.

Dinner was served after Vespers.

"Darcy," Grégoire said. "You can leave tomorrow."

"What?"

"I'll oversea the removal of his things. You can do the rest from England."

Darcy replied simply, "Did you read any more of the journals?"

"Yes."

There was silence again. Grégoire watched his brother move the food around on his plate.

"Did you hear what I said?"

"Yes, I did!" Darcy said. "He was my uncle, too."

"Because I can—"

"*He was my uncle, too!*" The sound of the glass slamming on the wooden table was enough to startle both of them. They let the sound fade into an uncomfortable silence as the cook took their plates. "Excuse me," he said in a much smaller voice as he excused himself, leaving Grégoire at the table.

"Is the master all right?" said the cook.

~ ~ ~

Grégoire eventually found his brother on a bench by the sea, without his hat or overcoat, staring out into the inky ocean of night.

"You can approach," Darcy said. "I don't bite."

Grégoire sat down beside him, a folio in his hands. "I'm sorry. If you want, we'll burn them."

"Do you think it is what he would have wanted?"

"I have no idea. I didn't know him. He did not know himself." Grégoire smoothed his hand over the cover of the folio. "I do suspect that he helped you at one time, and that he might not have been as ill as we have believed. Anyone would go mad from the torment he describes."

"You seem well."

Grégoire managed a half smile. "Thank you for the compliment, but you know very well my intention." He handed the folio to Darcy. "This is the rest of what I've read. There is far more."

27 March 1769

Geoffrey visited today. He did not look well and I did not look well, so it was mutual. Father is dead. He died in his sleep. Would I be so lucky. I think constantly of death. Did I wish it on Father, even by accident? Do my thoughts have power? Will any of this affect anyone? The plan was to remove me from the picture. Were we successful?

29 March 1769

I do not understand why I have these thoughts that are so terrible that I cannot transcribe them. I am shamed. I did not think this way at Pember—I cannot write it. It hurts too much. I was afraid. I was irrational. I had thoughts there that were bad, but not like this. Now I think things in my boredom that any person should think are crazy. I am no longer borderline. I am beyond the pale, as they say.

14 April 1769

Excuse my absence. I was detained for some time after bashing Dr. ____ in the head when I believe he attempted to bleed my brain. My brain! I need my brain! It is all I have left, even in its tarnished form. So they tied me to the bed and left me like a naughty child to be punished. They took away everything sharp. They would not let me go outside. I decided not to be the master of Pemberley's fate—can I not be the master of my own?

3 June 1773

Geoffrey visited. He is engaged to be married to an earl's daughter. The family, he does not care for too much, but he is in love. I could see it on his face; it lit up when he talked of her. I hope it lasts. I hope that all of his wild oats have been sown and there are none left.

He agreed to stop the treatments. I am all joy! Though some of me remains flesh, my spirit is happiness, and my blood is on fire—and it will stay in me! I take a tonic for sleep, or if I am agitated, but it is of my own choosing. He also changed my nurse. I like her better, though she does treat me like a child; anyone would be preferable to the previous woman. I can rest now.

"Does it go on like this?" As usual, Darcy's calm voice masked a wellspring of emotions.

"I imagine so."

Darcy handed back the folio. "Then let us keep reading."

~ ~ ~

The handsomely paid solicitor returned the next day on a boat laden with trunks and another filled with men to do the packing. There was a library to rival Pemberley's in this strangely constructed house, and it would not be an easy task. Darcy looked at each title as he passed it on, to be packed with great care. The duplicates would go either to Grégoire's private collection—if he ever desired to have one—or a poorhouse school. His uncle had been quite well read.

Grégoire sat at the desk, reading through the letters his namesake had set to ink for some reason or another. At lunch, he shared some with Darcy.

5 July 1773

Interesting to note that there is general improvement in my health since the end of my treatment. This is, of course, coming from a man whose word cannot be trusted. After all, I am insane. But I have more energy, and feel calmer. I go outside more. There are wonderful ruins on this island. Like me, they are slowly turning to dust, but at least the moss on them is quite beautiful. Yesterday, I saw a bird. I wrote to the executor in London to inform Geoffrey that if they have a book on birds native to the Isle of Man, then he should send it on.

3 December 1773

My brother did send me a large shipment of books that arrived just today in a great trunk, and I must assume they were selected at random, because there is no lack of variety here. For some reason beyond my admittedly flawed comprehension of this world, a large stack of them were women's novels, the sort that make me think the printing press a contemptible invention. There was a book on the birds of Scotland, for which I am (relatively) grateful. Perhaps most interesting was a copy of Bede's Ecclesiastical History of the English People, *a rather old translation, but one I can read well enough. It came in two volumes, one which seems to be just a collection of his letters about his travels to other churches.*

14 January 1774

I am fascinated by this St. Bede, the father of English history, not for his tales but his experiences in the Dark Ages, wandering around the isle and the people he met along the way. He records a lost culture, which at his own time was dying; I wonder if he knew that or considered it. He must have. I will write the solicitor to see if more books are available.

29 October 1774

Large shipment of books of every sort. I am to be a truly enlightened madman if I manage to read them all, and I think I shall. There is little else to do with my time besides this journal itself, and what do I have to record? The time of the tides? The servants are not much for conversation. I feel well. Did I make a mistake? Did my isolation cure me? I sought escape and have found it, and it is most unsettling.

4 June 1779

The truth is confirmed: I am not fit for human contact. I am too afraid. It is a relief in a way, confirming the rightness of the path I chose, though in looking back I can see that Father was most persuasive about it.

Geoffrey came just yesterday and brought his wife, Lady Anne Fitzwilliam, and his son, Fitzwilliam Darcy (poor soul, such a name!). I do not think Geoffrey was mistaken in his choice of bride in the brief moments we spoke, but she was terrified of me and I of her, though I made an effort to hide it. She was wearing Mother's jewels. This is Mrs. Darcy now. Geoffrey is Mr. Darcy of Pemberley and Derbyshire. He has assumed the role meant for me, and he has made a presentable depiction of a happy family.

His son, not six, looks much like him, but with tousled hair, as permitted in youth. Either no one told him my condition (why would they?) or he did not understand it, because he had no hesitation in talking with me. I spent nearly an hour talking to him in the sitting room. I held him in my arms, and I kissed him. Would a son of my own have been so precious?

I cannot spend much time on contemplation of this sort, as it makes me ache. Geoffrey is himself in turmoil. I pray that this is not new information to the reader, but he confessed to me that he was not three years into his marriage before he had a bastard son. With his steward's wife, of all people! Poor Isabella Wickham. Poor George Wickham, unknowing in all of this. He thinks it's his. The ruse has worked perfectly. George is too good for this; he does not deserve the deception. Neither does Lady Anne, but I do not know her, and I have many fond memories of George, who was trained to be my steward with my father's consent.

5 June 1779

I grapple with all of this deception. My death was a deception. My brother's affairs (for I do not know truly how many he is having, but I will venture a guess that he will have more than one child outside of wedlock) are a deception. He said he would not tell Anne because he needed her to love him, for at least their son's sake. "A son should have two parents who love each other," I believe he said. And Geoffrey does love Anne, but has never been the master of his base instincts.

It is with deception that Our Lord and Savior was arrested and crucified—but then again, he knew all along and did not alter the course of events one bit, though well he could have. I have never considered myself a religious man, but I do not know any religious men—except those who appear in books, so I have no real scale by which to judge. I know the Bible well enough, and I have my selections of ecclesiastical books. What was Jesus thinking, on the cross? Did he not think, What a fool I was, not just to be rid of Judas. But of course not; he died for a higher cause. He allowed it all to unfold because he knew the path of fate, but he was alone in that. I do not know the path of fate; it unfolds before me after I have already made my choices and cannot retract them. But that is true of all mortals. Do we truly make mistakes, or has God already decided all of our paths and we merely follow them, unwittingly? What were his designs for me then? Or—the more appropriate pondering—why did he choose to give me this illness that boils my brain? There is a key somewhere; I do not see it. I will ask him when I die. It will be the first question out of my mouth.

"You remember it?"

"It is not something you forget," Darcy said. "They did not tell me he was mad. They just said I was not to speak of him to anyone else, even Nurse."

"What did Lady Anne think of him?"

He shrugged. "That memory, my mind did not store. She was my mother. I was five. She was not yet a person outside me, just my mother." He continued, "I've seen the book he discusses—the one by St. Bede. It's been packed to be sent to Pemberley. I imagine you'll have some interest in it when we return."

Grégoire nodded.

On their third day, Darcy did not find his brother in the bedroom, or any of the others. When he asked a worker, he was told his brother was outside.

Grégoire Bellamont was not immediately found. The bench was empty. Darcy walked along the shore. He had played here as a child. The ocean seemed endless on a misty day. In the distance, he could see ruins. Yes, that was right. There had been a monastery on the island, before the Dissolution of the Monasteries by King Henry VIII. Moss grew over the remaining stone frame. Only a few arches still stood. Grégoire sat on a fallen column.

"He starts his story from the beginning," Grégoire said, not looking up from the text. "I would warn you before reading this."

Darcy was startled but said, "I am not afraid. Let me see it."

17 May 1780

Perhaps I should have begun at the beginning. Hello, Journal. My name is Gregory Darcy. I am the son of Henry Darcy and the grandson of Philip d'Arcy, who came from France to marry the sister of the second Duke of Devonshire, and as part of the dowry, was granted plentiful lands in Derbyshire. I remember little of my grandfather. He was the nephew of the one before him, on the side of the family that remained in France. But are we not all Frenchmen? If civilization began in the Fertile Crescent, then perhaps we all come from there, and the last stop before England could only have been France.

But I am probably going on about the less important things. I was raised at Pemberley, with my younger brother, Geoffrey, as my playmate, and we did manage to get ourselves into a good deal of trouble, for there was no person better at boyish pranks than young Geoffrey was. In this regard, I stood in his shadow. I preferred the shadows. I am told I was lively enough as a boy, but rather shy.

As I stood on the threshold of manhood, being two and ten, I began to have thoughts that disturbed my tutor when I expressed them, so I promptly stopped, as any child does when they sense they are doing something wrong. I do not remember what I first said, but I definitely asked him if he was intending to kill me at some point. I do not know if I really thought that. Often things fly in and out of my head. The tutor was changed, and I said nothing to the next one. I became almost silent and, of course, this itself was odd. I was afraid to say anything, not able to tell what was a good thing to say and what was bad. My answers were often restricted to positive and negative replies in single words or a nod of the head.

My father brought in a man to inspect my ears, and I played along. Of course, he found no irregularity, but he prescribed some concoction that made me monstrously ill. After two days of losing my stomach, in my delirium, I told my nurse everything. It was not so much a confession as it was a series of things I no longer could hold myself back from saying. I have no recollection of it whatsoever, but she reported it all to my father, who questioned me thoroughly when I recovered my senses and asked me why I had said those things. I could have said I was delirious (it was true), but I have never been good at lying to anyone and I confessed that some of the things he told me I said were true, in that I believed them, or at least thought them. I thought people talked about me behind my back and conspired against me, not just to undermine me but to do me physical harm. I was afraid.

He brought in a doctor, whom I immediately disliked, and my fears this time were not unfounded. He prescribed a diet for me of milk and bread and nothing else. I remember my first bleeding. I was now four and ten and of some stature, so my natural reaction was to strike him to get him away from me, which only tore my skin and he broke his arm in the fall. I was tied to the bed and remained there for three days on nothing but bread and milk, a prisoner in my own house. My father visited me, looking concerned. Then the doctor bled me in a vast quantity, this time with my limbs already tied. In my weakened state, I started talking nonsense, or so I am told. But then the doctor was called away and I recovered without his presence. I said felt better than I did, and for a time, was believed.

I cannot bring myself to write about the first ball I attended. Please do not ask that of me. Suffice it to say, the doctor came back, and again I was deemed ill, and again I suffered, and again I recovered.

Geoffrey was my lone supporter. Not that my father had no care for me, but only my brother believed me when I said that the doctor was an evil man who made me worse. My little brother was blessed with all of the social graces I was not. He emerged in society to attend his first ball at just five and ten, and charmed all of the ladies, and then at great length described to me exactly what charming a lady could result in later in the evening, when he had her alone. He did not understand his own debauchery, the innocent rake. I myself could not dream of such a personal connection. I would not let my servants see me naked, much less a woman, must less touch her.... How could I have an heir?

At this point in my history, I suggested to my father that I was not fit to be master of Pemberley. He seemed to age right before my eyes in that one meeting, his despair flooding the room. He begged me to go through one more set of treatments. I don't wish to dwell on them, as even the memories are painful. There are scars on my arms where they cut me. By the end of the month, I was thin as a rake (not the kind my brother was) and sometimes my eyes failed to focus. Finally, Father relented, and the whole scheme was cooked up and presented to Geoffrey.

Though in these pages I record my brother's dalliances and adultery, he was truly a brother to me in every way, readily assuming the yoke of Pemberley and our half of Derbyshire, so that I could rest. He did not want the position, but he did not say as much to our father (at least in front of me). He easily could have refused, but this boy of six and ten set his whole life on a sterile course from which there could be no variation. He did this so that I might know peace. There are no words to say how grateful I was and still am. Father eventually agreed, and so quietly we signed all the papers disinheriting me, should I ever choose to show my face in England again and try to reclaim my lost throne. And then I went riding. We covered the horse with pig's blood, and I rode away from the only home I had ever known in a wagon. It was the dead of night and the last time I saw my father alive. I could not write my brother directly—only through a solicitor in London, who did not know my real identity. I was in anguish until Geoffrey wrote me, assuring me that everything had gone well, and that he would always care for me, and he would visit me when he could. I was not, it seemed, to be completely forgotten. He refused to do so. I saw him once before our father's death, and then immediately afterward. I wished him only the best and I still mean it.

Darcy handed back the papers. "That is enough for today." Without explanation, he walked off. Grégoire did not follow. No explanation was needed.

That night, Darcy could not find sleep. He did not have his sleeping draught with him. He wandered the long hallway of sitting room after sitting room. Most of the books had been packed and taken away, or were lying in open trunks. At the end, only moonlight illuminated the bedroom. Neither of them wanted to sleep in it.

Grégoire was asleep, but if he was still adhering to his wild schedule; he would be up for prayer in a few hours, even in the dead of night. For the time being, Darcy was alone. He carried his candlestick in and used the flame to light the old candle at the desk, not quite melted all the way down. He set his own stick down by the dresser and opened the drawer. He had not been thoroughly through it, and the objects were foreign to him, especially in the dim light. There were many small miniatures, carved out of wood—clearly his uncle had whittled as a hobby. There were numerous birds, horses, and a few human figures, not distinct enough to recognize. Perhaps they were not meant to be a specific person.

He would have all of the items put in his own luggage and taken back to Pemberley. He had already decided it; there was no need to dwell on it now. He turned to the desk and opened it. Only one folio remained, still covered in dust. He wiped it away and saw the date. Darcy must have been four and ten, maybe five and ten—this was the last journal, unless Grégoire had removed another one. He sat down and brought the light up closer as he began to read it. It was mainly theological or philosophical arguments Gregory seemed to be having with himself (Gregory himself commented that he was not sure whether he was mad or just bored).

Why am I doing this to myself? He could see that only a few pages were left. There was no need to guess at why that was. *Perhaps I am as torturous to myself as Grégoire is to his body.* He sighed and turned the sheets over with great care until he found the last two entries.

16 July 1790

Lady Anne Darcy, formerly Lady Anne Fitzwilliam, is dead. If that were the least of the news, I would be satisfied. She left behind a daughter, Georgiana. She died cursing her husband—she had discovered his infidelities (there were now two bastards as living records of it), one with her own maid. Geoffrey visited me, not in anguish over it, for this actually happened two years ago. Between then and now, there was no contact between us, except for him to send me books.

I saw him yesterday and he looked older than me. Still distraught over his wife's death, he cursed himself as easily as she had cursed him, but that was not even his main concern. His daughter, whom I have never met, is apparently well, but Fitzwilliam is not. Or so Geoffrey says. There are hints of the same affliction that seems to curse our bloodline. He said he had not taken Fitzwilliam to a doctor, as his memories were as tainted as mine. Geoffrey could not imagine inflicting that horror on his own son. Instead, he wished me just to talk with Fitzwilliam, who was having trouble in school, not because of an academic failing but because he did not move easily among people he did not know, and had trouble getting to know them.

I did not relate to my nephew the extent of my sufferings, or the nature of my illness, though he did know why I lived here and that I was mad. In fact, he seemed surprised that we had a somewhat normal conversation, where I did most of the listening and he told me about school and his sister and his friend George, the steward's son (I held my tongue! I bit it until it bled, almost). Slowly, I prised from him some of his innermost thoughts, and was not shocked to find they mirrored some of my own. I told him to dismiss them. He had no younger brother; he had no options. He did not believe himself to be sick. Perhaps without a doctor's pronouncement, he never would be. He would just be a shy boy who would turn into a shy man without many social graces but with a strong sense of responsibility, as he already seemed to have. Hopefully, he would marry well, produce an heir, and run Pemberley quietly and happily.

Or is that how it was supposed to happen for me?

I cannot wait any longer to find out. It is decided.

23 July 1790

How little I have to say to the world as I pack for my exit. Should I curse people? Bless people? Should I leave my servants and nurses a tip? Especially considering that they will be the ones who must deal with my corpse.

I have had enough. There is nothing more left for me, except to take up space in this room that I cannot bear to leave. In fact, I have more business with God, though I will be doomed to hell for this. Or perhaps we are wrong, and I will not. Either way, I have some questions for him, and some requests of him—that Geoffrey should find some peace within himself for his crimes, that all three of his sons and his daughter should live well, that Fitzwilliam should have a normal life, and that Lady Anne is in heaven after all of her sufferings as a wronged wife.

There is one last flash of insight. Most men do not get to finish their own stories according to the schedule that they choose. I do.

FINIS

"Darcy?"

It was like coming out of a dream. Perhaps he had fallen asleep. But no, there they were, the final letters large on the page.

"Grégoire." He looked at his watch. "Oh yes, of course. Which one is this?"

"Vigils."

Darcy slumped back into the chair. "I won't keep you."

Grégoire looked down at the open folio, and then at Darcy. "I have some time. Is it so terrible?"

"It depends. He was a suicide. He is doomed to hell, is he not?"

Grégoire swallowed but did not answer. He read the pages in silence and put the folio down. "Have you been to his grave?"

"I confess not."

"I found it today. Do you want to see it?"

At half-past three in the morning? Why not? "Yes."

The grave was near the abbey walls, so close that it might have been on consecrated ground. The stone had only his name and birth and death dates. The day of death was a day later than the journal entry—they must have discovered him the next morning. The hour he had died was a mystery that would never be solved.

Grégoire said his Latin prayers, whatever they were. When he was finished, Darcy spoke.

"Hello, Uncle. We've come to bring you home."

CHAPTER 24

Joseph Bennet's Proposal

"OH, EDMUND, WHAT A FINE THING FOR OUR GIRLS!"

"What?" Mr. Bennet said, hardly looking up from his paper. "Has Netherfield Park been let at last? Again?"

"Oh, Mr. Bennet! You tease me so! You will drive me to distraction!" she said, and rushed over to kiss him on his forehead.

"Always my intention, my dear," he said, and she hurried off to do some errand, real or imagined. It did worry him that her brain had been damaged by a stroke, and that sometimes her words or actions could not be properly accounted for. But in this case, Mr. Bennet knew precisely what she was talking about. Dr. Bertrand was leaving, set to head back to Town, and she was watching his departure from the window.

His serious daughter entered the sitting room, a book in hand, so he did not even have to get up to find her. "Mary," he said, in the sort of fatherly tone that got a daughter's attention, "why do you play with that man's emotions? At this point, it's positively rude."

"Papa!" she said. "I am not. I have been completely civil to him."

"Nonsense. He has been coming several times a week now for almost a month to call on you. You are in love with him. He is in love with you. Yet you have given him every subtle indication that if he made an offer of marriage, you would reject it. That is my conjecture, anyway, or he would have done it weeks ago."

She pursed her lips. "It is not so simple."

"Please." He gestured. "Sit down and explain to me the complexities."

"There is—well, he lives in town, and I could hardly—"

"Yes, leave Longbourn while I am still alive. I agree with you on this point, if you would be so kind as to grace us with your presence and Joseph's presence. I dread the idea of an empty nest. Have you said as much to him?"

"You mean, have I told him that I have no wish to leave Longbourn until I am forced by the entail?"

"Precisely."

"Yes," she said.

"And what did he say to this, our Town doctor?"

"He said he would manage."

Mr. Bennet nodded. "He's a young fellow and the situation would be temporary. Apparently, he does not think fifty miles that far at all. What other nonsense bothers you?" But instead of responding, she looked away. "It cannot be Joseph. He adores the man. And if you think he is too young to realize that you may well marry Dr. Bertrand, you are underestimating your son."

"He may not wish it. I promised myself that Joseph's wishes would always come first."

"He *may* not? You have not had this conversation with him?"

"I have not. No, Papa."

"Goodness! What are you waiting for? Ask the poor boy already and be done with it!"

"Papa!"

"Mary," he said a bit more sternly, "the best way to decipher his wishes is to ask him about them. All of these studies will do you no good if you are not capable of reaching that logical conclusion."

She colored at this.

"Now ask him. Not this moment precisely, but by dinner at least. Or I will tell your mother that Dr. Bertrand is really Mr. Collins, and she will insist that you marry him immediately and save us all!"

She protested but it worked. Four of his daughters had married without much help from him. Now, at least, he could be of assistance.

~~~

After pacing for some time, Mary finally entered the nursery, where Joseph was finishing lunch. "Mummy!"

"Joseph," she said. "Come. We are going to take a walk."

Of course, it was not so easily done, as it was now October and he had to be bundled up properly, something Mary did herself. At last, they made it out the door and walked slowly down the path that circled the grounds. "Joseph," she began, "what do you think of Dr. Bertrand?"

"I like him a lot," he said, looking up at her. "Are you going to marry him?"

Feeling her face go red, she turned away.

"Mother?"

"I'm not sure," she answered. "What do you think? You know that I will always love your father, but that does not mean he is here." She looked down and saw his frown. She stopped in her tracks and knelt down to face him. "What is it?"

"I like Dr. Bertrand. I think he knows a lot of things and he makes you happy and I think he likes me. And I know it's different because my father isn't dead, but Isabel says that after Aunt Bradley remarried, and had her own children with Uncle Bradley, it was *different*. As though…she forgot about them."

"Did George say anything like that?"

"I haven't asked him, but he seems lonely. His brother is a baby!"

She chose her words carefully. "Joseph, you are my son. My wonderful child, my first child. That would never change. Even if I were to have children with Dr. Bertrand, I could not forget about you, not for a second."

"But Aunt—"

"Your aunt is a different person from me," she said. "You realize that, don't you?"
~~~

"Of course."

"Your aunt and I have our different ideas about marriage. Let's leave it at that. Mr. Wickham died and left her penniless and with two young children. Had she had no family, her situation would have been desperate. She *had* to remarry if she was ever to leave Longbourn. But I have no obligation to find someone to take care of me and you. I consider Dr. Bertrand only because he might be a good man to be a father to you. You see how that is different?"

He mulled over it, and then nodded. "But you promise you will always love me, even if you have children and they're really special?"

"*All* children are special. And I do promise." She kissed his cheek. "To my last day, you will be my first concern. I love you." She hugged him. "I love you more than you can imagine." She wiped her tears away before releasing him. She loved her son, but was not given to displays of emotion. "And it will always be that way."

He did seem somewhat convinced. "All right. You can marry him now."

"Darling, I have to wait for *him* to ask *me*."

"Why is that?"

She stood up and they resumed their walk back to the house. "Because that's the way things are done."

"Well, if he doesn't ask, then I'll tell him to!"

"Joseph Bennet, you will do no such thing!"

"All right," he said. Then he mumbled, "But I will if I *have* to."

~ ~ ~

Joseph did not have to. Andrew Bertrand came on time for services on Sunday, and then asked Mary to walk with him to see the changing leaves at Oakham Mount. It would have been hard to argue that a woman with a child needed a chaperone to keep her virtue intact.

"I thought you were Catholic," she said. "What do you think of our services?"

"The last time I went to Mass was for my first Communion," he said.

"But you wouldn't mind—"

"No, I wouldn't mind. Though, people do get sick on Sundays as often as any other."

"So when is your day of rest?"

"When I manage it," he said. "Like now." He stopped in his tracks. "Are you decided?"

"Decided?"

"I apologize, Miss Bennet. You are at times easy to read. Until today, I could not be sure if you had formed an opinion of my character. But now, I'm fairly sure you have."

She said nothing.

"Mary Bennet, will you marry me?"

She looked up into his eyes, hers already welling up. "Yes, Andrew, I will."

They kissed for the first time, with the leaves blowing around them. The kiss was soft and gentle, but lingering. "What would you have done?" Mary said at the end of it.

"What?"

"If I had not come to a decision about your character."

"I would have asked anyway," he said with a smile. "I could hardly have waited any longer."

~ ~ ~

"Well, my goodness," Mr. Bennet said, not rising from his chair as Dr. Bertrand entered. "At least take off your hat first. Manners, Doctor."

Dr. Bertrand blushed and removed his hat and gloves.

"Technically, you do not need my consent," he said. "She is of age. But as her inheritance is somewhat conditional, you might want to ask for it."

"I am not after her inheritance," he said. "But I would like your consent to marry Miss Bennet."

"The last one," he said somberly. "The last Miss Bennet there is, and shall ever be in my lifetime." He shook his head. "But of course, you have my consent." They shook on it. "There is, of course, the matter of your profession as a royal physician."

Dr. Bertrand had prepared for this. "Dr. Maddox and I have already discussed it. Because it is Mary's intention to live in Longbourn until your, um—"

"Long-predicted death, yes. Go on."

"Yes. Well, of course, I do not propose otherwise, though I may be in Town for a few days every now and again. Or we may just hire someone new to add to the staff. Either way, it will be worked out to everyone's satisfaction."

"Except perhaps the Prince's, what with his doctors always abandoning him," Mr. Bennet said. "But my chief concern is my daughter and grandson and *your* concern is now my daughter and grandson. The inheritance, however, is still conditional. You will receive fifty thousand pounds with the marriage, and the other half when I die."

Dr. Bertrand was dumbstruck.

"Joseph's father was quite generous in the settlement for ruining my daughter's virtue and reputation," he said. "I confess that Longbourn was a shack compared with what it is now, and I was a man who was nearing debt, but we have been living happily off the interest from the account—that and only one daughter to support. Two, when Lydia was still mourning Mr. Wickham, but she was hardly doing *that*." He studied Bertrand's expression. "You really had no idea. No suspicions whatsoever."

"I knew about the trust for Joseph."

"Yes. And he gave that before the child was born. Mr. Mastai—that is his name, though we never utter it here—is very penitent. Perhaps because he is supposed to be celibate. Yes, Mary had possibly the largest dowry in England, but we never made it public. If she had wanted to, we would have. You've struck gold, Dr. Bertrand."

"With all due respect, Mr. Bennet, that is not the real gold I struck today," he said. "And my name is Andrew."

~ ~ ~

Although the engagement of Dr. Bertrand and Mary Bennet was no surprise to the Derbyshire crowd, it was an excitement nonetheless, especially in Elizabeth's dull days with Darcy gone. Well, they were hardly *dull,* with one son and three daughters, but they were less full.

"Where will we spend Christmas?" Jane asked as she sat with her sister on the terrace of Kirkland, discussing the news. "The wedding is close enough that we must stay in Hertfordshire."

"If Hertfordshire can hold us. And if they do not have a Town wedding," Elizabeth said. "She writes that they have not decided. His parents may demand it. Or the very opposite, when they see the English commoners that their son is marrying into." She was interrupted by Monkey jumping up on the serving table and grabbing a scone in his mouth. "Monkey!"

"What's this about English commoners?" Bingley said, as Monkey's arrival could only mean that he was not far behind.

"Dr. Bertrand's parents are French nobility. Their name isn't even Bertrand. They changed it while hiding during the Revolution. So they must not think much of us, whatever our fortune," Elizabeth said.

"Is that right?" Jane said, reaching for her husband's arm as he stood by her side and Monkey climbed back up onto his shoulder, taking the scone with him. "Would they consider us commoners?"

"To be noble, you must have more ball gowns than you could ever wear and be deep in very fashionable debt. You are neither, my dear, so I suppose we do not fit the bill and are unsuitable company for Mr. and Mrs. Bertrand," he said. "What's this about the wedding? Finally?"

"I think the only one still in a state of indecision was Mary," Elizabeth said. "The rest of us were soundly aligned long ago. What a family she had to contend with!"

"He is a sweet man," Jane said. "And he helped to save Grégoire's life."

"Speaking of him," Bingley said. "Any idea when they'll be back from—where did they go, Scotland?"

"The Isle of Man."

"The Isle of Man?" Bingley shrugged. Darcy had many holdings in many places and didn't discuss them. "So—any news?"

"The last I heard, they would stay for a few days. If they've written to say that they've departed, it has not yet reached me, sadly," Elizabeth said.

"Well, I suppose we'll hear soon. Mrs. Darcy." He bowed with as much dignity as he could with Monkey clinging to his arm, and went back inside. He and Georgie had just returned from the visit with the Maddoxes, and he had been restless ever since.

"Your husband has lost his playmate," Elizabeth said, and Jane did her best not to laugh about the reference to Darcy's absence. She was not entirely successful.

~ ~ ~

The post being what it was, Elizabeth received a letter that they were leaving the island to come home only a day before they made their reappearance. The Darcy carriage was followed by wagons of shipping boxes, and one carrying a wooden box that could almost be mistaken for a coffin. But as both brothers got out of the carriage, it could hardly be that.

"Papa!" Because her legs were longer, it was Sarah, not Cassandra, who made it to Darcy first. Anne Darcy was now seven and did not run around like an enthusiastic toddler. Most of the time, that was. She was third, though, to greet her papa. Then the adults emerged to welcome Darcy and Grégoire.

"Lizzy," he said with his second daughter in his arms, and leaned over to kiss his wife on the cheek. "Georgiana. Lord Kincaid."

"Mr. Darcy. Mr. Grégoire," Lord Kincaid said. "I trust the trip was a success."

"Yes," Grégoire said. "We stayed only long enough to reclaim some personal items left on the site before it could be sold."

"Books," Darcy said. "Lots of books." He turned to Mr. Reed, who stood quietly at his side. "Have the last wagon brought up alongside the chapel."

As they entered, Darcy and Grégoire were brought up on the latest news about the engagement, which delighted Grégoire. Darcy said that it was a fine—a very fine—choice. "Where is Geoffrey?"

"He is at Kirkland," Elizabeth explained, and they sent someone to summon him. As they left to refresh themselves from a long journey, Darcy made a strange request—that Elizabeth, Georgiana, and Geoffrey join them in the chapel at two. They said yes, and he left to get cleaned up.

An hour later, the specified people gathered in the tiny chapel. Elizabeth realized that everyone but she was a Darcy by blood, and Lord Kincaid had been excluded.

"Geoffrey," Darcy said gravely, "we decided that you're old enough to be part of this, but you're not to say a word of this to anyone without our permission." He cleared his throat. "Even Miss Georgiana Bingley. Understood?"

Geoffrey nodded.

Darcy sighed and continued, with a look of encouragement from his brother. "Our father—Geoffrey Darcy—had an older brother. We had an uncle. His name was Gregory."

"Why have I never heard of him?" Georgiana asked. "When did he die?"

"You were two," he said, "and by then, any traces of him had already been erased from Pemberley's records. I knew of him because I met him twice, first when I was a little boy and again when I was fifteen, just before he died. On the Isle of Man." He continued before they could question him further. "He was mad. His death was faked when he was of age and he was removed from the records so it wouldn't…hurt our father's marriage prospects. By the time of your birth, Georgiana, the only ones who knew of him were our father, our mother, and me. The house where he lived remained in the ledgers until recently, when someone made an offer for it. And seeing that Father named Grégoire after his brother, whom he loved very much, I decided to…take him there."

"He left a journal," Grégoire said as the audience sat quietly, attempting to absorb this terrible information. "When he was a child, he was raised to be master of Pemberley, but when he started showing signs of mental illness, a doctor was brought in who probably drove him mad with his treatments. When he turned seventeen, he asked to be disinherited. Father would inherit, and Uncle Gregory would disappear. All of Gregory's portraits were burned. The only ones we have are some tiny ones we found on the island."

Georgiana was the first person to speak. "Darcy—you met him! While I was alive! Why didn't you tell me when I came of age?"

"Father told me never to speak of him, and I listened," he said quietly. "I would never have spoken of him again, but this sale came up. It was the way they both wanted it. Georgiana, I'm sorry. I truly am."

Elizabeth raised her objection. "Why did you not tell us when—"

"I did tell Dr. Maddox," he interrupted. "I told him in Austria, when I lost my senses. I made him swear never to speak of it to anyone. Apparently, he kept that promise."

They fell into an uncomfortable silence, each with his or her own thoughts. Elizabeth looked at her husband. He looked tired, and not from traveling.

"We decided—if everyone here agrees—that he should be written back into the family," Grégoire said. "Or, at the very least, reburied here at Pemberley. Along with all of his books and his notes and his personal effects, we've brought *him*. What's left of his body, that is."

"Did he want that?"

"We'll never know," Darcy answered. "He never said, and there's no one alive who can answer that question. Geoffrey, you are not to tell your sisters what happened to Uncle Gregory and why he lived far away. Your mother and I will tell them when they're old enough. And Georgiana, you should tell your husband."

She nodded numbly.

"I'll tell George," he added. "Just him. He deserves to know the whole of it." He didn't need to say why. Those who knew understood perfectly.

They filed out in silence, each with his or her own thoughts. It was time for Grégoire's prayer. So their last wagon had been carrying a casket after all, even if it was filled only with bones.

The next day, they had the workers from the Isle of Man pull the edge of one side of the fence around the Pemberley graveyard back far enough to dig a grave. The tombstone would come later. Grégoire put up a wooden cross with his uncle's name on it. For the time being, it would suffice.

"Why can't he be buried alongside Father?" Georgiana whispered to Darcy.

"Because he can't be buried in consecrated ground," he said. "He committed suicide."

She leaned into him, and he hugged his little sister as a local vicar said prayers over the barely covered grave. Gregory Darcy, lost for so many years, was finally buried in his home soil, near generations who had come before him and leaving space for generations who would come after him.

CHAPTER 25

The Last Bennet Girl

ON DECEMBER 15, 1817, Dr. Andrew Bertrand and Mary Bennet were joined in marriage in the same church where her four sisters had all been wedded to their *current* husbands. As Mr. Bennet gave away his last daughter, there was nary a dry female eye in the house. Normally, children were not invited to a wedding ceremony, but an exception was made for Joseph, who looked nervous until his mother smiled at him as she walked down the aisle.

Dr. Bertrand's parents did attend the wedding, and made a point of speaking only French at the wedding breakfast afterward. To their horror, almost all of the people present spoke at least some French, and understood them perfectly. The newly married couple were too happy to be distracted, and no major social disasters occurred before they left for a week in Town, leaving Joseph behind (in a shower of kisses) with his family.

Christmas, it had been decided, would be at Longbourn this year—no one would be missing, no one abroad, no one ill (aside from Mrs. Bennet, but they were all adjusted to that reality), no one dying, and no one ready to give birth. For that, everyone was grateful. All five former Bennet sisters under one roof, with their children and husbands, were quite enough. Lord and Lady Kincaid had returned to Scotland, taking Grégoire with them for a time. The Hursts and Dr. Daniel Maddox and Caroline Maddox, along with their children, were at Brian and Princess Nadezhda's estate.

Some of the children were not happy with this news. They loved their crazy aunt and uncle and their crazy guest. "Christmas comes every year," Bingley reminded his children. "If you got *everything* you wanted one year, then the others wouldn't be special."

The Bertrands returned in time to complete the party. Charles and Eliza Bingley turned eleven, and Charlie Bingley seemed surprised that he did not wake up taller that very morning. He was evidently jealous of Geoffrey, who was now starting to look what was deemed "adult-size." Georgie gave Geoffrey an occasional cold look, as she had always been taller and now it was no longer so, and probably would never be again. She did not verbalize her feelings; he understood it perfectly well without a word. And George, of course, was only a year or so away from officially being welcomed into the parlor, and an additional year from being a man of great wealth. All he had to do was hold any of his cousins' foreheads at arm's length and they would be unable to touch him, to the amusement of everyone but the person trying to do it.

"George, stop showing off!" his sister said. He smiled, which was a rare thing.

So great was the confusion with so many children and so many nurses that the older ones managed to liberate themselves from authority while their parents dined and the younger ones wailed. They gathered in the library, mainly because it was available and no one would likely come looking for them there, and feasted on all of the Christmas pudding that Charles and Geoffrey, in a concentrated effort, had managed to sneak from the kitchen.

"Monkey, no! Not for you!" Eliza Bingley screamed as he leaped into the pudding."

"Oh, now we can't eat it," Geoffrey said. "I'm not eating monkey pudding!"

From his position, an inch deep in the pudding, Monkey just howled at him.

"You have to be nice to him," Charles said, "or he'll—" and that was when Monkey, half covered in chocolate pudding, leaped right onto his arm, ran up his shoulder, and made a nest of his blond hair. A muddy, chocolate nest. "Make a mess."

"I'll get him off," Georgiana offered.

"It'll make it worse," Charles said. "Might as well let him sit there until I find somewhere to dunk him. Monkey! Sit!" And Monkey lay down on his head, which took some grappling. "Mrs. Murrey is going to be so mad."

"Who's Mrs. Murrey?" George asked.

"Our governess," Eliza said. "And she wouldn't be as mad at you as she would at us."

"I didn't know you had a governess."

"It's for Georgiana," Eliza said, at which Georgiana Bingley sneered. "*And* for me. And for Charles, because his penmanship is so bad that even his tutor can't get him to correct it."

"Hey!"

"Enough. You know it's true. And you don't even try."

"I *am* trying!"

Isabel said to Geoffrey, "Do you have a governess?"

"I have tutors. When Anne turns ten my parents said they'll hire one. They've been putting it off."

"Because governesses are royal pains in the—"

"Georgie!"

Georgiana just frowned and slumped into the armchair.

"Georgie doesn't much care for Mrs. Murrey," Eliza announced.

"The feeling is mutual," her older sister said with a grumble.

"Well, if you're just going to complain all night, I'm going to enjoy myself," George said and pulled back what was apparently a false set of books to reveal a bottle of port and several small glasses.

"George!" Eliza cried in shock!"

"How did you even know this was here?" Geoffrey said, transfixed.

"I used to live here, remember?" he said as he poured himself a glass. "Why are you all looking at me? I'm not three and ten for nothing."

"I want some!" Charles said, jumping to his feet.

"Absolutely not. Would be terribly irresponsible of me," George said, towering over his cousin.

"He can have a sip and see how foul it tastes," Georgiana said to their surprise. She was normally protective of her younger siblings.

She was correct in her assumption, however, as George let Charles take a tiny sip of port, which he spat out. "This is terrible!"

"When you have an adult tongue you won't think so," George said.

"Adult! You're lording your year over us just because your mother got a head start," Georgiana said. "Give me a glass."

"A glass!"

"C'mon! 'Snot like I've never had whiskey before."

He held up the bottle. "This is *port*. You can tell by the color."

"Well, how would I know?"

"You just said you were a scholar of the spiritual arts!"

"Spiritual arts? What is this nonsense? One glass and you're cup-shot!"

"*How would you even know?*" George spat back. Geoffrey took the bottle out of his hands. "No, I really want to know!"

"Good Lord, you are a toper," Geoffrey said, pouring himself a half shot glass of port and downing it with a frown of distaste. "We got slightly drunk on her last birthday, when everyone else had gone to sleep and her father was in India. She said she was lonely."

"I was!" Georgie said.

"Where was I?" Charles asked, leaning for the bottle, but Geoffrey put it way on the top shelf, far out of his reach. Monkey finally leaped off Charles's head and went right up on the top shelf with the closed bottle.

"Asleep in your cradle," Georgiana said.

"I do not have a cradle! Edmund has a cradle."

"Well, the point is, you were asleep. And so was Mama. And the Darcys were over, remember? To make it seem as though Papa weren't gone. But then *they* went to sleep and we got drunk."

"*You* did," Geoffrey said. "I could still—pronounce things. And stand."

"Stand!"

"I had to carry you back to your room," he said, and Georgiana colored. "Sorry. I wasn't supposed to tell, was I?"

She just turned away from him and crossed her arms.

"I—I think it's lovely," George said, smiling. Unlike Geoffrey, he had had a full glass on an empty stomach.

"What do you mean, lovely?" Geoffrey replied, confused.

"You'll understand—when you're *older*," George said, slapping him on the shoulder.

"You drunk," Georgiana said. "You're going to turn into your father."

It was not the right thing to say in front of George Wickham. Geoffrey could only move fast enough to barely keep George from getting his hands around Georgiana's throat. "Don't you *ever say that!*"

"George—" Isabella pleaded softly.

"Let me go!" he shouted, in a louder voice than they had ever heard from him. He was taller than Geoffrey, but he lived in Town and his main preoccupation was reading. Geoffrey fenced, rode, and shot, and he had inched upward from his growth spurt, too, so he was fairly successful at knocking George against the bookshelf and holding him there. "She has to take it back! Let me go!"

"I will not let you touch her," Geoffrey said calmly and quietly as he held him back. Books were coming down off the case now.

"Geoffrey!" Georgiana said.

"My father may have been a drunk," George said, "but *your* father is a murderer!"

There was no one who could move quickly enough to stop Geoffrey Darcy from dropping his hold on his cousin and instead punching him in the chest. George doubled over and dropped to his knees, to be caught by his sister just in time.

No one said a word. There was just Geoffrey's heavy breathing, the girls frightened in their seats, and George coughing up alcohol.

"Geoffrey Darcy!" Georgiana said. "What did you do?"

He rushed to explain himself, "He—he called my dad a murderer; what was I *supposed* to do?"

"Your father *is* a murderer!" she said, rising to George's defense. Perhaps out of a bit of guilt. "And my papa is a sop. And George's father was a drunk and a gambler and now he's dead. So what? It doesn't matter to us." She turned to George—who could get his head up only with the help of his sister—and curtsied. "Mr. Wickham, I'm sorry I called Uncle Wickham a drunk."

"You shouldn't speak ill of the dead," Charles said.

"*Or* the living, if they're relatives," she said, and turned to Geoffrey. "You've got all your tutors telling you things. What's the master of Pemberley supposed to do when he punches his cousin?"

"I—he's supposed to apologize, I suppose," he said, trembling. Georgiana's disapproving stare could do that to him. "George, I'm sorry. I got upset."

George just nodded. He had stopped coughing up things, and Geoffrey picked him up and helped him into an armchair. "I know," George said quietly. "I—got upset, too."

"I've never seen you attack anyone," Isabel said. "What were you thinking?"

He was too rattled to answer anything but the truth: "I don't want to turn into my father."

"For God's sake, you're nothing like your father, and we all know it, even if we don't remember him very well," Georgiana said.

"Or at all," Charles said.

Monkey squawked and leaped from the shelf. Actually, it was not so much a leap as a drop; only Georgiana's reflexes saved him as she caught him. "Monkey! You're drunk!"

They looked up, and indeed, the bottle cork had been removed, and the port spilled out onto the shelf.

George was the first to start laughing. It was not long before they all joined in. Monkey was passed to Eliza, who held him like a doll. "Monkey?" But Monkey just squealed and pawed for a strand of her hair but failed to grasp it. "Monkey! Oh, what if he has a headache in the morning? We don't have any monkey medicine!"

They laughed until their sides hurt, because it felt good, even with their sides actually hurting. Then the night really set in, with the fire going low, and Georgiana told her younger siblings to go to bed. "I am sorry," she told George, kissing him on the cheek before carrying off a sleeping Monkey in her arms.

"I'll be fine," George told his sister, and she hurried off to bed. He stayed in his armchair for a bit while Geoffrey played with the fire, bringing it back up a bit.

"I am sorry," Geoffrey said, wringing his hands. "Very sorry."

"I know."

"I know my father is a murderer. He feels bad about it, but he is."

"I know. I mean, I know he feels bad." George's head lolled to one side. He was still clutching his stomach as Geoffrey pulled up a chair across from him. "And I know my father—had it coming. My mother won't stop talking about it."

Geoffrey couldn't imagine what it would be like to have a mother like that. His mother never said *anything* that didn't seem to be funny or clever or comforting. "You're not like him. You're like Father—quiet, respectable, intelligent. No head for alcohol."

George smiled. "True, I suppose. But that's just because I'm not—I don't have friends beyond my family. I'm not *sociable.*"

"Like Uncle Gregory?"

"You mean Uncle Grégoire? You can't pronounce his name?"

"No, I mean—Oh, God. He said he was going to tell you."

"Who?"

"Father," Geoffrey said in a panic. "He said he was going to tell you about Great-Uncle Gregory. But—I guess he hasn't had a chance."

"I did just get here. Who's this Gregory?"

"God, no. I shouldn't be talking about this."

"Now you *have to*. You've said it. You can't leave me there."

Geoffrey stood up, collected what was left of the bottle, and poured himself another half glass. "You did not hear this from me."

"Then who did I hear it from?"

He ignored the comment. "Father came home from this trip and just announced that he had this uncle that nobody knew about. Our grandfather's elder brother. He lived in some kind of island asylum. He was mad, and they covered up his existence so that Grandfather could inherit Pemberley instead and find a good prospect for marriage. You know, he couldn't do that if anyone knew there was *illness* in our family." He finished the glass and put it aside. "Great-Uncle Gregory left all these journals—and Father and Grégoire found them and read them and decided to bring his bones back to Pemberley. But they couldn't bury him in the graveyard proper because he committed suicide." He squinted. "What sort of nonsense is that?"

"Which part?" George said, intrigued. "The leftover papist nonsense or the nonsense about worrying about marriage prospects?"

"I don't know," Geoffrey said. "I wasn't supposed to tell you this. Father probably has an appropriate speech prepared. He wasn't going to tell Isabel. I don't even know why—"

George interrupted him. "No. I know why." He shook his head. "My mother said that your father—they almost put him away after he came home from Austria."

"I don't know—maybe—they kept me out of it. I just know that Father was sick, but he recovered." He said, "Aunt Bradley talks too much."

"I know. But she says interesting things," he replied. "I don't want to fight with you over our fathers. Or our grandfather. Or anyone else."

"I know." It was Geoffrey's turn to say that.

"They were all fools and it's in the past. Can we leave it at that?"

"Yes." Geoffrey offered his hand. "You need help to your room?"

"Do you?"

They shared a laugh, and slowly meandered back to their quarters, both a little tipsy. And leaving the mess behind them.

~ ~ ~

"Charles?"

"Mmm?"

"What did I say about Monkey in my chamber?"

It took him a moment to recall. When she said his name, after all, he had been fast asleep, and waking up beside his wife the day after Christmas, he didn't wish to be alarmed by anything. He snaked his arm across her belly. "Why do you ask?"

"Open your eyes, dear."

Reluctantly he complied, and his eyes came to focus on Monkey, sleeping on their pristine white sheets in the space between their legs. He was mostly covered in something brown that looked like mud and his trail to the bed was obvious by the tracks. "Monkey?"

No response.

He sat up and picked up his animal, who stirred with a little squeal and then settled into his chest, and he lay back down.

"Charles?"

"What? Oh, come on, he's been so good as of late, we can't—Is that chocolate? It smells like it. And something else, too." He picked off a mushy lump and licked it. "It's Christmas pudding. And…port, I think."

Jane cracked a smile. "Do we even want to know why our animal is covered in Christmas pudding and spirits?"

"So you admit he's *our* animal?"

"Only if you will bother to notice he's staining your lovely Indian bedclothes."

He patted Monkey on the head. "I would, but as it seems I will be spending the day interrogating our children as to how this came to be, which is not something I relish, I will enjoy this moment, in bed with my wife and a chocolate-covered, possibly hung-over monkey."

~ ~ ~

Many hours later, when it was all sorted out that some of the children had gotten into the port and the pudding and then let

Monkey into both (the last being hardly the least of their crimes), the children were sent to their respective chambers to sit (on pillows) and think about what they had done, and their parents were left to endure the laughter from the parents of the children who *had* behaved.

"The first time I was drunk was with Wickham, and I was but nine," Darcy said. "So we must keep a sense of perspective."

Eventually, the animosity between parents and naughty children receded, and life returned to normal as they awaited the approach of the New Year. It was during that period that it snowed at Longbourn, to the delight of the children. While most of the staff were outside, making sure that the children didn't hurt themselves or get sick, Darcy noticed that George was alone in the library (where the mess had been thoroughly cleaned up and the port moved), staring out the window as his younger cousins played.

"George," he said, "there is something I should tell you."

George did his best to hide that he knew something of what was coming. Fortunately, it turned out that there was enough new information to intrigue him. Either Geoffrey did not know the half of it, did not understand it, or had not been told the contents of Great-Uncle Gregory's journal. Each possibility could be real, but he did not speculate. There was too much to think on.

His Uncle Darcy's unspoken message was clear; he understood Gregory Darcy's suffering and he knew that George did, too, on a level that the others didn't. It was just too painful to actually say.

"Our conclusion," Darcy said, "was that what could have been a minor social handicap was exacerbated by incompetent doctoring. Many people would be driven mad by the treatments he describes. He even wrote that he begged your grandfather to stop the treatments, and he agreed." This was not an easy subject for either of them. Darcy mostly looked away, out the window or toward the fireplace. "For all of my father's faults, which are detailed in the journals, I believe he did learn from watching his brother suffer, and could not bear to subject me to the same thing. Which is why

I am here today, a family man with a wonderful marriage, a healthy estate, and a horde of screaming children. And not on some island."

"I don't want this burden," George said in despair.

"I know." Darcy put a hand on his nephew's shoulder. "But you have something that Gregory did not have—you are not alone. And never will be. That, I promise you."

Fitzwilliam Darcy was not known to make promises lightly. That knowledge alone made it so much easier to bear.

CHAPTER 26

A Sight for Sore Eyes

~ ~ ~

GRÉGOIRE, WHO HAD NEVER been so far north, passed the holidays with the Kincaids at their estate in ____shire. Not only could he shower attention on his youngest nephew, he also found that William Kincaid was a scholar in his two favorite subjects, religion and history. William Kincaid was a staunch Presbyterian, but only in the way that debates with Grégoire amused him. One afternoon in early January, they discussed predestination: people were selected for heaven before they were born and there was nothing anyone could do to change their fate.

"We must assume that the Lord knows who is saved and who is damned before they are even born, because he is omnipotent. So our fates are decided."

"Not *decided*," Grégoire said. "Just *known*. I still prefer to think that my actions in this life determine my fate in the next life. Otherwise, we're wasting our time, and might as well be off fishing or something."

"The lake is frozen."

"Then skating. I don't know!"

"So we have reached a tie," Kincaid said as his wife entered, carrying their son. "Dearest, you must settle this debate for us. We need a deciding vote."

"There is no tie! You just refuse to give in to logic!"

Georgiana cast an amused glance at her brother, and then said, "And what are we debating?"

"If we have any chance of salvation by being good people or if we should all just go skating instead," Kincaid said. "Or ice fishing. Yes. I suppose we could do that."

"Can't we do both?" she said. "Go skating and still go to heaven?"

"I like her opinion," Grégoire said.

"I agree," Kincaid said. "Georgiana, you have won the day."

"Then be a dear and take our son off my hands for a few minutes!"

"Let me," Grégoire offered, and took the infant into his arms. Robert was now six months, and could stand—with help—on Grégoire's knees. "Look at you. Are you bothering your mother?" Robert giggled as Grégoire tickled his stomach. Georgiana took a seat at their long table and poured herself a cup of tea.

"You're so talented with children," William said. "I suppose your family has already mentioned the idea of having some of your own."

"Mentioned it, yes," Grégoire said. "I...well, I was never in a position to think of such things before. Besides, there are many orphans who need a parent."

William shook his head. "You're so intent to bypass the fun part? There's a worthwhile debate with a logical conclusion."

Grégoire just blushed, and Georgiana put a hand over her husband's own. "Leave my poor brother alone. He gets enough of this from Darcy." She turned to her brother. "Do you have any more mundane ideas for what you might like to do in the spring?"

"Yes," he said. "Go to Ireland."

"Indeed!" his sister replied.

"I have traveled most extensively, but never on my own and without a Rule to guide me. And I have never been to Ireland. St. Bede wrote extensively about his travels and their merits."

William shook his head.

"Yes, the father of English history," Grégoire said. "Excuse me, the father of the history of those invading Saxon bastards."

"Grégoire!" Georgiana cried, but her reaction was muted by the sound of her husband's laughter.

"So," William Kincaid said, "what is it about St. Bede and Ireland?"

Grégoire balanced his nephew on one knee. "He never visited the place, but he knew of it, and the church there, which had yet to be fully Latinized. There are many holy sites in Ireland."

"You want to make a pilgrimage, then?"

"I doubt that any of the sites are still there except the actual ground itself," Grégoire said, "but yes, perhaps I do."

The Darcys and the Bingleys returned before the hard snows set in, but when they did, they received no visitors, only the occasional postman with a stack of late letters. Grégoire had returned in time as well, and for months they were all prisoners together within the walls of Pemberley, emerging only occasionally to go to Kirkland or Lambton, but no farther.

In February, an alarming letter came in the post. Or, it would have been alarming, had it been phrased in a less nonchalant manner, but as the authoress was Caroline Maddox, the offhandedness could only be expected. It was sent to Jane, with permission to give the news to her family and the Darcys.

Dear Sister,

Forgive the delay in this information, but we decided not to tell anyone until the procedure was all over, so as to not leave you in unnecessary suspense.

Two weeks ago, Dr. Maddox consulted his physician about the loss of some vision in his left eye, which was apparently caused by a cataract. Fortunately, the doctor whose specialty is this particular surgery was in town to treat His Majesty, and did the procedure here instead of making Dr. Maddox go up to Cambridge for it. It was a brief procedure, but we will not know the results for a few weeks. Frederick and Emily are taking great delight in calling their father a pirate until that day comes.

If the roads clear and you feel compelled to visit, do not feel so obligated, because Dr. Maddox is intolerably cranky. He has refused to use pain medicine, the one exception being the day of the procedure. He is staring at me this very second, and in a moment he may inquire what I'm writing about him.

The chances of infection are low, but please remember him in your prayers. Mr. Maddox and Her Highness (and, unfortunately, Mr. Mugin) are keeping us company to help pass the time.

Caroline Maddox

They replied that, of course, they would keep him in their hearts and minds and await further news. Many people went blind in their old age. But Dr. Maddox was not old, and had said on any number of occasions that he was determined to see his daughter go out, and that was that.

~ ~ ~

"A sorry lot we are," Brian said to his brother, who was attempting to read the paper. "I'm a cripple and you're missing bits and pieces. We have opium and someone's keeping it locked up as though he were the chief guard of the Tower of London—"

"If you have any lingering pains, please tell me," his brother said calmly.

"I *did*."

"Well, this time, don't be such a noticeable liar."

Brian laughed. Dr. Maddox did not. "Is there anything to do around here that does not involve reading?" he asked.

"At your house?" Brian replied. "Hardly—though I could give you some suggestions, but you would find them all rather improper," he said as he poured Daniel another glass of whiskey. "Why don't you visit your infamous patient?"

"He's just been lying in bed, crying since his daughter died," Dr. Maddox said. "The illness is not physical. In addition, he would laugh at me." He did look ridiculous with a cloth patch over his eye and a bandage tied around his head to keep the patch in place.

"You'd be comforting a mourner."

"I failed to do so when I was in perfect health. I see no reason why I should do it now."

"Are we just going to argue all day?"

"We're hardly *arguing.*"

"You're contradicting everything I say."

"That's your imagination."

"There you go again." He stood up and opened the door, just in time to catch Mrs. Maddox about to enter. "Mrs. Maddox."

"Mr. Maddox. What are you up to?"

"Well, I tried to get your husband drunk, but he hasn't had the second glass yet. Maybe I'll shut the door and you'll be more persuasive."

"Bugger off," the doctor said. He did, however, take another sip. As Brian left, Caroline kissed her husband on the part of his head that wasn't bandaged and sat down next to him.

"It is ten in the morning," she pointed out.

"And this is Town. Plenty of people are cup-shot at ten in the morning."

She put her hand on his forehead. "No fever. What else am I supposed to ask you?"

"Is there any pus leaking from the eye?"

"Oh yes. Is there?"

"For the record, no." He put his hand over hers. "I feel completely fine in every respect that you should be concerned about."

"Not every respect that I'm concerned about."

"You know what I mean."

She smiled slightly. "Finish your whiskey. Perhaps you should get drunk—you might be less argumentative."

He finished the glass and pulled her into him. Even through all his layers of warm clothing, she could still feel his heart beating as he whispered, "I'm sorry."

"I know," she replied, her voice softer. "You're suffering."

"I'm worried," he said. "This will be the second time. And I'm older now. Maybe I won't be so lucky."

"You have another eye."

"It's not particularly good."

"You *are* being argumentative," she said, but without any dismissal in her tone. "You promised you would make it to Emily's presentation before court, and I'm not sending my only daughter out when she's fifteen, like some country girl."

"I wanted to make it to her wedding, but I like making reasonable goals," he said. "And I am also rather fond of watching my *other* children grow up."

She smiled. "But you won't see me wrinkle up into a knobby old woman with horribly dyed hair."

"I will not stand for that," he said. "I love the smell of your hair. If you dare dye it, even tomorrow, I will not speak to you for a week."

"You would not. You could not."

"I would try."

She managed to laugh. Daniel was silent, but she sensed that some of the tension was gone from him. Every day, his pain decreased a little and his anxiety about the results increased some more. It was a horrible balance.

"The last time I did this," he said, "I didn't have a wife to comfort me. Despite my mood, I *much* prefer my conditions this time around."

One crabby week later, and after many conspiracies to drug Dr. Maddox's tea (all of which he discovered before they could come to fruition), it was time to visit Dr. Hunt at the Royal Society of Medicine house. Daniel Maddox was very methodical that morning in his usual preparations. Dr. Hunt, like most doctors, did not believe in washing around the eye, but Dr. Maddox did, as close as he could get. By the end of it, his hands were shaking.

"Your eye will be fine," his wife said. They had not removed the bandage, so he had no idea if the eye worked.

"And if it's not?"

"Your eye? It's not as if you don't have another one."

He smiled and kissed her. "I will try to remember that."

It was Brian who took him to the doctor. It was as if he were four and ten again and Brian were his guardian. He was there to stand by him (but this time, not hold his hand) when the doctor removed the patch and inspected his eye—all of which, he could see. There was a quick exam of his distance vision with cards, and he was declared, aside from his severe myopia, to be in good visual health.

But his real joy came when he arrived home and his children ran down the stairs. Little Danny outpaced the other two in his excitement. "Father!" He was small enough to still be picked up.

"Look at you," he said.

"A sight for sore eyes," Brian said.

The servants, who held their master in esteem, were all relieved and quickly set him down with something to drink for his tribulations. He toasted with his brother, wife, and sister-in-law.

"You know," he said to his sons, "one reason I became interested in medicine was because I went to so many doctors when I was a child. Do either of you want to be doctors?"

"I want to be a samurai!" Danny said, to which Brian laughed, earning himself a frown from everyone else in the room.

"I want to be a fencing champion!" Frederick said.

"I think I liked the samurai idea better," Caroline replied. "At least it involves some bizarre honor system."

"At least it involves regular exercise," said Dr. Maddox.

"At least he didn't say he wanted to be king," whispered Brian, and his brother was in too good of a mood to do anything but laugh.

Winter eventually became spring, and the snow and ice melted, and once again the roads were cleared for travel. The early spring was a time for many birthdays, the most significant being Georgiana's and Geoffrey's, who both turned three and ten. The following fall, Geoffrey would be attending Eton. Georgie now hovered in the precarious stage where she was no longer a child and not yet a woman, when she had to wear a wide-brimmed hat and not talk to men in the streets or even be introduced. Whether she resented any of this or not, she said nothing.

George came up to Derbyshire for their birthdays. When asked what he was doing alone, he replied that his mother didn't care where he went and then quickly changed the subject. At the end of Geoffrey Darcy's first day as someone three and ten, young Mr. Darcy and young Mr. Wickham stayed up much later than the rest of the household and helped themselves to the good whiskey that the older Mr. Darcy kept in his study, having learned the lesson about port well enough. By sunrise, they were still awake and utterly in their cups. Whatever rift caused by the fight at Christmas had been mended. When Master Darcy rose, Mrs. Reynolds quietly informed him that his son had been found passed out cold on the terrace, and would probably sleep through the whole day. The master's reaction to this was uncharacteristically mild. He did speak to Nurse and told her that when Geoffrey was to be woken (preferably by dinner), it should be done very loudly, with some kind of drum if at all possible. Otherwise, he had no comment.

At the end of March, when all of the significant dates had passed, Grégoire Bellamont was seen off. Darcy went with him all the way to the coast, where he would take a boat to Ireland. He had spent months reading literature on the land and the history of its church. On more than one occasion, Elizabeth had to quietly remind her husband, "He is a grown man and can do as he pleases," as he tried to oppose Grégoire's plan.

This time, Grégoire took something besides his prayer book, his spectacles, and his cloak. He took a bag of money—his own money, from his own account. Some had already been sent to Dublin, where it would sit in an account if he needed access to it. His route was established and he would write if he varied from it, so it would be not so hard to find him. Darcy had declared that he would let him go only with Dr. Maddox's permission. Unfortunately, the doctor would not be in on the conspiracy and said Grégoire was well enough to travel. It had been more than eight months since his injuries and though his back was mainly scar tissue, it did not cause him pain or impede his movement.

"When can we expect you back?" Darcy said as they walked along the docks to the waiting ship.

"When I find what I'm looking for," he replied.

"And what are you looking for?"

"That, I also must find." He shook hands with Darcy. "Good-bye, Brother."

"Write me if you get into trouble. Or if you need anything. Or if you get sick. Or if—"

"I will write."

Darcy nodded, composing himself. "Good-bye. And good luck." He added, nervously, "Go with…God."

Grégoire smiled from the plank. "I will do my best."

CHAPTER 27

Saint in a Box

~ ~ ~

"SIR, ARE YEH AL' RIGHT?"

Grégoire was not. The walk from Dublin to Drogheda had worn him out. Usually, walking thirty miles over two days would have been no trouble for him, but perhaps he had not recovered as well from the previous summer as he had presumed. He was still standing only because of his staff. "Yes." His voice said otherwise, and he looked sideways at the priest who had come up from behind him. "Just let me—" Without question, the priest came and helped him to the pew before the shrine. He cried out as his back hit the hard wood. "I will be fine. Thank you."

Now that he was sitting, he was sure he would be all right. He still could see the gorgeous shrine before him, with the afternoon sun just coming through the stained glass, and all the candles lit around the relic. Behind the glass was the head of Oliver Plunkett, the Catholic protestor who had been martyred by English authorities in 1681. There was talk about making him a saint, but nothing could be done without England's consent, and England would hardly consent. Or, that was what the man at the entrance told him in a thick brogue.

Grégoire crossed himself. He had missed Mass, as it was already late afternoon when he arrived, but he heard one in Dublin the day before and to his great delight. The last Catholic Mass he had heard was in July of the previous year.

"Yeh al' right?"

This time, it came from the man next to him, who had just sat down. This man was no priest, just an ordinary fellow in shabby clothing who had knelt before the altar first. "I'm a little tired."

"Yeh nade a draink?"

He nodded.

The man passed him a flask, which apparently contained very watery whiskey, which quenched his thirst somewhat, even though it lit a fire in his throat. "Thank you," he whispered, passing it back to him.

"Wha yeh from, fella? Yisser accent is fierce quare."

"Lots of places," he said. "France. England. Bavaria. Spain. Pick what you like."

"Been travelin' donkey's years, den?"

He nodded again. "Yes." He felt better now, sitting, and with the whiskey dulling the pain. "Why do you come to this shrine?"

"I suppose a noggin in de box is bloody disturbin', isn't it? But we 'av ter git our relics wha we can git dem."

To think that he had once taken relics for granted. The Irish and English relics had all been destroyed in the Dissolution of the Monasteries, and the bones of saints finally buried, often in unmarked graves. "Yes, I suppose that's true." He smiled.

"Hugh McGowan."

He shook the offered hand. "Grégoire Bellamont."

"Gray-wha?"

He laughed. "It's French for Gregory."

"Yeh nade a place ter stay, Gregory?"

"Just for a few days, yes." Whatever the rate was, he could pay it. That was not his concern. His concern was that he could barely stand. Hugh took his arm and put it over his broad shoulders.

Hugh lived nearby. And the tiny apartment on the outskirts of town was not far from St. Peter's Church. "We're startin' dat hostin' business," Hugh announced to the woman in an apron standing in the doorway. "All we got is a cot an' food. 'S that all right, Mr. Graywar Bella—Bellamen—"

"Just Gregory," he said. "And yes, anything is fine."

He was introduced to Mrs. McGowan, first name Nora, before he asked to rest before supper. The night before, he had slept on the side of a road with his bag as a pillow, so the fur-covered cot was a vast improvement.

When he woke, it was dark outside. A single wax candle was burning on the wooden table. There was no separation between the kitchen and the sitting room where he was housed. A room in the back was presumably the couple's bedroom. Mrs. McGowan sat alone at the table, and rose when he joined her. "Al' we 'av is sum stew. I wasn' 'spectin' visitors."

"Anything you have would be lovely, Mrs. McGowan."

He couldn't tell what was in the stew, aside from potatoes, but he didn't care. He was used to either a monastic diet or the fancy ten-course Pemberley dinners, so it was a nice medium. After grace, he ate his portion, and then a second. "Thank you."

"Yer English is very—English."

"I learned it from my family," he said, "on my father's side. Before that, it was more like yours."

"An' yer ma?"

"French."

"So what're you doin' in back-end Ireland, Mr. Gregory?"

He smiled. "I don't know, properly. There are some places I wanted to visit. Pilgrim sites I read about."

"Answers ter yer spiritual questions. Most people go elsewhere for dat."

"I've been to Rome," he said. "And I don't have the strength to go to Jerusalem. So here I am."

"An' yeh git a noggin in a box."

"I suppose it's better than an empty box."

They shared a laugh and chatted about the local sites before he said, "Excuse me. It's time for prayer."

"It's noight, Mr. Gregory."

"I know—Compline," he said, and excused himself to the other side of the room. Mrs. McGowan disappeared to give him privacy as he sat in prayer. When he was finished, he rose to drink some local beer.

"'S a monastic thing," she said. "Innit?"

"Yes. I used to be a monk." When she showed no disgust at the idea that he had left his religious order, he continued, "Some habits are hard to break. Nor do I wish to break them. Good night, Mrs. McGowan."

"Gran' noight to yeh, Gregory. Sleep well."

Her prediction was accurate. He slept like the dead.

~ ~ ~

The next morning, Hugh offered to take Grégoire to Mellifont Abbey, Ireland's oldest Cistercian monastery. The ruins were open for tourists, but Hugh's guidance was necessary to find the place. Beyond that, Hugh could only guess at what the various ruins were, but Grégoire was able to recognize most of the decaying structures. The gray stone of the columns from one row of cloister arches remained intact, standing alone beside stone floor and grass. The only fully standing building was the chapter house, though the windows were long gone, and there were birds roosting in the inside grooves of the arches.

"What were yeh?" Hugh said. "I mean, before?"

"Benedictine. But I was a novice as a Cistercian in France. That monastery dissolved. Then the one in Bavaria did. There are some left in Austria, but I went to Spain instead," he said, looking down at the floor of the chapter house and noticing the indentations where the heavy wooden pews had sat. What had happened to the wood after the Dissolution? Had it been chopped for firewood, or was it sitting in the house of some aristocrat, himself unaware of its holy origins?

They made it back to Drogheda for High Mass at St. Peter's Church. Hugh, who was out of work until the summer harvest, took Grégoire back to his house. There, Grégoire wrote a brief letter to Darcy, saying he had arrived safely in Drogheda. He did not anticipate a long stay.

The next day, they traveled to Monasterboice, an abbey of a different sort, dating back to before the Norman invasion and containing one of the many unexplained round towers and beautiful Celtic crosses of stone. Carved in relief were the stories of Eve tempting Adam, Cain slaying Abel, Moses striking the rock, the life of Christ—almost the entire Bible on the great Muiredach cross. It was Grégoire who was tour guide now, easily able to decipher the pictography.

"What do ya t'ink dey mean?" Hugh asked, pointing to the round tower.

"I don't know," he said. "I have a relative who traveled to India, where there were thousands of towers like that. I forget what he said they were called, but the Mohammedans pray five times a day, so five times a day, a man with a loud voice would climb to the top and call them all to prayer."

"Loike Saracens?"

"Yes. This was in India. Here, we have bells to tell us the time, but the principle is the same, I suppose."

"Kinda a heretical ting to be sayin'?"

"If I were a monk, I suppose so," he said with a smile. "Alas, I am not."

~ ~ ~

After they returned from High Mass, Grégoire decided that he would leave the day after next. He had to begin his path west to see the ancient burial sites of Brú na Bóinne. He spent most of the afternoon resting, and enjoyed a final hearty meal with the McGowans.

When he rose at half past three in the morning for Vigils, Nora McGowan was up. She had gone to bed earlier, but she was sitting up now at her kitchen table with a cup of mead.

"Mrs. McGowan," he said and bowed. Not quite sure what the decorous thing to do was, he sat down across from her and she filled a cup for him from the pot. It was not hot or cold, and had the flavor of honey, but otherwise was fairly tasteless.

They sat in silence for a while. She seemed hypnotized by the single burning flame of the candle that lit the room. He sipped his mead.

"Why did yeh leave de church, Mr. Gregory?" It was not an accusation; it was a question.

"A mixture of the politics of Rome and my own zealous devotion nearly killed me. I'm not damned, just forbidden to take holy orders." He added, "I didn't know how to find the balance between physical devotion and preserving my health, and no one would teach me. Instead, they cast me out." When she seemed satisfied with the answer, he asked, "Why does your husband go to pray at the shrine every day?"

She did not look at him. She had not been looking at him for the entire conversation. "Our only current bun—de wan sprog dat lived—didn't cum 'um from de war."

"He died at Waterloo?"

"Maybe," she said. "Maybe not. 'E's not on de rolls. 'E just went missing. Could be alive, fer all we know."

"Have you tried going to London? They have more official registries there." She turned to him. "Do ya t'ink we can afford ta go ta London?"

"I'm sorry." He put down his mug. "What was his regiment? Do you know? Do you have all of his information?"

"Aye, why?"

"Because I have relatives in London. I could write them and ask them to look." It had been three years—he was most likely dead, buried in a mass grave in France. But unless his whole regiment were in the grave with him, someone would know. They knew that—they had to know that. "It's no trouble," he said to her start of a response. "Just give me all his information, and I'll write it down and send it to my brother."

"We wouldn't want ta be beholden—"

"It's no trouble, I assure you," he said, and could not be persuaded otherwise. He did not excite her hopes of finding their son alive, or at all, but if there was information to be found, it would be in London.

When they saw him off the next morning with a few days' worth of food packed in his satchel, it was with tears, not because of how well he had paid his bill, but because of his promise and the letter he had sent out by courier that very morning.

"Jaysus bless yeh, Mr. Gregory," said Nora.

"I hope that he sees fit to do so," he said.

Following the River Boyne, Grégoire slowly made his way to Brú na Bóinne, called Quarters of the Boyne in English. It had no Christian significance, but he knew that there was God's glory in any beautiful sight.

There was no guide. So he wandered alone among the stone tombs, with their intricate carvings of spirals and knots.

He had once had a theological discussion with the abbot in Bavaria. "What about all the souls that came before Christ? Was it only the Israelites who were saved, or all people?"

"Our Lord God spoke to other people before he sent his son to earth. Even before Abraham, he gave Noah laws. If people followed them, they went to heaven."

"What if they had never heard of Noah? Did God speak to other people we don't know about?"

The abbot answered, "Everyone knew Noah. He was the only one to survive the Flood!"

"Of course! Thank you, Father!"

Grégoire smiled at the memory as he sat on the grass before a burial mound. It had all been so simple, the answers all waiting for him. *I should have asked about the people who came before the Flood!* he thought, and slapped his leg in amusement.

~ ~ ~

He wandered south, chasing ruin after ruin of worlds that had passed on. There was Boyle Abbey, the monastery of Clonmacnoise, and finally he went east again to see the Jerpoint Abbey, another Cistercian abbey founded after the Norman invasion. The structure still stood in stone, without windows and with a new floor of grass. He was hardly the only tourist there. He silently said the words along with the guide as the man laid out the *Carta Caritatis* (Charter of Love)'s basic principles—obedience, poverty, chastity, silence, prayer, and work. With disappointment, Grégoire noted that he fulfilled only one or two of those principles, prayer and perhaps work. He nevertheless felt calmed by the beautiful structure, covered in moss and ivy.

Upon leaving the grounds, he felt a certain despair—he had seen many relics and ruins, but had he learned anything? Had his time been well spent?

He wandered north, unconsciously heading back to Dublin, stopping at inns as he went, occasionally staying with a family or out in the open. He had been traveling for more than a month when he stopped at a house in a small farming community and asked if there were any religious sites around. He would offer to do chores for a meal. He would chop wood and milk cows, and sometimes he would stay the night.

At this particular house, he inquired after any churches around, or places of interest, as he had already missed High Mass. The small structure housed a working family—a husband and wife and several children running around behind them. The father introduced himself as Mr. O'Muldoon.

"There's ruins out back," he said, pointing. "In de woods. Yeh can't miss de wee stone tower."

He thanked them and left, wandering into the forest. This was the place where legends had it that fairies roamed, but he did not believe in such nonsense. It was starting to rain, so he was nearly in despair as he spotted the little enclosure that might have once been a church tower. It was no more than what had probably been the nave of a church, but some of the stone arch was preserved even if the back was not, so that he could sit beneath it and be dry. There were, he noticed now, lumps of fallen stones elsewhere in the grass, with dirt over them. This site had been long abandoned, but tonight, it would be his home.

As the rain came down, he lit his only candle and set it carefully in the corner, on the stone floor. There was something there. Taking the candle in one hand, he began to wipe away the grime and dirt to find a tiny mosaic portraiture of some saint, not clearly defined but recognizable for his traditional tonsure and golden halo. He had a staff in one hand and his other hand pointed with one finger in some direction. Was it Patrick? It was probably Patrick. He crossed himself. "It is just you and me tonight," he said to the saint, and began Vespers. Afterward, he ate a little black bread. After Compline, he extinguished the candle and drifted off to sleep. The rain had let up, but he was hardly going wandering through the wet woods at night, so he rested his head on his sack and slept.

When he woke for Vigils it was sudden, and the candle was lit again. Had he not put it out? It was thick enough to not be burned down. In a haze he sat up, and stared at the saint. *He's pointing.*

Grégoire barely remembered saying prayers or going back to sleep. He woke for Lauds and it was light out. The candle was out, and had not burned down, and it was dry and sunny, but the saint was still pointing. "Thank you," he said, crossing himself, and projected the exact angle of the finger in the mosaic set in stone. It led to a path—not the one he had used to get there, but one going in a similar direction.

He left the woods hungry. He was out of food, having not thought to acquire it from the O'Muldoons. When he stepped onto the dirt path, he tried to point himself according to the saint's direction.

His stomach was growling terribly when an hour had passed and he came upon a small, isolated house with smoke coming from the chimney. There were also some chickens running around, and he heard the bell of a cow from behind the wooden building. There was some attempt at a vegetable garden on the right side, but the crops were not doing well.

Grégoire readjusted his satchel, which hung over his shoulder and by his side instead of on his back, and stepped up the stairs to the porch and front door. "Hello?" His hand was still on the door from the knock when it pulled back to reveal a woman with strawberry blonde hair, long and straight, standing there as if she had been expecting him. Clearly, she had seen his approach.

"'Ill yeh be 'avin' sumt'in'?" she said, arms crossed.

"I am terribly sorry," he said, bowing, "but I will gladly perform some labor for you if you would feed this hungry pilgrim."

She looked him over—he could not be anything *but* a strange Christian pilgrim in his odd dress. "We don't 'av any grub."

"You—you have a cow. I could milk it for you."

"Dat coy 'asn't given me milk in days," she said. She stood mainly in darkness, her house unlit, but he could tell she was thin. "We don' even have any fuel for de fire ta cook yer food."

"I could chop wood," he said. "If you have an axe."

"For what? For free? I told yeh—we don' have any food!"

He stepped back. "I'm sorry." He lowered his eyes, looking down at her bare feet. "I'm doing penance. Let me cut some wood for you and I'll be on my way." She needed it more than he did. He had a sack of coins in a pouch under his shirt.

"Yeh're doin' things for free now?"

"St. Benedict said that work was a form of prayer," he said, trying to give her whatever answer she needed to accept his offer.

That one seemed to work. "There's 'n axe in de back, in de shed, I t'ink."

He nodded. "Thank you."

There was plenty of wood—trees had fallen down everywhere and had been left uncut. He didn't know who else was living in that house, but they were clearly incapable of manual labor. He worked until his back began to ache, which coincided nicely with

Sext, when he took a break and surveyed his work. He had cut enough firewood for several weeks. Perhaps that was why he was so exhausted. He leaned back and closed his eyes. If he nodded off, at least there was an axe by him.

"I got sum milk," the woman announced, and he opened his eyes to her standing over him, blocking the sun. "Guess de coy jist needed rest."

He nodded and stood up, but he needed his staff to do it. "I'm sorry," he said, as she looked surprised by his apparent exhaustion. "I refuse to accept my own limitations." He limped back with her to the house, where he was finally permitted entrance.

It seemed to have only two rooms—a bedroom and the main room, which was much larger. "Does anyone else live here?"

"No," she said. "But I 'av ter say dat when fierce quare men cum ter me door."

"Common sense," he said, taking a seat at the half-broken table. One leg was missing and a stump held it up. "I'm sorry. My name is Grégoire Bellamont."

"Yeh expect me ta pronounce dat?"

He smiled. "I can't pronounce Irish, so we're even. You can call me Gregory." He took the offered cup of milk and drank it hungrily.

"I loike it. It's exotic. Gray*ware*."

He chuckled. "Your accuracy is stunning, Miss—"

"Caitlin. MacKenna."

"Miss MacKenna."

"Yeh sound so proper—but yer not English, yer French."

"Born in France. My father's English. He…had an affair with his maid." The last made her chuckle and spit out her milk, which made him laugh.

"So wha yeh live?"

"Raised in France, went to England, and then Bavaria, and then Spain, and then went home to England…and now here. Why? I just try to walk in God's path."

"Yeh soun' loike a priest."

"I used to be a monk."

"You left de church?"

"The church left me."

She did not inquire after that. It was too loaded a question. "Well, dere's nuthin' special out here."

"There are some ruins in the woods about a mile back."

"Really? I don'—I don' wander around." She took his empty cup from him and refilled it. "Suppose you'll want ter know wha' me family is."

"I met the O'Muldoons," he said, "but they didn't mention you."

"Noice couple. Laddies are screamers, but not really brutal."

He nodded.

"Jaysus, yer polite."

"Do you want me to be otherwise?"

"It makes me unaisy."

He looked down at his cup and then up at her again. "How far along are you?"

The question did not strike her as hard as he had thought it would, but she did look as though something had hit her. "T'ree months."

He nodded.

"Am I showin'?" She wore a shapeless, ratty blue gown.

"No, but you keep putting your hand over your stomach."

She laughed. It was nice to hear. "Yer a smart bugger." She poured the last of the milk into her cup and sat down across from him. "Me ma and pa didn't approve whaen we said we wud git married. Wanted nothing ta do wit' me. And he didn' want nothing to do wit' me, either." She put a hand over her forehead, blocking eye contact. "He bought me some medicine ta get rid of it. I said no."

He crossed himself, but only gestured for her to continue.

"So he kicked me out. But he gave me a wee nicker for de road, an' I bought dis gaff wi' it." She looked down. "An' 'ere I am."

"Is there a town around here? Somewhere to buy food?"

"'S about foive miles down de road."

"Is the market still open?"

"'Til dusk."

He stood up. "Then I had better get going. Thank you for your hospitality, Miss MacKenna. I will return, with God's help, in a few hours."

"I can't pay yeh."

"Money means nothing to me," he said. "Too many years as a monk, I suppose." And with that, he abruptly left her presence and set off to town.

~ ~ ~

When he returned, it was getting dark, and his back ached again from being laden with packages. She looked shocked—almost horrified—to see him politely enter and then set the packages down on her kitchen table. "There's bread—and grain, for the cow and chickens—and some mead, and some whiskey, and sugar—"

"*Sugar!*"

"And I don't know, some other things." He collapsed into a seat, the day's events wearing on him, and it was almost time for Vespers. "Excuse me. It's time for prayer." Without another word, he walked out the door and to the side of the house, where he recited the entire service by heart to the setting sun. She had opened all the packages and the contents were scattered, but she was standing there, quite uncomfortable in her own house. "I'm sorry. Have I done something wrong?"

"Yer always apologizing," she said. "I can't pay fer dis."

"I told you, you don't have to—"

"Yeh even a pilgrim? Who are yeh?"

He sighed. It was always about his blasted money. "My English family is quite wealthy. My brother will give me whatever I want. But possessions mean nothing to me, besides the necessities of life. That's the way I was raised and it remains my mindset," he said. "Food *is* a necessity—for *both* of you."

"Do yeh—do yeh *want* somet'in'?"

He sighed. "I'm very tired. May I sleep on your floor tonight?"

"That's it?"

"Yes, Miss MacKenna—that is it." He rubbed his eyes. "And if you will excuse me—I am very tired, and would like to sleep a little before Compline."

"Oh. Yes. To be sure," she said, and disappeared into her room, emerging with a rug. "I'm sorry—"

"It will be fine. I can sleep on stone. Thank you." He laid out the mat and a small pillow from his bag.

"Dere's nothin' else?"

"No, Miss MacKenna."

"Yer sure?"

"Yes."

She did not seem to believe him. Perhaps she had calculated how much he had spent and knew that it was a small fortune. He lay down, but she would not let him sleep. "Are yeh still a monk or somethin'?"

"What? No, I said, I've actually been…" It dawned on him that she was hovering over him in a particular manner. "No, no! That was not why I came here." He could feel his cheeks burning. "That is not what this is about. If I behaved inappropriately—"

She stepped back, a little alarmed. Perhaps they were both embarrassed. "I just—I didn't know. Fer sure."

"No, please! I assure you, nothing of the kind. I am not under any…vow, but that was not why I came here. Please believe me."

Her face was red now, too. "I believe yeh. I'm sorry, I t'ought— It doesn't matter. Forget it."

He nodded, unable to think of anything else to say, and she disappeared into her bedroom. He did not, however, find sleep before Compline, only afterward, and it was an uneasy one at that.

Grégoire rose, as he always did, for prayer in the dead of night. He lit a candle so that he could find his way and not trip over half the kitchen. He was not successful and knocked over a chair.

"Yeh need anyt'ing?"

"No!" he said, embarrassed again. "I just...am very clumsy, trying to find my prayer book." He turned and saw her in the hallway leading to her bedroom, holding her own candle.

"Well if yeh don' mind—I'm starvin'," she said, and began to tear through the bread, starting with the white and moving to the black. "Oh, God, I've been so hungry."

"A normal human response. I get hungry and I'm accustomed to fasting for any reason."

She downed her bread with milk. "Yeh were really a monk? Robes and everyt'ing? Funny haircut?"

He ran a hand over the top of his head. "It just grew back, actually."

"Why did they keck yeh out?"

"Many reasons, but mainly, I think I would have killed myself with my monkery," he said. "Martin Luther said that, but it was true for me, too. Without the heresy."

She finished off the milk. "It wud ha' ben a shame."

"If what?"

"If yeh'd killed yerself. Yer such a good man."

"Thank you."

The awkward silence lasted a long time. He wasn't counting, but it must have been a good twenty seconds before she kissed him, and he put up no sacred or religious resistance. They practically toppled over the table. "Careful of my back," he said. She was right; he wasn't a monk anymore. At that moment, he certainly didn't want to be.

"I didn't come here for this," he said, forcing himself to pull away from her for a brief moment. It was also to catch his breath. "Everything I told you was true. Do you want me to go?"

"Stupid monk," she said. "Am I *actin'* loike I want yeh ter *leave?*" She paused. "Is it 'cuz of the—"

He shushed her, taking her hand away from his shoulder and putting them both on her stomach, where there was a small swelling. "No. I just—am not very experienced with women."

His confession did not seem to put her off. Grégoire did not leave the house, nor did he return to his mat on the floor.

CHAPTER 28

Missives from Ireland

THE DARCYS RECEIVED A number of correspondences from Grégoire, as he had promised. Some came in clumps, others did not, but he was nothing if not a prolific writer about the places he went and the sites he saw. It was the first and the last of the letters that concerned Darcy. Along with his travelogue meant for the entire household, he included a letter to Darcy.

Dear Brother,

I need to make an inquiry but am unable to do so from my present location. If you employ your steward, I would happily compensate him for his time.

I was hosted by a couple named Hugh and Nora McGowan. Their son, James, served in the ___ regiment in His Majesty's armies. They do not know how to read, so he did not write them while abroad, but the last they heard, his regiment had been sent to Waterloo and there it suffered many casualties. However, they have never been informed of his death, and he has not returned or sent message that he is alive. Although they are not believing him to be alive, they would like to know what became of him. They do not have the finances to travel to London and conduct further inquiries. I, of course, offered them my services. With the information enclosed (physical description, etc.), perhaps something can be dug up in London, or one of the members of his regiment can be spoken to about his death.

I also include their address. Please use it if it can be concluded that he has passed on to the next life. If he is alive, some effort could perhaps be made to get him to visit his grieving parents.

When I am at a location where I can be reached, I will let you know. Otherwise, I leave this task to you. If you do not have the time, I open my accounts for someone to be hired to investigate it. Spare no expense.

Thank you.

Grégoire Darcy-Bellamont

That Grégoire was championing the cause of some lost soldier's parents was no surprise to his older brother, who showed it to his wife.

"So kind of him," Elizabeth said. "What will you do?"

"Have a solicitor sent to London," he said.

The next notable letter, beyond traveling tales, was remarkably brief.

Brother,

I have decided to stay in County Carlow for a little while. I find it very pleasant here. I have opened a box, so that I can receive posts from you. Write to me at Tullow, Box Number 0828.

God Bless.

Grégoire Darcy-Bellamont

"His lack of explanation is stunning," Darcy said. It was the sort of letter Darcy would write, but not Grégoire. Or, it was not in the style of letters he had been writing.

"Maybe he met a girl and he doesn't wish to admit it."

Darcy returned Elizabeth's look, and then both broke into laughter at the idea.

~ ~ ~

Two weeks before, the paper on which he would write the final letter was still rolled up in Grégoire's sack, unused. He stirred for Vigils with no desire to get up; it was just his body's natural reaction and he rolled over, trying to ignore it. He did not want to wake from his dream and find himself alone in that little shelter of a ruin, beside the saint. It seemed so wet and miserable, and this was much better, even if the bed wasn't exactly high quality.

He swallowed all of his alarm when he realized that it was not a dream and there was a woman beside him by reminding himself, *You are not a monk.* If this was the way he had to get used to it, it was not such a terrible thing.

Caitlin did not stir beside him, even when he removed his hand from her belly, where it had roamed in his sleep. It was barely daybreak as he yawned and reached over to open the shutters, bringing the morning sun into their faces.

"Ow!" came a cry beside him. "Why—what time is it?"

"Time for Vigils," he said. "I'm sorry—my body just knows." He made a move to rise, but she grabbed him by the cross around his neck and pulled him back down. "All right, all right."

"I don' want ta be alone," she said. "Is dat so brutal?"

"No," he said. In fact, he didn't think it was terrible at all. There was something to be said for waking up next to a live person and her warm body, no matter what the outside temperature was. He had only one other experience with it, and it had been so guilt-ridden that he barely remembered the specifics.

"Why—why did yeh do al' dis for me?"

He assumed she was referring to his stocking her kitchen for a month. "I would have done it for anyone. I have the money. I can't take it with me."

"Really?"

"Really," he said, facing her. "As for the rest of it—I suppose I'm not much of a monk after all." He smiled and kissed her head. Her hair needed a wash, but it was a lovely color of red and blonde together, and not curled or pinned up like the hair style of an English gentlewoman.

She giggled and leaned into him. "Yer shirt is so soft."

"It's cotton." It was more than a little worn because he had washed it often, but it was softer on his skin. He wore it as an undershirt at the abbot's orders and Dr. Maddox's strong suggestion.

"I 'ave never felt cotton before."

"Neither had I." He was used to only wool and linen.

She laced her fingers with his. His were calloused from long hours of various kinds of manual and scriptural labor, hers the same. She was not a soft English rose. She had probably grown up on a farm and done her share of chores.

"Why do yeh 'ave cuts on yer arms?"

She was referring to the scars on his forearms, which went up nearly the length of them. "Oh, that was from where they had to take skin—" He stopped. "It's not a pleasant story."

"Neither is me gettin' knocked up an' Neil leavin' me."

"I'm sorry."

"Yeh always say dat," she said, "and I t'ink yeh mean it. I 'ave never met anyone loike yeh."

"And I have met no one like you, Caitlin."

That must have been the right answer, because she kissed him. He had largely lost all linear thought when he had to stop her from pulling up his shirt, the only thing he was still wearing besides his religious jewelry. "Don't."

"Why?"

"Because—I don't want you to see it." The mood—at least on his end—was temporarily discouraged. "When I said I almost killed myself in my discipline, I was serious."

"So you've never shown anyone?"

"A lot of doctors, my brother, and my entire abbey, but I don't remember it. And even then, I was ashamed." His grip on her hand unintentionally tightened.

"All right," she said, letting go of his shirt. It stayed on.

~ ~ ~

They were both ravenous, and dove into all available food. Grégoire went out to feed the chickens and the cow. Those animals seemed to somehow convey surprise at his presence and his actions. He returned to the house with a pail of fresh milk. Caitlin drank to the point of being ill, and he helped her get outside in time, holding back her long hair.

"'S been this way since—yeh know," she said. "But it wus less, cos I wasn' eatin'."

"You need to eat. Even if it makes you sick." He carried her back into the house and set her in the only chair with a back, providing her with a little mead, which he had thrown a shaving of ginger into. "Sip."

"How do yeh know so much aboyt *afflicted women* or whatever yer callin' it in England?"

"I've known many women with child. Relatives and townsfolk near my abbey in Spain," he said.

A little worn from her recent experience, she sipped the concoction before setting it on her lap. "Are yeh 'eadin'?"

"Leaving?"

She nodded.

Did he know what he should do? Certainly not. Did he even know what the right thing to do was? She was an increasing woman—unmarried, and in need of someone, and no child would result of their union. "Today? Not unless you tell me to."

She did not. Did he know what he was doing? No. Did he care? Not in the least.

~ ~ ~

The next day, Grégoire was on his way back from the trip to Tullow to set up his post box when he encountered Mrs. O'Muldoon, who greeted him: "Mr.—I'm so sorry—"

"Grégoire. But you can call me Gregory, if it pleases you," he said, bowing to her. It was not something to which she was accustomed, and the plump Irish housewife forced herself into a curtsy. "Mrs. O'Muldoon. How are you?"

"I wasn' 'spectin' ta see yeh here."

"I am planning on staying in the area. For how long, I know not."

"I 'eard a rumor—are yeh at—nearby ta us?"

"With Miss MacKenna, yes," he said. So he admitted to living in sin. "This is probably inappropriate of me but—what do you know of her?"

They continued down the path away from the market toward their homes, where she pulled him to the side. "She com here 'bout two months ago. Bought de house for a song—de animals wi' it—'cuz the owner 'ad jist lost 'is struggle an' strife—his wife, yeh know—an' wanted ter move ter de city. He was lookin' for any deal he could make." She took his arm. "She was in a real bad way. I suppose she told yeh dat."

"She did tell me the circumstances were difficult, yes."

"She's a nice lass—can't say much for her livin' alone, but she wus shuk. We woulda taken 'er in, but we have a baby and we couldn't afford it, yeh know—"

He nodded kindly. "I know, yes. Of course."

"She wus al' banged up; bruises and the loike. She could barely walk straight. She towl me a wee aboyt her paddy not takin' well to her leavin', but not much. We talk about these t'ings, women. Yeh know."

He nodded again. "Since then?"

"She's been alone. Not seen a soul fer all we know. She used ta go ta market, but den she stopped."

"I understand. I just wanted to know—"

"Terrible t'ing, to be all alone. But that doesn' mean yer obligated in any way, Mr. Gregory—"

"No, I understand," he said. He was just trying to confirm Caitlin's story—dirty as he felt in doing it. It was something his brother would do. "Thank you, Mrs. O'Muldoon. I'll see you at church."

"Jasus bless yeh, Mr. Gregory."

"God bless you."

They parted and he continued down the path to the house.

~ ~ ~

Was it physical satisfaction he felt, or was it something more? Either way, he liked the feeling, even if he could not distinguish it properly. Nothing tied him to Caitlin; he could leave her at any time, and if he felt generous, even leave enough money to get her through her pregnancy without making a dent in his annual income. He didn't tell her that, but he didn't lie about his finances, either—she had enough sense not to ask. He was content in a way he had never felt before. *It must be physical affection.* He had known the love of brotherhood, of God, and of family. A woman had been beyond his experience. His one night in Bavaria did not count; he could see that now.

How am I to go to confession? It was the thought that truly bothered him. *How can I confess to a sin with no intention of reform?* He did not want to ignore the orders of a priest, but then again, hadn't he done that before?

He went each morning to Mass in the local church, or High Mass if he was too lazy to get up, but it was several days before he stepped in the box and crossed himself. "Before I begin, I must ask—Father, are you a member of any of the monastic orders?"

"No indeed, me son."

"I am excommunicated from my order and would be unable to speak to you if you were. That was why I asked," he said, and crossed himself. "Forgive me, Father, for I have sinned. It has been two months since my last confession." He did not go through his entire history with this priest—he had confessed all those sins long ago and did not wish to go over them again. "I am living with an unmarried woman who is carrying another man's child."

"Who is dis oither lad?"

"I do not know him. All I know is that he told her to get rid of the child, and she ran away from him, and was living on her own before I found her."

"Where is 'er family?"

"She said they would not speak to her after they discovered her condition."

The priest paused. "Yeh 'av relashuns wi' this woman?"

"Yes. Forgive me, Father, but I would be lying if I did not say that I have every intention of continuing."

"Yeh intend ter marry 'er?"

He leaned back in the box. For some reason, he had not anticipated this question. "At this stage, I do not know. Marriage is a sacrament. There is more to it than physical pleasure or financial necessity."

"Yeh are supporting 'er?"

"Yes."

"In exchange for deese favors?"

He colored. "No. She was starving and I bought her food with no intention of things proceeding as they did. I was just returning from a pilgrimage to Jerpoint Abbey when I encountered her. I had no intention of staying in the region."

"If yeh intend ter continue dees carnal relashuns, yeh must make an honest woman out av 'er."

Grégoire swallowed. "I need time to consider it. I take sacraments very seriously."

"But sexual prohibishuns, less so."

He bowed his head. "Forgive me, Father. I was a celibate monk for most of my adult life. This is the first time I have ever been in a…relationship with a woman, aside from one other time, and I repented, and was forgiven. And that was when I was under oath. Now I have no such restrictions."

"Yeh 'av de restricshun av bein' a Christian lad."

To this, he did not have an answer. He had not looked forward to this, and he would not look forward to future sessions. But he could not marry Caitlin—he barely knew her. "If we are meant for marriage, then I will happily make her my wife and raise the child as my own. But as of now, I cannot answer you."

It was the turn of the priest to stop to consider. "Yeh are rational and considerate, and doin' the woman a generosity. 'Owever, yeh are still livin' in sin an' must examine yer motives for doin' so. We are meant ter learn from sin—it leads us astray, but in doin' so, lets us see wha de right path wus so we can reclaim it," he said. "Say ten Hail Marys and attend Mass at least once a week."

"Thank you, Father."

"Go wi' God, me son."

He had never felt as though that box were such a prison, and never so relieved to be free of it. It was not the punishment—which was nothing in comparison with anything he had experienced in his past—so much as what the priest had said. If this continued, he would have to marry Caitlin. On the other hand, if this continued, maybe he would want to.

~ ~ ~

After a brief refresher course with Mr. O'Muldoon and acquiring the right materials, Grégoire set to work repairing the floorboards of the kitchen, especially the ones that had a tendency to pop up when one stepped on the other end. The project would take hours. *Work is prayer.* So said St. Benedict, even though Grégoire was still required to set aside time for prayer itself, and to attend Mass, and, of course, services on Sundays.

"Are yeh sure yer not still a monk?" Caitlin said as he finished Sext and joined her in the kitchen for lunch. With the right spices and after some failed attempts, she had finally managed to get some good dishes together.

"Why? Do you want me to act like one?" he said, kissing her.

"T'be sure not," she said, and began putting out the food. "It's just—all the people I know who are runnin' to church are either priests or so—"

"Self-righteous?"

"Aye." She stopped her conversation and bowed her head as he said grace in Latin, and then they ate at a leisurely pace.

Caitlin took a sip of tea. "I jist mind dis lady hittin' me wi' a rod for runnin' up an' down de aisles whaen oi wus wee."

"I don't think Christ would have hit you when you acted like a child," he said. "I don't think he would ever have hit you."

"Yeh shoulda told *'er* that," she said. "'S like, yer just all good, nothing bad in yeh a'tall—" She stood up. "Excuse me."

He was used to her running outside after eating—she was with child and not used to such good food—but he sensed something was the matter. When she was done being ill, she sat down on the front steps, weeping.

"Caitlin? What is it?"

She just shook her head, trying to shoo him away. He would not be shooed, and sat down beside her, wrapping an arm around her. "What is it?"

"'S nothing."

"It is not."

She tried to meet his eyes, but failed, collapsing into his tunic. "I'm so sorry, so sorry—I shouldn't be doin' dis ta yeh. Yer so good—"

"You're not doing anything to me," he said, "except making me happy."

But she just kept sobbing, until she was so exhausted that he picked her up and carried her to her bed, where she remained for the rest of the day. Grégoire looked at the abandoned floor project and shook his head. He spent the rest of the day in prayer, even if he did not know precisely what he was praying for.

CHAPTER 29

Sacred Sacraments

~ ~ ~

THERE DIDN'T SEEM TO BE ENOUGH hours in the day. He had prayer, Mass, Caitlin, and chores around the house. He needed to get it into some semblance of shape. She was consuming food at the normal rate of a woman entering her fourth month, so it was not a surprise that he was at the market almost every day. Initially not a good cook, she was a fast learner, and Grégoire was a happy teacher.

One day, shortly after he had returned from the market and was trying to properly spice the potatoes before they went in the stove, she asked, "Why do yeh go ta Mass every day? Is it so Jasus 'ill fergive yer sins?"

"Every person is a sinner," he said, "but no, that's not why I go. I go because it's a sacrament."

"Dat's somethin' the priest used ta say."

It didn't mean, of course, that she understood it. He turned to her, wiping the last of the salt from his hands over the pot. "Through performing the sacraments and leading good lives, we thank the good Lord for all that we have been given. Even when it's not much, even when it's so terrible we can hardly bear it—it's the only life we have."

"Yer 'onestly believe dat?"

"Have I ever said anything I did not believe?"

He put a cover over the pot. The potatoes could sit for a bit. "Let me take you somewhere."

She was all obliging as he led her into the forest, to the little ruin where he had spent the night. It was much easier to see inside now, with full daylight instead of rain. Some dirt obscured the mosaic, and he wiped it clean again. "When I was lost, I found this."

"'S St. Patrick," she said. "I seen it before. In other churches."

"I thought it might be. You see where he's pointing?" He gestured. "In the direction of your house. I didn't know which way to turn, so I followed him to you."

Caitlin giggled, and then, realizing that he was serious, leaned into him. He kissed her. "I don't know what I would have done without him."

Time passed, but Grégoire did not pay much attention to the calendar. He went to Tullow to check his mail and found a response from his brother, saying that he would be looking into the business of the missing soldier.

The summer heat was beginning to set in, and he was sweating by the time he returned to the house. Dropping off his bundle on the porch, he took the soap from it and headed off to the stream behind the house. The cow mooed at him as he passed; she was doing much better now that she was regularly fed.

Only in the privacy afforded by the forest and the bushes around the stream did he remove his outer tunic, and then his undershirt, which he proceeded to wash carefully in the tiny flow of water. Afterward, he hung it in the sun to dry and then sat down by the stream, bare chested. Removing his sandals, he let the water cool his aching feet.

"Didja get de feed?"

He scrambled to his feet, which involved a lot of splashing, to reach for his tunic. "Caitlin, please don't—"

She was standing in the sun, a wrap covering her hair. "I've seen de rest of yeh, yeh know."

He held his tunic up over his bare chest. "I know—but this is quite different."

"Well, now it's out, yeh might as well not be hidin' in shame."

He blushed. "It is not…" but he couldn't contradict her. It *was* shame. "I'm sorry."

She held out her hand, and he sighed and put the wool tunic in it. They sat down together on the grass, waiting for his shirt to dry. He had not seen his back in a long while—not since once in the mirror at Pemberley, some months earlier—but there were scars that would remain, and times when it was still tender and easily made raw.

"Does it 'urt?"

"Sometimes."

Caitlin removed her headscarf, which was little more than a random piece of yellow cloth anyway, and dipped it into the stream. She took the soaked cloth and gently applied it to a shoulder blade. Beyond the initial contact with cold, he stopped flinching and his body relaxed.

"Does it fale better nigh?"

"Oh, goodness, yes," he said. "I've never—I never had anyone else to do this for me. I mean, doctors did it, but it wasn't quite the same." He played with his rosary as she applied the compress to his back. The feeling was heavenly. "Most of it I did for myself. The white stripes are from where they sewed me up the last time. I was being punished for disobeying the Rule—the monastic rule book—and my flesh was too weak. It broke. There was so little left after infection that the doctors had to take skin from my arm. That part, I don't remember. There are some things in between—I remember the abbot telling me he had to excommunicate me from the order. I remember talking to the archbishop of Oviedo. I remember sitting on the coast." He shook his head. "It is all a jumble. I dreamed I was being hammered on an anvil, and it was the saints, taking turns with the—" he broke off. He couldn't continue. He had dreamed many dreams as he lay in fever, but he remembered only a few, and all of them haunted him.

"Some t'ings—'tis best just ta forget," she said. He had a mental flash of what Mrs. O'Muldoon had told him about Caitlin when she came to the area, broken and bruised, not to mention with child. Meanwhile, the actual Caitlin put down her cloth and leaned over to kiss him. "Yer not so terrible ta look at. Not loike yer missin' an eye or somet'in'." She smiled. "In fact, I kinda loike the way yeh look."

He returned the kiss. "That is comforting to know, as I find you beautiful."

~~~

His shirt had dried by the time they stepped back into the sunlight. Grégoire's mind was in a pleasant haze as he dressed himself and they returned to the house. While Caitlin sorted the packages and prepared lunch, Grégoire reread the letters from his family, which included one from Georgiana, eager to know if he would return home in time for Robert's first birthday. Had that much time really passed?

"'Sat from yer brad'er?"

"Sister," he said. "Her name is Georgiana. Her first son was born last spring."

"Yeh never blather aboyt yer family," she said as she put his soup in front of him.

"You never talk about yours."

"I 'ad a brad'er, little Connor, but 'e died of de fever a few years ago. And me ma and pa, but dat's it. Nothin' excitin'. Just a little farm. Not loike a great English house."

"I didn't grow up in England," he said. "I was born and raised in Mon-Claire, which is a wasteland at the top of a mountain in France. My mother went into exile after being fired from her job as a maid. I never would have known about my father if he hadn't come before he died to meet me. I was ten, I believe."

"Why did 'e coom?"

"He was trying to make amends for the things he had done in his life. My mother was his wife's personal maid. She was with
~~~

child with Georgiana when I was conceived. When Lady Anne found out, she fired my mother on the spot, and never forgave my father. She died after childbirth, and her last words were to curse my father."

"And your brad'er?"

"He's more than ten years older than me. He inherited everything and found out about me through some odd banking reports about an account in France. This was nine or so years ago. It came as quite a shock to him."

"But he didn't toss you off?"

He shook his head. "He embraced me as though I were his real brother, not his fathers's…bastard. He did everything he could do for me—everything that I let him. He would have let me use the Darcy name if I could, legally."

"'S not a noble, is he?"

"His mother was. And our sister married an earl." He saw her look down in embarrassment at her plate. "It does not matter to me. I have no rights to anything under English law, being born out of wedlock. Father was just being kind when he left me an inheritance."

"'An *inheritance*,'" she said, as if the notion itself were absurd. "Can I ask yeh a question?"

He smiled. "Of course." The soup was a little heavy on the ginger. She was not yet familiar with many roots and spices, but there were more successes than failures.

"What are rich people loike?"

He laughed. She hadn't meant it seriously—there was no way that she could have. That didn't mean he was exempted from providing an answer, so he took a piece of potato floating in the soup and put it in his mouth, chewing on it to give himself time to mull over the question. "Do you wish to know a secret?"

She squealed. "Aye!"

"They are terribly, *terribly* bored."

Neither of them could hold back their laughter at that. He was glad that he had swallowed his food properly, as he could not have held it in. "They have their servants do every menial task. They do not even dress themselves, and are left with nothing to do. So they read books and go on walks and then sit down for long dinners where they discuss reading books and going on walks. And then write people about it, because writing takes time."

"Yer jokin'!"

"I was once privy to a discussion of how they were planning on replanting the garden so it might look more in fashion with something someone had read in a magazine. I nearly fell asleep! I mean, there is intelligent conversation, but still..." He shook his head, still smiling at Caitlin's bemusement. Whatever amused her amused him.

"One day, ye'll read me a letter."

"One day, you'll read it yourself," he said.

Time and time again, she resisted his attempts to teach her to read, mainly because of her own prejudices against her intellect, and because it seemed to be such a wasteful thing to do with her time. The unspoken message was clear: she did not know where her life was going beyond the birth of her child, if she even lived. They seemed to be neck-and-neck in terms of their esteem of themselves. Perhaps that was why it was so easy to relate to her, this other lost soul.

The days and nights fell into an easy pattern. He went to church without her. She had her own reasons, both societal and personal, not to show her face in the house of God, especially beside a man who was not her husband while carrying a child that was not his or a husband's. "Pray fer me," she would say, and kiss him good-bye every Sunday.

Maybe she noticed all of the little improvements around the house and kept track of them and what they would have cost her, or maybe she didn't. He never fully revealed his wealth (she would have found the number imaginary), but he found ways to slip things into her life on some pretense or another. They needed a new leg for the table, so he found one. They needed new sheets for the bed, so he bought them. Expensive items, such as soap and sugar and even chocolate, found their way onto the shelves. After a bad rain, he had Mr. O'Muldoon come over to help him repair the roof.

"The Missus is goin' ta ask me, so I might as well ask yeh—are you t'inkin' a marryin' her, or are yeh not de type?"

"Marry your wife? That would present some difficulties."

The man laughed so hard he nearly fell off the roof, but insisted on an answer to the question.

"I don't know," Grégoire said. "I have no experience in this area."

"Who has experience in marryin' someone before dey get married?"

He could not fault his logic there. "I suppose you're right. I just never imagined I would be considering this question."

But he was. He would be lying to himself if he thought otherwise, and his confessor (the only priest in the church) kept reminding him of it. If Caitlin was not married in four months, her child would be a bastard. Although Grégoire was himself a bastard, he could not imagine what Caitlin would do. Mr. Darcy had given his mother money to go back to France—enough money for her and Grégoire to live on for years in Mon-Claire.

However, marriage was more than charity. It was a holy sacrament, not to be undertaken lightly, at least ideally, even though it often was done lightly or for any number of convenient purposes. Darcy, who had a reason to marry and produce an heir to Pemberley, had avoided it until he was eight and twenty. But then again, Darcy was not a social animal and mistrusted everyone, while Grégoire heedlessly saw only the good in people, often to his disadvantage. He tried to see Caitlin in shades—she was scared, she was tough, she could be moody, and she had little tolerance for stupidity (in terms of customs, not learning, of which she had basically none). She was not demure. She was not soft (even though her skin was). She was not a churchgoing woman, but she did have faith, even if it had only a subtle means of expression. He could not have a discussion with her on the influence of the Council of Trent on doctrine, but he could talk to her about God and she would listen. It was not that he sought to alter her character, but rather that he had a need to express his feelings to *someone.* And she was always a willing listener, and often would see the obvious where he could not. He told her of the places he had visited, the things he had seen, the things in the world he could not understand and could not be explained in books. It was not a structured debate over a dinner table or in a parlor room, but a confession and an earnest response.

"What do you think of predestination?" he said to her on a whim, and explained the concept.

"Why worry 'bout a silly thing like dat?" she said. "Either 'tis true or 'tisn', but I'm not goin' go around wonderin' if people I meet are destined for heaven or hell or just goin' there because of somet'in' dey did. 'Twould be downright rude of me."

He laughed and tightened his hold around her. It was getting harder for them to lie close together, at least at the torso, and he put a hand over her swelling stomach and kissed it.

"I luk loike I ate somethin' wrong."

"You look beautiful. Also, you look as though you're with child, which should not come as a surprise to you." It was his business to make her laugh. Otherwise, she was often increasingly anxious about her condition. They didn't speak of his staying on, or their relationship—that subject remained too uncomfortable, as neither of them had the answer. She didn't ask him to stay, but he didn't leave of his own volition, and for the time, they were both happy with that.

Late one day in the early summer, Grégoire walked to Tullow, to find not only a letter from Scotland but one from Darcy, which was longer than usual.

Dear Grégoire,

My steward has located James McGowan. He is alive but in debtor's prison outside London. I do not know the specifics in their entirety, but in a particular engagement with the French, he had a fight with his superior and made a movement interpreted as running from battle, a punishable offense. He was fined, and his pay after Waterloo was smaller than he had assumed, so he borrowed money to pay it and found himself in debt overnight. His debts are 600 pounds; there may have been other losses from gambling or drinking while he was afield. I understand that many other soldiers from his regiment are also housed in the same prison along with him.

I await your decision as to how to resolve this.

Your brother,
Darcy

He purchased paper on the spot, penned a response in the post office, and sent it express.

Dear Brother,

Please see to it that the 600 pounds is removed from my account to pay his debt, and any others he may have incurred. Also, purchase him a ticket to Dublin, and some money for travel to Drogheda, to be given on the condition that he is to return to his parents immediately. They are desperate to see him. Do not mention my name at any point in these proceedings.

Your grateful brother,
Grégoire

P.S. I apologize for the brevity of this letter. A longer one will follow about far less pressing matters.

If he were face-to-face with his brother, Darcy would probably say something against it, even though it was a small amount for Grégoire. But then Grégoire would just remind him that Elizabeth had once told him that Darcy had paid off their brother (not knowing the brotherly connection) with ten thousand pounds, just to save a girl's reputation.

Grégoire was apparently still smiling when he returned to the house, because Caitlin immediately grilled him on his grin. "My brother. Pound wise, penny foolish."

The next morning, he forced his sister's letter upon Caitlin as they lay together in bed. "So—So ha—"

"He."

"So he seen—"

"So he *can.*"

She shoved the letter in his face. "Jist read it."

He collected his sister's letter, and kissed Caitlin on the cheek. "You did very well."

"Rubbish!"

"I am most serious. I always am. Except when I'm not." He squinted, as he was without his spectacles and was not eager to remove himself from his position to retrieve them.

Dear Brother,

It is so strange that I miss you most terribly even though you are now only a short distance away, in comparison with Spain! I accept your apologies that you will not be attending Robert's first birthday. We do not need to hold him up so he can stand now; he does it on his own! Only with much falling over, so that I worry horribly for him, but William only laughs and the housekeeper tells us that all children are the same way, covered in bruises as they find their footing. I can't imagine our brother or Elizabeth allowing their children to run about at such a young age, but I will hardly contradict my husband or the nurse.

Brother may come up and bring Geoffrey, but Elizabeth is reluctant to be so far north with her mother unwell, even though her condition has not changed. We have not had many English guests, but the Maddoxes and Mr. Mugin came up, as they were traveling the country a bit. Mr. Mugin is set to leave in the late summer, and he had never been to Scotland. I am told the Japanese love to travel—much like you, I suppose!

Mrs. Wallace from the next estate has been over often to advise me on my garden, which I am afraid has been in neglect since my confinement, and she says that perhaps—

"It goes on about this for a while."

"Yer sister sounds sweet," she said, "but spare me, please."

He closed the letter and put it on the new nightstand.

"What have yeh been tellin' 'em?" Because clearly, he had not been telling them the whole truth.

"This and that. That I am happy here, near the shrine of St. Patrick, and am contemplating my future. All of which is true." He gave her a reassuring smile. "The English talk about many things in their letters, but not the things that are most personal. Only if the circumstances are dire."

"So is dat why yeh always take forever ta get ta de point?"

He laughed and kissed her.

CHAPTER 30

Intruder

NO PART OF HIS BROTHER'S REQUEST surprised Darcy, but nonetheless he was not pleased to visit a debtors' prison. He had been there twice for a different half-brother, and under much more frustrating (and expensive) circumstances.

The door to a cell was opened. A sandy-haired man, still in partial uniform, emerged, looking tired and confused as he was told by the officer that he was free.

"Your debts were paid," Darcy said, "courtesy of an anonymous donor who happened to meet your desperate parents, who've had no word of you since the war, Mr. McGowan." He did not wait for the man to respond before shoving some bills and a ticket in his hands. "Your ship leaves in the morning for Dublin. This was all done on the good faith that you would return home to them as expediently as possible. You can make up whatever lie you like to explain your absence, but that would not be in the spirit of your patron. All I will tell you is that you had better be there for that ship's departure and you had better be in Ireland by the end of the week. Your parents are sick with grief, or so I'm told."

The former soldier looked down at the money and then up at him, wide-eyed. "And who be yeh?"

"His brother," he said. He had no desire to associate with this man. "I'll be there to make sure you get on that boat, Mr. McGowan."

"I will." He crossed himself. "I didn' mean ta wind up—"

Darcy raised his hand to stop him, to telegraph, *I don't care. I'm just doing this for my overly charitable brother.* Something about prisons put him in an especially bad mood. "Tomorrow, Mr. McGowan. Eight sharp." He left without another word to the soldier he had just freed. He wanted only to be free himself of this task. He would remain to see James McGowan off, and then return to Derbyshire.

It was early yet, and he saw no reason to open the townhouse for just a few days, so he was staying at Bingley's—who had needed to take a trip to Town for business, so they had traveled together, and dined with the Maddoxes. In the old days, Bingley had been trailed by his status-obsessed sisters and perpetually cup-shot brother-in-law Mr. Hurst. His traveling party was now much smaller, but no less annoying to Darcy.

"I have to bring him," Bingley said in the carriage, petting Monkey, who was on his lap. "Otherwise, he'll drive Jane insane. He gets terribly upset when I leave."

"So between me and your wife, you must choose your wife."

"Of course, Darcy."

"A proper choice, I admit. However, I must remind you that your wife is less capable of throttling you."

Bingley shrugged. "I'm not certain that you're correct."

When Darcy returned to the house after his task at the prison, the first person he was greeted by was not a person at all, though he did try to stand up like one. He announced himself with a squeal.

"I don't care for you, either," Darcy said, and poured himself a glass of wine as he waited for Bingley to emerge from the study.

Bingley finally did, and Monkey climbed up him and onto his shoulder, which he took no real notice of. "I take it that it went well?"

"As well as could be expected," Darcy said, closing his book as Bingley sat down next to him. "I'll know for sure tomorrow morning if he's true to his word. Though I didn't ask for it. Still, he can't cash in the ticket."

"And then you'll write Grégoire? Assuming he's still in Tullow?"

"Yes. Wherever that is," Darcy said. "I suspect that he is wandering around the area or has holed himself up somewhere nearby. He's not been terribly forthcoming."

Bingley nodded. "How does he sound?"

"Happy. Or so Elizabeth assesses—she's better at reading between the lines than I am. But he's not going on and on about Irish monastic history anymore."

"So you don't know what he's doing."

Darcy was happy to have a friend who said the obvious, so he didn't have to say it. "Correct."

"I take it he has not set a date for his return."

"No."

A servant offered Bingley a biscuit from a tray, which he took. Monkey immediately grabbed the treat. "Monkey! Give that back!" But the monkey just squawked at him. "I suppose I don't want something that's been in your filthy paws anyway." He took another biscuit for himself and dismissed the servant. "Well, if he continues to write regularly and he sounds well, then that is a great improvement. I would not worry."

"You would worry if one of your children were in Ireland and behaving in a way that was out of character ."

"Grégoire is not your child. He is your brother, and is a grown man." Bingley frowned. "He is not sophisticated, but he is nonetheless capable of making his own decisions. Has he wasted away his entire inheritance gambling?"

"No."

"Has he attempted to rejoin the church, perhaps under a different name?"

"No."

"Then you have no reason to worry."

"I am not worried."

"Darcy," he said, "I've known you half my life now. I can read your indifferent stares better than your own sister can. The only one who can best me at that is Mrs. Darcy."

Darcy said nothing, confirming Bingley's initial assertion, but not willing to admit *that*, either. Instead, he changed the topic. "Speaking of children—"

"Oh, please do not tell my sister."

"I'm sure she will get the truth of it out of you. Which, by the way, is?"

"That we had an incident in which we had a change of governesses." He scratched Monkey's tiny head. "As in, we no longer have one. Know of any?"

"Was she dismissed or did she storm out in a rage?"

"A little of both, actually."

Darcy gave one of his half smiles. "How did Miss Bingley manage it?"

"This will impress you: hunger strike."

"*What?*"

"She had nothing but well water with lemon in it for three days. And locked herself in her room. *And* left the key in, so I couldn't open the door without removing the hinges."

Darcy continued smirking. "I admire her fortitude."

"It was a very…admirable…effort. In a way. And it did work. Mrs. Murrey gave up shouting through the door and was gone on the fourth day. Left a note of where to forward her last week's pay."

"Do you have any idea what brought it on? The particular incident?"

"Georgie does not like piano. Beyond that, no one is eager to ask her."

James McGowan was good to his silent vow and boarded the boat bound for Dublin. Darcy witnessed his departure and then returned to the house to write a letter to Grégoire relating this event. Darcy whiled away the rest of the day fencing at the club. He was finally getting good enough on his left side to face his old opponents properly, a source of satisfaction to him. Every year, Geoffrey came closer to besting him. He knew that one day his son would beat him—but he wanted to at least make him work for it.

The next day, he took George out for his birthday. It was not George Wickham's actual birthday, but it would occur within the month, and Darcy was not often in town. George Wickham would be four and ten, and he was obsessed with entering Oxford as soon as he could. Legally and financially, he could do it—Darcy had promised to front him the tuition while they waited for George's trust to open—but George had not the tutoring to be ready for a university-level education. Nor did Darcy think that a young man not even halfway through the tens should go to university. Geoffrey would not begin Cambridge until he finished at Eton, and he would begin Eton in the fall. Darcy suspected that it was more that George wanted to get out of the house than he desired to further his education. He wanted to say, *Don't rush into adulthood. It has responsibilities beyond your imagination.* But he could not express this, and instead he listened to George as he took him on a tour of the bookshops and purchased for him whatever he liked and did not already have.

"How is Mr. Bradley?" Darcy asked, leaving the broadness of the question open to interpretation.

"All right. Mother's with child again, if you hadn't heard."

He hadn't.

"Well, they're not sure yet, but they're fairly certain. I guess that is why there's been no general announcement."

"Your mother is certainly resilient," he said.

"I know—I mean, I've read, I've asked—it's not something she can control, but I wish…" he trailed off. Darcy let George find his words. "I wish she would slow down. For her health." He didn't specify physical or mental, if there was any specification to be made.

"What does Mr. Bradley think?"

"I haven't asked Mr. Bradley what he thinks!"

"Of course not," Darcy said as they walked down the street toward Gracechurch. "What do you think he thinks?"

"He seems…content. And he's concerned about Izzy, wants her to become a dignified lady. And he hired me a French tutor, so… he does what he can."

"I am pleased to hear that," Darcy said. *Very pleased indeed.* They arrived at the apartment, and were greeted by the sound of young Brandon wailing.

Mr. Bradley emerged when they entered. "Mr. Darcy."

"Mr. Bradley. I trust all is well."

"As it ever is," Mr. Bradley said with a roll of his eyes. "George, did he happen to buy you any new clothes, or was it just all books?"

"Next year, Mr. Bradley," George said.

"I will buy him a very smart suit," Darcy said, "but not until I do not fear him outgrowing it."

"Uncle Darcy!" Isabella Wickham came barreling down the stairs, bypassing her stepfather to curtsy to her uncle. "Did George keep his promise?"

"You should ask him that, Miss Wickham," he said as George produced the embroidery pattern she'd been begging him for. He had insisted it was part of his own birthday present. Darcy did not discourage George from spoiling his sister, as no one else seemed to be doing so, and he did the same with Georgiana. It was not clear yet whether Isabella would take the path of her mother or follow in more sensible footsteps, but it would definitely be close.

"I don't like to disappoint you, Izzy," George said, and she hugged him and kissed him, which he didn't seem to care for, big man that he now was. He was wiping it off as Lydia Bradley made her appearance, holding Brandon Bradley's hand.

"Mr. Darcy," she said, not bothering to curtsy.

"Mrs. Bradley," he said and bowed.

"I assume you wouldn't be staying for dinner, even if I offered?"

He did not want to fight with her—not ever, but especially not in front of her children. "Unfortunately, I am engaged elsewhere and am returning to Derbyshire tomorrow. Do you wish any messages delivered to your sisters there?"

"Tell them they have a new nephew or niece on the way to spoil, if they feel inclined to stop by," she said. "Feels like a niece."

He did not attempt to smile. It was not something he did. He merely bowed politely. "Congratulations, Mrs. Bradley. Mr. Bradley."

Mr. Bradley was beaming. Lydia Bradley's expression was harder to interpret, and Darcy had no wish to do so. He excused himself and left.

~ ~ ~

Darcy's missive made it to Tullow in good time. Grégoire, who had opened the post box in Tullow almost three months earlier, put down payment for another month. He had spent the day in town, but not shopping for groceries. Unfortunately, he had found no jewelers to his taste, and had to send out for information elsewhere. That did not dampen his mood as he returned to the house.

The sun was still up and dinner was on the table, but he did not find her waiting for him. He checked the bedroom, but still nothing. Eventually, he found a note on the nightstand. In scratchy handwriting, Caitlin had written,

In te roen

Curious more than worried, he headed out on the path to the woods and the church ruins with the mosaic of St. Patrick. There he found her, leaning against the old stone wall, a shawl over her shoulders. "Caitlin," he said, immediately noting her red eyes. "What is it?"

"I—I don't know." She did not protest when he sat down beside her. There was just enough room for the two of them in that little shelter—them and St. Patrick. "I'm shuk."

"What scared you?" He knew what really scared her, but he wanted to know what had set her off.

"It kicked."

This did not shock or alarm him. "It did?" She nodded.

He put his hand over her belly. She was now in her sixth month. "Did it do it once or—"

"It stopped. But I mean, it did it."

"Caitlin," he said, "that's wonderful." He laughed. "It's wonderful."

"It's still scary." Her voice was weak. "I don' know if I can do dis."

"Of course, you can."

She shook her head. "Not alone." Part of him was almost offended. "You're not alone; you know that. I won't leave you." He kissed her forehead. "Caitlin, I love you. I am not leaving you."

She put her head down so he couldn't see her face. "I shouldn'a got yeh involved. I'm so sorry." She was crying again. "So sorry."

"Shh, you don't have to be—" "I shouldn'a let yeh do all t'ese nice things for me, I shouldn'a let yeh get attached—"

"Caitlin—"

"But I love yeh," she said, raising her head back up. "I love yeh so much. I can't let yeh go."

He took her hand, the one she was trying to cover her face with, and kissed it. "You don't have to let me go. I am not trying to leave."

She shook her head. "Don' say it. I know yeh want ta. Please don'. Don' make it worse."

He nodded, even if he didn't really understand. He certainly had his suspicions. They had been together for months, she was increasingly due, and they were devout Catholics—even if Caitlin did not attend church—so the word *marriage* didn't really have to be uttered before it was being thought of by both parties. Still, they hadn't said anything, not in words.

"You're shivering," he announced. "It's not good—for the child or for you." Without allowing her to stop him, he picked her up, a feat he could still manage—barely, and carried her back to the house. He tucked her into bed and brought her some fresh milk. "Drink." She obeyed him, but otherwise was silent.

By the evening, as he went about making himself supper, she emerged from the bedroom, looking more composed. "Sorry."

"You don't have to be."

"I got rattled—I don' know." She looked at him with a weak smile as he ran his hand through her hair. "I don' deserve yeh."

"I would say the same," he answered, sitting down across from her. "If you really want me to leave, then say so. It will hurt, but I'll do what is right. But I won't leave unless you push me. I love you too much for that."

She said nothing, but squeezed his hand.

~ ~ ~

"Forgive me Father, for I have sinned. It has been two weeks since my last confession." Grégoire crossed himself and immediately began, not looking through the screen, even though he knew very well who the priest was. They rarely talked person to person; it was too awkward. "I have decided to ask Caitlin to marry me."

"Dis is a pure, gran' step, me sun."

He sighed. "I don't like the circumstances. It should be a happy time, but she's increasingly ill from her condition. Her emotions are everywhere. We haven't spoken the words, and yet she begs me not to ask for her hand—and I know exactly what she means. Then she tells me she loves me, and I know she means it."

The priest did not hold back. "Why do yeh t'ink she is confused? Yeh 'av toyed wi' 'er emoshuns for months nigh."

"Father, I would never—"

"Yeh tell 'er yeh love 'er?"

He turned to the lattice that kept the priest from him, his voice near anger. "Yes. Every day."

"An' do yeh continue ter nu 'er carnally, even in 'er condishun?"

"Yes."

"An' yeh continue ter provide for 'er. In every way, yeh are 'er 'usban' except under Jasus. Dat step, yeh seem reluctant ter take."

"I just said I would take it!" he shouted and then stopped in horror, crossing himself. "Forgive me, Father, for I have sinned. I just yelled at a man of the cloth." It lightened the air just enough for the conversation to continue. "Is this what love is? This torrent of emotions?"

"Many people 'av said so, me sun."

"I wanted this to be happy. I didn't plan it, but I suppose in the back of my mind, I wished that the time that I chose to take a wife would be the happiest moment of my life—and yet I am also so confused."

"Den yeh must truly be in love," said the priest. It was one of the most clever things he had said in their short but complex association. "Yeh will recall the story of Jacob and the angel."

"Yes, of course. He fought with him and won, and earned the name Israel."

"Yes.'N' yer man wept, as well. 'Is life ter dat point wus av doubt, for stealin' 'is brother's birthright by trickin' 'is owl lad an' den runnin' away. But he wept not whaen he wus on de road ter redempshun, but he did not weep until de final moment whaen he physically wrestled wi' 'is emoshuns through de aingayle, an' prevailed. So God blessed 'im an' from 'is seed came de twelve tribes av Israel, an' from de tribe av Judah, de ma av our Lord Jasus Chroist," he said. "Doubt an' de despair dat follows it whaen yeh dwell on it too long withoyt actin' are failures, but dey can be reversed an' overcum, an' den yeh truly becum de paddy God intends yeh ter be."

Grégoire swallowed this information, and was silent for a few moments as he did so. It did not dismiss all of his emotions—or any of them—but it made his path clear. "I think I understand." He leaned forward. "If I ask and she says no, what will I do then?"

"'Av feth in Christ an' hill show yeh de way," the priest said. "Say ten Hail Marys fer de sin of fornication. Jasus bless yeh, me sun."

"Thank you, Father. Go with God."

He did not linger. He said his prayers and left the church. When he returned home, he had no more questions. He had only a beautiful woman with dinner waiting.

~~~

Caitlin's emotions evened out again when she became accustomed to the baby's kicking, even when it disturbed her sleep. Grégoire laughed as he put his hand over her and felt it. "I think this child will be doing a lot of dancing."
~~~

The next Sunday, he went to church and prayed. On Monday, after early Mass, he went to Tullow to pick up the ring he had ordered. It was a gold band with emeralds set in it so that they looked sewn in, like the knots he had seen on the old crosses of Monasterboice. "I'll take it," he said, and put the box in his pocket.

It was a long way back from Tullow. He stopped on the road for none prayers, and hoped to be home in time for Vespers, which were followed by their supper. It was summer and the days were long, so he did not worry about light. The fields thinned out and the forest became thicker, until at last he came upon the house.

He did not smell dinner cooking. The fire was not even going. The place was a mess, as if it had been torn apart, and he stepped inside and set down the bag in shock. He barely had a moment to react to being grabbed by a strong set of hands and hurled against the wall, which was enough to knock him to his knees, but not onto the floor entirely. A hulk of a man backed away.

"Who are you and what have you done with Caitlin?" Grégoire demanded.

"Yeh must be the one keepin' 'er 'appy wit' yer fancy gifts. I'm not the best 'a men, but yer scum!"

Grégoire grabbed the table to help stabilize himself. He was nearly a head shorter than this man, and had never struck a man in his life. He would not win in a fight—not a physical one, anyway. "You have not answered my question. Who are you?"

"Caitlin? Yeh want ta tell 'im who I am?"

Caitlin emerged from the bedroom. To Grégoire's horror, her clothes were torn, with some pieces bloodied, and her face was red and swollen. "Please jus' let 'im go."

The man had red hair like fire and his personality was similar—easily brought to the peak of destruction. "Yeh tell 'im who I am!" Grégoire looked at her as she came forward, shaking, to take the man's side, but not to touch him. Her voice was a whisper. "E's me 'usband."

CHAPTER 31

The Unmentionable Thing

"IT'S NOT POSSIBLE," GRÉGOIRE SAID.

Mr. MacKenna grabbed Caitlin by the arm so hard she cried out. "Why don't yeh tell yer rich lover de trut'h?"

Grégoire could see that Caitlin was wavering. The man did not release her arm, and eventually she raised her terrified eyes to face Grégoire, "I—'tis me husband. He tol' me he didn't want anoder mout'h ta feed, but I wouldn' do it."

"An' what did yeh do, Mrs. MacKenna?"

"Ran away," she whispered, but loud enough for them all to hear.

"And?"

"Stole de money ta do it."

Mr. MacKenna was still angry, but he did cast a triumphant glare at Grégoire, still backed against the wall.

"Cait-Caitlin," he stuttered, "your family—"

"Died wi' me brah'der, whaen I wus twelve. I didn' have any-body—'cept Neil."

"Normally, I'd be mighty inclined ta quid da man who's been feckin' me wife," Neil MacKenna said, "but I'll make an exception dis time. Now, go runnin' back ta England or wherever dey make cheatin' fecks."

Grégoire wanted to apologize—legitimately, as it was called for—but he looked again at the beaten, sobbing form of Caitlin, swallowed, and said, "I will not let you take her."

"*What?*"

"I said I will not let you take her." He stood up straighter. "I understand now she is your wife and I respect that, and I will never touch her again, but if you treat her and the child this way—"

"'S gonna sell da baby. Or kill it,"Caitlin wimpered.

"Shut yer *bake!*" her husband said, and struck her.

This, Grégoire would not stand for. Not in the place he had come to think of as his home—not anywhere, for that matter. He tried to come between them, which only earned him a smack on his face hard enough to knock him to the ground. MacKenna released his wife long enough to take a knife from the kitchen counter and drive it into Grégoire's arm, pinning him to the wall. Grégoire wasn't sure what bothered him more—his cry or Caitlin's own.

"Yeh don' come afta 'er," MacKenna said. "Yeh leave with yer loife, English."

In what seemed like a blur to Grégoire, the MacKennas left. He remembered only the pleading, apologetic look on Caitlin's bruised face, and the scrap of rag she dropped on the floor as she left.

It was not until they were gone that he was able to pull the knife out, not so much because it was lodged in him but because it was lodged in the wooden wall. He set it on the ground and pulled up his shirt. The wound wasn't bad—just a pierce through the top layers of flesh on his upper arm, barely more than a graze compared with earlier wounds. He pulled himself up with his good arm and scrambled for a piece of cloth. Eventually, he removed the window dressing and tore off a length, wrapping it tightly around his arm to stop the bleeding. The pain in his arm and the sting on his face were not nearly as bad as the ache in his heart, just beginning to set in.

No. He needed to concentrate. That was what Darcy would do. He needed to find a surgeon to sew him up, and then he had to follow them. He looked around at the looted room. All the good items appeared to be gone. As he stepped over it, he remembered the piece of cloth and picked it up. It was not cloth—it was paper with the word *dreser.*

He stumbled to the bedroom, which had also been ransacked. The mattress had even been overturned. On the dresser, in a pile of things apparently deemed worthless—his clothing and the like—he found a note scribbled so quickly it was barely readable. But his name was spelled correctly, as he had taught her.

Grégoire

Im sory. i lovd you. it was to hard to sey.

Dublin east. talbot stret. 37.

He knew if he gave into his emotions, he would lose too much time. Instead, he swallowed them as best he could, stuffed his bag full of the things he thought he needed, and left, Caitlin's note tucked in his satchel.

~ ~ ~

"Mr. Gregory!"

Even though the walk had not been far, Grégoire collapsed at the O'Muldoons' door, one hand clutching the bleeding arm. Fortunately, Mr. O'Muldoon caught him in time, and helped him to a seat at their table.

"I—I need a surgeon," he said, his voice a hoarse whisper. A glass of whiskey was set before him and he took a good gulp. "It's small but the bleeding won't stop."

"Yeh know who attacked yeh?"

He didn't want to look at either of their expressions when he said it, so he just looked at the table. "Caitlin's husband." He sighed. Now that he was sitting, and panic was not giving him strength, he was starting to fade—not from blood loss, which by his standards was relatively minor, but from emotional exhaustion. "I didn't know."

"'S not right," Mrs. O'Muldoon said. "We woulda told yeh, if we'd known."

"I know."

They didn't ask him any further questions. Mr. O'Muldoon instead announced he was leaving for another farm, where he knew he could borrow a horse that could get him to Tullow.

"I was—I was robbed," Grégoire said. "I cannot pay right now, but I…have money. In Dublin."

"'S all right, Gregory. Ya jest rest."

She put a blanket over him because he was shivering, and he finished the whiskey and had another glass. He was nodding off into a sad, comfortable haze when the surgeon arrived. Being sewn up was enough to properly wake him, but it was quick and clean. As the O'Muldoons paid the surgeon, Grégoire began to remove his paper and writing implements from his satchel.

"Oh no, Mr. Gregory, yeh should rest—"

"I have to write … my brother," he said, "to meet me in Dublin. I'm going after her."

"Gregory," Mr. O'Muldoon said, laying a strong hand on his shoulder, "I can't even imagine what yer goin' t'hrough, but she's a married woman."

"I know," he replied calmly as he opened the ink jar. "I know I can't…He felt the oncoming torrent of tears, but swallowed them back. "Even so, Mr. MacKenna is going to kill or sell the baby and maybe kill her in the process. I will find some way to protect her." He crossed himself. "God help me."

It took him more than an hour to write the letter. It was brief, but his mind wandered, and once the tears began, it was hard to continue. He hoped what he wrote would be comprehensible. After many blots from tears, he folded the letter and requested a candle to melt the wax. He barely had the energy to stamp the Darcy symbol into the soft seal. "For tomorrow's post; I may oversleep."

Mr. O'Muldoon took it with some evident reservations, but not enough to stop him from holding his tongue as his wife escorted their tired, wounded, and tipsy guest into one of the children's rooms, where he was given their bed for the night. "Compline," he said to no one in particular. "Oh, goodness, Compline." But the words didn't come. "*In te Domine speravi...*"—"In thee, O Lord, have I put my trust..."

Beyond that, he had nothing left in him.

~~~

Elizabeth Darcy knew something was wrong before anyone else in Pemberley, outside the two people in the study. She knew even before elderly Mrs. Reynolds, still sharp as a tack, managed to swing by with a concerned look to indicate, *Maybe you should go check on your husband*. Even though Elizabeth was upstairs, trying to convince Cassandra to settle down for a nap, she knew she had to get to her husband before he was forced to come to her. It was better that way.

She opened the door to the study to find him discussing pounds with his steward, who was still seated as Darcy paced anxiously by the window. Seeing her, he said, "Five thousand, it is. I need it by the end of the day. I do not care how you acquire it." That was a nod for the steward to leave. He forced a smile for his wife. "No one in this family is ever permitted to leave Britain again. Travel is nothing but trouble."

"Is he—"

"His letter," he said, holding up a tear-stained letter with the Darcy seal still attached to one edge. "He is as well as can be expected." Clearly, nothing would offer explanation but the letter itself, so he handed it to her and returned to the window, pacing and staring out at the rolling hills of Pemberley as Elizabeth sat down to read.

Dearest Brother,

I have not the time or strength to spend on an adequate explanation for my unforgivable actions. I plead only for your assistance, despite what I have done. I have not the wit or experience to complete this mission without you.

As you know, I have been living outside Tullow for three
~~~

months now, but not in any kind of spiritual retreat. In my travels, I came upon a woman who was not only starving, destitute, and with child all alone, but the most beautiful creature I have ever seen. She said her family had thrown her out, and the father of the child had abandoned her when she refused to end her pregnancy. Her name is Caitlin.

I have never been in love before. I did not know the symptoms, other than the physical ones, which I shall not elaborate here. I confessed my sins and the priest said to marry her expeditiously. I was more hesitant to enter into the eternal union of marriage if I was not sure. She was only three months along when I met her. I gave her every attention even when she asked for nothing. When we came to an understanding of our love, I went to buy her a ring.

The day that the ring arrived, I returned home. Yes, I considered it my home. There was a man there who identified himself as Mr. Neil MacKenna, her husband. In the time since I had left he had beaten her to the point where she was bruised beyond recognition. When he pressed her, she told me everything. She has no family. They died years ago. She married Mr. MacKenna, but he did not want the child, so she stole his money and ran away. She could not bear to tell me. She left a note saying she . . . I cannot say it. To return to the moment, he made to strike her again for some perceived insult and I tried to get between them. He stabbed me in the arm (only a graze, I assure you, now sewn) and left me pinned to the wall, taking his wife with him. He said he would kill me if I followed.

I can have no intentions for her. She is a married woman and I, once a monk, am now just an adulterer. The fact that I did not know has some relevance, but I have no time for that now. She said he is going to sell or kill the baby when it is born. He may kill her. The part of me that remains a good Christian cannot let that happen. Perhaps we could pay him to separate from her? I have faith that you will think of something.

I will be in Dublin. She left his address behind. I taught her to write. I will be staying at ______. Please write me at Box 22 or find me there.

No, I will not come home until I have seen her to safety. I am sorry, but in response to your question, I WILL NOT LISTEN TO REASON.

This poor sinner,
Grégoire

She looked up from the letter, her eyes not particularly dry. "When are you leaving?"

"As soon as I have enough money freed up. Tonight should be long enough. If not, then tomorrow morning."

"Should I write Georgiana? He doesn't mention her."

"What do you think?"

This was a woman's realm—he could not divine what his sister would think of this, though he knew that she would be sympathetic. Grégoire had been wronged by the woman he loved, and she had been wronged by the man who controlled and owned her, for all purposes. Elizabeth said, "I think she should be told as soon as possible."

He nodded. He was trying to focus on the task at hand—getting to Dublin quickly. He fell into methodical planning when he could not bear the emotional consequences of doing otherwise. Grégoire was right—Darcy was good at getting things done, even things that seemed impossible. "In all likelihood, the husband is sufficiently poor that he can be tempted to send his wife away to raise the child elsewhere for the right amount of money. We would have to hire a protector to make sure it happened—it could not be Grégoire. Even he must know that."

"There is absolutely no way that the marriage could end?"

"My understanding of Catholic law is that we would have to find sufficient evidence that the marriage was falsely done or incestuous. Of course, I suspect it was neither, or Grégoire would have said so. No, they are married until one of them dies." He paused. "I must get to my brother."

"Darcy, you know he wouldn't—"

"I know. But he would put himself in harm's way for her—he's already done so."

"Do you wish me to go?"

He stopped pacing. He seemed to be considering it. "Dublin is not far by boat. In all likelihood, it will be a financial exchange and we will leave. If I need you, I will write for you."

They exchanged looks.

"I will take a pistol this time," he said. "I'll take two."

"So why is he going to Ireland?"

"I don't know," Geoffrey said, plucking up the grass in front of them as they sat on the hill. From there, he could see his father riding away on his horse, westbound. "Something about Uncle Grégoire."

"*Of course,* it's Uncle Grégoire," Georgie said. "Who else do we know in Ireland?" She repositioned her shawl, which protected her dress from the morning dew. "Is that what it means to be master of Pemberley? You always have to be abroad, rescuing relations?"

"Apparently."

Grégoire was staying at one of the best hotels in Dublin, apparently aware that his brother would prefer nothing less. The former monk was staying under the Darcy name, perhaps for his own safety.

To Darcy's surprise, as he entered the hotel suite, Grégoire was neither in intense prayer or openly sobbing. He sat in the armchair, a bottle of fine whiskey beside him, untouched. Darcy had never seen him with a real beard, the kind a man grew out and trimmed properly. It made him look older, but what made him truly aged was the look around his eyes, as if he had cried until he had nothing left in him and was now just a shell of a man, grasping his rosary. His clothing was clean but unchanged. He was worn out in other ways. "Brother—"

"Grégoire," he said as they embraced. "I came as soon as I could."

"Thank you." There was something strangely calm about Grégoire. Perhaps he was just out of other emotions. "My arm is healing. The stitches can come out early next week. He only grazed me."

"Thank God."

Grégoire crossed himself. So he had some faith left.

Darcy had only a few bags, which were soon brought up. Dinner was ordered. The stew that arrived was inedible, but Grégoire didn't seem to mind. Neither of them spoke, Darcy not sure which topic to broach first and Grégoire lost in his own thoughts.

It was the younger brother who broke the silence. "I bought her a ring." He put it down on the table, as though it were hot to the touch. Darcy picked it up.

"It's beautiful," he said, at a loss. It seemed fitting for an Irish lass. "What do you want me to say? That it will go well on someone else's finger?"

"I don't know. I don't know anything." He looked down. "I went to confession. The priest—a priest here—he said I should say prayers and give to the poor in penance for my sins. But I've always done that. And I refuse—" He choked up. It seemed he hadn't exhausted his tears after all. "I know it was a great sin, but that doesn't make what it was at the time any less wonderful. I cannot feel sorry for something I do not feel sorry about."

"You didn't know," Darcy said. "She did not tell you."

But Grégoire did not seem to want to be comforted. Darcy reflected: Had he wanted someone around while he fell into the bottle after Elizabeth's rejection of his initial proposal? The only reason he had sobered up at all was to keep a good face in front of his sister and not let Pemberley go to ruin while his heart quietly lay broken. No, he had come here for a purpose, to help Grégoire do his real penance—to save this woman he loved from doom (or at least determine if the doom was real).

Darcy fell back on his habit of being brutally honest. "I can find no words to comfort you. There are none for a man with a broken heart," he said. "But on this mission, I can help you."

"That," Grégoire said, "is all I need."

CHAPTER 32

The Business at Hand

FOR TWO DAYS, DARCY had staked out the East district. It was near the docks, so most of the people were workers, and accustomed enough to a wealthy Englishman walking through on his way to a better part of town—but with his distinct accent he said little. Grégoire's address was confirmed—there was a Mr. MacKenna living in an apartment complex on Talbot Street, a dockworker and handyman, currently a step away from the workhouse (a description that matched most of the men in the area). His wife was in residence, but had not been seen or heard from in days.

Grégoire was sensible enough to understand that he ought not go with Darcy on his trips. They would not risk a chance encounter with the man who had assaulted him. In addition, Darcy convinced him to shave. Pressing charges would be difficult, especially with MacKenna as the cuckolded husband and Grégoire as a wayward man of the cloth. Even with the Union Jack flying over their heads on the pole above the hotel entrance, this was not England. Grégoire went to Mass, and spent most of the day in the cathedral. He seemed to be returning to his normal self. It was a strange comfort to Darcy. This Grégoire was at least familiar to him.

As he sat in the tavern across from the docks, sipping awful beer and pretending to read the paper, he mused on all of this.

"I thought you were the great reconnaissance expert. Might as well write, *I'm a wealthy, spying bastard* on your forehead," said the man sliding in next to him. "And don't start with the 'Lord' business."

"Kincaid," he said, not frowning but not smiling as William Kincaid joined him. "Is Georgiana here?"

"Came as soon as we heard. She's with her brother. So have you seen the woman in question?"

"Not yet. I have only her description. She is not leaving the flat, which, considering her condition, is no surprise."

"Not everyone cares about propriety, Darcy."

"Did I give my sister away to an earl or not?"

William smiled. "What about the landlord and landlady?"

"Lives on the first floor. Just the wife. Husband is dead, I think."

He nodded. "Did you talk to her?"

"She said they arrived last week and Mrs. MacKenna has not been out since."

"Not even for groceries?"

Darcy shook his head.

"I don't like it."

"Neither do I."

"You go forward with your plan," Kincaid said. "I will be your back."

"That may prove difficult. They did rob my brother, but I doubt they spent the money on a chandelier."

When Darcy returned to the suite, Georgiana did not rush to him, as she used to do. She was embracing her own younger sibling, who was sobbing. Darcy said nothing, slipping in silently. Whether they noticed his presence or not mattered nothing to him. That Grégoire had been able to unload his feelings on someone was a relief; that it was not himself sparked something he had not felt in a long time: sibling jealousy. But he was the responsible one, wasn't he? The one whom others turned to when they needed help? He mulled it over with a glass of Irish whiskey, which he shared with Lord Kincaid.

"We should be done with it," Darcy said. Two days had been painful enough, and now that they had the location confirmed, they had no reason not to make their move. Grégoire was willing to pay anything, but Darcy would do the negotiation, so that the numbers did not begin in the thousands. MacKenna had probably never seen a hundred-pound bill in his life.

"Has she ever seen you without whiskers?" Darcy asked as Grégoire emerged from prayer, dressed in a white shirt and vest. He looked more normal these days, less the penitent monk who had come home from Spain.

"When I first arrived in the area, yes."

Darcy nodded.

Georgiana gave both her brothers and her husband a good-luck kiss good-bye. "You will be fine," she assured Grégoire. Assuming he did not put himself in harm's way, he would not be in danger.

The Darcy brothers set out just as it was getting dark. Kincaid would meet them later; that was part of the plan that Darcy dearly hoped would not be necessary. He also hoped they would not be robbed on the way there, as that would be exceedingly unfortunate (except for the thief, who would then presumably retire to a private isle in the north). They took a coach down Talbot Street; there was no reason to conceal themselves further as foreigners. They were not stopped at the entrance to the building, or even on the stairs. The walls were thin on every floor and in the building next door, which was no more than a foot away. The noises were all indistinguishable, one from another.

The flat that belonged to Mr. and Mrs. MacKenna had no sounds coming forth from it, but light spilled out from under the door. The stairway was lit only with moonlight through the broken window, and they stopped in front of the door. Grégoire crossed himself and nodded as Darcy removed his hat and knocked on the door with his walking stick.

"What do yeh want?"

"To speak to Mrs. MacKenna."

The door opened so hard it slammed against the inside wall, and Darcy found a pistol pointed at his face. A small one, but a pistol nonetheless. Grégoire remained on the staircase, out of view.

Darcy betrayed nothing but calm and confidence. "If you shoot me, you will hang. If you do not, you will be a very rich man."

The man facing him—red-haired and red-eyed, slouching in an intimidating manner in his soiled workman's clothing—was not quite twice his size, but it was apparent who would win in a brawl. Still, Darcy didn't move for his own pistol, plainly tucked into his belt, or anything else. He stayed still and let the logic sink in.

Neil MacKenna finally lowered his pistol, but did not put it away. "Who are yeh?"

"Mr. Darcy," he said, "of Pemberley and Derbyshire."

"Never 'eard av either o' dem places."

"Fortunately, I am not here to discuss them. I am here to discuss your wife."

"I'm not runnin' a brothel," MacKenna said, backing up just enough to let Darcy a step or two into the room. There was no evidence of the wife in the immediate room, but he saw there was a side room with light beneath its door as well. MacKenna was not as slow as he looked, at least mentally. "I'll bite. Where's de bugger whose been feckin' me wife?"

"Wary of being stabbed again," Darcy said.

MacKenna put the pistol down on the parlor table, or what was supposed to be a parlor table but was dented and worn and probably a century old. "Fine. On me honor."

"On your honor," Darcy repeated, as he heard Grégoire emerge behind him, not standing nearly as tall or as proudly as his brother. MacKenna watched him, but did not move against him. "Now. We are here to make a deal."

"I towl yeh, she is not for sale."

"But you would agree to a separation from your wife, perhaps. She would live somewhere else—in the west, maybe. Wherever she likes. And you would stay here. And I would make it worth your while, and we will all be happy."

"An' 'er fella 'appy too, aye?"

"Sir," Grégoire said, "I swear under God in heaven that I did not know that Mrs. MacKenna was your wife, or anyone's wife. Marriage is a sacrament. I would not willingly violate it again." He swallowed. "I would never see her again. She would live separately from both of us. You could even employ a guard to make sure I did not violate my oath."

"And I would employ a guard to make sure you do not violate yours," Darcy said to Mr. MacKenna.

"Sounds dear," MacKenna said. The fish was considering the bait.

"Quite. And for the sake of Christian charity—what with you giving up seeing your adored wife and future child—I would not have you in poverty." Darcy carefully reached into his coat, and removed the first packet of bills, laying them carefully on the parlor table beside them. "Five hundred pounds."

MacKenna did the math in his head—or gave the appearance of doing so. "For 'er, maybe, a wee house. But dat wud leave me here, in dis shitehole, if I split it."

"Of course," Darcy said. He removed another packet. "A thousand."

"But yeh're forgettin' the kid. Kids're expensive little buggers until dey're old enough fer de chimneys. And that's a few years. And if I decide to have some of me own? *Sacrament* of marriage an' all, we're all men 'ere."

Darcy nodded as if everything this man said were reasonable, and removed another, larger packet. "Two thousand for Christian piety."

"Whattaya know about Christian piety, English? Yer *kings* get divorced. Yeh gotta lot of makin' up ta do."

He rolled his eyes and looked at Grégoire, who did not even have to nod. "Five thousand pounds." He held up three more packets of a thousand in hundred-pound notes. "More money than you would ever see in your life, even if you worked the best job in the city from dawn 'til dusk, Mr. MacKenna." This time, he did not put it on the table. He held it up for MacKenna to drool at. "I want to see Mrs. MacKenna."

"What?"

"I have to know she's in good health before I put down money for her long life in solitude."

MacKenna looked at both of them, and crossed his arms. "Six thousand."

"Perhaps you do not know the definition of 'see'—"

"Six thousand. Yeah, so, a thousand to see me wife." He nodded in the direction of Grégoire. "I know he'll pay it. Yer lucky I'm not chargin' fer both eyes."

This was no small sum—except to Grégoire, who just nodded.

"Six thousand pounds," Darcy said, putting the money on the table and offering his hand.

MacKenna looked at the gloved hand, spit in his own, and shook it. "Done." He immediately picked up the bills and began stuffing them into his shirt.

"Not quite," Darcy reminded him. "Your more immediate part of the bargain."

"*Caitlin!*"

The woman who emerged was much as Grégoire had described her, good and bad. Wearing a filthy blue dress that did not even attempt to disguise her condition, she emerged barefoot from what was likely the bedroom. Her hair, a reddish blonde, was long and straight and flowed down her back, probably making her look younger than she was. Grégoire had said that she had told him she was twenty. Her face was swollen on one side, and she crossed her arms as if she was shivering, trying to make it to her husband's side.

She had not looked at Darcy except in passing; Grégoire was her only concern and his with her.

"Mrs. MacKenna," Darcy said, bowing to her. She was, after all, a lady.

"Mrs. MacKenna." Grégoire's voice cracked as he bowed.

MacKenna grabbed her by her thin, frail arm. "If yeh excuse me, I'd loike a moment ter make sure me struggle an' strife understands everyt'in'..." Caitlin whimpered as MacKenna pulled her along to the bedroom. In thirty seconds, he was back. Darcy sensed Grégoire tensing beside him.

The husband turned back to Darcy and tossed him a five hundred–pound packet of notes. "Ta be fair—fer de child."

Darcy barely had time to piece together what he had meant by that before he heard the scream. Where was Kincaid?

Grégoire, of course, rushed heedlessly forward to the doorway before Darcy could stop him, only to face MacKenna turning to him with his pistol drawn. "You can buy me wife, but not me child!"

The crash of the window was what startled MacKenna, and his shot at Grégoire went astray, hitting the wall instead as William Kincaid leaped into the room in a swathe of tartan. "What in feckin' hell—"

"Feckin' hell is where you're going," Kincaid said, but did not run him through with his claymore, the "great sword" of the Scots Highlanders. Instead, he bashed him on the head, hard enough to knock him out. Grégoire was just fast enough to avoid the gigantic Irishman crashing down in front of him. He leaped right over the body and into the bedroom.

"Handle him!" Darcy told Kincaid, and entered the bedroom to find Grégoire over Caitlin, who was still screaming.

"Shh," he told her as he slowly drew out the knife that had been stuck into her stomach. "It will be all right—"

"Feck no, Grégoire, it will not be feckin' all right!" she screamed. Darcy was impressed that she actually pronounced his name correctly.

He turned to Kincaid. "I'll get a surgeon. MacKenna?"

"If he rises, I will make him regret it."

Darcy nodded and bolted out the door.

This had not been the plan.

~ ~ ~

When he returned with the surgeon and a constable, both the MacKennas were unconscious. Grégoire sat on the bed beside Caitlin MacKenna, pressing down on the wound in a desperate attempt to make it stop spurting blood. He was pushed aside by the surgeon and collapsed on the ground in exhaustion. "She is still breathing—"

"What in the hell is this all about?" said the diminutive constable, who was far too calm for Darcy's liking. At least he was English. He turned to Kincaid, who only raised his sword.

"Lord Kincaid of Clan Kincaid, Earl of _____shire," he said. "This man stabbed his wife and tried to shoot that man over there, Mr. Bellamont."

It was yet another stroke of bad luck that Mr. MacKenna chose that moment to return to consciousness, and this time the presence of the constable prevented Kincaid from beating him back. MacKenna quickly backed down from whatever he had been planning when he saw that he was on the floor and disarmed, and he was also facing Kincaid, Darcy, and a man in uniform.

"What's all this?" the constable asked, rightfully, of the man who owned the apartment.

"These men—they came to take me wife!"

"That's not true," Darcy said. "He agreed to a monetary transaction and separation from his wife—"

"Because your feckin' friend seduced her! Me wife!"

"Sir," Kincaid said, "this man has stabbed his wife and shot at my brothers-in-law because of a conversation."

"Is this true?" the constable asked MacKenna.

"I—I did try to shoot him," MacKenna said, pointing to Grégoire in the door frame, "after he stabbed me wife! She's carryin' 'is child!"

"That's a lie!" Grégoire shouted. "You stabbed her! You wanted to kill the baby!"

The constable's whistle brought them all to silence as his men stamped up the steps. By now, most of the other houses had heard the screaming and quieted down so that they could listen through the window, especially the family across from the apartment, who had allowed Kincaid to jump through their own window to get to MacKenna's. "Men," the constable said, "take these two into custody." He gestured to MacKenna and Grégoire.

"*What!*" Darcy resisted the urge to shake this little man—this man whom he had brought to arrest MacKenna—"That man is a liar! My brother has done nothing! You cannot lock him up for trying to save a woman's life!"

"A woman he got with child? A woman not his wife?" the constable said skeptically.

"That's not the story—please, just listen to me, and I will tell you everything, and Lord Kincaid will confirm—"

"Course you will," the constable said, apparently thinking himself a brilliant detective, "because he's your brother. Now I just want to talk to both of them and all of this will be sorted out—"

The thing that kept Darcy from taking a swing at the man was Grégoire's voice. "Darcy! Don't!" He was not resisting as the officers shackled him. "Let it all come out. Just take care of *her* now."

"I will not see you in a cell!"

"I lived in a cell," Grégoire said. "The truth will be sorted out. Just save her!" That was his last plea before they pulled him away.

"Come on, Darcy," Kincaid said, putting away his blade and tugging at his shoulder. "The walls are thin as paper here. Everyone in the neighborhood heard us. We can gather enough witnesses to have Grégoire out by first light."

Only the distraction of Caitlin's scream as she woke was enough to shake him from his horrified stupor, and he did not care for the world it brought him into.

~ ~ ~

Grégoire's interrogation began immediately. A skilled confessor, he recalled everything in neat order, showing his wound from the earlier knife fight in the house near Tullow. Yes, he knew she was with child. No, he had not known that she was married and had not touched her since he found out she was. He named all the people who knew her story of abuse and neglect, and all those he had spoken to since he met her—names and locations, one after another.

"You never told her what you were worth?" the constable said, appropriately astounded by the number. With interest from years he had not spent his fortune, Grégoire was worth about 50,200 pounds.

"The desire of money is truly the root of all evil," he said, "if this is all it brings." Mercifully, they had allowed him to keep his rosary, and he worried the beads with his fingers the entire time he spoke. "I tried to buy her health when she was starving. I tried to buy her happiness when she was upset. I tried to buy her freedom when I found her enslaved to a man who said he wanted her child—his child—dead. And now I am in jail and she is, for all I know, dying. What has money brought me but misery?"

Everything that had happened in Dublin, he explained. Their plan had been, as they had said to MacKenna, for him to agree to a separation, the only thing that would keep his hands off her and her future child, and they would pay anything for it to happen. In fact, had Mr. MacKenna not been so vengeful, he would have simply walked out the door a very wealthy man.

"And the Scot?"

"My brother-in-law was protection—in case something terrible happened." He tried to cross himself, but his shackles prevented him from doing it properly. "If she dies, you might as well lock me away, because my life will be nothing."

When they were satisfied, they put him in a cell, different from his monastic cell only in that it had bars, and he was chained to a wall. There, he collapsed. The cell boasted a tiny window, and he could see only the sunlight of morning. There was no food for him.

"Forgive me, Lord, for I have sinned," he said. "Most recently, I missed Vigils because I was being interrogated. But before that, I did terrible things, for which there is no accounting." That was how he began Lauds, the prayer for the sixth hour of the day, which he recited from heart on his knees before collapsing on the wooden board that served as a cot and slept. His body was relentless—he woke again for Terce and yet again for Sext. He thought maybe he would go through the entire monastic cycle before he saw another person. Then, as he was finishing his psalms, he heard boots against stone and the constable came around the bend, followed closely by Darcy, who lost his color upon seeing his brother. Grégoire absent-mindedly realized that he was still largely covered in Caitlin's blood.

"Mr. Bellamont," the constable said, "you are free to go, but are requested by the department not to leave Dublin proper until Mr. MacKenna's trial, as you will be called to witness."

"Of course, officer," he said. He couldn't believe how weak his voice sounded as the constable unlocked the heavy padlock and then the locks that held him to the wall. "I swear it."

Darcy helped him up. "She's alive," he whispered. Darcy was cleaner, but beyond that did not look much better than he did. He looked profoundly tired. "She's lost the child."

It sank in Grégoire's chest harder than any of his shackles. "Was it a boy or girl?"

"Does it matter?"

"*Was it a boy or a girl?*" He was surprised by the insistence of his own voice.

"Boy," Darcy said grimly. "She will likely live, but she will not have children again." He was now supporting his brother, half carrying him out, as Grégoire had lost most of his strength hearing those words.

"Lord, what have I done?"

Without hesitation, Darcy answered, "You have saved her life."

CHAPTER 33

The Promise

FROM A CERTAIN PERSPECTIVE, Darcy felt it was fortunate that Grégoire could not be present for the events immediately following his arrest. He did not want his brother to have those memories to add to his other painful memories.

The initial surgeon on call had merely stitched up Mrs. MacKenna to stop the bleeding. For a bit she seemed to recover as they gathered her things for her and transported her to the hotel, but by the time they reached their room, she had suspicious cramps. Fortunately, Darcy had prepared for the worst and already found and had the card of the best surgeon in Dublin. When the surgeon arrived, two hours had passed and she was exhausted and nearly delirious, clinging to Georgiana's arm and screaming Irish curses.

The surgeon immediately pronounced the baby dead and her body in a pseudo-labor. This idea, Mrs. MacKenna did not take well, even though she must have expected it. She was tired, distraught, and in great pain. She grabbed Darcy's hand and squeezed it so tightly he was relieved it was the lame one. "Yeh take care a' Grégoire. Yeh promise me."

"He's my brother. Of course, I will."

"*Yeh promise me!*"

"I promise," he said softly.

In the background, the doctor was mixing up his concoction for pain, probably some cheap version of laudanum. She did not seem particularly aware, just focused on Darcy. "I didna' mean fer him ta get involved. It jest *happened*."

"I know," he said, but probably not in the way that she thought he knew. This was not the first time that Grégoire had gotten himself in over his head.

"I love 'im," she said. "I loved 'im. It wasn' right, but I did."

He had less argument with how she felt about Grégoire and more with the massive deception for a period of months that had nearly cost his brother his life, but Darcy didn't say that. This was not the time to say that. "I will tell him."

The surgeon gave her a healthy dose of whatever was in the glass, and when that wasn't enough, he made her sip whiskey. It knocked her out. William Kincaid escorted his wife out of the room; she had every right to sit by a normal labor, but this was not a normal labor and the only thing in question was how badly it would end.

They stayed in the sitting room of their suite and waited. Occasionally, she would return to consciousness and wail, until the doctor found some way to knock her out again. They sat in silence because no one could think of anything to say.

At last, the surgeon emerged and handed a bag to his assistant, who quickly left. "I've done the best I can."

"Will she live?"

"If she is fortunate, yes. I do not think she will bear children again—that part of her is too damaged."

Darcy nodded and paid the surgeon. He had to leave to begin collecting people to speak on Grégoire's behalf and submit his own statement, but he felt the need to at least see her first.

To his surprise, Mrs. MacKenna was awake, if barely, in the bed. The hotel would not be recovering the sheets. "It was a boy," she said with what remained of her voice.

"I am very sorry, Mrs. MacKenna."

"I felt 'im kick. We laughed about it—now he's gone." But she had no energy left even to cry. She just let the tears fall. He briefly squeezed her hand, and excused himself to collect his brother.

It was nearly twelve hours later when he returned to the hotel. Darcy had not slept at all since the previous morning, and Grégoire, evidently little. Fortunately, witnesses were not hard to gather—the family who had let Kincaid jump through their window were immediately questioned, as was the landlady about Mr. MacKenna's regular behavior (none of which spoke well of his character) and his shouting threats at his wife. There was also the matter that the knife was an old soldier's blade, from the war of 1812, in which he had fought. With the evidence stacking against the other suspect, Darcy convinced them to release his brother, and the two of them numbly returned to the hotel.

His impulse was to somehow get Grégoire cleaned up before Georgiana saw him, with his clothing and hair still caked with dried blood, but Darcy was tired and that impulse occurred far too late to make any difference.

"How is she?" were Grégoire's first words to his sister, who, all things considered, was taking the sight of him incredibly well.

"Resting. You heard about—"

"Yes."

Nothing else needed to be said. Kincaid offered his condolences, and Darcy had hot water and a tub brought up as fast as possible. In the changing room, they left Grégoire to himself, perhaps to find some peace in a tub of hot water.

With Grégoire safely released and Mrs. MacKenna out of danger, general exhaustion overtook the party, and somehow, clothed or with at least their outer layers removed, Darcy and the Kincaids fell into their separate beds.

Grégoire padded out of his room, clean and shaven, and back in his normal clothes. His fingers ran through the rosary beads as he crossed the parlor and slowly opened the door to Caitlin's room, bringing the light from the parlor in. She was pale and even from a distance he could see her strained features, contorted in pain as she slept.

He was too distracted to pray, and he had no right to bless her. He turned to leave.

"I know yeh won't come in," she said, "and I am sorry—so sorry."

"I'm sorry, about the child," he said. "I think…I think I understand why St. Patrick pointed me to you."

"What?"

He looked away. He could not look at her, even in her distressed state, and not see beauty. "I had to save your life. It cost you the child, and it broke my heart, but it saved you from him," he said. "I only wish I could dismiss my task and move on." *God help me, I still love you.* "I am sorry—I have to go." He could not stay alone with a married woman—one he loved, and had loved, in every sense of the word.

"I love yeh," she said. "I can' not say it."

"I know," he replied, and left. As he padded, barefoot, back to his own room, his chest felt heavy. His limbs felt leaden. The weight of it all was just so terrible. The world had turned dark around him, and he felt the same way.

~ ~ ~

As they waited for supper, Darcy composed a letter to Elizabeth, relating the events of the past days and explaining that they would likely be in Dublin for the duration of the trial. If it would be long, he would ask her to come. He had not made that assessment yet. He did not know the speed of the local courts there.

Grégoire was still sleeping, and their guest was being attended by a nurse. Georgiana joined Darcy in the parlor, wearing a shawl of the same tartan that Lord Kincaid had worn earlier. She kissed her brother's cheek and then sat down across from him. "What will happen, do you think?"

"Mr. MacKenna will either have a long sentence in Australia if the law is exceptionally kind, or he will hang." He did not mince words with her. He did not have the energy, and she was not a little girl anymore, even though she had a slight build.

"Then Mrs. MacKenna might become a widow."

"I know." He had been considering that possibility from the first moment of rational thought after the arrest. If MacKenna went to the gallows, Mrs. MacKenna could not be expected to wear jet for long. And then she would be available. "I think Grégoire should return with us to England, after this is settled. Immediately."

"Brother! You are cruel!"

"He needs distance to think," Darcy said.

"You would not approve of their marriage."

"I do not approve of the way their relationship came about," he said, though what she said was not untrue. Although it was amazing that Grégoire was thinking of marriage at all, did it really have to be a barren Irish peasant girl? "It was all deceit."

Their voices were hushed. "Not *all* of it," she said. "Just one important detail."

"*Very* important."

Georgiana smiled. "But consider what our relatives would think if he brought her home. Caroline Maddox might have apoplexy."

"Georgiana," he said sternly, but not all that sternly. "He needs time to think. If this is truly a love that knows no end, he will merely sit in a stupor for a few months while she publicly mourns her husband—and then rush back to her the moment he gets a chance. A man can take only so much heartbreak."

They were in limbo for nearly two weeks. Mrs. MacKenna was seen again by the surgeon, who was pleased with her recovery. Darcy stood in the room as he gave his pronouncement, but it clearly brought no comfort to the woman who had just lost her child and any chance of another one. She sat in despair at one end of the hotel suite and Grégoire the other, and the two did not meet. Grégoire went to Mass every day, and he prayed. He did little else.

Darcy bought him books to tease him into occupying his mind, and both the Kincaids tried to make conversation with him, but he would have none of it. His stitches came out and the bruises on his face faded and he was pronounced a healthy man, to which he said nothing.

Because Mrs. MacKenna could not be moved, her account of the events of both nights in question—and all that had preceded them—was taken down by the clerk for the judge. The twisted tale of the man who had killed his own unborn child to get back at his wife for cheating on him with a monk was the talk of the town, which made their isolation that much more unbearable. Darcy wrote his wife but did not ask her to come; by the time she had arrived, they might be ready to leave. After posting the letter, he came to regret it; what would he give for one night with Elizabeth?

At last, Grégoire was called to testify. He was calm, as if in a trance. Maybe the events had cut some emotional nerve, because he was silent all the way to the crowded courthouse. Darcy escorted him and sat beside his brother in anonymity until Grégoire was called by baillif: "Mr. Grégoire Bellamont." The English officers of the court spoke French and could pronounce his name. The rabble, who were following the case closely, hollered and hooted as Grégoire silently took his place before the judge.

As he gave his testimony, he looked and sounded numb. Although Darcy was happy that Grégoire did not break down in tears or make emotional pleas in front of the discourteous crowd, it bothered him to see his younger brother so distant. It also bothered him to notice that some of Grégoire's hair had fallen out, on the top, but he hardly had time to think on that now. The only time Grégoire showed emotion was when Darcy told him of all those who had come to Dublin at their own expense to testify to his good character—the O'Muldoons, the priest from the Tullow church, many people in Tullow, and some people from Drogheda. Darcy turned his head at the sight of James McGowan, a man he had never expected to see again, now out of uniform and with an older couple, who were clearly his parents. They had come to see Grégoire, having already testified to his charitable and pious character.

"Thank you, Mr. Bellamont. You may be seated."

The judge apparently did not need any time. Mr. MacKenna was called to stand before him as he donned the black cap over his massive wig. "Neil MacKenna, for the most heinous crimes of assaulting three people, one being your own wife, with intent to kill, and for the murder of your own unborn child, I sentence you to be hanged at the gallows at noon tomorrow."

The gavel striking the wood seemed almost to physically strike Grégoire, who leaned on his brother for support. Although Darcy had no sympathy for Mr. MacKenna, the cuckolded husband would soon burn in hell, and that was no easy pill to swallow. The crowd was cheering and laughing, however, and the judge had to rap his gavel many more times to restore order so that Mr. MacKenna might be escorted back to jail.

"Your Honor," Grégoire said, and even though his voice was soft, it was heard. "Might I approach the bench?"

The judge eyed him skeptically. "You may, Mr. Bellamont. Be brief."

This was not anything that Grégoire had discussed with Darcy, but Grégoire was always surprising him. Grégoire passed the shackled MacKenna and whispered to the judge, who whispered back, apparently confused by what he had said. There was hardly an ear in the room that wasn't tuned in to try to hear them, but no one did. Grégoire stepped away, bowed to Mr. MacKenna in passing, and returned to his place in the rows beside his brother.

"By special request," the judge said, "Mr. MacKenna is to have a private execution in the prison. This court is adjourned."

Darcy looked at his brother, but Grégoire offered nothing in public, and they were forced to focus on making a quick escape from the furious crowd, who had been denied their spectacle. It took a long time to restore order; and the masses were still swarming and yelling as the brothers ducked into a carriage and began the ride back to the hotel.

Because Grégoire would not, Darcy broke the silence. "You were under no obligation to request such a thing."

"I am the guilty party in that I made him more of a spectacle than his crimes alone did. He can hardly be expected to meet God with the sounds of the mob still ringing in his ears." He looked out the window of the carriage. "Every person deserves at least one moment of peace in their life."

"Even you," Darcy said. Grégoire said nothing.

Mrs. MacKenna did not attend her husband's execution or his burial. She still could not sit up for long, much less leave her room. The news was delivered to her, hours later, by the priest who had administered final rites in the prison. He closed the door behind him when he spoke to her, and then he delivered the news to the rest of them. "His Excellency, the bishop, upon reviewing the matter, feels that three months is an appropriate time of respectful mourning for the man to whom she was joined in matrimony, along with the her unborn child."

They thanked him and he left. Now there were arrangements for them to make. The widow MacKenna would live—her stitches had come out only the day before. What kind of life she would lead would be up to her, but Grégoire said he would pay for any arrangements she wanted, both for her mourning period and beyond. He did not, however, say this to Mrs. MacKenna. The plans were drawn up without her and presented to her the next day, with his notable absence.

Caitlin MacKenna, wearing a dressing gown dyed black, was sitting up, and nursing her aches with fine whiskey. "Is 'e really goin' back ta England?" was the first thing out of her mouth. Unlike Grégoire, she did not appear to be emotionless. In fact, the very opposite.

"That is between you and him," Darcy said, and presented her with an offer to set her up wherever she liked, with a certain number of servants, and an annual income from a large account. She gaped at the money. "I—" she said and broke off. "It's all him, isn' it?"

"Do not think he is the only person who cares for your good health," Lord Kincaid said, carefully dodging the question.

"Fine. Just—take me outta Dublin. I 'ate dis place. I always 'ave."

They nodded. Darcy sent out a solicitor provided by the hotel, and a house was purchased in a small town on the coast, south of the city. She deemed herself well enough to make the journey, and seemed insulted when they implied that she might not be. Darcy sighed and insisted that they would all have to accompany her there.

It was nearly a day's ride in two separate carriages. Georgiana, who had developed a friendship with Mrs. MacKenna while attending her, rode in the carriage along with Mrs. MacKenna and Lord Kincaid. The Darcys rode in the second carriage.

As if she were not tired and ill enough from the ordeal and the journey, Mrs. MacKenna nearly passed out at the sight of the house—modest by any of their scales, but what she announced to be a "feckin' palace." A seat had to be brought for her to sit on and recover herself before she could even go in.

Darcy and Grégoire did a quick inspection of the house, which the latter had purchased, sight unseen. It was a fine house for its size. "She will consider this a luxury," Grégoire said. "She deserves this happiness." It was his longest speech since the trial.

"And you?" Darcy asked, given that Grégoire seemed to be in a talkative mood as they stood in one of the empty bedchambers, looking out at a field. "Or have you contracted the Darcy curse and must be without emotion?"

Grégoire seemed almost to smile as he watched Mrs. MacKenna being attended by her servants on her new front lawn. "I came here to do something and I did it. By all logic, I should return and go on with my life." He sighed. "I suppose you will oppose this match."

"Her character is a little...questionable." He had to say it. "She lied to you, Grégoire. I wouldn't dare say it was for your money. I don't doubt she had and still has feelings for you. But she was entirely remiss in not divulging her marital status."

"Thank God she did not," Grégoire said, "or I might have missed her on my path." He turned to his brother, acknowledging his plan for the first time. "Three months. Two, technically, and twenty-seven days."

"And you must give her a day to take off her mourning dress."

"I hardly think that takes a day. Maybe half a day, from what I've seen of your guests at Pemberley."

Darcy found himself laughing—partly out of relief that his brother had made a joke and partly because the joke was amusing. "Before we say our good-byes, I would ask a question."

"Of course."

"What is happening to your hair?"

Grégoire reached up to the growing bald spot on the top of his head. Even doing so dislodged hairs, and he took down a few strands. "I'm getting older, I suppose. Perhaps my grandfather Bellamont was bald." He shrugged. "I have many concerns. This is not one of them."

"As long as it's not on *my* side," Darcy said, unconsciously running his hands through his own hair, which, despite being partially gray, was still very much attached to his scalp.

"What will I do without yeh?"

Mrs. MacKenna had recovered and was standing not far from the water with Grégoire, alone with him for the first time since the night he had returned from prison. "You could try knitting. Or sewing. Or painting china cups. Some fancy-lady activities."

She took his hand and he did not resist. "Do I have ta keep sayin' I'm sorry or can we jest let it go?"

"I know you are," he said, and raised her hand to kiss it. "We are all following God's path—I know that now. And as terrible as it is sometimes…there are some moments that make it worth it." He let her arm go and removed his silver cross from his neck—the one he never removed, not even when bathing. Before she could say anything, he put it over her head, where it got a bit lost in her black lace veils before finding its way to her neck. "I give this away only because I intend to reclaim it."

"So yeh—"

He kissed her—and not on the hand. That stopped conversation for a moment. "Now I've ruined your reputation and must make amends by marrying you as soon as possible." They laughed together in relief. It was good to feel some happiness after so much death—not just of her husband, but of her baby, as well. "Good-bye, Caitlin."

"Good-bye, Grégoire," she said, her voice wavering.

"Will you take me when I do come back?"

She grinned. "Even if yer bald by then."

CHAPTER 34
Mourners

SADLY, MRS. MACKENNA was not the only one to wear jet that summer.

The Darcys had not been home a week (and were still deciding exactly what details of their trip they would explain to their larger family, and a good time to do so) when Darcy entered his study to read the day's mail and found Elizabeth there, weeping. She held up the letter, which was in Mr. Bennet's handwriting. "Mama," was all she said as she fell into her husband's arms. Little more than a year after her first stroke, Mrs. Bennet had suffered another. This one had felled her.

The Kincaids, fortunately, had already left, and the Darcys could leave immediately without having to see them off. Darcy inquired of his brother if he wished to go and pay his respects to Mrs. Bennet, whom he had not known well, and Grégoire said he would. Darcy barely had time to order all the arrangements for Elizabeth's wardrobe when they returned to Pemberley, whenever that would be.

He did have time to confer with Bingley, whose house was also in an uproar when Elizabeth and Jane met to share their sadness. The letters were the same and very brief—Mrs. Bennet had been struck down when trying to get up from a chair and had died only a few hours later. Even Dr. Bertrand's immediate intervention could do nothing. She would be buried as quickly as her daughters could come home.

"Have you heard anything else?" Darcy asked. He had been caught up in estate matters since their return from Ireland.

"No," Bingley said. "The letter arrived just this morning. I did write to Louisa and Caroline, though I imagine that Caroline received a letter from her father also."

"They're at their country house?" Darcy said, referring to the Hursts. The Maddoxes still lived in town full time.

"Yes. I doubt that Louisa and Mr. Hurst could arrive in time even if they received a letter."

"The Kincaids will just send their condolences. They've been away from home for quite a while, and it's a very long journey for them."

"And Grégoire?"

"He wishes to pay his respects."

Bingley nodded. "So when is it going to be an appropriate time to ask about Ireland?"

"He met a girl."

"I would think that you would say that with a bit more excitement."

"He's waiting for the end of her mourning period," Darcy said. "Whether he wants anything else to be public is his business."

Grégoire had largely returned to his good humor, but kept to himself, and his thoughts seemed elsewhere—and with good reason. Only Elizabeth knew the whole story.

The next morning, many carriages set out from Derbyshire for Longbourn. The weather was good (if a little hot), so there were no delays, and they were the last ones to arrive, completing the set of former Bennet daughters. There would be no Mrs. Bennet again until Joseph married. He looked the saddest of all the grandchildren, having had his grandmother as a constant presence since he was born. Mary and Kitty had mourned together before their other sisters even arrived.

As for Mr. Bennet, he had retired to his study and said he would receive their condolences after the burial. That he was beside himself was apparent, and they had no choice but to respect his wishes.

The Collinses arrived just in time, with their four daughters in tow. If Mr. Collins had been disappointed about hearing *which* Bennet had expired, he showed none of his emotions in that regard. There was only a moment of awkwardness when he assumed that he would be giving the sermon, only to discover that Mr. Bennet had already asked the local rector.

The next morning, a somber, large crowd gathered to pay their respects to the husband and five daughters of Mrs. Bennet. In age order and all in black gowns sat Mrs. Jane Bingley, Mrs. Elizabeth Darcy, Mrs. Mary Bertrand, Mrs. Catherine Townsend, and Mrs. Lydia Bradley. Mrs. Bennet's life work was complete. Her five daughters were all married (happily, even!) and all provided for by their husbands (to varying degrees, all acceptably).

"She outpaced me in everything we did together," Mr. Bennet said after the rector had finished his sermon. "She was always the more active one." He paused before continuing. "By circumstance, the happiest years of my life were our first year of marriage and our last year of marriage."

He seemed to have more to say, but he could no longer stay standing, even with the help of a cane, and several of his sons-in-law helped him back to his seat, where he collapsed in tears. Mercifully, the remainder of the service was short and the sobs of the various Bennet sisters (with the exception of Lydia and Kitty) were muted as all five sons filled in the grave.

The reception was almost as brutal as the funeral. Mr. Bennet, never a fan of public gatherings, was uncomfortable as much of Hertfordshire came to pay tribute to Mrs. Bennet. All of Hertfordshire knew her and her daughters, and of course her newly wealthy husband, who had come into a great fortune only a few years earlier.

"I just had a thought," Bingley said to Darcy as they stood at the back of the reception while their wives received condolences. "Of all of us, Dr. Bertrand is the only one with both living parents, and he's much younger than us. When Mr. Bennet dies, we'll be... the old people."

"I prefer *distinguished,*" Darcy replied. "You can call yourself 'old.'"

At last, the reception came to a close, and those who were not family said their good-byes. Everyone who was not necessary made themselves scarce—except Mr. Collins, who barged in on Mr. Bennet in his study when he was sitting with his favorite daughter, pouring himself a glass of wine, his first real peace of the day. "Mr. Bennet. Mrs. Darcy. I hope I am not interrupting anything."

"No," Mr. Bennet said. "However, it is very late and I am very tired, Mr. Collins. If you would be brief."

"I thought perhaps now, while I am in Hertfordshire, we might discuss matters of the estate—"

If Mr. Bennet did not have the will to intervene, Elizabeth would. "Mr. Collins, this is not the best time—"

"Indeed," her father said, capping the bottle of wine. "Come back when the correct Bennet has died, Mr. Collins, to discuss matters of the estate." More lightly, he added, "And you cannot inherit Longbourn just yet, sir. You are one daughter short."

Taking a glare from Elizabeth as his cue (she was, after all, his patroness), Mr. Collins most politely excused himself. Then he rattled on about how sorry he was to lose such a wonderful woman as Mrs. Bennet until he finally did shut up and actually take his leave.

"With all of my daughters settled and Mrs. Bennet now... settled, he has no concerns except waiting for me to die, which he has been doing for years," he said, and then immediately changed topics. "Your mother did talk of having a place in Meryton. Or Brighton, perhaps. Or she would stay with Kitty—she has always admired Netherfield. It's nothing compared with Pemberley, but it has its charms."

"She was being brave about the prospect of being tossed from her own home, Papa," she said. "Now she does not have to suffer that."

He nodded. They sat in silence for some time before he spoke again. "Did you see Lady Lucas?"

"Yes, I received her."

"I mean, did you see her with *me?*" He shook his head. "She could have been a bit more subtle."

"You are an eligible bachelor now, Papa. She was mercenary before her husband died, and now I fear it is worse."

"On the day of the burial! She's not cold in her grave..." he said and trailed off, leaning on his hand. Elizabeth rose and hugged her dear father, who was crying again. "There will never be another Mrs. Bennet. For all of the years I complained of my marriage, I could never imagine having any other."

"Papa," she said.

"This is my happy ending," he said. "My daughters are all married to good men and have children of their own I am most proud of. My wife will not have to worry about a place to live after I die. Poor Mr. Collins will have to contend with raising at least four daughters under the roof of Longbourn—the perfect irony. There is no better way this could have happened. And yet, why am I so miserable?"

"You are *sad*. We are all sad because we had not the wit to know a truly great thing until it was gone," she said.

"Perhaps we cannot be faulted for that," he said. "For many years, she cleverly disguised it." His wistful laughter seemed to settle him a bit—and her. "There will never be another Mrs. Bennet."

"That I think we can safely say is true," she said with a somber smile.

~~~

When all the guests had departed and it was just family—still a large crowd—there was one final matter to attend do. Not so serious, but in many ways, still a blow to them all. Mr. Bennet announced that he did not wish to live at Longbourn without his wife rattling on and on, and because the Bertrands had more business in Town than in the country, they had decided to buy their own townhouse, and would lodge with the Bingleys while they searched for one. Longbourn would be closed until Mr. Bennet wished it reopened or his death.
~~~

He said he would travel to see all his daughters, but they knew he detested traveling and would likely just stay at Pemberley once he reached it. The former Bennet sisters reluctantly agreed—although they could not stand the idea of Longbourn being closed up, they could not imagine keeping it open for nothing but memories.

All the arrangements were made, and with final good-byes to his southern-living daughters, Mr. Bennet departed with the Darcys for Derbyshire. The Bingleys briefly delayed their departure to Kirkland to help the Bertrands choose a suitable place. Darcy said to Dr. Bertrand in private, "I hope Bingley has learned to make that kind of decision."

"He is just giving advice."

"Well, it cannot *all* be praise."

Mr. Bennet insisted on riding in the carriage with Grégoire, whom he had not had a chance to grill about his adventures in Ireland. He had heard only through gossip that he had met someone there.

"Tread lightly, Papa," Elizabeth said. "The end result was reached only through the most painful circumstances."

"Is there any other path to true love?" he replied, smiling for the first time since his wife's death.

~ ~ ~

"Mugin-san! Mugin-san!"

But Mugin-san was not outside, where he usually was when Georgiana Bingley made one of her visits, no matter how unannounced. He always just knew. Sometimes he sat on the porch of the Japanese wing of the Maddox house and smoked a long pipe, but today, there was no pipe and his geta shoes were just outside the door, meaning he was inside.

"Mugin-san? What are you doing?"

He was sorting through his small bag. Mugin always traveled lightly. He had no house to put things in; he was a nomad. "Leaving."

"But you weren't supposed to leave until September!"

He did not look up from what he was doing. "I am leaving tomorrow instead. So sorry, little ookami. I have business at home, and this is not my home. I will always be a stranger here."

She grabbed his hand and tugged him away from his packing, which only happened because he allowed it to. "For a thief and a criminal you're no good at lying."

He smiled. "I have—how do you say—overstayed my welcome."

"Did you gamble all of Uncle Brian's money away?"

"No."

"Did you get into too many fights?"

"No."

"Did you kill someone important?"

"No."

"Did you sleep with every prostitute and now you're bored?"

Mugin laughed. She was now too big for him to casually pick up, the way he had in the old days. Instead, he just walked around her and slumped onto his bed mat. "See, this is why I go. I am a bad influence on you."

Georgie could not comprehend him. "*Why* are you leaving?"

He picked up his pipe from the nightstand—more of a low stool—and began to pack it with tobacco. "I just told you. Weren't you listening?" He took the matchbox she handed him and struck a light. "I told him everything."

"Who? Papa?"

"Not so bad. Brian-chan."

"Why? Why would you do that?" Her surprise and confusion quickly turned to horror.

"Because I was drunk, Jorgi-chan. Very, very drunk. Like you say, in the drink."

"In the cups."

He shrugged. "Whatever. I was drunk and he asked. Maybe he is not as dumb as he looks."

"And he's making you leave?"

He inhaled and then exhaled a long stream of smoke, not in her direction, as he rose and stepped out on the porch. She followed him. "He is very mad. He thinks he's a samurai but he's gaijin at heart, with all of this—how do you call—propriety. You are supposed to be a good little girl who is to be a good little lady, not a warrior. He knows your father will be very angry if he finds out. He is very mad that I was teaching you otherwise, and I do not like being around angry armed samurai whom I am not allowed to kill. It is a tricky situation."

"But Mugin-san—"

"He wants to strike the wall. I do not want to be the wall," he said.

"Will you come back? When he's not as angry?"

He looked in her eyes. That was all it took.

Georgie abandoned all pretense and hugged him, grabbing hold of his waist and burying herself in his silk jacket. "You can't leave me! I won't let you!"

"You could try to make me stay," he said, "but you're not that good. Yet."

"That's why you can't go."

He tried to smooth it over as he forced her to release him. "There are things I cannot teach you, Jorgi-chan. There are things I do not know, or do not know how to express. You have to find your own way." He chuckled. "Besides, if I stay, we might have to get married—"

"*Mugin!* Don't say that!"

"And then *everyone* would be upset at me," he said. "There is a trunk in the corner of my room. After I go, it is yours."

"Can I see it now?"

"No. When you need it," he replied.

"I'm coming to Japan," she said, trying not to cry in front of him. That would be the worst thing—to cry in front of Mugin. But if it made him feel bad, it would be worth it. "I am going to come find you." Tears sprang to her eyes.

"I know," Mugin said. "I'll be waiting."

CHAPTER 35
English Gentlefolk

IT WAS AFTER GRÉGOIRE WAS GONE that Caitlin became anxious. She considered herself a stable, tough person in general, but since the beginning of her pregnancy, things just hadn't been the same. Grégoire, who seemed to know more than any of her acquaintances, said it was completely normal. She assumed that the anxiety would disappear as she healed from having her child cut out of her. She had made out well, she was safe, and she had more money than she knew what to do with. If Grégoire was true to his word (and he was *always* true to his word), he would return to her. Everything was fine for her now.

So why wasn't she happy? It wasn't physical pain that spontaneously made her break into tears. She was accustomed to pain. In fact, the fancy laudanum they gave her helped her soar through the first week. It was only when she emerged from the haze that doubts began to creep in. What if Grégoire *didn't* come back? What if he didn't want her? What if his brother talked him out of it? She knew she was damaged beyond the scars on her stomach. She didn't bleed anymore, or have courses, or whatever they called them in decorous England. She never felt clean. Somehow, she felt less innocent than she had as an adulterous woman with a child on the way, lying to her lover about her husband.

She did not know what to do or what to say to the servants. They made her uncomfortable, doing her errands as though she were an invalid. When she was suitably recovered, she tried to dismiss some of them (leaving someone for laundry—she *hated* laundry), but they cried and *begged* to keep their jobs. They wanted to serve her—or at least get paid. She was a good mistress. She was kind to them and treated them very respectfully. They did not want to leave. How could she say no? So she kept them on.

Caitlin went to church every Sunday. Circumstances had prevented it for the past eight years, since she had met Neil. At the time, she was only twelve. She had been out of the habit, but the service was familiar. It was soothing because it reminded her of her early childhood and because it reminded her of Grégoire. He had never pestered her about church—he had asked her once in a while if she wanted to join him, and her response had always been negative, and then he would nod with understanding in that way that said, *I understand everything*. It wasn't rebellion—she knew she didn't belong in the house of God, listening to the priest talk about sin. She had sinned enough and been sinned against. She would have returned home from services and sinned again. She didn't need to hear about it. If there was one thing Caitlin MacKenna had no tolerance for, it was listening to things she didn't feel comfortable with, or thought were silly or stupid. Sometimes, Grégoire had beliefs that seemed silly, or even stupid, but he said them with such earnestness that it was hard to dismiss them. He believed they all were following divine destinies; he believed that saints could intervene on people's behalf.

He didn't belong to her; he belonged to the church. They would take him back and he would disappear back into a monastery. That was her constant nightmare—that he would devote his life to God again. What kind of person did that make her, to want to stand in the way of *that?*

But she couldn't imagine her life without him. It was too lonely and terrifying a prospect.

By the end of the third month, she was trying not to fully panic. She also realized quite suddenly that her whole wardrobe was black.

What she had been wearing before her husband's death could not be mended or cleaned. That was when she burst into the laundress's workroom and begged, "I need somet'in' ta wear!"

Rose laughed—not at her, but at the silliness over it. This woman had been ill and depressed after trauma, and now she was worrying about her clothing, when Grégoire would probably show up in the same tunic he always wore. Should she wear makeup? "No, ma'rm, the English gentlefolks don't much care fer such things."

So many things to worry about, and the only dress she could find on such short notice was an earthy brown and had to be tailored on the spot, as it had belonged to a much heavier person who formerly lived in the house, and Caitlin was a stick. It was her first day out of jet, and she tossed off her black mourner's veil with no emotion about that except impatience. But Grégoire hadn't wasted any time, and her dress was only half sewn to fit her when she heard the doorbell. "De pins! Hurry, please!" It was in that shabby, half-patched gown that she raced down the stairs, still not entirely sure if she was not armored by tiny needles, straight into Grégoire's waiting arms. There were no pretenses of greetings. He had his arms open and she leaped into them. It was like receiving a dear husband who had been gone for years. "Yeh came back." She buried her face against his shoulder so he wouldn't see her tears.

"I always keep my promises," he said. "I wasn't...quite positive how you would still feel about me, but I prayed to the saints."

"What did de saints say?"

"Nothing. So I just trusted my instincts," he said. "That is, if you would still have me."

"Yer messin' wit' me," she said, "and 'tis not noice."

"So you would?"

"Why do yeh 'ave ter ask?"

He looked away shyly. "Because—well, I never thought I would ask this question of anyone, but will you be my wife?"

"Didn't yeh promise yerself ta de church?"

"The church did not accept my application." He held out his hand. In it was a gold ring. "Which was most fortunate. But you haven't answered me?"

"Are yeh daft? Aye, feckin' aye!" She snatched the ring and put it on her finger, kissing him. In a slightly more sedate tone, she whispered, "Aye."

Could he really have doubted it? Either way, the relief on his face was evident. "Now, of course, highborn English couples must be chaperoned during their engagement most strictly, so as to not be tempted into anticipating their vows?"

"What?"

"So they don't make love."

She laughed. It was something only he would say to her, a private world they shared. "I t'ink we covered dat."

"And neither one of us is highborn English gentry. Thank goodness for that."

There were plans to be made—so much planning for something so far away. Unfortunately, at least part of Grégoire was, in fact, highborn English gentry, because his brother insisted on a three-month engagement, and the past three didn't count. "And when he gets in a mood, it's best to just put up with him."

She wanted to cook him dinner, but she was too distracted. He confessed to being exhausted and hungry from his travels, so they shoveled in whatever the cook was serving. "I don' want ta 'ave a cook," she said when they were in private. "I want ta cook for yeh."

They slept together, but not in the optional sense. "I'm not—you know." She, who had been so uninhibited on their other first night together, was shaking at the idea. Not because it might have consequences, but because it might not.

He tucked his hand inside her robe. "Don't!" she cried.

"I showed you my scars," he said. There was such a gentleness in it that she could not help but relent. In the lamplight, she pulled apart the robe for him to see the scar, now almost four months old, from where the doctor had cut her open to remove the snuffed-out life inside her. He traced his thumb along the scar so carefully that it tickled instead of hurt. "I'm sorry."

"Grégoire." She swallowed. "I don' t'ink—I don't know if yeh want laddies—"

"I want children. Whether they're of my blood or not makes no difference to me." He kissed her cheek. "And I'd rather test the surgeon's theory myself."

"'E said it would take a miracle."

"Good," he said. "I believe in miracles."

The next morning, they tackled the immediate matter of what to do with the house. Caitlin was surprised when he said he rather liked it. "I t'ought—"

"I feel no obligation to live in England," he said. "Here, I am close enough to my family."

She had not even considered that she would stay in the house—that it might be *their* house. It was not that the concept appalled her—it was just so foreign and unreal. "'S big."

"You've not seen my brother's house," he said with a smile. After they wandered around the empty rooms, they went outside and sat on a bench by the coast. "If it is too big, I can sell it and get something smaller."

"'S not t'at," she said, leaning against him. "I don't—it feels fierce quare, wit' servants and de loike."

"They could find other work," he said, "but the house is bigger than you're used to. Perhaps we could keep one or two servants."

She interlaced her fingers with his. "I do 'ate washin' clothes."

"So a maid. And a man, to do the heavy work," he said.

"Dere's so many rooms."

"I have a brother and a sister," he said. "They'll visit. And I have books." He kissed her on her neck. "I want to build a chapel."

"God forbid yeh need to go too far fer church."

He laughed. "And a garden. I used to have an herb garden in

Spain. I liked it very much."

They circled the grounds. The property itself was not very large, but it was isolated, surrounded mainly by a forest and a single road going in two directions. One way eventually led north to Dublin. In the south, there was a town that was large enough for a poorhouse and an orphanage. The rest of the land was farmed"If you are truly uncomfortable with the house—" he said that night.

"No," she replied. "It just took gettin' used ta."

They slept in the same bed again, but did not make love. Caitlin was not sure she was fully healed. And Grégoire seemed to want to wait until after the wedding, which made Caitlin laugh.

Caitlin MacKenna, whom he considered to be the strongest woman of his acquaintance, timidly brought up her fears of meeting his family. "I don' have anyt'ing really nice to wear."

"We'll get something in Dublin."

"And I don't know how ta act."

"Be yourself. I would not expect anything less from you," he said, and kissed her. "Though you should probably keep the swearing to a minimum."

She giggled. "They're not goin' ta loike me, are they?"

"My family is full of good people. If anyone looks down on you, I will be extremely disappointed in them."

Geoffrey didn't want Nurse to pack his trunk. He didn't officially keep a manservant yet, but he felt like a baby whenever she did something for him that he was capable of doing himself.

He snapped the locks shut, and jumped back at the sight of the person sitting on the windowsill. Her red hair made it all the more jarring a visual in a room with dark wooden panels. "Stop doing that!"

Georgie smiled. "So. You're to Eton, then?"

"No, I'm to the Orient. What do you think?" he said, not truly annoyed but wanting to rise to her challenge. "You weren't with your family when they came to say good-bye. They said you had a headache. Isn't that what women say when they don't want to go somewhere?"

"Yes, but I was more subtle than that. I said I had my courses."

"Your what?"

"Girl's thing." She looked at the ground. "So are you looking forward to school?"

"Yes, I love tests and I hate the country." He wasn't in the mood to play the usual game with her. She was interested in him now, but she had snubbed him only a few hours earlier. "What do you think?" Honestly, he didn't know what she thought. Sometimes it was as though he couldn't talk to her anymore. "They have female seminaries, you know, if you're so jealous."

"Shut up. You know that isn't what I meant."

"Then stop gloating because you get to stay in Derbyshire while I have to go to school and take exams and face bullies and teachers who won't like me because I lack a title."

Her expression softened. "I wasn't gloating. I'm sorry."

He sighed. All of the fight was gone from him. "Georgie—" But when she raised her eyes, he stopped in his tracks. He couldn't face that stare. "Listen—we've established that I don't want to go and you don't want me to go—but I'm going. Because that is what my father did and...well, I don't know if they had Eton then, but if they did, Grandfather Darcy went. There are *expectations.*"

"Do you always do what you're told?"

"I pick my battles. Which is why I remain in good standing with *my* parents."

It was the wrong thing to say—in fact, it was the worst possible thing he could have said. This time, her eyes were lowered and so she couldn't stop him with her gaze. He came forward and embraced her, letting her lean against his chest. "I'm sorry. It was the wrong thing to say." He sighed. "I'll be a terrible master of Pemberley. My father never says anything wrong."

"That's because your father never says *anything,*" she said, some of her good humor returning, even when her voice was cracking.

She pulled back, wiping the tears away. "I have to get back. I'm supposed to be resting in bed."

"You could try *occasionally* being honest with your family," he said with an encouraging smile. "It might work."

She rolled her eyes. "Your advice is sage."

They embraced again. "I'll see you at Christmas," he said. "I'll try not to be *much* taller than you, but this I can't promise."

She kissed him on the cheek. "Good luck."

"Try to keep Derbyshire in one piece for me."

"No promises. We own a monkey," she said, and released her grip on his hand before sneaking back out the door. He didn't know why, but the sensation of her touch on his palm stayed with him a long time.

Nothing was as frustrating to Elizabeth about Grégoire's engagement (or the events surrounding it) as the fact that Darcy was reluctant to speak of it except in purely factual terms. She had become accustomed to his opening his heart and mind to her when he would with no one else, which made his refusal to do so now all the more cutting. Georgiana was the one who supplied all of the details of their trip to Ireland—even the gruesome ones—and Darcy did confirm them later, but did not add his own commentary.

For the three months that Grégoire spent waiting for Mrs. MacKenna to leave her mourning days behind her, he exhibited all the traits of a man besotted and denied his passion. This was tempered only by his quiet determination and his reticence about a subject close to his heart (he was, after all, a *Darcy*). He was overflowing in his emotions, but he would become lost in a smile whenever she was mentioned. Darcy offered Grégoire no suggestions, but on the other hand, did not discourage his brother from his affections.

It was not until Grégoire was gone that Elizabeth confronted Darcy in her favorite place to do so—in bed, with the sheets twisted around them. "If you truly disapproved, you would have said something to him by now."

The look of defeat on his face meant she had planned the discussion's location correctly. "I suppose. But must I remind you that I have *never* approved of any of Grégoire's choices?"

"True."

"Of all the life-altering decisions he has made, I find marriage to be the least detestable of them. So I am willing to compromise on his choice of an Irish peasant."

The wedding would have to be in Ireland and, of course, be Catholic. That would not be in open discussion until Grégoire returned, assuming he found Mrs. MacKenna alive and well and assuming she accepted his offer of marriage. That would limit the guest list considerably, but she imagined Grégoire preferred it that way. And he would not be taking his wife on the grand tour of town. "He might have to wear real clothing for that," was Darcy's reply when she playfully suggested the idea.

Though the Bingleys and the extended family were aware that Grégoire had found a potential wife in Ireland, the specifics were not public knowledge, nor was the date of his return, which was only an estimate. They were not in communication with him until he reappeared, two weeks after he had left.

Caitlin MacKenna did appear at first to be the typical Irishwoman. Her hair was long, straight, and reddish blonde. It flowed down her back, which made Elizabeth initially think her younger as she approached Pemberley, hiding beneath her wide-brimmed straw hat. While they were still out of what she apparently assumed was earshot she said, "Now *t'is* is a feckin' palace."

Grégoire laughed. Whether Darcy heard it or not, he said nothing as they approached. "Grégoire. Mrs. MacKenna." He bowed to both of them. "This is my wife, Mrs. Elizabeth Darcy."

Mrs. MacKenna curtsied.

"Please come in, Mrs. MacKenna. Grégoire, welcome home." Darcy had told the servants not to make a fuss, but that did not keep more than a few of them from finding a reason to walk by as they entered Pemberley proper. "The Kincaids have been delayed by the weather in Scotland, which washed out the roads. They should be here in a few days."

Mrs. MacKenna was introduced to the Darcy daughters—Anne, Sarah, and Cassandra. "My son, Geoffrey, has just left for school," Darcy explained.

"How is he? Has he written?" Grégoire asked.

"Unfortunately," Darcy said, to which Elizabeth rolled her eyes. "He is terribly homesick, of course. That's Eton for you. I will not deny that I was any different."

Mrs. MacKenna said little, noticeably intimidated by Pemberley and her future family. Propriety was preserved, but she did occasionally grab Grégoire's arm, which he never stopped her from doing.

"And this," Darcy said in the portrait gallery, "is our father, my son's namesake."

It was a picture of Geoffrey Darcy when he was young and dashing—he resembled Darcy, except that he was wearing a wig and long coat. Beside it was a portrait of an exquisite blonde woman. "My mother," Darcy said. "Lady Anne."

Mrs. MacKenna did not inquire about Grégoire's mother. She did not have to, and it would have been awkward if she had.

Elizabeth was eager to get to know Mrs. MacKenna, but Grégoire would not leave her side, and so there was no opportunity on the day of their arrival. It took conspiring with Darcy to get him to drag his brother off somewhere. In a few days, the Kincaids would be arriving.

She finally cornered Caitlin in, of all places, the chapel. Mrs. MacKenna was not praying so much as sitting in the final row and knitting. "Mrs. MacKenna."

Her guest quickly rose and curtsied. "Mrs. Darcy."

"We have not had much time to talk," she said, "and we are soon to be sisters. May I sit?"

"'S yer chapel, Mrs. Darcy."

Elizabeth took a seat on the hard wooden pew. "What are you knitting?" It did not appear to be embroidery.

"A shirt fer Grégoire," Mrs. MacKenna said, "since 'e likes ta dress all medieval." Despite the skill with which she handled the needle and thread, her hands were shaking and she pricked herself. "Shite!" She shook her hand and put the thumb in her mouth. "I'm sorry, Mrs. Darcy. Christ, I promised Grégoire I wouldn't curse. I'm not—I'm not normally like t'is."

Elizabeth had a feeling that she was, but she was under enormous pressure to present herself as otherwise, though probably not from her betrothed. It was just an unavoidable circumstance. "I apologize if I am making you nervous, Mrs. MacKenna."

"Yer not," she said untruthfully. "Besides, everyt'ing's makin' me nervous. I don' know why."

"I was at my wit's end by the end of my engagement," Elizabeth said. "Everyone was telling me what to do and what to say and, of course, Darcy's family didn't approve—"

"Why? Yer a perfect lady."

"Maybe in your eyes," Elizabeth said, "in which case, I am honored. And Georgiana, Fitzwilliam's sister, did like me, but barely knew me. Darcy's aunt, Lady Catherine, expressed her disapproval before he even made the second offer, on account of our lack of connections to society. He was her sister's son and she wanted him to marry someone of a higher station."

"Wait—de second—?"

"Yes." Elizabeth blushed. "Our long courtship was full of misunderstandings. The first was that he thought I would be obligated to accept his offer because of my family's inferior social status, and the second was that I thought he was a stubborn, arrogant man whom I could never come to love. His first proposal, I rejected." She added, "The circumstances were bad, and we both said things we could not take back, but it led us to a greater appreciation of each other. Oh, and I had opinions of my own. Apparently, his aunt thought this was too high-spirited of me."

Mrs. MacKenna smiled at that. "But it did—I mean, it has al' worked oyt."

"Yes. But it has worked out because we have worked to understand each other. Also, Darcys are not known to give up on love."

After a moment, Mrs. MacKenna said, "An' afterward?"

"Mr. Darcy is an adoring husband and most loving father to his children—"

And that was when it broke. There was a tension lurking beneath the surface that was more than social awkwardness for this woman from Ireland. The shirt abandoned, Mrs. MacKenna broke into sobbing that was so hard she was unable to speak for some time. It was only with Elizabeth's embrace—which Mrs. MacKenna did not resist—that she was able to gain some control over herself. "Sorry. I'm so sorry, Mrs. Darcy—"

"Mrs. MacKenna, you do not have to be sorry, but you must tell me what is bothering you."

"I 'ate that name," she said, trying unsuccessfully to wipe her tears away. "I 'ate him. I 'ate me dead husband. 'S that so terrible?"

"No, not at all," Elizabeth replied. "Caitlin, tell me what is bothering you, besides that."

"I—'e says it's not a problem. I know 'e means it because 'e's just so good, but—" She faced Elizabeth for the first time, her eyes red. "Why would 'e want a banjaxed doll? Is he gonna say, down de road, I want laddies? He loved de other one and it wasn' even his. He loved ta feel it kick. I 'aven' been bleedin' since it al' 'appened," Caitlin MacKenna said after a long pause. Elizabeth held her tongue at hearing courses referred to in such a way (for it seemed that this was a difference between them that was not so easily bridged). "I just want ta make 'im happy. I don' wan' 'im ta regret anyt'ing."

Elizabeth pondered her response before giving it. "Caitlin, Grégoire has made many tough choices in his life, and no matter what their outcome, he has never regretted any of them."

Caitlin could only nod, but it was clear some understanding had been reached and some nerve had been soothed. "If you are worried about it still," Elizabeth said, "you should know that we have never seen him as happy as he has been since he met you."

"Even if I made 'is 'air fall oyt?"

They shared a chuckle. "That mystery remains unsolved," Elizabeth said. Grégoire had returned to England with a bald spot that had not been there before, but it did not seem to be spreading. The loss of hair had abruptly stopped. "I once heard Grégoire describe the tonsure as the crown of the church. He was upset when he was told that he was no longer allowed to wear it. We all saw how devastated he was as the hair grew back. That the tonsure has mysteriously reappeared is not something I am wont to question." She added, "Though, I have had to reassure Darcy almost daily that it is unlikely to happen to him. He is *terrified*."

Their laughter filled the little chapel of Pemberley for some time before they rejoined the men.

CHAPTER 36

The Dress

"NOW, JUST BECAUSE YOU are not my actual grandchild does not mean I find you any less adorable," Mr. Bennet said to Robert Kincaid, sitting on his lap. The toddler could now sit up and even balance himself on someone's knee fairly well, and was beginning to shout things that resembled words more than random cries. At the moment, though, he focused on putting his hand in his mouth. "Especially when you do that," Mr. Bennet added.

The master of Longbourn had taken up what seemed like permanent residence in an armchair in Pemberley's library. He expressed relief that, since coming to Derbyshire, he had yet to receive the attentions of another woman determined to marry.

He was there for Elizabeth when Geoffrey left for Eton. Though she smiled encouragingly until her son was in the carriage, tears came as the carriage pulled away. Darcy comforted her, but he had been to Eton himself. It was part of his heritage; it was what boys did.

It was Mr. Bennet who was able to say the right thing to his daughter. "Your son will be home soon, and I sense he will never truly be far from Pemberley. As for your daughters, take heart in the fact that my son will never let them out of his sight, much less marry and move away." He was able to soothe his daughter's heart better than anyone else.

The day after the Kincaids' arrival, the earl was invited to shoot with Darcy and Bingley, as was their custom, especially in the fall.

"If we are to be invited for dinner," Bingley said, "it is on the condition that I will not be subjected to Irish jokes the entire evening."

"What are you, daft? You can't make jokes with an *actual* Gael in the room," Kincaid said. "Besides yourself, of course."

"She has lighter hair than you," Darcy said to Bingley, who had not met Mrs. MacKenna yet. "Nearly blonde."

"What about Grégoire?"

"You know very well what he looks like, Bingley."

Bingley gave him a look. "How is he?"

"How would you expect? Besotted," Darcy said. "And no, I have no intention of interfering with the match, despite all reason."

"Not all *reason,*" Kincaid said. "She is a sweet woman and she is devoted to him, and he has no need of a dowry."

Darcy said nothing, firing at a stray duck flying south but missing.

"She *is,* Darcy," Kincaid said, the only one who could speak with any authority on the subject present. "It is not just gratitude. She could easily have lived a life of comfort with the money he gave her."

Bingley, who had been privately told the particulars of the courtship (if one could call it that) of Grégoire and Mrs. MacKenna, could add *something.* "Great marriages have been built on less than gratitude. In fact, I am surprised you haven't thrown a grand ball in celebration of the fact that he is marrying *at all.*"

This did manage to soften Darcy, who had been even more guarded than usual, and had been since his brother had returned from Ireland. "They are to be married by Christmas."

"A felicitous time," Bingley said, having been joined in marriage with Princess Nadezhda at the same time of year. "In Ireland, I assume?"

"Yes."

"Do you wish us to take the children while you are gone? I am assuming you are not taking them." The Darcy daughters were all still younger than twelve, and would be out of place at adult ceremonies, unless they happened to be held at home. "I think Jane could use the distraction."

"So I am to assume that Miss Bingley took Geoffrey's departure as expected."

Bingley smiled sheepishly. "Between her cousin and Mugin-san, she's lost her two best friends."

"She's scared away all her governesses—you might consider sending her to a school in London," Darcy said.

"It was discussed." Bingley's tone was dismissive. Meaning, his daughter had put her foot down against it. "Stop smiling, both of you."

"I didn't say a word," Kincaid said, though he was smiling. Darcy was smirking, which for him was quite a lot.

~ ~ ~

Dinner arrangements were more complex on the Bingley end, because they were bringing their children along to see their grandfather and meet Grégoire's betrothed. Though they had tutors, the four Bingley children were currently sans governess, and had only Nurse. Only Edmund Bingley was still young enough to not put up a fight—not that Charles or Eliza Bingley had any reason to fight.

The problem was, of course, Georgiana. She refused to get dressed for the evening and was perfectly capable of scrambling out of anyone's hold (not that her father wanted to try). She was four and ten, and her foul mood had begun when Mugin abruptly left England, and deepened when Geoffrey left for school. Jane and Bingley faced the daunting prospect of doing something beyond both of their characters—yelling at their child. It was still on the horizon, but it was there. Darcy, they were sure, could simply give any of his children a stare and they would obey, no matter what their age—but he was Darcy, and they were Charles and Jane.

They were stuck in a debate about how to approach the situation after all arguments through the door had failed when Charlie, now one and ten, knocked on his sister's door and was granted entrance. They decided to listen in and face the consequences if they were discovered.

Young Charlie, the elder of the Bingley twins, resembled his father in almost every way except his hair, which was blond. He also hadn't had his growth spurt yet, much to his annoyance.

"Hello," he said, announcing his presence. After unlocking the door, Georgie had returned to her bed, put her bare feet up on the dresser, and buried her face in a book.

"Did they send you in?"

"No."

She said nothing.

"Listen," he said, mustering what courage he could. His sister was still taller than him, her voice was less squeaky, and she was an intimating person in general. "You're not the only one who misses him. I didn't want him to leave, either."

Georgiana put down her book.

"He is my best friend. And he was the only other boy around here," Charlie continued. "What am I supposed to do, play with Edmund?"

"You could try," she said.

"You could spend time with your sister," he countered. Georgie and Eliza Bingley were not known for their close relationship. "You could do…sisterly things."

Georgiana's response was a look.

"I know you're upset," he said, "but Mother and Father are now really upset because you're upset, and you really shouldn't make them upset." He frowned. "Did that sound stupid?"

"Yes," she said, but smiled. "Are they really upset?"

"What do *you* think? You won't even put on a pretty dress."

"I hate that dress."

"Mother says we shouldn't use the word *hate*."

"Mothers say those sorts of things."

To this, he had no response. She had stumped him. He frowned;

she always managed to do that, because she was older. "I do not understand why you won't—"

She sat up. "I will enlighten you. I have to put on a very pretty and very expensive dress—which I *hate*—to meet Uncle Grégoire and Mrs. MacKenna. Uncle Grégoire dresses as though he made his own clothes and all he had was brown wool because he doesn't care about money or looking fancy. Mrs. MacKenna was so poor when she met him that she was starving to death. Do you think it makes either of them comfortable to see all of their relatives dressed up in fancy clothes?"

"I didn't know that," he said. "About her, I mean. Should I know that?"

"I heard Papa talking about it. There was other stuff, too, but it was complicated." She shook her head. "The point is this: I do not understand why I have to get dressed up and feel uncomfortable to make other people feel uncomfortable. Does that make sense?"

The only response he could manage to find was, "Did you tell Mother that?"

"She wouldn't understand."

"Now, you're being mean. You're not smarter than she is!"

She did halt her speech. "What I meant to say was, she—I don't know. Adults act differently. They do things just because it's the thing to do. They don't *think* about things."

"Or they do it because it's the right thing to do."

Georgiana looked away. "Are they *really upset?*"

"Our parents? Yes."

She sighed. "Get out. I have to change."

"Should I send—"

"I can do it myself."

All the Bingley children were present at Pemberley that night, including Georgiana, who was complimented for her very pretty dress, and she curtsied and thanked her aunt. When asked how he had gotten his sister out of her room, Charlie admitted that he had no idea.

~ ~ ~

After the introductions were made and the Bingley children sent to eat with their cousins, the gathering of four couples and Mr. Bennet sat down to eat. Mrs. MacKenna was silently judged to be incredibly shy, which was not entirely unexpected, and she generally stayed quiet until the subject of the wedding was brought up. Although it was to be in Ireland, they wanted some celebration in England so that people whom Grégoire wanted to attend could do so. They were, however, faced with the peculiar problem that all of the hosts were in mourning for Mrs. Bennet, and could not hold a reception, and the Kincaid castle in Scotland was too far.

"There's the Maddoxes," Bingley suggested. "They are only a few miles from town and have never had a chance to host anything."

"Is the house large enough?"

"Have you seen the renovations?"

"Did they ever finish that wing? The Oriental one?" Mr. Bennet asked.

"Always under construction."

"You're not thinking of doing something to Kirkland are you, Mr. Bingley?" Elizabeth asked.

"No," Jane answered before Bingley could. She gave him a soothing look, which silenced his opposition.

"If we turn England into the Orient, perhaps everyone will be less inclined to go there," Darcy said, "and come back with all sorts of...things."

"Monkey is not a thing!" "Anything you can toss is a thing," Darcy said, and took a sip of his wine.

"Who's tossing Monkey?" Elizabeth said, with an accusing look at her husband.

"*Thinking* of tossing it," Darcy corrected.

"Who in the world is Monkey?" Lord Kincaid finally asked. He was seated next to Caitlin, who was similarly clueless.

"His name is very self-descriptive," Jane said. "He's our pet."

"Somehow he was left off the invitation list for tonight," Elizabeth said. "Because someone banned him from Pemberley."

"Someone didn't appreciate having to chase him around the house while he was covered in mud before he woke half the house—"

"If you hadn't upset him—"

"There is nothing upsetting about telling an animal to leave. My dogs would do it on command—"

"You tossed him out the window!"

"He was in my hands. He *leaped* out the window. And then back in. Just to annoy me. Do you have any idea how long it took the maids—"

"Fortunately," Elizabeth said, interrupting the argument between her husband and brother-in-law, "it will not be your decision as to whether Monkey is invited to the celebrations, as they will be held elsewhere—"

Grégoire cleared his throat. "Speaking of—Would you all mind terribly if I *asked* Her Highness and Mr. Maddox if we could use their property before we begin to plan an event there?"

Mr. Bennet laughed. "That does seem the polite thing to do, no?"

"Her Highness?" Caitlin finally said, her first words in three courses. "Yer all *royalty?*"

"Mr. Maddox is married to a minor Hungarian princess," Darcy quickly explained to his guest and future sister-in-law.

"She is much less intimidating than you might think," Georgiana Kincaid half whispered to her. "Oh! Except for all the swords."

Caitlin nodded politely and kept silent for the rest of the meal.

"I can't do dis."

"You can."

Grégoire and Caitlin had found the chapel to be the best location to be unchaperoned. Even if someone came upon them, nothing could be suspected of them, especially given Grégoire's religious devotion and respect for sanctified places. There they could sit in the pews and he could put his hands over her trembling ones. "They're just people," he said. "Their clothing is different and their speech is different and sometimes even I get confused by all of the titles and orders of names, but we are all the same on the inside."

"Do yeh t'ink dey loike me?"

"If they have any sense at all, they think you're a sweet, polite woman who will make me a wonderful bride," he said, kissing her. "And if they don't...well, we are all foolish sinners, and of that sin I will absolve them."

"Of bein' idiots?"

"Assuming so, yes," he said with a smile. "You don't have to impress them. You are not marrying *them*."

"But if—"

He kissed her to silence her. "No 'if's.' They are good people and you are a wonderful woman and you make me happy. For that alone, they already love you." He squeezed her hand. "They have seen me poor, filthy, half starved, beaten, and even harmed by my own hand. And yet my brother, who may seem to the world a pretentious, arrogant English gentleman, loved me as a brother from the moment we met. He gave me advice but he never stopped me from doing otherwise—even when he should have."

She bit her lip. "'As 'e said somethin' 'bout me?"

"He does not find conversation easy," he replied. "It is not in his nature. Nonetheless, if he truly disapproved, he would have said something months ago. And even if he had, I could have replied that he had been bothering me to leave the church and get married since the day we met in Mon-Claire. So there is no high ground for Darcy on this subject." He added, "Nor do I truly care."

"Den why don' we run off an' marry?"

"Because," he said and sighed, letting her lean into him and wrapping his arms around her, "when I wrote to him of our situation and asked him to come to Dublin and put his own life and reputation in danger for a woman he did not even know, he did not hesitate or ask a single question. He made our union possible and if he wants to be a part of it, who am I to stop him?"

She rested in his arms. It had been a tiring day. "I wish I'd had a family ta love so much."

He kissed her hair and said, "You're about to have one."

CHAPTER 37

The Princess

≈ ≈ ≈

IT WAS A YEAR AND A SEASON since rescuing Grégoire from certain death in Spain that the Maddoxes opened their house to receive him and his bride-to-be.

"I should warn you," Grégoire said to Caitlin as they approached the doors of the non-Japanese side of the house, "Mr. Maddox dresses as if he were mentally unbalanced. He is not."

"Den why—"

But Caitlin didn't get to finish her question, because the door opened and Brian appeared in his usual garb. "Hello, Grégoire. Mrs. MacKenna, I presume."

She curtsied. "Mr. Maddox."

"Please come in. You must be freezing," he said. "Excuse my wife—Nady is cooking. She insists on subjecting us all to Transylvania's finest—"

"*Subjecting!*" came a heavily accented voice from the other room. Princess Maddox emerged, wearing her Romanian dress and jewelry, looking majestic but for the fact that she was wearing sandals and an apron.

Brian smiled apologetically at his wife, "Nadi-chan—"

"*Subjecting!*"

"Not everything *necessarily* needs sour cream—"

She rolled her eyes and turned to her guests. "Grégoire. Mrs. MacKenna."

"Your Highness," Grégoire said, bowing, and Caitlin followed with a curtsy to the princess, a little confused by the couple before her—a man in a skirt and bathrobe wearing two swords in his belt and a woman in an embroidered gown and with her hair covered in silk veils and a gold circlet.

"Welcome to our home," she said. "Mrs. MacKenna, would you like to join me in the kitchen while my husband runs away in fear of my wrath?"

"I love you," Brian said, kissing his wife on the cheek before quickly running away to show Grégoire something or another, leaving Caitlin with her royal host.

Caitlin smiled shyly as she followed Princess Nadezhda into the kitchen, where servants were running around. "He says otherwise, but he likes my cooking," Nadezhda explained. "Besides, English food is so plain. In my homeland, at least there is some flavor." She spooned some soup off the top of the pot. "Here. Too much cream?"

Nervously she tried it. "No. 'S quite good, actually."

"Good. It is your party," she said.

"T'ank yeh fer hostin' it, Yer Highness."

"We are honored," she said, removing her apron and handing it to the cook. "Anything that makes Grégoire happy makes us happy. I do not know what you did to him, but he is not the same man he was when we found him in Spain, or even when he had recovered from Spain."

Caitlin looked down at her feet. "Not al' of dose t'ings were good, Yer Highness."

The princess did not look concerned. "To be together, Brian and I went through a lot and put our family through even more, but now everyone is happy. And now Grégoire will be happy. He has suffered so much." She shook her head. It was a little hard to understand her because of her accent, but then again, Caitlin imagined that her own Irish accent might be sometimes hard to understand. "You know, in Spain, they thought he was a saint."

"I can imagine."

"No, I mean that very seriously," the princess said. "They were going to let him die and put his bones in a reliquary. The abbot excommunicated him from his order to save his life. Of course, I'm not Catholic, so I don't understand. But I don't think anyone does." She shook her head. "The abbot thought it was better to have a living man than a dead saint. He was a good man, I think, this abbot." She was interrupted by the distinct sound of something shattering. "And my husband, who is twice my age, is a child with our things and is always breaking them. That or the Bingleys have arrived. Should we find out?"

They should, Caitlin said.

One smashed crystal decanter later (because Brian's carpentry skills were not what he thought they were), order was restored, just in time to receive the guests from London. Even without their children, the Darcys, the Kincaids, the Bingleys, the Maddoxes (both couples), and, of course, Grégoire and Caitlin themselves made up a gathering of respectable size.

Caitlin was introduced to perhaps the oddest couple she had ever met, in terms of sheer mismatch. There was the spectacled Dr. Maddox, tall and thin as an overgrown weed and shy but rather pleasant. Beside him was his wife, Charles Bingley's sister, a head shorter than her husband and with everything about her perfect—her hair, her gown, her matching bonnet, and her jewelry. Everything except the smile, the only one at the gathering that seemed a little false, but as she was to be only distantly related to this woman, Caitlin was not overly concerned, and a smile from Grégoire dissolved her unease. The Maddoxes (the hosting ones) had no children, just a large house filled with oddities from their travels abroad, and they seemed quite happy with their situation.

Separated by gender from her betrothed on the premise of discussing "womanly" things, Caitlin sat on the wooden porch with the other ladies. She was the only one with her hair down (all attempts to pin it up nicely had failed) but had a bonnet on, at least, so she did not feel so out of place beyond where her accent already put her.

"Have you selected a location for the wedding?" Jane asked.

"Somewhere—near. Ta de house," she said. "Any church."

"But Catholic," Mrs. Maddox said. "Of course."

"'Course," she replied. "Yeh can come, if yeh want, but I know 'tis a long way. Yeh know."

Mrs. Maddox said, "I'm afraid I haven't been, Mrs. MacKenna."

"What're yeh talkin' about? Don't yeh 'ave family dere?"

Mrs. Maddox colored, and Mrs. Darcy and Mrs. Bingley quickly put their hands over their mouths. "No," Mrs. Maddox said coolly. "I'm afraid I do not."

"Yeh sure? Yer t'e most Irish-lookin' fancy lady I've ever—"

Mrs. Maddox excused herself so quietly and quickly that it was hard to make out her actual words as she left the porch. It was well that she did, because she was barely back in the house, with the sliding door closed behind her, when everyone around Caitlin burst into laughter. "What'd I say?"

"Only the obvious," Mrs. Darcy said.

"We're being cruel to my sister-in-law," Mrs. Bingley said between giggles. They were laughing so hard they were almost crying.

"Well, I think it was worth it all the same," Princess Maddox said, and that, of course, brought on a whole new round of laughter.

Sometime after Mrs. Maddox had been calmed down—and how that was done, Caitlin did not inquire—they sat down for dinner and Grégoire's relatives toasted the couple, who were to be wedded in the coming weeks, after the arrangements were complete. Only in privacy did Caitlin admit to herself and Lady Kincaid that she might like to be married in one of those pretty white dresses (even if she hardly deserved to wear white). A white wedding dress was, she believed, what a princess would wear, even if the only princess she knew didn't seem to act much like she had imagined princesses would. Grégoire came to the table with red eyes, as his loving relatives had conspired to get him a little drunk, and he consented to every toast, and insisted that one be made to St. Patrick, who had brought them together, and St. Sebald, who had brought him home to England, and to St. Buddha, whoever that was, and St. Bede—and he was lucky to make it to dessert before passing out cold on the settee.

"The soul is always in a state of joy for the love of God," Brian Maddox said, "and alcohol allows the body to join the soul in that joy. It can be spiritually uplifting in the right circumstances."

"I know many churchmen who would disagree with you," Darcy said, the least drunk of them all, having had hardly anything. "Where in the world did you hear that? The Orient?"

"Russia. From Rabbi Zalman of Liadi," he said, raising his glass. "We spent a winter in his house. His congregation used to drink and dance every Friday night until the sun came up."

"And spend Saturday sleeping it off," his wife added. "The rest of the week, they drank much less. Only for special occasions."

"I think that when a monk marries, it is a special occasion," Mr. Bingley said. "Or at least a very rare one."

The party dispersed to return to their respective homes in town. It was during this shuffling about (and carrying, in the case of Grégoire) that Darcy stopped in the darkness beside Caitlin and Grégoire's carriage. "You have made my brother very happy, Mrs. MacKenna."

"T'ank yeh." He rarely spoke to her, and so was very intimidating.

"As you seem to be the only one capable of doing so, I will be pleased to see the two of you wed," he said, and stepped into his own carriage before she could respond.

~ ~ ~

"There's no reason to be in a snit—"

"She assumed I was Irish!"

Dr. Maddox, who had had more than a few drinks and was still feeling the effects upon retiring to their chamber, said only, "She is certainly not the first and I doubt the last."

Caroline growled and climbed into bed beside him, but before she could slip away from him, he pulled her close. "If you are so upset, dye your hair. But it will not match your fine skin and I would be very annoyed with you, because I would not have you any other way than you are now."

"Says the man who can hardly see."

"I can see well enough still." He kissed her on her forehead, and could feel some of her anger abate. "If you really wish to be a snooty Englishwoman, you should know you married a Welshman with a proud heritage of clan Madoc. So it is a hopeless case." He chuckled. "Do you really have any other reason to dislike her?"

There was a long moment of silence. "I suppose not. And Grégoire is visibly smitten," she said. "Will she ever have children?" They knew only minor details of her history with her previous husband.

"The doctors in Ireland said it would take a miracle," he replied. "Fortunately, Grégoire is known for them."

~~~

As an unspoken peace offering, Mrs. Maddox escorted Mrs. MacKenna to all of the best shops for wedding dresses, and between that and the pre-wedding gifts of jewelry, the women of Grégoire's extended family conspired to make her a very modish bride.

"I hope that someone is helping Grégoire purchase suitable attire for his own wedding," Elizabeth said in passing as Caitlin's gown was being pinned up by the dressmaker. "I don't know where he gets his clothing—"

"I make 'is shirts," she said. "But I don' 'ave time before—I mean fer somet'ing fancy—"
~~~

"It is a royal tradition in England," Princess Maddox said, to their surprise. "What? The queen is supposed to make the king's shirts. Catherine of Aragon and Anne Boleyn fought over the right to do so for Henry VIII. Don't you English know your history?"

Jane and Elizabeth exchanged giggles. "I suppose we do not, Your Highness."

"I do not think Caroline of Brunswick will be sewing any shirts for the Prince of Wales," Elizabeth ventured.

"If he makes it to the throne," Caroline Maddox said, and returned their looks with her own indignant stare. "What? I am only repeating the gossip columns. You know my husband tells me nothing, only that he is not yet allowed to retire."

"The curse of being too good a physician," Princess Maddox said. "Has he tried again?"

"He was asked to lecture next term at Cambridge on anatomy," Caroline said. "If he ever plucks up his nerve, he might ask the Prince to officially release him, but as he has backed out twice now, I will not hold my breath."

"Men are so easily unnerved," Elizabeth said. "Mention our daughters and the word *out* in the same sentence, and Darcy will flee the room."

"My husband is afraid of standing up to your husband," Jane said to her sister.

"Taking responsibility," Princess Maddox said.

"Being outdrunk," Georgiana Kincaid said.

"Losing de rest of 'is hair," Caitlin said, and then covered her mouth in horror. "I shouldn'tna said that!"

"We won't say a word," Elizabeth assured her. "We promise."

The weather was much colder in Ireland when Grégoire and Caitlin returned than when they had left, this time joined by his brother and sister and their spouses. Despite all of her history, which made her anything but a naive virgin, Caitlin MacKenna still managed to be a blushing bride in the church not far from her new home. Aside from the Darcys and the Kincaids, there were no other guests because of the weather and the location, but all they wanted was a small crowd, having already suitably celebrated and eager to get on with the matter. Their only local guests were the O'Muldoons, who had to travel some distance (for them) to the ceremony, bringing along their many children. Grégoire and Caitlin sent a carriage for them.

"From the moment I saw yeh in town, I knew yeh would do right by her," Mrs. O'Muldoon said to Grégoire, who wore a very nice and appropriate vest over one of Caitlin's tunics, the best of the lot.

Lacking anyone else, Mr. O'Muldoon gave Caitlin away, and the service was, of course, in Latin. Darcy's only comment to Elizabeth about that when he returned from standing up as the best man was that he found it delightfully shorter than English services, where the vicar might have a tendency to go on and on about the sanctity of marriage. If it had been said in Latin (and neither had any idea if it had), it was brief.

On 1 December 1818, Grégoire Bellamont and Caitlin MacKenna were joined in holy matrimony, with the approval of his family, their friends, and the church. After a celebratory luncheon, the couple were given their space, and the many presents packed in trunks from England were dropped at their doorstep by the Darcys before their departure.

"There are some that couldn't get here in time," Darcy said to his brother. "Too many. You should invest in bookshelves while you wait," he said, slapping him on the shoulder. "If she makes you happy, she deserves you."

"She is my wife," Grégoire said with a smile. "It is no longer conditional."

Georgiana gave her little brother the tightest hug she could manage. "You'll come in the spring."

"We are not so far away," he reminded her. "And I want to hear about my nephew."

"He is fine!" Darcy shouted from his carriage.

"*Both* my nephews," he corrected himself. "And tell George to feel free to write me. Or visit. But perhaps not for a few months."

She nodded and kissed him and his new wife good-bye. The couple watched their guests depart in their carriages for Dublin. "Do you approve of my family, Mrs. Bellamont?"

"Who cares?" she said, and pulled him into the house with a tug, followed by a kiss. "My dress itches. I want outta it."

He grinned. "I would be happy to assist you."

"How many books do yeh *need?*"

Grégoire laughed at her comment and his situation, surrounded by trunks and trunks of books. Not only did he have his own collection, and many gifts of a similar sort, but Darcy had also sent him the entire library from the Isle of Man. "These belonged to my Uncle Gregory."

"De mad one?"

"The very same." He closed the book on Greek history, and a dust cloud came forth from the binding before he put it on the shelf. The others would have to wait—the wood had come, but he had yet to finish the bookshelves. He was only a week married and other things consumed his time, but he wanted to build them himself. He owned the house and he wanted to make it truly his.

"Jesus was a carpenter," he said to his wife.

"Really?"

"Really."

"Dey don't mention dat in church."

"I think the other things he did might have been more important."

The construction of the chapel would wait until spring, when the weather was better. The household staff was reduced to two maids and a doorman who also fulfilled the role of groundskeeper. The unpacking of their wedding gifts the Bellamonts did themselves. They received many fine wines for the basement. Grégoire, who was still a Frenchman on some level, appreciated it. There was, of course, some confusion about what came from whom. At a certain point, they decided that the origin of some items would forever be a mystery.

"Grégoire," Caitlin said, passing him a framed painting. It was St. Patrick, in the same pose from the ruin, pointing to his left—a common enough picture in Ireland. "It doesn' 'ave a note."

"I like it very much anyway," he said, and hung it in the main hall, so he would see it every day when he entered.

Their life settled into a happy routine, similar to the one they had before but far less desperate. By the first snowfall, merely a dusting before Christmas, they were quite settled, even if every last shelf had not been put up and every cupboard had not been filled. Caitlin wanted to attend midnight Mass, but it was cold and she was not feeling well, so he insisted she stay behind, and he walked there and back by himself. By the time he returned, it was nearly time for Vigils. Even if he sometimes missed the early morning prayers, being otherwise engaged, he always knew when they were. The moon was bright and he could hear the waves of the sea even from his front steps, so quiet a night it was. When he entered, the house was silent, with the servants sent home for the holiday and his wife asleep.

Grégoire was restless; he saw Caitlin nestled under the covers but was not yet ready to join her. He planted a kiss on her forehead before searching for another room, where he would have a better view of the moon. He'd moved the desk—which was little more than a writing desk—in the study to face directly out.

When I pass away, he thought, *will all of the magic that brought about this time in my life be forgotten?* His own life, he believed, would have meaning to others in the distant future—but how could he be sure? He could not bring himself to write anything too personal—too much love and too much pain, none of it designed for the paper he pulled out before him. Instead, he inked his pen and began to write:

This poor sinner,

Comes to think, on this holy night, how I came to be here, and what meaning might be gleaned from all of the things that have occurred—not just the events, but the method in them of bringing me from one place to another. Can I begin to fathom the holy plan, if indeed there is one for me? I used to think so, but now there is only a simple life for me. What is my existence to mean, then? If I am to have no lasting impression, how should I conduct myself in the time that I have, to live life as joyously as it deserves to be lived?

He was still writing when the sun rose, but he hardly noticed. The first thing to break his concentration was his wife's hand on his back. "What're yeh doin' up so early?"

"I would say the same for you," he replied, looking up at his wife and her pale complexion. "Of course. Would you like me to make you some tea?"

"Just a little," she said. "If yeh don't mind."

He took her hand and kissed it. "I never do."

CHAPTER 38

The Knight

~ ~ ~

"TODAY I WILL DO IT," Dr. Maddox whispered as they entered Carlton House. "Today."

"I can hear you," Dr. Bertrand said with amusement. "You should perhaps ask him at night, when he's likely to agree to any request."

"I will not ask important decisions of a man while he is in a state of severe inebriation," Dr. Maddox said. "Especially if he has the ability to go back on that decision when he has a bad headache the next morning."

The Prince of Wales, still Regent as long as his dying father continued dying, was usually in such a condition when one of them visited him. Since the dual deaths of his daughter and her child (and his heir), he had not been so inclined to his usual schedule of indulgent parties, but that had not curtailed his drinking or his liberal use of opiates for any perceived pain. The fact that he stayed mainly in his bed in fits of panic did not help his weight, to the point where there was real speculation if he would see the throne before the aged King George III passed away. Neither physician added to the gossip filling Town, but the servants of Carlton did the job well enough.

"There is also the matter of my conscience," Maddox admitted to his protégé, "for abandoning a patient I so utterly failed to treat."

"You cannot force the heir of the throne of Britain to exercise unless you manhandle him, it seems."

"They did that to his father," Maddox said, shaking his head, "and look how he turned out. Madder than when they started."

They silenced their conversation upon entering the prince's chamber. The Prince Regent was, of course, still in bed despite it being two in the afternoon, and with no intention to do otherwise. It took a lot of coffee, a lot of prying, and some actual manhandling to get him upright, dressed, and sitting in a chair for the doctor's inspection.

"You are actually quite well today, aside from the obvious," Dr. Maddox said after completing his inspection. "I am worried about the bump on your knee, but there is nothing to be done for it at the moment. And, of course, you should wean yourself from your laudanum, cut back on your drinking, control your portions, and get regular exercise."

"That is hardly news," the Regent said. "You give me the same advice every week."

"Because you never take it."

The Regent smiled. He had excessive amounts of gray in his hair for someone his age, due to stress and his poor diet, most likely. He had just lost his only daughter and grandson to complications in childbirth. Still, he had not been a healthy man when it happened, and there was always talk of his inheriting his father's illness—talk that Dr. Maddox did not believe to be true. The Regent wasn't mad—just under stress and corpulent.

"How is my father?"

"I do not know, Your Highness," Dr. Maddox said. "I do not read the gossip papers, and I am not in regular contact with his doctors."

"But he is still alive? I am not king?"

"No, Your Highness. You are not."

The Regent put his hands on his temples. "Thank God for that." His old humor seemed to briefly return, if only briefly. "I suppose someone would bother to inform me if I was made king."

"Sometime before the coronation ceremony, I'm sure."

The Regent smiled. "The only ones who have not forgotten about me are my doctors, and I sense they have a mission today."

So the Regent's senses were not totally lost. "Your Royal Highness, I have been offered a position as a guest lecturer at Cambridge in place of their old anatomist."

The Regent nodded slowly. "And I suppose this would be a springboard to a full professorship."

"If I found it to my liking, it would. Assuming I was relieved of my duties here, which, of course, are my first and only real concern."

"You've been trying to be rid of me for a year now, I think," the Regent said without malice. "And, of course, I've put up a horrible fight. No, Dr. Maddox, I would not be comfortable if you were not in my service—however limited your role was," he said. "Dr. Bertrand would assume most of the responsibilities. You have worked this out between yourselves?"

"Yes," Dr. Bertrand responded. "I have taken a house in town with my wife and son. My patient list is limited, and would be even smaller if I had additional responsibilities to Your Highness."

The Regent nodded, mulling it over. "I assume this guest lecturer position would be limited hours, in case I needed you."

"Cambridge is not terribly far from town, Your Highness."

"So you would take up residence there?"

Dr. Maddox nodded. "Although I would retain my house in town, I feel that my family would benefit from a manor in the countryside, not far from Cambridge. We would be closer to our relatives in Derbyshire as well."

Again, the Regent was silent for a time, a very nervous time for Dr. Maddox. "I suppose your protégé can manage the task of giving out advice that I never seem to take. With a new salary for his new position, of course. You will, however, retain your own position of chief physician to the extent that if I call on you, you will come immediately."

Dr. Maddox tried to hide his joy. "Of course, Your Highness. Thank you, Your Highness."

Their examination done, the doctors were dismissed with a wave of the Regent's hand. They were nearly out the door before they heard his voice bellow in the chamber. "Oh, and I suppose I cannot have one of my own physicians presented to the world as anything less than a knight of the realm. Be here tomorrow, the same time. And you can invite your wife and brother, but there will be no big ceremony. I despise ceremonies." He continued, "And there is a royal holding of some land in Chesterton. If it is to your liking, there will be a designation for you."

Dr. Maddox bowed, now legitimately awed. "Thank you, Your Highness."

"Enough! I have no patience for ceremony. Go and be overwhelmed somewhere else, Doctor, and I will see you on the morrow."

Brian Maddox's first question was, "Can I wear my crown?"

"Your crown?"

"I do have one, you know. You've seen it. I am a *prince*." He frowned. "Or a count. I was never clear on that. The point is, I never get to wear it."

Dr. Maddox was in too good a mood to refuse anyone anything. "I will still never call you Your Highness, you understand."

"Easily understandable." They embraced, and toasted his good fortune. "And I assume Caroline is—"

"Still recovering from her faint, yes." In actuality, Caroline Maddox was busy scribbling letters to everyone she knew, but her excitement had not waned.

"She's really willing to give up Town?"

"For part of the year, yes. It will be good for the children to not be breathing smog all the time, and Emily is years from going out. Thank God." He raised his glass to that. "An estate in the country. I never imagined I could do it."

"There is no one more deserving. Hell, I have one, and we all know I am a contemptible rogue and probably a madman. Congratulations, Danny." He was as pleased with his brother as Maddox was happy for himself. "Perhaps we should invite the Earl of Maddox around sometime. You know, I do outrank him."

"In a small area of Transylvania, you might, but in England, he would say otherwise," Dr. Maddox said.

"Hey! Unlike him, I earned my title."

"*Earned?* You married it!"

"Yes, completely free and without complications," Brian said. "Well, cheers to you. If you don't want me to show up in royal garb, uninvite me now."

Dr. Maddox smiled. "I wouldn't dream of it."

"I hope he'll show," Brian said.

"I hope he'll be at least partially sober," Dr. Maddox said, fidgeting nervously in his dress clothing. It was nothing compared with the awkward metal crown Brian was wearing, more of a helmet than a circlet, and studded with ancient jewels and stones that looked more bashed in than carefully placed, with an Orthodox cross at the top. In his Romanian costume and with his very distinguished wife beside him, Dr. Maddox had to admit that his brother did look sort of...*royal.*

"Your brother gets a crown," Caroline Maddox said on the other side of him. "What do I get?"

"To be called Lady Maddox for the rest of your life," he said with a shrug. "It was the best I could do."

She gave him a smile that indicated she was more than happy with the situation.

The nonaristocratic Maddox couple bowed at the announcement and entrance of the Lord Chamberlain, the Marquess of Hertford. "Prince and Princess Brian and Nadezhda Agnita of Sibui," the royal servant said.

"May I present His Royal Highness George Augustus, the Prince of Wales, Earl of Chester, and Prince Regent to His Majesty

George III," the royal servant continued.

The Regent entered upright and actually walking without a wobble, which surprised Dr. Maddox somewhat. In fact, he looked the best he had in weeks, perhaps because much of his girth and ill look was hidden by the royal robes and crown. The Prince Regent, who an hour earlier had been seen sobbing in his bed, was quite capable of assuming the character of a man in control of his life and his country when required. He did so regularly during ceremonies he could not avoid, the number of which would only increase when his father died. Despite his usual casual nature, Brian had the good sense to bow to his future sovereign.

"Your Royal Highness," the equerry said, "Dr. Daniel Maddox is known for his dutiful service to the Crown in the field of medicine."

The Prince Regent, who was not known to stand on ceremony despite being required to do so on a regular basis, gestured for Dr. Maddox to kneel before him. Fortunately, between the gin and the laudanum, he still had enough coordination to wield the sword. "I knight thee Sir Daniel Maddox, Order of the Garter." He touched each shoulder and passed off the sword to his equerry and took from him the chain, putting it around Maddox's neck. "You may rise, Sir Maddox."

"Thank you, Your Highness."

Fortunately, the regent did not stay to see how choked up his doctor was, and left with the servants carrying the ends of his robes. In the haste of it all, there was no reception. Dr. Maddox, an intensely private man, hadn't wanted one anyway.

"I used to read him stories about knights when he was recovering from eye surgery," Brian whispered to his wife as Sir Maddox was embraced by his own wife, "and now he gets to *be* one—without all the fighting. Same amount of gore, though."

~ ~ ~

"Papa, if you're a knight, where's your sword?" Emily Maddox said as her father sorted through his medical books for the ones that would go to Cambridge. "And your armor! You have to have armor to fight dragons."

"I don't fight dragons. I'm not that sort of knight."

"Uncle Maddox has a sword."

"Uncle Maddox thinks he lives in Japan," he replied to his daughter, who was now ten, "where he would need a sword, I suppose."

A week had passed, and Sir and Lady Maddox had received the congratulations of their friends and relations in Town in person and their Derbyshire relations by post, on account of the winter weather. Grégoire and Caitlin Bellamont probably had not even received the announcement yet. The spring term would start soon, and he was due in Cambridge three days out of the week.

"Mr. Wickham to see you, sir," the servant announced, and George Wickham entered the study.

"Sir Maddox," he said and bowed. "Miss Maddox."

"You can do that nonsense with my wife, but not with me," he said. "I've always preferred 'Dr.' anyway. I worked hard enough to earn it." He turned to his daughter and gestured for her to shoo. "Mr. Wickham. What brings you by? Are you intending to loot my library again?"

"If I did, I wouldn't have any room for the spoils, Dr. Maddox," George said with a shy smile. "I've come for your advice about university."

"I told you not to worry about your credentials, Mr. Wickham," Maddox said. He pulled another volume off the shelf, dusted off the cover to see the title, and replaced it. "Not everyone who enters university went to Eton or Harrow, or even knows half of what you do if they had private tutors. I didn't go, your Uncle Bingley didn't go, and my brother attended only his first two years. I honestly think those schools might exist just to get ill-mannered boys out of the house for a few years, before they can go on to university and become ill-mannered men." He added, "Excepting your cousins, of course, who are always on their best behavior." But the expression on George's face was not that of a man soothed. Dr. Maddox sighed; young Wickham was so distant and stubborn—not always to negative ends, but once he had a notion in his head, it was hard for him to shake it.

Maddox put the book in his hands down, and placed one hand on George's shoulder. "So—are you still set on Oxford, then? Not that you don't have time to decide."

"Yes."

"It is a fine school. My father went there." He was never quite able to figure George Wickham out. "Not that you are tied to any choices now. You have some ways to go yet, Mr. Wickham. And if life has taught me anything, it is not to assume too much responsibility unless you absolutely have to. Otherwise, you might end up a gambler and a drunk, and eventually marry a princess and walk around with a set of swords as though you're some kind of medieval knight."

George gave one of his rare half grins. "Says the knight himself."

"I *hope* it is merely an honorary title, and I will not be called on to don a suit of armor," Dr. Maddox said.

~ ~ ~

Because of the speed with which it had been given, Sir and Lady Maddox were not able to celebrate their titles with the family for some time, and put it off until the next family gathering, which was not until early summer. Dr. Maddox was back and forth between Cambridge and Town, and as predicted, was offered a full professorship in medicine for the fall term. Lady Maddox spent much of her time with her sister, surveying properties outside Cambridge before selecting a manor, which would undergo renovations to her tastes.

The families gathered in Derbyshire for various celebrations, one of them to mark Geoffrey Darcy's completion of his first year at Eton, which he did not want celebrated, at least not in the form of all the adults telling him how much older he looked and what a wonderful young man he was turning into. He was more interested in relaxing with his cousins—fishing in the pond with Charles and Georgiana, with his loyal hound by his side. And that was what he did.

"So how is it?" Charlie Bingley asked eagerly, as he would be attending the following year.

"Fine," Geoffrey said. "A lot of work, and some of the boys are snobs, but it's all right."

When Charles was reassured, he left to collect more bait, leaving Geoffrey and Georgiana to themselves. Georgiana Bingley, who had no real interest in fishing, always sat against the tree and played with the flowers, tearing off the petals and tossing them into the water to make them float. "Nice sandals," he said of her wooden geta shoes.

"Thanks," she said.

"They were a gift?"

She nodded.

Geoffrey sighed. He hadn't been able to really talk to her over Christmas break, either. Then, he hadn't understood why. Now, having been gone for almost a year, he understood a little better. "I need you to teach me how to fight."

That got her attention, and some of that old amusement. "You *know* how to fight."

"I know how to fence. That is different."

"Since when have you taken an interest in pugilism?"

"This isn't pugilism. I just want to be able to...get out of a fight."

"The aristocracy of Eton knocking Geoffrey Darcy around? Your father wouldn't stand for it! Think of the family honor!"

He grinned. "I'm not saying I can't throw a punch. I'm not Uncle Bingley."

"Papa fought a master pugilist in China!"

"I heard he lost."

Georgiana smiled. "So what you mean to say, in your dignified and roundabout way, is that you want to be good at it, in case some older boy decides to thrash you for fun?"

"Yes. That is what I am saying, in my dignified and roundabout way."

"Pity I can't be there to protect you."

"I wish you were there," he said, and then uncomfortably changed course. "So will you teach me?"

"I might," she said. "Violating all the bounds of decorum, of course."

"I've never known that to stop you."

"Then it's agreed. Unless you're to Ireland?" she said. "Why can't Uncle Grégoire come here?"

"Mrs. Bellamont is completing her confinement in August. Or September. They're not sure. And I know how it works now. How a baby is conceived."

"Oh, really?"

"Yes, really. I don't know what school was like when Father went, but some of those boys have filthy—" He reddened. "I can't talk about this."

"Talk about what?"

"Don't tease me. You know."

"I really don't."

"Well, I can't really—" He couldn't look at her. "You should ask your mother, if you want to know."

"Oh," Georgiana said. "No, she wouldn't say a word. This is the sort of thing a woman is supposed to learn only on her wedding night. Though it's positively mystifying—"

"Well, maybe it should be," he said defensively. "Wait—how do you know?"

"Because Papa has a locked drawer in his study that isn't *always* locked and has some interesting literature in it," she said. "All kinds of pictures of monsters. I thought it was some kind of Indian fantasy book. Plus, George has all these books—"

He interrupted, "How do you know what dirty books George Wickham has?"

Georgiana straightened. "Because Izzy told me," she said. "I didn't ask him about them, if that's what you're implying."

"Then why are you asking me if you won't ask George?"

"Because I like to torture you. Of course, you can keep all your Eton secrets, which are probably all wrong anyway. You didn't really think I would ask you seriously about that sort of thing?"

He smiled. "No. I mean—I wasn't sure."

"Even though you just asked me to help you punch people."

"That is not precisely what I said, but yes. And it's still different."

"I suppose," she said, and returned to a more restful position as her brother returned.

The Darcys and the Kincaids—minus their children (Geoffrey was a last-minute decision)—arrived in Ireland to find the Bellamont house quite different from the way they had seen it after the wedding. Not only was a stone chapel under construction, but the house had its halls lined with bookcases and pictures—mainly of saints. The furniture was wooden, some of it carved. "Grégoire's really obsessed wid t'is carpentry business," said an increasing Caitlin MacKenna, to which her husband smiled. She walked about the house and grounds as she wished, but did not seem eager to do much of it. Their dinners were cooked by a chef, for which she was apologetic, despite the fact that none of them expected it of her. "I would do deh cookin,'" she said, "but 's hard ta stay on me feet."

Their rooms were not grand, but they were clean, and they were decorated. Grégoire and Caitlin had dedicated themselves to making the house their own. It was not the grand sort of renovations like the ones that Lady Kincaid planned for her house outside Cambridge. The drapes were not made of the finest materials, the carpets did not necessarily match, and there was less organization to everything, but everywhere, there was a touch of something that was clearly either Grégoire's or Caitlin's handiwork.

Darcy looked at the writing desk in the study, which faced the window and a view of the ocean, and picked up one of the wooden figures on the shelf. It was a man with a beard and a halo surrounding his head.

"I'm not very good," Grégoire said, "but I rather like the process."

Darcy replaced the figurine. "This desk looks familiar."

"It is not the one from the Isle of Man," Grégoire replied, "but it has a similar arrangement. I do like looking out at the ocean when I write."

"I've been reading your columns," he said. "The paper will protect you?"

"If there is anything to protect. I doubt new ramblings about the saints and modern day religion would upset anyone." He smiled distantly. "Then again, I have always been naive about what is upsetting to people. Especially the church. Yes, they will protect my anonymity." Grégoire had published several sermonlike columns in a Catholic paper in Dublin, under the name A Poor Sinner, despite the fact that Darcy would describe him as neither. They were philosophical arguments, generally rather uplifting, and had some popularity with the inspirational crowd, apparently. "I have written nothing controversial and have no intention to do so. Nonetheless, if the church wishes to say something to me, I must only remind them that I have been excommunicated from my order, and that will end the conversation."

"How convenient."

"Very," his brother said. "The local daily in Belfast has also picked up the column."

"You will be careful?"

"I will not make that promise," Grégoire said, "as I always seem to break it. But no, Darcy, I am not making trouble."

"Good," Darcy said with a tone of finality, "because I'm sick of getting you out of it."

They were fortunate to have come far enough to laugh about it.

~~~
~~~

Precisely nine months after her marriage to Grégoire Bellamont, Caitlin's labor pains began. That she had become with child at all stumped the local doctors. They were all encouragement. Grégoire did not announce the pregnancy until after Christmas, when they were sure.

What he was less thrilled about was the prospect of staying downstairs with his brother and brother-in-law throughout his wife's travails. Darcy finally agreed to go upstairs and ask his wife how things were proceeding. He was within twenty feet of the door when he heard a steady stream of sailor's curses in the form of one long shriek. His ears were still burning when he returned to the study. "She is fine," he said, pouring himself a drink.

"That feckin' gobshite! I should've na'even 'ad kids—'s what the doc said," a distressed Caitlin said to Elizabeth, her brogue getting heavier as she became generally less lucid, to the point where not even Georgiana or the midwife's soothing voice could begin to calm her. "I 'ad ta marry a stupid feckin' saint with 'is stupid feckin' miracles and 'ave a stupid feckin' miracle kid! I'd like ta stab *'im* in the stomach—"

Elizabeth pressed a cloth to Caitlin's brow. "You would hardly be the first wife in this condition to curse her husband." Despite her distress and her reddened face, Caitlin still looked too young for all of this—one and twenty. The same age Elizabeth had been when she had given birth to Geoffrey. Had she really been that young?

"For feck's sake, let dat idiot up 'ere and I'll feckin' do it meself!"

The midwife encouraged her otherwise, and by the end of the day, the wailing of another person, who had never wailed before, filled the Bellamont house. A slightly inebriated (maybe more than *slightly*) Grégoire bounded up the stairs before either of his brothers could follow him and charged into the room. Fortunately, there had been enough time for the baby to be properly cleaned and bundled before the appearance of his father. Grégoire stumbled at the sight, and was quickly grabbed by Kincaid, who helped him into the chair to receive the baby, which he was informed was a son.

"Drink dis, ma'rm," the midwife said as the others offered their congratulations and excused themselves from the immediate presence of a very exhausted Caitlin Bellamont, who could only crane her head at the sight of her husband and the child wrapped in a blanket in his arms.

Grégoire's first response was a laugh, as he very carefully released one hand to stroke the few strands of brown hair atop his child's pink head. "If I had known that such a wondrous thing could exist on earth, I would have said my prayers of thanksgiving so much harder throughout my life. I certainly shall now." He looked to his wife, who smiled weakly back at him, her voice, for now, silenced.

~ ~ ~

The very next day, the local priest baptized Patrick Bellamont in the newly consecrated, still half-constructed chapel. Lord and Lady Kincaid stood as godparents. The service was basically the same as an Anglican one, and little Patrick was as oblivious to it as any newborn. Caitlin, who leaned on her husband, had knitted the white outfit herself the month before.

Despite the expected exhaustion, Mrs. Bellamont recovered her health relatively quickly. The largest of the gifts, which had been packed most carefully and remained hidden in the carriage for days, was a wooden cradle with the Darcy seal on it, a little aged but otherwise in perfect condition. "It might have held my husband, for all we know," Elizabeth said to Grégoire. "Or Mr. Wickham. There were only a few cradles at Pemberley that we could find."

The Darcys were lodged in the room next to the new parents, and overheard an argument—not a mean one, but with loud voices—between husband and wife over the hiring of a nurse.

"I can raise me own laddie!"

"I'm not saying you cannot—"

"I'm not sick!"

"I was not implying that you were—"

Elizabeth had to glance at her husband and share a laugh at the experience of his younger brother and his wife. After two nights, Mrs. Bellamont relented and agreed that maybe another pair of female hands was "a good idea."

On the final night of their stay, Darcy woke very early, long before daylight. Looking at the grandfather clock he had sent from Pemberley as a wedding gift, he saw it was half past four, later than the earliest monastic office of the day, Vigils. Grégoire was up, of course. Darcy found his younger brother sitting in the study, facing the window. In one hand was a pen, scribbling on paper, and the other balanced his sleeping son in his lap. Darcy approached cautiously.

"He is quite soundly asleep," Grégoire said in a lowered voice. "After all the racket he made a while ago. I hope he did not wake you."

"No," Darcy replied, and raised his candlestick to get a better look at his newest nephew. Although, after four of his own, the sight of a baby never left him unaffected, the fatherly glow on Grégoire's face was even more moving to him. "I suppose he is named after the saint?"

"It was St. Patrick who brought me to Caitlin," Grégoire said, discarding his pen for the moment to wrap his other arm around his son. "Now things come full circle." He rocked the baby, who shifted in his arms but did not wake. "I am truly a blessed man. I could not have imagined being a husband and father would bring me such joy." He looked up at Darcy. "Everything I could possibly ask for, I have received. What am I to do now?"

"If you are lacking occupation, I would remind you that you will be quite busy until the day he leaves for university," Darcy replied, "though it may happen sooner than you think."

The two brothers sat together in the study, facing the ocean and the morning light that rose on the horizon, and Darcy had his turn holding his nephew Patrick, the newest grandson of Geoffrey Darcy.

CHAPTER 39

One Year Later

ABBOT FRANCESCO had been composing a reply to the Roman bishop, but he was lost in thought again, as often happened of late. A product of getting old, he supposed. His wandering mind was focused again as Prior Pullo entered. "Father, there is a priest here to see you. Father O'Banon."

"Father O'Banon?"

"He says he has come a long way. From Ireland."

He nodded, although not in understanding. "Thank you, Brother Prior. Send him in."

The man who entered was all in black, except for his collar. His red hair and his clothes looked a bit disheveled from his journey, but otherwise he was quite composed. "You are Abbot Francesco Chiaramonti?" he asked in Latin.

"I am."

He bowed. "I am Father Michael O'Banon, from Belfast. Please pardon my intrusion."

The abbot gestured for him to sit. "What brings you to Spain, Father O'Banon?"

The priest opened his sack and nervously removed a tiny bound book, which he held reverently in his hands. "On behalf of the archbishop of Belfast—and myself, I admit—I've been making inquiries into the author of a series of anonymous editorial columns of an inspirational nature that have been published in the local papers for two years now. They've become so popular that the first set were recently compiled into a book, which is now a best seller." He set it on the abbot's desk. The abbot opened it, but it was in English. "The author calls himself A Poor Sinner. His real name is Grégoire Bellamont."

That name had never been far from the abbot's mind, so he recognized it, even mispronounced with an Irish brogue. He flipped through the book, but his English reading was far worse than the little English he could speak, and it solved no mysteries for him. "Have you met him?"

"I have, in fact. He lives south of Dublin, and despite the fact that he wishes no attention for himself, he did greet me quite warmly." He swallowed. "I understand he was once a brother here."

The abbot closed the book. "He is excommunicated from this order. It is forbidden to speak of the monk who was dismissed from this abbey."

"So he said. I thought I would try anyway."

The abbot leaned back in his chair. "It is *not* forbidden to speak of this layman, assuming he has not taken holy orders in secrecy."

"He has not."

"Then how is—Mr. Bellamont?"

Relieved, the priest continued, "He is quite well. He is married and has an infant son, who is named after St. Patrick. As I said, he is not known as a literary celebrity, but locally, he is known as an extremely charitable man. He teaches at an orphanage. Besides writing, that is his primary occupation." He added, "There is something...unusual about him. He never says an ill word, and he is all reverence and joy, but also humble, despite what is clearly his vast scholarship in religion."

"So Grégoire is still as he was, in many ways," the abbot said with a smile. "You cannot fathom what it means to me to hear that he is well. But—he is under investigation for his writings?"

"No. Technically, yes, but it is a matter of curiosity. His writings are extremely popular, as I have said. Priests and preachers alike are known to use the material for their sermons. He writes of the joy of daily living, the ways to see how Christ and his saints influence our lives—all very positive, which is quite different from the hell-fire sort of speeches more common in Britain. But he has written nothing controversial about any church doctrine."

"And he writes—in English?"

"Yes. There was actually a question as to some of his quotes from Latin and Greek texts, as we did not recognize the precise wording. Then we realized that he was not quoting from direct translations, but using the original text and translating the work himself. Except for the Good Book, where he uses the Douay-Rheims because it's an *acceptable* English translation. When I asked him about it, he said he knew it would be blasphemy to do otherwise, and he knows better than to write something that upsets the church."

The abbot nodded. "Then he has learned well." He pushed the book back to the priest. "I cannot read English, unfortunately."

"The publisher said there would be a Latin edition next year. He is doing it himself."

"Very good. I would be eager to read such a thing," the abbot said. "So Father—how can I help you, given that you seem to know more about this layman than I do?"

The priest paused. "Though he discouraged me from doing so, I cannot help but wonder about the circumstances surrounding his excommunication from the Benedictines. He will not deny it, but he will not otherwise speak of it."

"Then he has a great deal of tact," he replied. "Grégoire was misused by the church and nearly killed by it—literally. Despite much penance, I have never forgiven myself for the events that led to his excommunication from the order—though, in all truth, it sounds as though it was the right path for him." He stood up and went to his shelves, where he found the scroll he needed, and returned to the desk, unrolling it. "This is my condemnation of his actions and announcement of his excommunication from the order of St. Benedict. My principal goal upon signing it was not to damn him or encourage penance, but to save him from Rome, which was ready to unofficially label him a living saint and use him for its own ends. Although I have never regretted my actions, they have always weighed heavily on me." He rolled it back up. "The precise circumstances of the excommunication do not speak well of anyone involved—myself, the bishop, or the archbishop of Oviedo. However, now that he is delivered into safety, there may not be a need to have a document condemning him. If I am to tear it up, I would like his opinion on it first. You say he lives south of Dublin?"

"Yes," said the priest. "Are you in need of transportation?"

One last journey for one old abbot.

"We should stop here," the priest said, and pulled the horses to a stop in front of a large building not far from the last town on the dirt road, deep in the forests of untamed Ireland. "He may be at work."

The abbot nodded and took the priest's hand to help him off the gig. He needed a staff to walk, especially on such a long journey, as they approached the building, which looked a bit—but not entirely—like a church. Made of wood and with a thatched roof, it lacked any signs, but it was evident enough from the chorus of children's voices that it was an orphanage. The abbot was helped to a bench as Father O'Banon spoke to the local priest in quick English, too quick for the abbot. At last, O'Banon returned to him. "The lesson is almost finished, if we would wait."

Abbot Francesco nodded. "We will wait."

They were offered beer, and accepted it to parch their thirst. Sitting in silence, they could make out some of the speech that was behind the closed door.

"And what letter is this?"

"Jaaaaaaaaaaaay!"

"And what does it stands for?" The children answered him in their thick brogue, "Jesus Christ, our Lord an' Savior!"

"Very good," said the teacher, who did not have the same accent. "Now I see it is time. You are all dismissed."

There were some cheers and the children came rushing out, but some of them stopped. "Mr. Gregory, candy!"

"Candy is for saint's days and Sundays, you know that. You'll ruin your teeth if you eat it every day." After some resistance, the last of the children emerged, to be herded by the head of the orphanage to the meal room. It was only then that their teacher emerged, and the two guests rose to greet him.

Grégoire Bellamont was not as the abbot had expected, but he had not been sure what to expect. The former monk was not dressed like an English gentleman, nor like a priest or a local worker. His brown tunic and belt made him look more like a beggar and the cross around his neck like a pilgrim, and there was a bald spot where his tonsure had been, but besides that, he was unchanged. He looked healthy but shocked, and after a moment, dropped to his knees. "Father."

The abbot offered his hand so Grégoire could kiss the ring. "Grégoire. It is good to see you."

"But we are forbidden—"

The abbot had already removed from his satchel the scroll, and held it before Grégoire, not waiting for him to recognize it (if he would at all) before tearing it in half. "I would do so not only to try to undo some of the damage that was done to you, but so that I could speak to you once more before I die."

Father O'Banon, who spoke little Spanish and therefore could not understand their conversation, sensed the mood perfectly as Grégoire and the old abbot eagerly embraced.

"My son," the abbot said, kissing Grégoire on the cheek. "It is good to see you well."

"I have you to thank for that," Grégoire responded. "Please, let me invite you to my home. Father O'Banon has told you of my situation?"

"Yes. I am pleased."

It was not far to Grégoire's house, and the abbot insisted on walking there. "I will catch up with you." The priest nodded and took the gig on the road.

"Come, Father, it is time for Sext. I end my class when I do so I can make it back on time."

~ ~ ~

Abbot Francesco and Grégoire Bellamont prayed together in the chapel that the latter had added to his manor house, a structure of Gothic stone. The abbot was surprised that Grégoire seemed to be keeping the monastic cycle, even though, as a layman, he was not expected to do so. Grégoire did not have stained glass, but someone had painted on the windows, and the paint was thin enough so that light could still come through, giving much the same effect.

"My wife," Grégoire said. "She likes to paint." He pointed to the different windows, all of which had paintings of men with halos. "St. Patrick, St. Bede, St. Benedict, and St. Sebald."

"Ah, yes, your old patron," the abbot said, referring to Sebald. He did not know another monk so dedicated to the Bavarian saint. He had not even heard the name until Grégoire joined his monastery.

"Dinner should be ready," Grégoire said, "and you have not met my wife—or my son."

"Yes, of course."

They made their way through the side door into the house, where the smells of food filled the room leading to the kitchen. At the sound of the door shutting, a woman emerged, wearing an apron over her dress and a scarf over her head. In one well-practiced arm she carried a boy, looking to be about a year old, with brown hair like his father. "I didn' know we 'ad company."

Grégoire kissed his wife with no shame, and took his son from her before turning back to the abbot. "Father, this is my wife, Mrs. Bellamont. Caitlin, this is Father Francesco Chiaramonti, the abbot who saved my life in Spain by ordering me away."

She curtsied to the abbot, who bowed a little nervously. He had never met a former brother's wife before.

"And this, of course, is Patrick," Grégoire said of his son, who was currently pulling at his hair and babbling. "Named after the saint who brought me to Caitlin."

"'E believes all t'is stuff, about saints guiding 'im, as t'hough they 'ave nothin' else ta do wit t'ere time," she said, her local accent quite distinct. It took all of the abbot's English vocabulary to understand her. "And honestly, I'm startin' ta believe him."

She excused herself to get their meal, and Grégoire guided the abbot to the best chair at the table, grabbing a pillow for his old back.

"God bless you," the abbot said.

"Do you wish to hold him?" Grégoire said in Spanish.

He had not expected this. "Yes." How could he say no? Why would he say no? When he was safely seated and comfortable, little Patrick was set carefully on his lap, and he stared up, wide-eyed, at the mysterious old man. "Hello, Patrick. You are a sight I never expected to see." His only memories of children came flooding back to him—of the occasional child he had christened, but mainly of holding his younger brother, now the vicar of Christ, as a newborn. Had his brother been so precious? Had his own father exhibited the same glow of pride that was so clear on Grégoire's face? For a monk, pride was a sin. For a father, surely there was no sin in that. "He is wonderful, Grégoire."

"He is a blessing from God."

"Blessin' from God what keeps stickin' t'ings in his mout'h," Mrs. Bellamont said. Patrick had just grabbed a wooden spoon from the table and shoved it in his mouth, and she moved swiftly to remove it, at which point, he began to cry. "'Scuse me, Faither."

"Of course."

She lifted Patrick out of his arms and into hers, rocking him into complacency as they sat down to eat. According to Benedictine custom, no one spoke until they were all finished. That was when Grégoire showed the abbot his writing tablet, and some of the Latin translations he was working on. "I would be honored if you—"

"I would love to."

The abbot spent the afternoon going through the Latin translations of the columns, rough drafts though they were. The subject matter would vary, and Grégoire was wise enough to rely heavily on quotes from church fathers, rather than making the key points himself, but the undertone was the same. The joy he found in a humble, ordinary life was transmitted perfectly. The arguments ranged from simple to complex, and he had scattered notes about revisions in between the lines, but he had apparently found his calling—and an audience. That he believed that his entire life was destined to follow a specific path was reinforced by his stubborn attitude.

As he read, the abbot occasionally looked up and through the window. Young Patrick was still mastering being upright, and his father was helping him walk along the shore, the waves lapping at his tiny feet. Grégoire had finally found people to pour his love into—people who deserved it, and not just dead saints.

"My son," he said the next day, when it came time to depart, "can you forgive me for all the ways in which I have wronged you?"

Grégoire smiled. "Considering what the consequences were, I cannot help but thank you."

"I'm old, Grégoire. And tired. I want to step down as father abbot," he said, continuing despite Grégoire's look of surprise. "I have to move on, and I cannot do it without your forgiveness."

"You would be surprised by what you are capable of," Grégoire replied. "Father Abbot, I bear you no ill will. I never have."

They embraced one more time. The gig was ready to go, and the abbot was ready to leave. He left behind his staff, and Grégoire made him a parting promise to send along the Latin compendium of his works, and he sent his greetings to all the brothers he missed so much. Mrs. Bellamont curtsied politely to him, and Patrick's good-bye consisted of babbling as he flailed his free hand in the abbot's direction.

As the abbot boarded the gig to sit beside Father O'Banon, the priest remarked on the loss of his walking stick.

"In the presence of a saint," he replied, "you find yourself without need for further support."

The End

Historical Notations

~ ~ ~

ANY MONASTIC RESEARCHER will quickly discover that there is a great wealth of information on monastic life in the medieval period leading up to the Counter-Reformation (mid 1500s) and a good deal of material dealing with modern, post Vatican II (1962) monasticism. Between those periods is more of a gray area, and I've done my best to show life in a monastery in post-Napoleonic Europe, but I was probably wrong about a couple things.

A good deal of material was made up for the sake of narrative. There was no archbishopric of Oviedo. Spain in 1817 only had five archbishoprics. Some of the monasteries had been dissolved by this point, but plenty of them still existed, particularly Benedictines. Pope Pius VII may well have had an older brother, but the abbot in this book is pure invention.

Much of the material for the scenes in India are derived from the autobiographical accounts of Dean Mahomet, who moved to England and opened a shop in Brighton that is mentioned in this book. The scenes in China are similarly derived from late Qing Dynasty sources.

As noted in previous books, the Prince Regent (soon to be King George IV) had several children out of wedlock, or in wedlock with his Catholic wife (the marriage was not considered valid). Some of these were fairly public knowledge and some are more historical theories. Frederick Augustus Maddox is imagined, as his mother, so he certainly never met his grandfather King George III because he is not a real person, though to be fair, George III was quite mad by this time and probably met an incredible number of imaginary people.

Also, none of the events of this book occurred and the overwhelming majority of the characters never existed. So there's that.

Bibliography

Allen, John. *All the Pope's Men: The Inside Story of How the Vatican Really Thinks*. New York: Doubleday, 2004.

Atkin, Nicholas and Frank Tallett. *Priests, Prelates, and People*. Oxford Oxfordshire: Oxford University Press, 2003.

Beales, Derek. *Prosperity and Plunder: European Catholic Monasteries in the Age of Revolution, 1650–1815*. Cambridge: Cambridge University Press, 2003.

Brooke, Iris and James Laver. *English Costume from the Seventeenth Through the Nineteenth Centuries*. New York: Dover Publications, 2000.

Bury, J. B. *The History of the Papacy in the 19th Century*. New York: Schocken Books, 1964.

Callahan, William. *Church, Politics, and Society in Spain, 1750-1874*. Cambridge: Harvard University Press, 1984.

Cusack, Mary Frances. *An Illustrated History of Ireland from AD 400 to 1800*. London: Kenmore Publications, 1875.

Dorner, Klaus. *Madmen and the Bourgeoisie*. Oxford: B. Blackwell, 1981.

Duckett, Eleanor. *The Gateway to the Middle Ages: Monasticism*. Ann Arbor: The University of Michigan Press, 1988.

Howlett, D. R., ed. *The Confession of St. Patrick*. New York: Liguori Publications, 1996.

Mahomet, Dean and Michael Fisher. *The Travels of Dean Mahomet*. Berkeley, California: University of California Press, 1997.

O'Neill, Kevin. *Family and Farm in Pre-Famine Ireland*. Madison: University of Wisconsin Press, 1984.

Parker, A. A. *The Catholic Church in Spain from 1800 Till To-Day*. London: Catholic Truth Society, 1938.

Parry, David and Waal De. *The Rule of Saint Benedict*. Leominster, England: Gracewing, 1990.

Rochie, Edward Hardy. "The Dead Sea Discipline and the Rule of St. Benedict." *Journal of Bible and Religion*. Vol. 25, No. 3 (Jul., 1957), pp. 183-186.

Smith, E. *George IV*. New Haven, Connecticut: Yale University Press, 1999.

Sullivan, Thomas P. "Benedict on Authority." *Improving College and University Teaching*. Vol. 9, No. 4 (Autumn, 1961), pp. 179-180.

Tuathaigh, Geariód. *Ireland before the Famine 1798-1848*. Dublin: Gill and Macmillan, 1990.

Vidler, Alexander. *The Church in an Age of Revolution*. New York: Penguin Books, 1971.

Vidmar, John. *The Catholic Church through the Ages*. New York: Paulist Press, 2005.

Acknowledgments

TO THE LORD OUR G-D, King of the Universe: why can't You let me write on Saturday, huh? But I love You anyway.

All praise not normally reserved for a Higher Power of unfathomable nature goes to Brandy Scott, my best friend and editor, not always in that order.

Roger Savage worked very hard and at very last minute to clear up some American-isms in the manuscript and doing other editing that I could not have managed myself.

To my parents, thank you for keeping faith that there would be a fourth book in the series, even when I had almost given up.

Jane Austen deserves credit for writing one of the greatest novels of all time and allowing it to lapse into public domain.

To my Sensei, for providing most of the inspiration for Mugin.

Thank you to all of the patients of my father's office in Rutherford who keep buying my book and even telling my father that they liked it in a follow-up visit, with an occasional note to pass on the message to me. You should know that you're not actually required to buy your dermatologist's daughter's books to get a good appointment.

Aliza Gellar, my current roommate, gets an acknowledgment for moral support, which is what I say when I give my roommate a freebie for helping pay the utility bills.

A number of people at Ulysses Press need to be thanked: Keith Riegert, Bryce Willett, Karma Bennett, Claire Chun, and the additional behind-the-scenes people I don't know the names of.

Hillary King Chapin came through at last minute with some important Latin translations, and I'm very grateful for that.

To all of my readers: the original readers at Fanfiction.net and the various Jane Austen fan-fiction sites, thank you for reading from beginning to end, and for your continued support. Thank you to all of my Facebook friends, especially the ones who are also my Farmville friends and fertilize my virtual crops. Two birds with one stone right there.

Carey Bligard, Regina Jeffers, Abigail Reynolds, and Lynn Shepherd deserve thanks for helping me with some last-minute historical research.

And if there's anyone I forgot, I'm sorry. And thanks for whatever I'm thankful for.

Other Ulysses Press Books

Darcy's Passions: Pride and Prejudice Retold Through His Eyes
Regina Jeffers, $14.95
This novel captures the style and humor of Jane Austen's novel while turning the entire story upside down. It presents Darcy as a man in turmoil. His duty to his family and estate demand he choose a woman of high social standing. But what his mind tells him to do and what his heart knows to be true are two different things. After rejecting Elizabeth, he soon discovers he's in love with her. But the independent Elizabeth rejects his marriage proposal. Devastated, he must search his soul and transform himself into the man she can love and respect.

Darcy's Temptation: A Sequel to Jane Austen's Pride & Prejudice
Regina Jeffers, $14.95
By changing the narrator to Mr. Darcy, *Darcy's Temptation* presents new plot twists and fresh insights into the characters' personalities and motivations. Four months into the new marriage, all seems well when Elizabeth discovers she's pregnant. However, a family conflict that requires Darcy's personal attention arises because of Georgiana's involvement with an activist abolitionist. On his return journey from a meeting to address this issue, a much greater danger arises. Darcy is attacked on the road and, when left helpless from his injuries, he finds himself in the care of another woman.

About the Author

MARSHA ALTMAN exists more as a philosophical concept than an atom-based structure existing within the rules of time and space as we know them. She is the author of four books set in Jane Austen's Regency England as well as the editor of an anthology of *Pride and Prejudice*–related fiction. When not writing, she studies Talmud and paints Tibetan ritual art, preferably not at the same time. She lives in New York, New York, and does not own any cats.